A STORM OF DOUBTS
A Rae Riley Mystery
By JPC Allen

M✝ Zion Ridge Press
Books Off the Beaten Path

www.MtZionRidgePress.com

Mt Zion Ridge Press LLC
295 Gum Springs Rd, NW
Georgetown, TN 37366

https://www.mtzionridgepress.com

ISBN 13: 978-1-962862-06-6

Published in the United States of America
Publication Date: March 1, 2024
Copyright: © 2023 JPC Allen

Editor-In-Chief: Michelle Levigne
Executive Editor: Tamera Lynn Kraft
Cover art design by Tamera Lynn Kraft
Cover Art Copyright by Mt Zion Ridge Press LLC © 2023

Rae Riley Mysteries
"A Rose from the Ashes" in *Christmas fiction off the beaten path*
A Shadow on the Snow
"Bovine," in *Ohio Trail Mix: Adventures and Inspiration Along the Ohio Literary Trail*

Dedication
To my sisters, Alicia, Laura, and Ellyn
Thank you for helping me try to solve the mysteries in this life

The House of Reuel and Lydia Malinowski

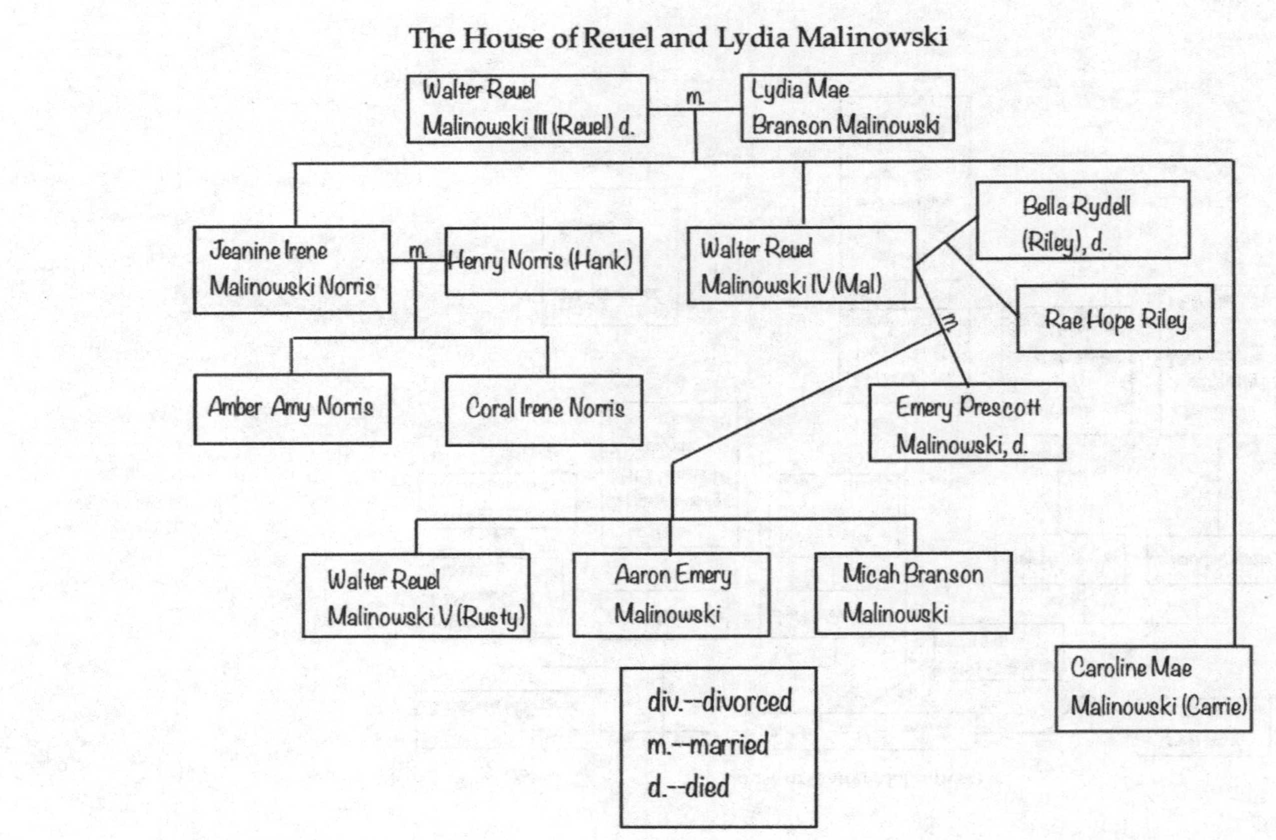

The House of Walter Malinowski Jr.

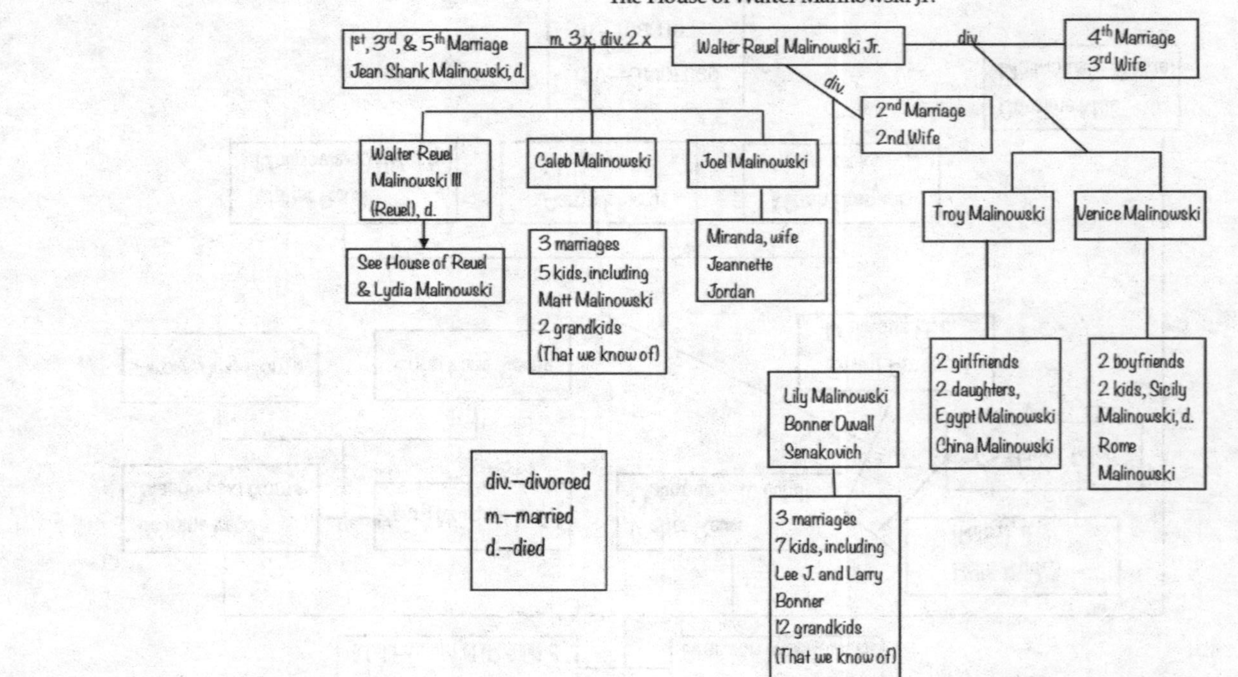

Residents and Visitors of Marlin County, Ohio

Jason Carlisle: Friend of Rae's family and owner of Carlisle Quarry and Concrete

Alli Carlisle: Jason's nine-year-old daughter

Richard Carlisle: Jason's seven-year-old son

Sylvie Carlisle: Jason's two-and-a-half-year-old daughter

Rick Carlisle: Jason's older brother and owner and editor of *The Marlin County Recorder*

Ashley Warren Carlisle: Jason's ex-wife and mother of his children

Steve Conrad: Ashley's fiancé and owner of car dealerships

Brad Schuster: State senator from the county

Bruce Schuster: Brad's younger brother and truck driver

Devon Majors: Rae's best friend and co-worker at the library

Barb Hanson: Library director and Rae's boss

Luke Norris: Father of Rae's uncle Hank

Eric Simcox: Chief of Police of Wellesville

Denise Harris: Chief Deputy and second-in-command at the sheriff's dept.

Chris Kincaid: Deputy and Rae's friend

Miguel "Houston" Blank: Deputy and Rae's friend

Chapter One

"Just stop it!"

The shout made me jerk and get poked by a dead branch of a honeysuckle bush.

Wasn't that a woman's voice? Not a girl's, not my cousin Coral's.

Swiveling on my hips, I sat higher and caught strands of my dark gold hair on the bush. The fox cubs or kits or whatevers I'd been photographing leaped and rolled over each other between muted beams of sunlight, undisturbed.

Two voices, one higher, one lower, slipped through the budding understory shrubs and bushes .

Who would be out in the woods on the morning of Memorial Day between my cousin's farm and my dad's? If we were still on family land. Coral knew exactly where we were, which was why I'd asked her to guide me after she told me about the fox babies. But Coral didn't care much for civilization and nothing at all for ridiculous things like property boundaries.

"Coral?" I called, long, white honeysuckle blossoms brushing my cheeks, their thick Easter-y scent clogging my nose.

When had she left me? I couldn't have been photographing foxes that long. Although she was the guide, she was only twelve, and I was just a day short of twenty. So it was my responsibility to return Coral home in pristine condition.

The voices continued, but too quiet for me to catch any words, their murmur blending with the faint rustle of leaves in the morning breeze.

So Coral might have met someone. But she knew not to talk to strangers.

I collected my camera and the small tripod it sat on and eased myself backward through the thicket.

Did not talking to strangers still apply if you met one in the middle of nowhere in the middle of a county as rural as Marlin County, Ohio?

"Coral?" I ticked up the volume.

"Leave me alone!" The woman's voice again. She sounded desperate, not angry.

"Did you call me, Rae?" Coral seemed to pop out of the morning air. She could move like a ghost in the woods.

"I wondered where you were." I closed my tripod. "Did you hear that yell? It sounds like somebody's in trouble."

Removing her baseball hat with a galloping horse on the front, she wiped copper bangs from her sweaty forehead. "Naw. Just some rich chick and her boyfriend."

My cousin Amber had mentioned that high school kids used an abandoned bridge as a party site.

"Did you talk to them?" I placed the camera inside my padded backpack.

"Nope. I just heard voices and followed them to see what was going on."

The distant hum of conversation continued to glide through the cool morning air.

"You stay here." I tucked the tripod into a pouch on the outside of the backpack. "I'll go see if the girl or the woman needs help."

"She looked more like a woman. But I said she wasn't in trouble."

"I know, but ... well, I'd like to see for myself. I mean, if I were in a lonely spot in the woods with someone upsetting me, I'd want help. Can you lead me to them?"

Coral squinted at me like I was a new species she'd stumbled across. Then she shrugged and headed for a short slope overgrown with young trees and dense stands of pawpaws.

An engine roared to life. As it pulled away, another one turned over.

"Hold on, Coral." I unzipped a pocket of my cargo pants. "It sounds like they—" Looking at the time on my phone, I gasped. "Coral, can we get back to your farm in twenty minutes?"

"What's the rush?"

I stared at her. "Amber and Dad are marching in the Memorial Day parade. He won't be upset if we miss him, but Amber will be. I promised her I'd take pictures."

Coral rolled her brown eyes. "Oh, yeah, I forgot. But she won't care if I don't come. She can't stand me."

"That's not true." At least, not completely true. The fights Amber and Coral had were more intense than the spats I'd witnessed between my three half-brothers. "Can we get back in time to ride into town with your parents?"

Coral studied a slug on a rotten log, a frown puckering her pretty, freckled face. "I don't think so." Now she looked worried, probably thinking that Uncle Hank and Aunt Jeanine would believe she deliberately wandered away to miss her older sister's performance with the band.

She raised her head. "We're not far from Walter's place. Do you think he'd drive us?"

My anxiety notched a few degrees higher.

That all depended on what kind of mood we found our great-grandfather in. And Dad and Uncle Hank and Aunt Jeanine would not approve of us going over there without one of them. We never knew which outlaw relatives might be hanging around Walter's house.

But if there was trouble, Coral and I could escape to the woods. Once Coral was in her natural habitat, chances of anyone keeping up were slim.

"Okay." I hitched the shoulder straps of my backpack higher. "We'll go to Walter's."

Coral crossed the small clearing we stood in and slid down a muddy bank. Then she leaped the trickling creek and grasped saplings and shrubs to climb up the other bank as skillfully as a squirrel.

I fell down the bank and landed on one knee in the creek. Then I struggled up the bank on the far side, slipping in mud and breaking off roots that only appeared strong enough for me to hold onto.

At the top, Coral turned from side to side, her face lifted, as if she was a human radar dish attuning herself to signals only she could detect. Then she broke into a jog, dodging the formidable trunks of towering sycamores and tulip trees and patches of spice bushes and honeysuckle, the heavy scent from their white flowers perfuming the entire forest.

The sun shot shafts through the stirring leaves, dotting the ground cover of dead leaves, baby wildflowers, and fallen twigs in an ever-changing pattern.

Despite the shelter of the canopy, sweat built up on my scalp and neck under my mop of hair, but I couldn't waste a minute to dig a scrunchy out of my backpack. We needed enough time to call the Norrises and Gram on Walter's landline, letting them know we were coming to the parade.

Coral quickened to a sprint, and I tried to keep up, pulling out my phone on the off-chance we might wander into a spot where I could get reception. Not much hope of that, though. The hills and cliffs we passed under usually blocked any signal.

I glanced at my phone. No service.

The terrain grew steeper, and Coral hurtled up it with the same ease she would on a sidewalk. Puffing, I fell behind.

Beside an oak or maple — the tree was too tall to tell which rustling leaves belonged to it — Coral studied the hillside, sunlight setting fire to her chin-length haircut. Then she darted up the slope again, and I lumbered along.

Fighting an urge to take a break, I spotted Walter's ramshackle one-story house through gaps between the wide trunks of mature trees. We ran out of the woods into the small clearing that surrounded the dingy gray house.

As we hurried across the patchy grass, someone opened the squeaky screen to the front door and sauntered onto the porch with a mug.

I skidded to a halt.

The man had shaggy, golden hair and a scruffy beard. Sipping from his mug, he studied us.

Although I'd expected to find a few of our relatives from the outlaw branch hanging out at Walter's house, it never occurred to me that our great-uncle Troy might be back in the county.

And according to Dad and Gram, Troy was a synonym for trouble.

Chapter Two

"You're trespassing." Troy's tone was casual, but his pale eyes locked on us as we approached the peeling porch.

"So are you." From the bottom of the porch steps, Coral watched him. "This property belongs to Walter Malinowski."

"Walter Malinowski Jr." I swung off my backpack. "Coral, this is our great-uncle Troy Malinowski. He's the father of Egypt and China. They live with Walter, so I guess he's here for a visit."

Troy lowered his mug. "You're Jeanine's girls?"

Jason Carlisle, a family friend, had mentioned that Troy looked like a surfer dude and although I'd seen photos of Troy, I hadn't realized how dead right he was. Troy was handsome in a beach boy kind of way with all that blond hair and a few days' growth of beard, making him look younger than he had to be, in his mid-forties. He wore his wrinkled t-shirt and ragged jean shorts with so much ease that he'd probably never feel comfortable in anything else.

"I am." Coral jerked a thumb at me. "She's Uncle Mal's daughter."

Tilting his head, he placed the mug on the splintered railing. "Mal doesn't have any daughters."

"What're you two doin' here?" Our great-grandfather Walter banged back the screen door. "Your folks'll have a fit." He stalked onto the porch, the floorboards groaning under the force.

I raced up the steps. "We've got to ask you a big favor, Walter." I explained how we lost track of time and needed a ride to the parade. "Can I use your phone to call Gram and Uncle Hank and Aunt Jeanine?"

Walter rubbed his enormous hand over the gray stubble that covered his thick, square jaw. "Yeah, I'll take ya." His harsh voice was so deep it seemed to echo in his throat. "I was plannin' on goin' after Jeanine called me yesterday and asked if I wanted to come see Amber march with the band. Phone's in the kitchen, Rae."

I passed between the two men. Troy must have taken after his mother, Walter's third wife, fourth marriage. He didn't have either Walter's imposing height or assault tank build. He was around my height, five-foot, eleven, with the trim body of a runner.

Dashing through the living and dining room to a kitchen that was so neat it appeared nobody'd had breakfast yet, I kept on guard for Egypt and China. The phone sat on the drab formica counter near the back door.

On the first ring, someone picked up.

"Walter?" said Uncle Hank.

"No, it's Rae. I'm calling from Walter's." I repeated why Coral and I hadn't returned to the farm. "Can you tell Gram?"

"Sure. I think she already left with your brothers. Thanks for fixing the situation, Rae. Amber was sure Coral was trying to make her mad. You two have to leave now."

"We will. Sorry we lost track of time." I hung up.

"Oh, no," said a fake, chipper voice. Wrapped in a faded pink bathrobe, seventeen-year-old China Malinowski ran to the small window over the sink and rose on her toes. "It doesn't look like the world's ending." She turned to me. "That's a relief. I thought only the end of the world would bring you to Walter's house." Her pale green eyes were as mocking as ever.

She must have been confident in my patience or manners or some virtue that I wouldn't pitch her out of the room. Being about a foot taller than she was, I could have done it without breaking a sweat.

"Can't stay to chat." I raced back through the house, and the screen door cracked behind me.

Laughter had Troy bent over, his golden mane falling beside his face. Nasty, taunting laughter. "So St. Mal had a one-night stand with the town tramp in high school and just now realized he'd produced a kid?"

My muscles steeled. I didn't like that. I didn't like that at all.

Walter said in a growl, "He ain't done nothin' you ain't done."

"I can keep track of my children."

Looking Troy full in the face, I said, "Dad thought I'd died, sir. Mom didn't tell me anything about who my dad might be until right before she died of cancer. She wasn't sure, but she left behind clues. I came to Marlin County to find him. When I compared blood types with Dad, we realized he was the only guy who could be my father."

Still chuckling, Troy said, "You didn't do a DNA test?"

"No, sir. It wasn't needed."

"And they've lived happily ever after, ever since." China sidled up against Troy. "Morning, Daddy."

"Morning, sweetheart."

They broke into the two fakest smiles I'd ever seen. Did either of them expect us to buy this devoted father-daughter act? Especially since Walter had had custody of China since she was thirteen.

Troy said, "This must have seriously tarnished St. Mal's halo."

Walter huffed a laugh. "He's a Malinowski. He's already tarnished. But Mal don't care." He pointed at Coral and me. "Go get in my truck. I'll be there in a minute."

As Walter put his hand on the latch for the screen door, Troy said,

"Of course, Mal cares. He's supposed to be this God-fearing Christian, and he's an elected official."

"Then he's doin' a funny job of carin'. He tells how he got Rae to anybody who asks, and he's building a new bedroom for her on their house." Walter stomped inside.

"C'mon, Coral." I ran down the porch steps.

"Nice meeting you, Rae." Troy's small knot of a mouth parted in a smile. "You can call me Uncle Troy or just Troy. I'm only five years older than your dad."

His smile softened, becoming—sad? No, not exactly.

"I knew your mom when she lived in the county." He looked past us to the maples and tulip trees gilded in morning light. "She was a good friend."

"Yes, sir."

Shifting his focus to me, he said in a wistful tone, if "wistful" was the right word, "You look so much like her, Rae."

That was a lie. In the six months I'd lived in Marlin County, trying to discover who my father was, not one person suspected I was any relation to the notorious Bella Rydell. Mom had been petite and beautiful, and I'm bony and built like an Amazon. We shared dark chocolate brown eyes, and that was it.

But I exercised my manners. "Thank you, sir." I spun on my heels and restrained myself from running down the short hill to the rutted drive.

I swung my backpack into the bed of Walter's red truck that was more rusty than red and chanced a peek over my shoulder.

The porch was empty.

I released a relieved sigh, but why? Troy was just one more outlaw relative among too many. Why did I feel so much better now that he wasn't in sight?

I opened the passenger door and held it.

Coral stared at the cab's shabby, gray interior, then at me. "You can sit in the middle."

"You're shorter. Shortest kid always sits in the middle. It's in the Constitution or Bill of Rights or something."

Shoving a navy blue baseball cap over his thick, iron gray hair, Walter tromped off the porch and across the yard like each step exterminated vermin. Except for his stiff gait, most people wouldn't have guessed he was eighty-one.

Coral's attention fixed on Walter as he approached.

I got it. She was nervous about sitting next to Walter. I wasn't all that thrilled either, but somebody had to.

Adulting with a sigh, I climbed into the cab and tucked my long legs to the right of the center hump.

Coral hopped onto the seat beside me.

Hurrying out the front door, Troy belted his black jeans. "I'll come with you. We'll take my car. China has to shower, so she can follow later in her car."

Walter glared at his son. "You got that right about China. I told her she ain't goin' nowhere with you. But if you're comin', you come in your own car. I ain't givin' you no chance to get after these here girls."

Troy's pale eyes — green like Walter's? — flew open. "Why would I 'get after' the granddaughters of my late half-brother?" He sounded honestly astonished.

"I ain't one of your marks, Troy." The sentence came out in a throaty snarl. "You can't con me."

Troy's handsome face saddened. "I understand. You're afraid Jeanine and Mal will be angry with you if you allow me near their daughters." He held up a hand. "I understand per —"

Cursing, Walter stormed up the little hill from the drive.

Troy watched with — I couldn't place his expression. But a smirk appeared to be forming.

Walter loomed over him. "Get somethin' straight, boy. I ain't scared of my own grandkids, and I ain't in no way scared of you. But if you want your head handed to you in a hurry, go after Mal's kids or his nieces."

"You terrify me." The smirk burst through.

Walter's calloused hands worked at his sides, as if itching for action, and then he marched back to the truck.

Twisting the key, Walter gunned the engine and roared backwards down the pitted drive to a gravel road.

Pressed up against the door, Coral fiddled with loose threads hanging from the cracked armrest.

Muttering under his breath, Walter tore around one corner after another. I fell on Coral, then leaned on Walter. Finally, I got the brilliant idea of gripping the dusty dash with my left hand to support myself.

Walter rammed the gearshift down a gear, his cinder-block face set in a fierce scowl.

I swallowed. "Thanks for taking us. And thanks for not taking up Troy on his offer to drive us. I — I don't think he likes us much."

"He don't like you at all."

The old truck screamed, climbing into a turn.

"How come?" Coral looked past me to our great-grandfather.

"You're Reuel's grandkids. And if that ain't enough, you're Mal's daughter and niece. Don't let his nice uncle act fool you. He hates you all."

Coral raised her reddish eyebrows at me.

Uneasiness, like a barbell, dropped through my gut.

Gram had said that most of the descendants of Walter's second and third wives hated the three sons and all the grandchildren who came from Walter's three marriages to my late great-grandmother, Jean Shank Malinowski. They seemed to think Walter preferred Jean's descendants because he kept remarrying her and was still married to her when she died. That made them jealous.

I'd never seen any preferences. Walter had gone to all the trouble to get custody of Troy's two daughters and the son of his daughter Venice when their parents had either died or run out on them. Walter acted tough and harsh with every family member I'd seen, not displaying an ounce of favoritism to anyone. Except for Aunt Jeanine. He softened a little around her.

I understood Troy's hatred of Dad, though. A con man would naturally dislike a relative in law enforcement. Dad was dead sure Troy was behind five of his cousins attacking him a couple of years ago. And I'd had enough experience with evil to realize that some people could spread their hate from their target to the target's friends and relatives.

Even when their target was a relative.

Chapter Three

As we passed the corporation limit for Wellesville, I texted Gram to ask where she and my three half-brothers were stationed to watch Dad and Amber. She texted back their location.

"Walter." I clicked my phone off. "Gram says she and the rest of the family are standing near the newspaper office."

"We ain't gonna be able to park nowhere near there. You two better be ready for a hike."

American flags fluttered from streetlamps above uneven trickles of people, who strolled along the sidewalk toward the center of the county seat. The sun glared from a milky blue sky, its warmth already prompting people to pat their faces and produce sunglasses. Too bad we hadn't made it back to the farm so I could get mine.

When we reached the barricade on Main Street to keep cars off the parade route, blankets and folding chairs lined the road as people pooled themselves into small groups and then dribbled away to form different ones. Walter turned and, after weaving his way through several streets, found a spot in the lot of the Baptist church.

As we climbed out, Coral rubbed her wet bangs off her forehead. "It's already humid."

I bit back a snicker. Ohioans had no idea what real summer heat and humidity were. Growing up in the South and spending the five years before I moved to Marlin County on the coast of North Carolina, I was a veteran of the summer weather wars. In North Carolina, this morning's weather would have been considered refreshingly brisk.

From the Baptist church, we walked to Elm Street, joining the trickles of people that flowed together into streams. When we reached Woodward Avenue, we began the climb to Main Street. With Wellesville built along the rolling hills of southeastern Ohio, any time you walked for more than a few minutes, you got a decent workout.

At the corner of Woodward and Main, the courthouse stood across the street like an ornate hill. The sidewalks along both sides of Main Street were packed, and we'd have to walk almost to the next intersection to reach the newspaper office.

A shot fired.

"That's the start for the parade," said Coral.

"Maybe we should watch from here." I wanted to get out on the street to take unobstructed photos of Dad and Amber and any other people or floats that caught my photographer's eye. "Walter, did you—"

But Walter forged ahead on the sidewalk.

Without him saying one word, people cleared out of his way, either pressing back against storefronts or stepping closer to the throngs lining the curb. Coral trailed after him.

For once, my great-grandfather's fierce reputation was an asset.

The intersection seemed like a good place to shoot from, so I didn't follow. I excused my way through the wall of people and crouched in the street next to the curb. I unpacked my camera and hung it around my neck. Down the sidewalk, I could see my youngest brother Micah perched on Uncle Hank's lean shoulders, the morning sun making his strawberry blond hair shine like gold.

"If you get any photos you like, Rae," a man's voice said above me, "email them to the *Recorder*. We like to publish local photos."

Shielding my eyes, I looked up.

Rick Carlisle, editor and owner of *The Marlin County Recorder*, stood above me. Wearing a beard, Rick's narrow face had lost some of its usual grimness since he'd come back from a mission trip to Haiti. The flecks of gray in it made him look older than ... he had to be over forty, since his younger brother graduated with Dad.

"Thanks. I'll see what I get." I'd never published any of my photos before, except on social media. But maybe I should consider it. "Are you here with Jason and the kids?"

"If I can find them." His lips jerked back in a smile, as if the action was unusual. "Nice seeing you, Rae." He jogged across the street.

I lifted my camera.

Rick had changed more than his facial hair since coming back to Marlin County. That was the most pleasant conversation I'd had with him since the confrontation I'd set up on Christmas Eve.

After a few more minutes, the lead police car rolled into view. Marching behind the car came the five-man honor guard, three of them carrying flags. A rustle went through the crowd as it got to its feet. But I stayed in my hunched position, lifted my camera, and clicked away.

Chief of Police Eric Simcox and one of his officers in navy blue dress uniforms with crisp white shirts marched on the right. Carrying the American and Ohio flags were Deputies Miguel "Houston" Blank and Chris Kincaid. On the left, towering above them all, strode Sheriff Walter R. Malinowski IV, looking like Thor had traded his Viking costume for the black and gray dress uniform and broad-brimmed hat of the sheriff's department.

Dad lowered his straight-ahead gaze a few degrees, looked directly into my camera, and winked.

Grinning, I snapped a photo.

As the five officers approached, sweat glistened on their faces. Now those guys had a reason to complain about the weather, wearing long-sleeve shirts under blazers that were probably made of wool. Houston and Chris might have regretted volunteering for honor guard duty to get the rest of the day off and join a group of us at the state park in the afternoon.

As the honor guard passed, I scooted back to the curb, taking random shots. The crowd gave off an odd vibe, different from the other parades I'd attended in town. Tension seemed to pulse through the spectators. Maybe it came from the effort to remain serious or respectful when the kids just wanted to run out in the street and collect candy tossed there from floats and fire engines.

I switched to my telephoto and scanned the crowd, searching for a scene that captured that tension.

To my left and across the street, I zoomed in on my best friend Devon Majors, sitting between Rick and his younger brother Jason. Jason's two older kids, Alli and Richard, and Devon's two daughters, Liberty and Serenity, sat on the curb, comparing the candy they'd snagged. Devon and Jason chatted, leaning back in their folding chairs, while Rick held Jason's two-year-old daughter Sylvie on his lap.

Jason gave Devon the full brilliance of his million-watt smile. That smile, combined with his perfectly sculpted dark hair and sunglasses, made him look like a movie star out among the little people. A pretty accurate comparison. The Carlisle brothers could be considered the celebrities of the county, easily its wealthiest citizens. Although Jason was a board member at the library, he didn't treat any of the employees like little people.

Devon said something with a grin, and Jason laughed.

Devon wasn't ... I mean, Jason wouldn't ...

My lens lingered on the group.

It wouldn't be impossible for Devon to fall for Jason. She'd gotten to know him while working at the library. Liberty and Alli had become friends. But Devon said she didn't believe in marriage, hadn't even married the father of her daughters, despite mourning him when he died. Jason was divorced, and I hadn't heard any gossip about him dating. At all.

I took some shots of a baseball team and reviewed the crowd again, sweeping by the Carlisles and Devon. I swung back. Something had changed.

Rick was sitting on the edge of his seat, saying something to Jason. He jabbed a finger at something or someone across the street while holding Sylvie against his chest. Jason was frozen to his chair, his hands clutching the arms, like he'd glimpsed Medusa among his friends and neighbors.

I turned my camera to that side of the street, but since it was the same side I was on, I didn't see much.

The clash of cymbals and the gut-punching pound of the bass drums signaled that the Marlin County High School Marching Band was about to take center stage. I scurried out as far into the street as I dared. The flutes were in front, and Amber happened to be on my side, perfect for my shots.

Even in her summer uniform of brown and gold polo shirt and sweatpants, her pearly pale face shining from the heat and exertion, Amber still resembled a storybook princess. Her red-gold hair, held back in a French braid, hung nearly to her waist, swaying to the beat.

After she passed me, I aimed my camera at the Carlisles again. But Devon and her daughters sat by themselves. Devon wore that thoughtful frown of hers, craning her neck to look down the street.

What had happened to the Carlisles?

A softball team strolled by, tossing candy to kids, who launched off the sidewalks like they'd engaged their booster engines.

Still crouched in the street, I took shot after shot, hoping to capture the mood of suppressed excitement and solemn salute.

At last, another Wellesville patrol car crawled by, bringing up the rear of the parade. The crowd fell in behind it to follow the parade to the town's biggest cemetery on the south side.

I grabbed my backpack from the curb but kept my camera around my neck.

"Got some good ones?" Gram swam out of the flowing crowd to me.

I looked down to her. "I haven't had time to review any of them. Too busy taking them."

"I understand why you and Coral went over to Walter's." Gram removed her sunglasses. "But you should avoid him and his place. You never know who's going to be there. Or what Walter will do."

Not exactly a new trending topic. Had Walter or Coral mentioned Troy was back?

Gram's wide, dark blue eyes were as clear and calm as the sky above us, her face just as relaxed.

No, Gram hadn't been told. I sighed. But she'd want to know.

"I know that, Gram. It was kind of an emergency." We ambled with the rest of the crowd. "And we didn't have any trouble. Even with — well, Troy's back."

All calm fled her face, and she halted so fast that Uncle Hank collided into her.

"Need to tap your brakes before you come to a complete stop, Lydia," Hank said with a grin.

"Troy's back," said Gram. "Where are the boys and Coral?" Then she darted away from us, her thin frame sliding through clumps of families.

"That ain't good." The laid-back grin had vanished from Uncle Hank's extra-broad mouth, and his extra-big brown eyes hadn't a glint of their usual humor.

Hank never got concerned, except the one time he thought my brothers and I were in danger.

A shiver tried to chill my spine.

If Uncle Hank was worried, there had to be something to worry about.

Chapter Four

Hank and I followed Gram as best we could, veering around strollers and wagons.

When I fell in step beside her, I said, "Troy didn't come into town with us. In fact, he offered to drive us, and Walter wouldn't let him."

"He could have come to town on his own."

"Lydia, I'm sure the kids are fine." Hank tilted the brim of his weathered cowboy hat lower on his forehead, scanning the crowd flowing past us. "They know to go to the cemetery. We'll find them there."

The crowd contracted as they merged to fit through the tall sandstone gate marking the official entrance to the Wellesville Cemetery. Inside, a flatbed trailer had been set up on the wide, flat ground between two mausoleums and the metal tablet embossed with the names of citizens who'd died in wars. A gently sloping hill provided a backdrop. With the way the ground rolled and heaved, dotted with headstones from tiny, plain gray stones to imposing obelisks, that piece of ground was probably the only level spot in the whole cemetery. Several people were seated in chairs on the flatbed as Mayor Teague studied his tablet on a lectern with a mike attached. The band and the high school choir lined up to the right of the platform while the honor guard stood at attention on the left. Sky-scraping oaks provided dappled shade for most of the stage, honor guard, band, and choir.

No sign of my brothers, Coral, or even Aunt Jeanine or Aunt Carrie.

I leaned toward Hank's ear. "I can climb that hill behind the flatbed and scan the crowd with my telephoto lens. I should be able to see everybody in the cemetery. If I see the kids, I'll text you."

Giving me a thumbs up, Hank moved off to the left.

I began walking in the opposite direction when the band and high school choir launched into the national anthem. Placing my hand over my heart, I sang with my fellow citizens, searching for my brothers and cousin.

After we all belted out "the brave," I worked my way to the edge of the crowd, and Mayor Teague opened the ceremony with a few remarks. Every so often, I'd stop, peer through the viewfinder, survey the crowd, and take a few pictures.

By a large pink granite headstone, Walter had joined his oldest daughter, Great-aunt Lily, her various kids and grandkids eddying around them.

The Carlisles were nowhere to be seen.

The mayor introduced State Senator Brad Schuster, and the crowd broke into polite applause, punctuated by a few boos. What were those for? Nobody I'd waited on at the library had hinted at any problems with the senator. If gossip surrounded the guy, I'd hear it from some patron as I checked out their books.

I reached the hill behind the platform and hiked a short way up the slope. Where in the cemetery could my brothers and Coral have got to? They knew their parents expected them to go to the ceremony and that Dad would have a heart attack if he didn't know where they were.

Below me, with his head bent as he listened to a Vietnam veteran talk about his war experiences, Dad stood rock solid in the honor guard.

A faint chanting reached me as I climbed higher, little kids repeating the same word. Their voices floated from behind the hill.

I reached the crest, crowned by a black obelisk twice my height, and the chant came to me clearly.

"Mi-cah! Mi-cah!"

At a mausoleum in a far corner of the cemetery, hidden by the hill, about twenty kids chanted and looked at a little figure clambering onto the roof of the building.

I groaned. Of course. My three brothers couldn't just suffer through the ceremony with the rest of the population. No, they had to find something to do, like climbing to the top of a mausoleum. At least, they weren't disturbing the audience or the speaker.

My youngest brother reached the peak of the mausoleum's roof.

"Mi-cah! Mi-cah!"

Why were the kids still chanting? Since he'd made it to the top, they should have applauded or something.

Someone raced from around the edge of the hill. Throwing off his hat, Dad pounded toward the group of kids like they were all fugitives.

Micah spread his arms.

So he wasn't just climbing to the top.

Letting my camera drop on its strap, I raced down the hill.

"Mi-cah! Mi-cah!"

"No, Micah!" Dad roared.

Several kids jumped with screams and took off as Micah threw himself into a swan dive from the roof of the mausoleum.

Dad bellowed again, scattering the rest of the kids, except for Rusty, Coral, and Aaron, who held a blanket taut. Micah landed in it, carrying all of them to the ground.

"Holy smoke," Dad said in a hoarse breath as he and I reached the snarl of kids at about the same time.

Hopping to his feet, Micah tugged on Dad's pant leg. "Did you see me, Dad?"

Rivers of sweat tracing his face, Dad dropped to his knees. "Is anyone hurt?"

"If we are, it's your fault, Dad." Aaron pushed Rusty off him and glared at Dad.

"My fault?"

"Yeah. You yelling like that scared everybody away." Indignation lit Aaron's light blue eyes. "There were a lot more of us holding the blanket to catch Micah, so he wouldn't hurt himself. You're lucky we all didn't run away." Scowling, Aaron folded his arms over his chest, the picture of a serious scientist thwarted by incompetents. Well, as serious as a nine-year-old could be as a scientist.

Bewilderment rumpled Dad's face, like it usually did when he stumbled across one of my brothers' adventures. Or maybe that was "misadventures".

"He wasn't jumping from that high up." Coral brushed grass clippings from her jean shorts. "You worry too much, Uncle Mal."

Dad said through his teeth, "I have reasons. Four of them."

"Oh, it's Mal's boys," someone said behind me.

I turned around. A good chunk of the crowd had skirted the hill, most likely to see what had made the sheriff take off at 50 mph. I bet no one was surprised it was my brothers. In the five months since I figured out Dad was my dad, I'd learned that Mal's boys were building a reputation for adding excitement to any situation.

Most people headed back to the ceremony, except for Houston and Chris, probably because they figured only a terrorist attack would launch Dad into action like that, and he'd need his deputies to back him up.

"Everything all right?" Chris asked in a bass that didn't match his average size.

"Everything except my nerves," said Dad, getting to his feet.

Houston nodded, and he and Chris followed the retreat to the ceremony.

Rusty, Coral, Aaron, and Micah had lined up by age, sunlight setting their four different shades of red hair on fire.

Peering at them one by one, Dad said, "Rusty, you're thirteen, and Coral, you're twelve. Didn't leaping off a roof from ten feet in the air seem dangerous to you?"

"I made sure it wasn't." Aaron couldn't have sounded more disgusted. "I experimented at lower heights to see if we could catch Micah in the blanket. He jumped off that." He pointed at a shiny black, box-like monument, about six feet tall. "And that." He indicated a nearby oak with low, twisting limbs. "Since we caught him both times, I knew he'd be safe jumping from higher up."

Rusty held one twig-thin arm. "And we had a pile of blankets under the one we were holding in case it broke." His toe pointed to a wad of blankets and towels on the ground.

"We're not stupid." Coral's tone was as sour as her frown.

"I know." Dad rubbed his sweat-soaked, blond crewcut. "But this stunt doesn't show how smart you all are." He looked into the four faces. "One of you could have broken an arm or a rib. And you aren't being respectful. Would you boys like someone jumping off your mom's headstone in the church graveyard? Or from the ones for your grandpa or great-grandmas?"

My brothers studied their feet, and Coral's frown lengthened.

"Taps" floated to us from the other side of the hill as Gram, Uncle Hank, Aunt Jeanine, and Aunt Carrie joined us. We remained quiet as the tune continued, the rustle of leaves the only accompaniment to the solo trumpet.

The last notes of "Taps" died, and then came applause.

"That's the show." Hank replaced his cowboy hat over his wiry, dark hair. "What made you take off like someone lit your pants on fire, Mal?"

"Another one of Aaron's experiments," I said.

Hank squinted at Dad. "You don't look hurt."

From getting hit by an alpaca when Micah tested a saddle to falling into Aaron's Santa trap, Dad was always on the wrong end of my middle brother's experiments.

I swung my camera under my arm. "At least this time nothing attacked you."

Wiping his forehead, Dad said, "Heat stroke's not an improvement."

Gram touched his arm. "Mal, Troy's back."

Dad's hand froze. "You've seen him?"

"No, but Rae has."

He spun to me. "Does he know who you are?"

His question was so sharp that I felt like it poked me. "Yeah, now. I introduced myself."

"Amber will be looking for us. She shouldn't be left alone." Jeanine walked quickly toward the dispersing crowd, Hank falling in with her.

"I'll be right there," Dad called after them. "Amber and I were planning on going back to my office to change for the picnic."

He returned his focus to the four kids. "Your uncle Troy—he's actually your great-uncle—is dangerous. You have to stay with an adult throughout the picnic. Understand?"

Rusty's blue eyes, the same dark shade as Dad's and Gram's, grew round, but Coral, Aaron, and Micah looked puzzled.

Aaron said, "Why's he dangerous?" Curiosity had extinguished his disgust.

Dad mussed my brother's dusty orange hair that had turned a deeper pumpkin color from sweat. "It's a long, long story, and I'm about to roast in this uniform. I'll explain after lunch. But you don't leave Ma for any reason." Dad moved toward the hill.

Stroking his cheek with one finger, Micah said, "What about if I have to go to the bathroom?"

"Get Hank," Dad called over his shoulder.

"What if I can't find him?"

"Ma can stand outside the door."

"What if Uncle Troy comes into the bathroom?"

"Ma!" Dad sent out an SOS.

Gram put her arm around Micah. "We'll be able to find Hank if we need him." She took hold of his hand. "The fire department's picnic is at the school, so let's—"

She looked up to the hill, and we all followed her gaze.

Uncle Troy and China watched us a moment, then turned and disappeared among the evergreen bushes and headstones.

Chapter Five

Lucky for Wellesville, the fire department was in charge of the barbecue at the elementary school. Their makeshift pit of concrete blocks gave off so much smoke that most people would think the school had caught fire.

"I was talking to Coral." Dad, now wearing jean shorts and a black camo t-shirt, joined me in the huge line that twisted a path along the edge of the playground to wait for barbecue chicken.

"I'm sorry we had to go over to Walter's house, but it was an emergency."

"I understand that." His gaze locked on mine. "What concerns me is that you were going to see if that woman or girl needed help."

That searching expression made me feel about seven. I rolled the hem of my olive green t-shirt. "She sounded really upset, and—well, I thought I should check to see if there was serious trouble."

"And if there had been—" Dad's normally booming voice grew strangely quiet "—what would you have done?" Worry lined his forehead.

Swallowing, I squashed a groan. Dad was going into protective mode. Actually, he was always in protective mode, but now he was dialing it to the max. And he wouldn't like my answer. "I—well ... we heard the cars drive away, so I didn't have to make that decision."

"A domestic disturbance is the last thing you should get involved in. Those situations are dangerous for trained officers."

"You don't know that's what it was." I turned sideways to him and looked down, allowing my hair to fall beside my face. "It just sounded like somebody could use some help. If my boyfriend and I were fighting out in the middle of the woods, I'd want some help."

"You'd have more sense than to go to a secluded spot to break up with a boyfriend." Dad sighed. "You have a very kind heart, Rae. God wants that. But don't let it fool you. You have to be wise and kind."

"Good to see you, Mal." A thin man with a high-bridged nose and bristling black high-top, frosted with silver, approached us and held out his hand.

Dad took it. "Been awhile, Brad. Rae, this is our state senator, Brad Schuster. He grew up in Marlin County but lives in Zanesville now, right?"

"As much time as I spend at the state house, it seems more like I live in Columbus and just sleep in Zanesville." His words were so smooth, as if all his speeches had worn off any rough edges. "And this is your daughter?" He offered a thin hand.

I shook it, and it was smooth too.

Dad said, "Yes. Rae Riley."

"That's the girl I was telling you about." Another man with black hair that looked like he had combed it last week staggered toward us, bumping against a young woman carrying a toddler and then ricocheting against an elderly man in a straw hat. His gut straining against a hunter green t-shirt with a leaping fish on it, the man threw a friendly arm holding a beer can around Dad's shoulders. "But what I can't figure out, Mal—if Bella was as drunk as all of us were that night you two hooked up, how could she be sure you're the chick's father?"

The fumes from his breath made me choke as my face flamed.

"That's none of your business, Bruce." Dad assumed his cop voice.

"A bit early, Bruce." The senator pulled the other man off Dad.

Standing side by side, the men were obviously related. They both had the same high-bridged nose.

"It's my day off." Bruce chugged the beer. "I don't get as many of those as you do. I ain't a politician."

Brad chuckled. "You're certainly not, and if you don't want Mal to arrest you for public drunkenness, you'll leave with me. Nice to meet you, Miss Riley. See you later, Mal." He guided Bruce away from us, and the crowd swallowed them.

"Don't you pay any attention to him." Taking my hand, Dad dipped his head to catch my gaze. "We share too many mannerisms and personality traits for you not to be mine." He squeezed my hand.

The flames on my face died as I squeezed back. Why couldn't people mind their own business? If our family was satisfied that Dad hadn't insisted on a DNA test before acknowledging me, that decision only concerned us.

I said, "I know better than to listen to a guy who's drunk. Are they brothers?"

"Yes. Bruce graduated with me. He's a truck driver. Brad's five years—" Dad suddenly straightened to his full height.

Troy and China stood a few yards from us. Aside from their eye color, I didn't see a resemblance. Of course, China might have been a blond under all the black dye of her pageboy haircut.

Gesturing with his Coke in the direction the Schuster brothers had gone, Troy said, "Did you give Bruce Schuster clemency?"

"Brad can take care of him. If he becomes a nuisance, then I can." Dad's cop voice returned. "What're you doing in Marlin County, Troy?"

Troy's small mouth formed an "O" of surprise, then he said, "My family lives here. It's Memorial Day weekend. Besides —" he pulled China next to him "—I missed my girls."

China delivered one of her tart smiles that made her look decades older than seventeen.

Dad picked up a paper plate from a table spread with a red-checked plastic cover. "Took almost two years for you to miss your girls."

"My work forces me to make hard choices. Just like yours."

Dad barked a laugh. "But mine actually *is* work."

Troy stared at me, reigniting the burn in my cheeks, and that dumb, wistful smile appeared amid his blond stubble.

Helping himself to pasta salad, Dad said, "I'm glad you came back, Troy. I needed to thank you."

Troy's eyelids fluttered, as if he had to fight to prevent them from flying wide open. "You needed to thank me?"

"Yeah. If you hadn't conned five of my cousins into jumping me right before the election, I doubt I would've won."

Troy sighed. "Maybe it's a hazard of being a cop to be suspicious of everyone, including relatives, but you have no proof I conned any of my nephews into attacking you."

"I have their statements. Of course, Matt and Larry were drunk at the time, so their memories were a little fuzzy about what you said to them by the time I arrested them. But Rome wasn't. He told me that you said I'd attacked Matt and Larry and you were calling 911. That's why Rome, Jack and Jesse joined the fight—they were on a rescue mission."

"I thought you had attacked them." He sipped from the can he was holding. "I'm sorry if I got that wrong."

"Your thanks doesn't sound very thankful, Mal." China's mocking tone made me grit my teeth.

"But I am." Dad inched forward with the line. "That fight convinced people I wouldn't play favorites with my relatives." He set his plate on one of the buffet tables and stepped out of line and up to Troy.

The loud chatter surrounding us dropped to a murmur as sizzles rose from the pit, and a redwing blackbird let loose its squeaky toy call from the maple overshadowing us.

"There are only two reasons why you're here." Dad glowered at his— what? Half-uncle? "You're either lying low from somebody who wants your hide or you're working a con. Either way, stay away from my family, especially my kids and Coral and Amber."

Troy's posture wilted. "Mal, I don't know why you think I've got some vendetta against you and your family. I admit when I was a kid, I disliked you and your sisters."

A disbelieving laugh spurted from Dad.

"But I'm forty-three now. We should put this kids' stuff behind us."

He held out a hand.

Dad gripped it. "I already have. But that doesn't mean I trust you."

Troy winced but smiled through it. "I've got another admission. It takes a lot of guts to acknowledge a long-lost daughter when you're an elected official."

Putting his arm around my shoulders, Dad said, "I had to. I'm Rae's father."

"I can see so much of Bella in you, Rae." His voice had grown husky. "I know most people didn't care much for Bella—"

"What're you doin' with him?" Walter's roar lifted half the crowd around us six inches off the ground and silenced the other half.

He stalked toward us, people scattering like leaves caught in a hurricane. "I told you, Troy. I told you. You can't take the girls nowhere. I don't care that Gyp's twenty-two. And since China's only seventeen and I'm her guardian, what I say goes."

China lost her mocking expression and folded into herself, like she'd been caught after curfew. Walter was the only person I'd seen who could make her do that. "I know, Walter," she said to the ground. "We drove separately."

He stomped to a halt. "You didn't ride with Troy?"

"I told her she couldn't," said Troy, "because of your rule about not letting the girls go anywhere with me."

He almost sounded respectful, but I caught a subtle trace of taunting. China might look nothing like him, but now I knew where her personality came from.

Walter watched his son. "China, that true?"

"Yes, Walter." Her words were dripped out. "I can show you I drove the Ford here."

"Nice havin' you listenin' to me for once." He folded his massive arms over his broad chest. "You're stickin' with me here at the picnic. Get your food. We're eatin' with Lily and her kids."

"Would you get me some chicken, Rae?" Dad handed me his half-filled plate. "Walter, while China waits in line, could I talk to you?"

Walter agreed with a grunt, and Dad led the way up a small hill to the entrance of the school but still in full view of the line straggling along the buffet tables and barbecue area.

I hadn't noticed before, but they walked exactly the same, except Dad's gait wasn't stiff. My friend Devon said I moved like Dad, so I guessed that meant I also moved like Walter.

Not sure I liked that.

Dad and Walter stood close to each other on the concrete slab leading to the doors.

A firefighter asked if we wanted white or dark meat, startling me. I got a breast for me and a breast and thigh for Dad.

"I ain't no kid!"

I jostled the two plates, and I wasn't alone. Walter's shout seemed to jostle a lot of people.

He stormed away from Dad, who remained rigid on the slab.

I brought the loaded plates over to the drinks table as Dad marched down the hill, his boyish face tense, but I couldn't tell if it was from thought or anger.

"I'm guessing Walter didn't like what you said." I handed him his plate.

"Yes, but I figured that when I asked to talk to him." He picked up a plastic cup. "I've told him before he shouldn't let Troy stay in his house because he's a bad influence on Egypt and China. He thinks I'm bossing him around."

He started to reach for the lever on the giant jug of lemonade but stopped, looking back along the line of people waiting for chicken.

Walter was leading China, who carried a plate piled with food, toward the side of the playground near the parking lot. Troy sauntered behind.

"What was Troy trying to accomplish?" Dad filled his cup.

"Trying to make you think he's here for an innocent visit." A breeze blew strands of hair on my lips, and with my hands full, I had to blow them off.

"Troy's no dope. He knows I don't believe anything he says. He was putting on a performance for somebody—either China or you or the citizens of Marlin County."

"Me? Why me?" I spotted Uncle Hank, Coral, and my brothers sitting on blankets under a spreading oak tree and headed for them.

"I've got no idea, but he went out of his way to compliment you and your mom." Dad bent his head toward mine. "You've got to be on your guard, Rae. If it was as simple as staying away from Troy, I wouldn't worry. Much." He released a self-conscious chuckle. "But Troy never does his own dirty work if he can help it. Someone you might not expect could stir up trouble, and it'd all be Troy's doing. So be aware." His gaze grabbed mine. "If you have any trouble at all, please tell me."

Since my hands were full, all I could do was give him a reassuring rub with my elbow against his forearm. "I won't turn into Nancy Drew again."

The worry in his face vanished as he gave me his lit-from-within grin.

Under the oak tree, Dad settled down among my brothers, and I sat beside Rusty.

Dad pointed at the four plates lying beside Rusty. "You must be starved."

Although four plates were overdoing it, Rusty could put on some weight. He was so skinny that he made tomato stakes seem obese.

Munching on a slice of cantaloupe, Rusty said, "Those belong to Gram and Aunt Carrie and Aunt Jeanine and Amber. They told me to keep the bugs off while they went to talk to people."

Aunt Carrie detached herself from the milling throngs and dropped down beside Rusty.

"I swear half my graduating class has come home for the weekend." Carrie placed her plate on her lap. "I saw three girls from my—I should call them 'women'. We're all at least thirty-four."

Carrie looked younger than thirty-four to me. If Dad could pass for Thor, Carrie would make a great Valkyrie. An inch shorter than me, with white-blond hair spilling over her shoulders, she had a powerful build, like a swimmer, and I could imagine her wielding a sword in a fantasy battle.

Carrie said, "I saw three women from my basketball team. Then I bumped into Barb Hanson."

"She was in your class?" I said.

Nodding, Carrie swallowed a big forkful of pasta salad. "Did you know she and Rick Carlisle broke up?"

"Yeah. That was back in the winter."

"Well, I didn't." Carrie chomped on a chip, her pearly pale complexion reddening. "Stuck my foot halfway down my throat when I asked how Rick was."

"Come on, Carrie." Dad's tone was light as he swatted a bee away from his lemonade. "Foot-in-mouth disease can't be new to you."

Chomping harder on another chip, she glared at Dad. "No, it's not new. What is new is explaining over and over again that the blonde walking around with my older brother isn't his new girlfriend, but the daughter he didn't tell anybody about."

Dad turned to stone, except for his lips. They barely moved as he said, "Not here."

Lifting a brownie from Aunt Jeanine's plate, Aaron said, "Didn't Dad tell you, Aunt Carrie, on Christmas morning about Rae? That's when he told us."

Carrie's glare lingered on Dad, and he returned it. Then she swirled the soda in her can. "Yeah, he phoned me on Christmas morning. It was the shock of my life."

Moving baked beans around my plate, I did my best to blend in with the grooved tree trunk behind me.

Carrie seemed mad only at Dad and had been since Christmas. She'd been suspicious of me—most of the county had—but the risks I'd taken to protect the family from the stalker seemed to prove to her I wasn't out to scam her big brother, and she'd been nothing but nice to me.

"Shoot, Carrie." Uncle Hank plopped his cowboy hat on Micah's head, making him giggle, and stretched his lanky, bowed legs. "Just have it out with Mal behind the school, and I'll make sure no cops come by to — oh, wait. That won't work."

My brothers and Coral laughed, and Carrie allowed the angry set of her jaw to relax.

Dad didn't join in. He looked pained, like his lunch was disagreeing with him.

I reached for his hand and squeezed it. The pain dissipating, he squeezed back.

Chapter Six

Pulling into a parking space at the lake, later that afternoon, I surveyed the swimming beach.

Families and groups of friends dotted the imported sand, clusters of wet, deep colors and pastels decorating the drab ground. Rick Carlisle tossed his seven-year-old nephew and namesake Richard into shallow water while his nine-year-old niece Alli paddled on an inflatable, pink swan. Under the picnic shelter on the edge of the beach, Senator Schuster chatted with an elderly man and scooped something from a vivid tangerine bowl. About twenty people milled in and out of the shelter from preschoolers to senior citizens, so it was probably a family gathering, rather than a political one.

A long line snaked from the cinder-block concession stand. Just beyond it, I spotted Liz Mehaffie, one of Dad's admins and organizer of our picnic, swatting at Houston, her golden hair appearing to cover more of her body than her red bikini.

All the women in our group wore swimsuits much more revealing than mine. Since Mom had raised me to be modest, and since I liked the idea of all my swimsuit coming out of the water with me, I wore the navy blue swimsuit I'd bought three years ago in North Carolina—boy shorts and a midriff top with a scoop neckline that only scooped to my collarbone. As soon as I took off my light blue t-shirt, I'd look like a fugitive from a nursing home.

Shouldering my camera backpack and the pineapple-covered one I'd borrowed from Gram for my swim stuff, I lingered where the asphalt met the sand.

"Is your family having a picnic?" Jason Carlisle appeared at my side, carrying his youngest daughter Sylvie.

Dressed in a vibrant yellow swimsuit with a floral skirt, her dark brown hair hanging in wet clumps, the two-year-old stopped wiggling against her dad's hold long enough to wave and say, "He-wo."

"Hey, Sylvie." A breeze threw a mass of hair into my face, and I brushed it back. "No, my friends are." That still felt odd to say since it was the first time in my life I could honestly claim I had friends.

Jason allowed Sylvie to slide to the ground but held onto her hand. Somehow, even wet, he looked stylish. His dark brown hair was slicked back smooth and his red swim trunks were neither too tight nor too baggy.

He said, "I haven't seen you in a while. Everything going all right for you at the library?"

"Haven't had any trouble at all."

Sylvie pulled out of Jason's grip. He dove for her, grabbing her arm and grinding his left knee into the asphalt.

"Are you okay?" I held out a hand.

Jason got to his feet without my help, Sylvie flailing against his embrace. Blood dripped from his left knee.

"Lemme go." Sylvie bent backwards, away from her dad.

"You should clean that," I said. "I can hold Sylvie if you want to go to the restroom."

"No." The word was so sharp for Jason. He shifted Sylvie to his other arm. "I have a first-aid kit in our SUV. I'll clean up there."

Limping a little, he wove through the parked vehicles, Sylvie pushing off his shoulder and groaning.

Odd. I'd often watched Jason's kids in the children's room at the library while he went upstairs to the adult books. He'd acted like my offer was out of place.

Turning back to the beach, I almost bumped into Chris Kincaid.

"Glad you could come, Rae." Chris's voice was deep, like a cave had discovered it could speak. Wearing only long black swim trunks, he gave me a full two seconds of one of his rare smiles.

Was he just being polite or did he honestly care I could come? I really, really hoped he wasn't just being polite, but his narrow, black eyes and fierce, taut face were impossible to read.

"I am too." I smiled back.

He led the way to where our group had spread towels around a small grill at the edge of the beach.

Liz dashed over and hugged me. "Great to see you."

"Here ya go." Houston held out a root beer. He was only wearing snug gray trunks, revealing a lot more muscles than I would have guessed from his tall, skinny build.

"Thanks." I straightened from spreading my towel and took the can from him.

He drained a can of beer. "Your brothers definitely know how to stir the pot."

I sipped soda to hide a grimace. "They do keep life entertaining."

"When I saw Mal take off," said Chris, "I followed but couldn't guess what was going on."

The three of us fell silent, like we always did in the last two months since the stalker case was solved. I'd had lunch with Houston and Chris separately, and the conversation flowed at a decent pace. But being a trio seemed to remind us of what we'd lost. Chris hadn't once invited me over to his house to help with renovations, let alone to play the outlaw country music we all enjoyed.

I would have loved to have gotten our relationship back to normal. Or some kind of new normal. But the pain must still have been too fresh for the guys.

"Houston," Liz called, adding flirty notes to her usual perky tone, "can you get the charcoal to stay lit? I thought asking a firefighter would be the best bet, but I guess not." She threw a pout at a guy with his red hair shaved to his scalp.

Houston broke into his good ol' boy grin. "Do I need to state the obvious?" His flirty notes brought out his Texas accent.

Liz fanned herself. "Yes, of course. I asked you, Houston, because you're the hottest guy here."

Throwing back his head, Houston strode over to the grill.

Watching Houston watch Liz, who watched back, as he tended to the charcoal, made me realize I should forget about swimming and keep my t-shirt on.

"I suppose," Chris said, "I don't have to persuade a North Carolina beach girl to go for a swim."

My cheeks caught fire, and I gulped root beer.

"Or—uh—sorry. I thought you liked to swim." He stepped back.

The first time in two months, Chris asked me to do something other than lunch, and I acted like he was inviting me to jump into a pool of jellyfish.

"I did. I do." Taking a deep breath, I pulled off my t-shirt, revealing my granny swimsuit. "I will." I tiptoed across the hot sand to where ripples in the lake lapped at my ankles.

Teen boys jumped off a platform anchored just inside the buoys that marked the swimming area.

Glancing back, I found Chris beside me. "I suppose the platform wouldn't be too far for a southern California boy." Did I sound flirty or just ditzy?

He didn't smile again, but the severe angles of his fierce face relaxed a little. "Not at all."

We waded to about waist deep and then plunged in. The cold water wiping the sweat from my skin, I stretched my limbs and fell into an easy freestyle stroke.

Chris pulled ahead and offered a hand when I reached the platform, which tilted and shook as the boys performed elaborate dives.

We occupied a corner facing the beach and turned our backs to them. Water beaded in Chris's thick, black hair and glistened on his powerful, mahogany arms.

"How's your new room coming?" he said.

Starting, I pulled my attention away from his arms. "With Uncle Hank busy with spring planting, it's slowed way down. My brothers and Gram and I help as much as we can, but my brothers and I don't know anything about construction."

Chris smoothed his wet mustache. "Too bad I can't help Mal."

"You've got too much work to do on your own house?"

"No. Nothing's critical there. But when I offered to stop over on one of my days off, Mal said he couldn't accept. There are so many people, powerful people, in the county who wish Chief Simcox had won the election instead of your dad that Mal thinks if deputies help at his house, those people would say he was coercing us to work for him. Someone might file ethics charges against him."

My mouth fell open. "But you'd be helping as my friend, not as his deputy. And you offered. Dad didn't make you."

"I know that. And Chief Simcox, Mayor Teague, and the others who'd make trouble would know that. That doesn't mean they wouldn't try to fabricate a charge out of it."

I flicked water with my foot. Being a Malinowski and winning his election by only two votes had made a very tough job even tougher for Dad. The worse part was that Chief Simcox was still seething about his loss, and their two agencies had to cooperate.

Despite our distance from the beach, the smoke from the grill Houston was working was easy to see curling into the sky. The white sunlight had mellowed to take on a golden tint.

Several of the other groups on the beach were packing up—probably heading home for supper. The Schusters remained, the senator and his brother setting up a corn hole board. Bruce seemed to have sobered. Or at least he didn't sway as he set baskets of beanbags on the ground.

A boy bumped into me.

Chris frowned at him. "How about a race to shore?"

As an answer, I dove off the platform.

Christ beat me, of course, and waited for me when I stood in the shallows.

"You can't hound us because we're in public." That was Rick Carlisle.

Chris and I turned to his voice.

Rick faced a man and woman near the concession stand, pure fury pulling his narrow, bearded face thinner.

"We're not hounding you." The man was tall with finely sculpted pecs and abs—so fine they looked inflated, as if he worked out for a hobby rather than worked hard for a living. His hair was cut so short it appeared painted on his skull. "Ashley wanted to see her kids. Public areas are the only places we can do that."

"Rick," Jason called, holding Sylvie as Alli and Richard jammed towels into a canvas bag. "Let's just go." His voice sounded strained, like he was fighting a deep pain in his gut.

"We can't run every time they show up." Rick glared at the couple.

The woman—Ashley—stood huddled in a bright teal jacket as if the breeze blowing over the beach chilled her. She lifted her hand and waved, but I wasn't sure at whom.

"Looks like trouble," Chris whispered, and then he strode over to Jason. "Can I help you, Mr. Carlisle? I'm Deputy Chris Kincaid."

Jason jerked toward us as Sylvie laid her head against her father's shoulder and sucked on her first two fingers. "Oh—uh, I know who you are, deputy. Uh—no. We're fine. We're just leaving. Rick, we need to go."

Alli crammed a shovel in the bag. "That's everything, Daddy."

Rick remained planted in the sand. "Just remember—if you violate the custody agreement, Jason will prosecute you."

The beach had grown quiet as people either moved away from the confrontation or watched it like a viral video.

"We understand the law," the super-fit man said. "We've done nothing wrong. You're the one yelling in our faces. Maybe I should bring a charge of harassment."

"Rick." Jason's voice sounded frayed. "Would you help Alli and Richard carry the bag and the cooler?"

Super-Fit Guy raised his voice. "Jason, Ashley and I are ready to sit down with you whenever you're ready."

"Daddy." Richard pulled on Jason's arm and said in his precise, quiet voice, "Is that our mom?"

I glanced at the woman. I knew Jason had full custody of his kids, and in the year I'd known him, he'd never once mentioned his ex-wife. But I hadn't realized she wasn't in the picture at all.

Jason's movie star face tensed. "We'll talk in the car, Richard."

Turning his back on the couple, Chris said, "Sir, if you have a custody problem, you should tell Mal."

Jason attempted one of his million-watt smiles, but it fizzled. "Thank you, deputy."

Stabbing a finger at the couple, Rick said, "Stay away from us." He barreled across the beach, gathered up the bag and cooler, and then marched toward the parking lot, his brother, nieces, and nephew trailing after him.

The couple lowered themselves to their blankets, the man stretching out his legs and leaning back on his extended arms. The woman, who wore her dirty blond hair streaked with gold highlights in a long pixie cut, curled her legs under herself. The man spoke to her with a faint grin, as if nothing unusual had happened.

Chris murmured, "Do you recognize the man or the woman?"

"No, but I've never seen Jason's ex-wife before."

We returned to our group, and I searched both backpacks for my sunglasses. When I didn't find them, I retraced my steps to the concession stand across the fiery sand. I walked behind it and found Troy leaning against the far corner, gazing at the families and friends spread over the beach. Or was he lurking?

I about-faced. I could take another route to the parking lot.

"Rae?"

I could pretend I hadn't heard. But I didn't want Troy to think I was scared of him.

I stopped, and Troy sauntered toward me, a Coke in one hand, the ends of his blonde mane fluttering in a sudden breeze, like he was posing for a commercial.

"Family picnic?" His lazy tone could make someone think he had nothing more important to do than stand on the beach and people watch.

"Friend picnic, sir," I said. "They're waiting for me."

"Oh, I won't keep you. It's just ..." He removed his sunglasses. "I can't believe I'm talking to Bella's daughter. I thought she died in that fire at the children's home. I was probably the only friend your mom had in the county." A tired breath drifted from his mouth. "I know she was mine."

That was a lie. "Mom never mentioned you."

"I'm not surprised. She was very unhappy here. She probably wanted to forget everyone and everything about the few years she lived in Marlin County. But I never will. I don't want to." Although his eyes were aimed at me, they focused inward for a moment. Then he brought me into view again. "I hear Bella in every word you say. I see her in every step you make."

"No." I crossed my arms. "I move like my dad. A lot of people have said so."

He chuckled. "It's obvious you're a Malinowski. When's your birthday?"

My arms loosened. "Tomorrow, sir."

"And you'll be twenty?"

The answer stuck against my teeth, but he could have found out a dozen different ways. "Yes, sir. Not that it's any of your business."

Mom would have cringed at my manners. Or maybe not, since she knew Troy.

"I'm supposed to be your great-uncle. Nothing wrong with me knowing the birthday of the girl my nephew considers his daughter." He slid on his sunglasses. "Happy birthday, Rae." He moseyed out from behind the concession stand and onto the sand.

I hurried to my truck, found my sunglasses under the driver's seat, and walked even faster to rejoin my friends.

Hayley, a dispatcher, sidled against Houston as he scooped a hamburger off the grill. Plopping the burger on her plate, he flashed his eyebrows at her.

Then he saw me. "Hamburger or hotdog?" The corners of his sea green eyes constricted. "Something wrong?"

I didn't want to answer Houston any more than I had Troy, and he was being nice. "I ran into Troy Malinowski. He didn't try anything, but I don't like talking to him." I picked up a paper plate. "Hotdog, please."

"Mal briefed me and Chris on your uncle at the picnic." He placed a hotdog in a bun and laid it on my plate. "If you need anybody to ride to your rescue, you know who to call."

With that accent, he should have tipped an imaginary Stetson. My heart seemed to pick up speed.

Sitting on my towel next to Chris and Hayley, I dug into my supper.

The beach was quieter with most of the families with little kids gone, although one group by the Schusters' shelter had amped up their phone so we could all listen to their country music favorites. The breeze strengthened, and the lake shimmered as the wind and sunlight twirled around each other.

I chewed a bit of hotdog. I wanted to enjoy the party — it was turning out so much less awkward than I'd feared — but Troy's words hung in my mind like a faint but definite stench.

What had he meant by he was "supposed to be" my great-uncle? And I was the girl his nephew "considered" his daughter? Weird choice of words.

"I was keeping these for later." Liz straightened from a cooler, holding a clear plastic container. "But the frosting is melting, so ..." Turning her back to us, she set the container on another cooler and rummaged in her purse.

The rest of us set aside our plates and joined Liz.

She picked up the container and held it out to me. "Happy birthday!"

A dozen cupcakes sat nestled in molded plastic, two of them holding lit candles shaped in a two and a zero.

Chris, Houston, Liz, and everyone else sang "Happy Birthday to You."

I stared at the candles. My first friend birthday party. Mom always made my birthday special, but we never had the money to host a party, and more importantly, I hadn't had friends to invite to one, even if we'd had a fortune.

The song died away with Houston's tenor and Chris's bass lasting the longest.

"Make a wish." Liz bounced on her toes.

"Oh. For sure." I tucked my wet hair behind my ears.

Mom ... wish you were here.

I blew out the candles, and my friends applauded.

Liz removed the two candles and handed me a cupcake. I took a big bite, frosting clinging to my nose, and everyone laughed with me.

Chapter Seven

We had to pack up before 11 p.m., but the red-haired firefighter, Noah, invited us to continue the party at his house.

As much as I hated to, I had to turn him down.

"I really want to, Chris." I carried my backpacks to the Rust Bucket. "But Dad's treating me to breakfast before work tomorrow, and I don't want to be too tired." I added quickly, "Can you do lunch tomorrow? Or are you on vacation?"

"My vacation starts Saturday. Let's try for tomorrow, and if that doesn't work, another day before I leave."

"Perfect. Where are you going on vacation?"

Chris shrugged. "I'm just going to drive and see where I end up."

I fell back against my truck. "Perfect."

"Really? I've told people at work, and they give me fixed smiles and polite nods."

"To just drive and see whatever comes your way? I'd love to explore the country like that. But," I sighed, "it's not as safe for a girl. And Dad would have a stroke as soon as I told him my plans."

"We'd appreciate it if you restrain yourself from killing Mal." Houston plopped Liz's cooler in the trunk of her car. "He's a whole lot easier to work for than Harris would be, and as chief deputy, I'm assuming she'd take over."

"Don't worry. I don't have anything like that scheduled."

As Liz pulled on a white sweatshirt, I said, "Thanks for everything."

She beamed, outshining the cones of light from the tall streetlights in the lot. "You are too welcome. Have a good time with your family tomorrow. It's your first birthday with them, isn't it?"

"Yes." And my third without Mom. "Good night."

I shoved my packs into the Rust Bucket. Why did that depressing fact have to intrude when I'd had such a good time?

I slid behind the wheel.

Chris began to turn away but then turned back. "That swimsuit looks good on you. Blue is a very good color for you."

Blood rushed up my neck, and my heart wanted to float free of me.

Mom always said to return a compliment for a compliment, but what could I say?

"Those trunks look really good on you," or "Black is a very good color for you," or "No shirt is a very good choice for you"?

Chris moved away.

Come on ... think. "You look good in anything."

He spun to me, the bright light revealing one eyebrow raised. In surprise? Irritation?

Shutting the door, I slumped over the wheel and turned the ignition.

A smile flickered under his mustache, and he gave me a big wave.

Straightening, I waved back and pulled away.

Through the deep quiet of the country night, I twisted my way through forests and fields that appeared as black walls unless caught in the illumination of my headlights.

Maybe Chris considered me more than a friend. Houston might too, but he seemed to flirt equally with any females of appropriate age in the near vicinity.

Considered me more than a friend. Considered ...

Why had Troy used that word? Was he one of those nasty people in the county who figured Dad was a dope for not insisting on a DNA test and thought I might not be his? But Troy admitted I resembled the Malinowskis.

I forced my hand through my damp hair.

Why was I ruining my great mood by thinking about Troy and his weird comments? He was a con man. He'd say anything to see what kind of reaction he could launch.

I turned onto the one-and-a-half lane gravel road and followed it to the dead end. Then I swung right onto the drive and passed into the shallow, open valley, rolling past the alpaca barn and up to the house.

I parked beside Dad's patrol SUV, already facing down the drive to head out in the morning.

I walked through the breezeway to the little screened porch and found the back door unlocked.

Someone had waited up, probably Dad, still getting used to dealing with an adult child. That and the fact that his wife had died in a car accident made him sack out on the couch until I got home.

I tiptoed into the kitchen, the light above the stove casting illumination on the tired, tawny linoleum.

Aunt Carrie lay on the fuzzed, brown couch in the big living-dining room, reading typed sheets of paper. Most likely a short story about deputy U.S. marshals from Aunt Jeanine, and she wanted Carrie to make sure she got her details about that branch of law enforcement correct.

Stuffing my keys in a side pocket of mybackpack so they wouldn't jangle, I said, "You didn't have to wait up for me."

Carrie swung her feet to the floor, hit one of my brother's trucks, and scooted it aside. "I know that. And Ma knows it. And I think, deep down,

Mal knows it, but he can't quite get it through his cement-lined skull that you're old enough to come and go as you want." She stood and stretched. "Doesn't my brother drive you crazy?"

I shrugged and placed the backpacks in a chair at the long, plank dinner table. "It's nice having someone look out for me. Mom always did and—" Memories of the eighteen months I was on my own after Mom died tried to choke me. I swallowed and fought to keep my voice from trembling. "So I like that Dad wants to make sure I'm home at night. I just wish he'd go to bed and let me wake him when I come in."

"He'll never do that. He's afraid he'll wake up at six in the morning and realize you never came home." Carrie blew out her cheeks. "I can't really blame him after what happened to Em."

Glancing away, she smoothed her hand over the top of her white-blond hair. "Sorry I got grumpy about explaining who you are to people at the picnic. That's nothing against you." A frown creased her pearly pale, round face. "I get why he didn't tell us about you when he was a dumb teenager. He was wrong not to let Ma help him, but I get it."

She flung out her arms. "But Jeanine and I aren't kids anymore. He can let us know the details of how you found him. I'm trained in law enforcement, just like he is. I can keep my mouth shut, and Jeanine doesn't gossip."

"He knows that. But he thought if he told you—"

"He'd have to tell Jeanine, who'd feel she had to tell Hank, and he might let something slip. Mal told me all that." Her dark blue eyes narrowed. "Did he tell Ma everything?"

Everything in me wanted to say yes.

Gram knew everything about how Mom tried to blackmail Dad, Jason Carlisle, and Professor O'Neil when she was pregnant with me. And that when Jason told Rick, Rick, on his own, tried to murder Mom and burn the abandoned children's home over her to cover up his crimes. And that Mom had written three notes before she died, apologizing to those men and forgiving whoever had tried to kill her. And how I let the statute of limitations run out on Rick's crimes when he was ready to confess because I knew Mom would want me to.

Gram knew all that but the names. Dad felt he had to explain the entire story to Gram so she would understand why a DNA test wasn't needed. He also felt it wasn't our place to expose all those long ago secrets.

But instead, I said, "I shouldn't say."

Groaning, Carrie dropped onto the couch. "Look, I don't blame you. You're trying to be a good daughter." She glared at the basement door, which led to Dad's room. "It's my brother I blame. He kept one secret for twenty years, and we end up with an extra relative. What's he keeping secret now?"

I shifted my feet. "Well, it's not another kid."

Carrie shot me a look and then flopped against the back of the couch. "I was a deputy marshal for eight years, chased fugitives all over California and Mexico—and believe me, you haven't chased a fugitive until you've done it in a foreign county. And Mal still acts like I'm his goofy little sister who can't keep her mouth shut and will die on duty some day because I'm not as cautious as he is."

I fiddled with a button on my denim shirt. "Sorry.

Carried studied me a moment. "No, I am. You don't need to endure my rant." Gathering up the sheets, she said good night and left to walk to the Norrises' farm, where she'd been staying during the holiday weekend.

I turned off the light by the couch, and in just the few feet between it and the door of my temporary bedroom, my feet stepped on a car, plastic bricks, and for some weird reason, a birdie to our badminton set. As I ran the water for a quick shower in the bathroom attached to the bedroom, the conversation with Troy replayed itself, over and over, until I wished I could reach in my brain and pull out the cells that had recorded it.

He hinted at something. But what?

I stepped into the shower, allowing the hot water to rinse lake gunk from my hair. After drying off and pulling on my pajamas, I was still too irritated to sleep. Since the stalker case, I'd had trouble sleeping anyway.

I picked up an anthology of sci-fi stories from my nightstand, went back to the living-dining room, turned on a lamp, and settled down on the couch for a good, long read. But the conversation with Troy sat at the back of my mind, like a little goblin, waiting for a chance to leap out and grab my attention again. And again. And again.

Chapter Eight

The next morning, I had to take another shower since I'd fallen asleep in a weird position, and my hair had dried in an even weirder one.

Throwing on a red t-shirt, I noticed Mom's cremation urn sitting on the corner of the desk. I swallowed a lump. I wouldn't let my third birthday without my mom ruin my first birthday with my dad.

I rubbed my hand over the urn and dredged up a smile.

When I came out into the living-dining room, Dad was already dressed in his summer uniform, a black short-sleeve shirt, no tie, white undershirt showing.

He gave me his lit-from-within-grin. "How's my — are you okay?" The grin disappeared.

A parent trained to read people was a major disadvantage. I wanted to say I was fine, but he wouldn't buy it.

He said, "It's your business, but I'd like to know."

The left side of my face contracted as I grimaced. I didn't want to spoil our breakfast. We didn't get many chances to hang out, just the two of us, between our jobs and my brothers.

"I'm just missing my mom."

Stepping around toy guns, socks, a boot, and plastic bricks, he put his arm around me. "Birthdays are tough."

Why had I forgotten Dad would understand since he'd lost his dad at ten?

I slipped my arm along the small of his back, which would have been impossible if he'd been wearing his fully loaded utility belt. "But this one is already better than the last two because I've got people to celebrate it with."

He squeezed my shoulders, a bit harder than comfortable. "Got that right. How did you celebrate your birthdays with your mom?"

We talked about Mom and his birthdays with his dad when he was alive as we drove to the lodge at the state park. If you wanted more than coffee, pizza, or sandwiches for a meal in Marlin County, the restaurant at the lodge was your only option.

The sun was already high, even at this early hour, touching new leaves and rejuvenated grass with a golden glow. Long stalks of butterweed, if I was remembering correctly what I'd looked up in one of Aaron's field guides, reached from the edge of the road to swipe the patrol

SUV.

I finally thought to ask, "Why was Senator Schuster booed by some people when he was introduced yesterday?"

"Couple of reasons I know of." Dad eased around a tight turn. "He just finished a messy divorce, and his ex-wife's from Marlin County. They were high school sweethearts, so people around here took sides. And there's talk of an investigation into his campaign finances."

"What'd he do?"

"Nothing. A person is innocent until proven guilty. The investigation is only talk at this point." Dad pulled into a parking space. "I've been in an elected position long enough to understand that talk may stem from an enemy making trouble, not from any wrongdoing."

As we got out, Dad opened the door to the backseat and took out a small, lemon-yellow gift bag he must have placed there before I got in his vehicle this morning. "You can open it over breakfast."

We walked down the slanted parking lot to the grand entrance of the lodge, which looked like a log cabin made of redwoods.

As we crossed the wide, two-story lobby, an overweight man behind the front desk spoke to Egypt Malinowski, who was wearing a housekeeping uniform and had a hand on a cart for cleaning rooms. The man broke off to say hey to Dad, and Dad returned it.

I looked straight ahead. She wouldn't spoil my birthday.

"Mal." Egypt pushed her cart toward us.

Dad turned to her, and I steeled myself for whatever insults she would unleash.

Like her half-sister, Egypt didn't take after Troy. Her pinched face with a chiseled frown and her long sepia-colored hair had nothing in common with her father's bleached, beach boy good looks.

"Morning, Egypt," said Dad.

"Walter said you know Troy's in town. Did you check to see if he's wanted anywhere?"

"First thing I did when I went to my office to change after the parade, although I didn't think it was likely. He wouldn't come back here, with me being the sheriff, if that was the case."

Egypt slouched by her cart. "I was hoping he'd done something you could grab him for."

Removing a card from a pocket on his belt, Dad said, "If Troy gives you trouble you think I can arrest him for, call me."

She recoiled from the card like it might bite her. "Malinowskis take care of themselves. We don't need no help from cops. Besides, Walter'd skin me."

"But you just wanted me to arrest Troy if there was a warrant out for him."

"Yeah. But that ain't the same as snitchin' on him to the cops."

"Keep it short, Egypt," said the man behind the desk.

Whipping around to him, Egypt bunched her lips, like she was readying an insult, when Dad leaned closer to her. "You said Malinowskis take care of themselves. If you call me, it'll be a Malinowski who'll take care of Troy."

She glanced from the desk clerk to Dad. "How come you're trying to help me?"

"Because you're my cousin, and Troy's unhealthy for you and China to be around. And it's easier for me to fight him than his own daughter."

Egypt stuck out her chin. "I could take him out if I had to." Her eyes moved from Dad to the card. She snatched it and hurried away with her cart.

The tension melted from my shoulders. Her ignoring me was a gift.

Dad held the door to the restaurant, and I walked through, then took hold of his hand as we waited for a server.

Surprise lit up his eyes, and he squeezed my hand.

When I'd gone looking for my dad, he could have been a million different shades of bad.

Thank You, Father, for giving me Dad.

Timbers soared to the extra high ceiling, and since we were the only customers, we picked a table by the mile-high windows, which gave us a view of Sycamore Lake. Plumes of mist rose from its surface as the sun cleared the dense towers of sycamores and maples.

The waitress walked — no, really, sashayed — to our table. "Saw you at the parade yesterday, Mal. You looked fine in that uniform." She raised pencil-enhanced eyebrows. "Looking fine in this uniform too."

"Thank you, Kelly." Dad focused on the menu as a blush invaded his cheeks.

Setting my jaw, I glared at the waitress.

"I'll start with coffee," Dad said. "Rae?"

"Tea."

"Get it for you in a jiff." Kelly winked and sashayed away.

"Order anything you want," Dad said.

Our food came quickly, and Kelly made more comments that turned Dad's complexion a deep scarlet, but she strolled away before I could form a reply that would hose her down.

I buttered my pancakes. "Is Kelly a local?"

"Yes. She graduated with Hank and Jeanine." He poured a few drops of cream into his coffee.

Jamming a fork into the stack of billowy pancakes, I said, "Then she knows you don't date."

Almost everybody in the county knew that because so many people thought it was strange that Dad hadn't tried dating since it'd been seven years since his wife had died.

Lifting his mug, he sighed. "Hazards of being a thirty-eight-year-old widower with three nice kids under eighteen."

I reached for more syrup. "When Kelly comes back, I'll drop kick her into next week."

Dad chuckled. "Thanks, but I have no desire to arrest my own daughter for assault."

Jason Carlisle entered the restaurant with Senator Schuster, both dressed in blazers with open collar shirts, as if ready to pose for a photo-op. They said hello and took a table set against the back wall.

I whispered, "Senator Schuster is hanging around Marlin County a lot. I saw him at the lake yesterday."

Dad matched my volume. "Probably trying to head off any bad publicity the rumors about a campaign finance investigation are generating."

Was he asking Jason for campaign contributions? Or some sign of public support? Made sense when Jason ran a successful, multi-county business.

Dad set the gift bag on the table.

I wiped my fingers on my napkin and started to pick it up.

"What are you doing here?" Jason's alarmed question turned Dad and me toward his table.

The couple stopped on the hunter green carpet as Kelly went on to a table in the corner.

"Ashley and I are staying here for a few days." Super-Fit Guy had his hand entwined with Ashley's.

"This is persecution." Jason pushed back his chair and stomped to his feet.

Super-Fit Guy looked puzzled. Or maybe he pretended to look puzzled. His face was flat, the tip of his nose, the slight bulge of his cheekbones, and the ridge of his eyebrows providing the only relief to the great plains of his face. "This restaurant is a public place. So are the beach and the parade. Since you won't let Ashley near her kids, those are the only places where she can see them."

"The court won't let Ashley near *my* kids."

Hanging one arm over the back of his chair, Dad stared with no attempt to hide it.

Shifting her weight from one foot to the next, Ashley clutched Super-Fit Guy's hand, looking everywhere but at the two men at the table.

"We haven't violated any court orders." Super-Fit Guy glanced our way, and for a moment, his gaze lingered on us. Then he said, "We'd like to talk with you, Jason. Just us and you, no lawyers. When you're willing to be reasonable."

He led Ashley to the windows and took the table in the corner where Kelly had placed the menus.

Jason murmured to Senator Schuster, and they both left their table. As they hurried to the entrance, Jason spoke to Kelly, and then they passed into the lobby.

Dad swiveled to his plate. "This is not good," he whispered.

The gift bag remained on the table between us, the tense situation seriously injuring the fun of learning what was inside.

"Let's get finished, and you can open your gift outside." Dad must have sensed my awkwardness.

He drained his mug, and I polished off the last of my pancakes. After he paid the check, we headed into the lobby. I told Dad about what I'd seen at the lake.

"Call it my cop instinct," Dad said. "but I got a feeling that guy and Ashley Carlisle are hanging around for something more than a sneak peek at Alli, Richard, and Sylvie. If she wants to change the custody agreement, she goes to court, not the beach." He held the door open for me. "Did that guy look familiar to you?"

"No." I passed outside.

Dad motioned toward a bench. "Have a seat and—"

Someone called our names, and Jason trotted to us from the parking lot. "Do you have time to talk to me, Mal? I need some advice."

Dad glanced at his watch, then to me.

I stepped back. "I'll wait in the car."

"It's nothing secretive." Jason pulled at the cuff of his shirt. "With my ex-wife and her boyfriend staying in the county, this mess will be public property in a few hours. If it isn't already."

"Did Brad leave?" said Dad.

"Yes. I needed to talk to you more than him."

We followed a sidewalk that wound toward several tennis courts. Jason looked toward the voices carrying from the courts and stopped beside a knot of tall fir trees.

He opened his mouth, closed it, straightened his already straight cuffs, and opened his mouth again. "This is such a mess. I should start at the beginning."

Dad shifted his weight off his weak knee. "Good place to start."

"At the beginning of May, Ashley and her fiancé contacted me. I hadn't heard from Ashley, not one word, since she left us four months after Sylvie was born. Before you ask, I have full custody, and Ashley has no visitation, so she has no right to be near the kids without my permission."

"I'm surprised a judge didn't give her some kind of visitation," said

Dad.

"Ashley had a drinking problem, and I provided witnesses in court, proving that. Judge Pollack agreed the kids shouldn't be alone with her. So they haven't seen their mother in over two years. Now Ashley and Steve—he's Steve Conrad. He owns eight car dealerships in Columbus."

Dad snapped his fingers. "I thought I'd seen him before. He acts in his own commercials. They're all over the TV when Ohio State plays."

Jason centered the heavy watch on his left wrist. "He's a man with money, which is the only man Ashley will have. When they first contacted me, they said ..." He began to take a deep breath but broke off, as if it hurt. "They said Sylvie isn't mine. She's Steve's."

Chapter Nine

I staggered back a step, and Dad's eyebrows darted to his hairline.

Jason rushed on, as if he was trying to get past the pain fast. "They want me to submit DNA samples of Sylvie and me for a private DNA test. If the test confirms Steve is her biological father, then we go to court, change the custody, and I'm supposed to hand her over like I haven't raised her by myself for two-and-a-half years." He looked to each of us. "She's a baby. She doesn't know any other parent but me. Ashley and Steve think she'll be perfectly fine switching families. How could they be so stupid?"

"So you haven't done a test?" Dad's usual penetrating voice had softened.

Jason went rigid. "Of course not. A test wouldn't change anything. It wouldn't change anything at all. I'm listed as Sylvie's father on her birth certificate. I have custody. That's all there is to it." His volume was close to shouting.

Jason's harsh response puzzled me. Dad had asked a reasonable question.

Still quiet, Dad said, "Are they threatening to get a court-ordered test?"

"Not yet." Jason's shoulders drooped. "I thought I could wait them out. Ashley has never stayed with anything in her life, including our marriage and motherhood. My lawyer thinks Steve would have a tough time getting standing to bring a court case. But I think one of the actual reasons for not hauling me into court is that Steve doesn't want the adverse publicity. Sylvie is a happy child with a happy family, and it would look awful for him to try to take her when he doesn't know for certain she's his. That's the other reason. I think—and my lawyer agrees— Steve doesn't want to go to all the trouble of a court case only to find out Sylvie is mine."

Sighing, Jason smoothed hair by his temple that was already smooth. "But I don't know if waiting will work now that they're here. They were at the parade and at the beach yesterday. Perhaps they're trying to pressure me into submitting samples for a private test by embarrassing me in my hometown. They know I don't want my kids wondering about why their mother is back. The more they keep making appearances, the more likely I'll have to tell the kids what's going on. Richard's getting upset, asking me if Ashley's going to move in with us. It's not fair to get their hopes up again." His sentence ended on a harsh note, his cheeks reddening.

He looked at Dad. "But Rick thinks the real reason they're here is to sneak a sample from Sylvie."

Dad's eyes widened. "If you caught them, you could bring charges. And a test like that wouldn't hold up in court."

"It's not for court. It's just so Steve would know whether he should invest the money and time to get a court-approved test."

Tugging on my earlobe, I said, "I don't think she's his, Jason. She looks a lot like Richard, and Richard is your clone. If they're trying to get Sylvie away from you to take a sample, they certainly aren't sneaky about it."

"They were at the parade. Rick just happened to spot them working their way through the crowd toward us. Both of them wore hats and sunglasses. They might have been hanging around to see if they could separate Sylvie from us in the crowd long enough to swab her cheek. It would only take ten seconds, if Sylvie cooperated."

"They weren't sneaky at the beach."

"Rick thinks that was an act. Once we'd seen them, they had to come up with some excuse for coming to the county. Saying they'd come to view the kids gives them a plausible excuse." He started to push his hand through his styled hair but dropped it. "Plausible if you believe Ashley is suddenly interested in the kids."

Dad said, "Unless you caught them trying to swab Sylvie, you can't charge them with anything. You can't get a protection order for their actions yesterday or today."

Jason's head lifted in a jerk. "Oh, no. That's not what I wanted your advice for. But that's good to know. No, it's about my babysitter for the kids this summer. My regular sitter is Angie Gibson, but she had rotator cuff surgery. So I hired Hannah Cervelli for the summer—she's home from UD. But I don't see how I can ask a nineteen-year-old to deal with this mess. What can she do if Ashley and Steve come up to the kids at the pool? Or the library?"

"Are you afraid of kidnapping?"

Jason swallowed. "No. Steve has too much at stake with his dealership empire. He wouldn't jeopardize that. But they might lure Sylvie away from Hannah, and I can't have that."

I pulled on my earlobe again. "What you need is a babysitting bodyguard."

"That'd be ideal." Jason's smile was dim. "But my kids couldn't know the person was guarding them. They know nothing about this."

"You know—" Dad tilted his head to one side "—my sister Carrie fits the bill perfectly. She has a Class A license as a private investigator, so she can do both investigative and security work. Guarding federal witnesses and defendants is what she did as a deputy marshal—when she wasn't chasing fugitives. And she loves kids. She's always telling my boys and Jeanine's girls how she's in the running for world's greatest aunt. Your kids would never know she was anything but the babysitter."

For the first time since he started the conversation, some hope filtered across Jason's tense face. "That would be a real relief. But it could be a long job, perhaps all summer, if we end up in court."

"From what Carrie's told me about the owner of the detective agency she contracts with, he'll agree to any job as long as it falls within the limits of an investigator's license and the money's right." Dad pulled out a card and pen and wrote on the card. "Carrie's staying with Jeanine and Hank until Wednesday. Call her and explain the situation. She's in between jobs right now. I'm sure she'd love the change of pace."

"Thank you." Jason took the card. "If Carrie wants the job, that'd be one load off my mind." He walked back up the path to the parking lot.

Dad and I waited until he was a decent distance ahead and then followed.

"I feel so sorry for Alli, Richard, and Sylvie," I said. "Richard didn't even recognize his own mother at the beach. Do you think Jason won't test Sylvie because the court would take her from him if the DNA test proves Super-Fit—proves Mr. Conrad is her father?"

"Possibly. Or maybe ignorance is bliss."

I lowered my eyebrows. "But he said the results don't matter. He's raised Sylvie. He's the only parent she's known."

"He may want to believe that. He's a decent guy. But he could be afraid that knowing Sylvie isn't his would change his attitude toward her. Jason knows that wouldn't be fair to a two-year-old, but he might not be able to treat her the same if he knew she wasn't his biological daughter."

My breakfast lurched in my stomach. "You really think that?"

Dad shrugged. "It'd be tough for any father."

We got into the SUV, and he handed me the yellow bag. "If you open it quick, you may get to your gift before something else interrupts us."

Chuckling, I looked inside and removed a small beige jewelry box. Glancing at Dad, I opened it. A necklace with a gold chain and a gold pendant shaped like a shell lay on the felt.

"It looks like whelk." I drew my finger along the pendant.

"What's that?"

"One of the big shells you can find along the coast of North Carolina where Mom and I lived."

"Open it."

"It's a locket?" I found the slit, pried open the wide part of the shell with my nail, and caught my breath.

My favorite photo of Mom and me. Although only our heads were in the photo, I knew Dad had taken it from the one I used as my home screen on my phone.

Touching the photo, I said, "I only have this shot in digital. How'd you print a copy?"

Dad grinned. "Well, I am a cop with undercover training. And most Malinowskis have a sneaky gene. It took the boys, me, Ma, and Jeanine to do it. I didn't know the shell was like ones you found in North Carolina. I picked it because I knew it would remind you of your mom."

A lump swelled in my throat, and my grip tightened on the locket.

"I owe your mom everything," Dad said. "She didn't abort you, she raised you without any grudge toward whoever your father was, and raised you in the church. I wish I could thank her to her face."

I compressed my lips because if I tried to talk, only sobs would pour out. Clutching the box, I flung my arms out to hug my dad and hit the computer sitting between us.

Dad leaned over it and kissed me on the cheek. "I'm glad you like it."

I kissed him back, clasped the necklace around my neck, and spent the trip to town pushing around my emotions to get them under some kind of control so I could wait on the public.

The houses grew closer together and more people appeared in front yards and sidewalks as we traveled along the main road that turned into Main Street.

"Thank you," I whispered and sniffed.

Dad told me there were tissues in the glove compartment.

I blew my nose and said in what I hoped was a calm voice, "I hope Aunt Carrie can take the job." My words shook like a blender was whipping them.

"Seems like the ideal solution." Dad turned onto Woodward Avenue and followed the slope down to the library parking lot behind the building. "Except for one thing."

"What's that?" I grabbed my backpack.

"Carrie and I'll be living in the same county."

Chapter Ten

I let myself into the library through the door of the walk-out basement and stashed my backpack in the employees' kitchen. Carrying my phone and a coffee-table book about Australia, I climbed the back stairs, walked through the children's room, down the hall, and entered the two-story lobby of the library, the morning sun flooding through the twelve-foot-tall windows.

That light glinting off the wide array of studs lining her ears, Devon Majors shuffled the sheets of paper listing the items we had to remove from the shelves and put on the hold shelf behind the check-out desk for patrons to pick up.

"Happy birthday!" Her moss green eyes shone. "Here's what I've worked out for your gift."

I placed the book on the counter. "What do you have to work out? All you have to do is hand me a package."

Devon released a noise that was close to a snort, flinging over her shoulder several of the many braids holding back her molasses brown hair. "My best friend deserves more than a sack with an object in it, especially after treating me to breakfast for my birthday." She set aside the papers. "I've got a whole evening planned. After work on Friday, you'll drive me home. Amber said she could stay late to watch the girls. I'll give you both supper. Then Amber can watch the girls while we go to a movie at the Opera House. I checked. They're running a Marvel movie."

My mouth fell open. I couldn't help it. My friends were overwhelming me with birthday love.

Devon fingered the stud with a blood-red stone in her left ear. "Is that a happy gape or a horrified gape?"

I snapped my mouth shut. "Happy. Very happy." I slid the Australia book under the scanner. "You don't have to go to so much trouble."

I couldn't say what I was really concerned with — how expensive this had to be for Devon. She made a little more than I did as a check-out clerk because she was full time, but she supported three people with that money.

"What trouble? I have to fix supper anyway, and the Opera House is close enough to walk to. The only trouble was if Amber didn't want to babysit my kids for twelve hours instead of the usual eight. But I told her she could take the girls to her farm to break up the day."

"Sounds perfect."

"That pendant is pretty. A birthday gift?"

As Devon and I hunted for items to place on the hold shelves, I managed to get out that Dad gave it to me at my birthday breakfast before tears choked me off completely. By the time it was nine, and Devon had unlocked the glass doors to Main Street, I'd pulled myself together enough so that someone could assume my red eyes were due to allergies.

A few minutes later, Rick Carlisle walked in with a stack of books under one arm.

He placed the books on the check-out desk in front of me, glancing around like he'd done every time he'd stopped by since coming home from Haiti.

"Can I help you find anything?" That's what I always said when I waited on him.

"Oh—uh—no." He scanned the wrought-iron balcony that overlooked the lobby. "I'll just browse."

He headed up the narrow stairs to the balcony.

Our boss, Barb Hanson, strode into the lobby from the hall that led back to the children's room. "Good morning, ladies. Devon." She slid down her lime green glasses that matched her blouse to peer at a paper in her hand. "Leandra told me you wanted to switch—"

"Good morning, Barb," Rick said from the stairs.

Barb whipped around like the greeting was a gun pressed to her spine.

"G—g—good morning." She hurried back the way she came.

The beard made his face harder to read, but I could still detect the disappointment weighing on his expression. Dragging his feet, Rick went up to the balcony and into the adult books.

"He needs to give up." Devon shook papers together. "Barb wouldn't even speak to him when he said hello to her at the parade. I've heard roughly a thousand reasons why they broke up. Have you ever heard the real one?"

No. But I knew the real one. And I knew Barb and Rick did not want anyone else to know.

Passing novels under the scanner, I said to the machine, "I've probably heard all the stories you have."

"I also heard it was mutual. Either it wasn't, or Rick has changed his mind."

The four Kenzora kids burst through the double doors, their mother panting behind with two large bags of books. All four demanded to know where they could sign up for the summer reading club.

Grateful for the interruption, I escorted them to the children's room.

Chapter Eleven

After work, Dad and I drove home. As we passed our barn, four horses—one black, one palomino, and two bays—grazed in one of the pastures the alpacas weren't occupying. The Norris family had ridden over for my birthday supper.

When we climbed out of the SUV, Carrie and Rusty were weeding among the peonies that flopped over in flowerbeds bordering the front porch.

Standing, Carrie wiped the back of her gloved hand across her smooth forehead. "Mal, I have to thank you for recommending me for the Carlisle job. The kids are sweet. It should be easy compared to tracking down deadbeat dads, swindlers, and lost relations."

"I don't know about easy." Dad untucked his short-sleeve shirt. "But it'll be much less dangerous for you."

"What's your work schedule this week, Rae?" Carrie said.

Odd jump in the conversation. "Tomorrow, twelve to eight. Thursday, 8:30 to five. Friday, 8:30 to four. Why?"

"Jason wants his kids to have as normal a summer as possible. So I thought the library would be a good place for our first trip. If I bring the kids, and Ashley and her prince come in, you could text me from the lobby and I can take the kids out the back door."

"Did Jason tell you Sylvie likes to take off?"

"Yes. But he bought one of those backpacks with a leash." She paused, pulling off a glove. "I suppose I shouldn't call it a leash."

"Carrie," Dad glanced with widened eyes at Rusty, who was still on his knees, yanking weeds, "maybe we should talk about this—"

"Rusty knows why I'm babysitting. Amber and Coral do too. They're too old to buy that I suddenly have a burning desire to switch jobs. It's unrealistic for Jason to think his kids won't find out what's going on. As long as they go out in public, somebody's going to let it slip. Alli may figure it out, anyway. She's sharp. By the way—" she slapped her removed gloves together, "—why'd you recommend me?"

Dad shrugged. "Because Jason needed a bodyguard who's great with kids."

Carrie blinked. "Uh—thanks."

"Why're you so surprised?"

"Because you've always told me how reckless I am—too reckless to be a good cop."

"I never said you weren't a good cop." Heat seeped into Dad's voice.

"Okay. You imply it every time I tell you about a case."

"Carrie, are you trying to pick a fight with me? Your gratitude doesn't mean a thing if that's what you're up to." Blood flooded into Dad's face.

Carrie thrust out her chin. "I don't have to pick a fight. I'll just flat out say it." She threw her gloves on the ground. "Rae, Rusty, can you leave us?"

"For sure." My own face was probably as red as Dad's.

I moved toward the breezeway, but Rusty remained rooted by the flower bed, a trowel dangling in his hand.

I grabbed him by one of his skinny arms. "C'mon."

Rusty stumbled after me, craning his neck to look over his shoulder.

As we entered the kitchen, Dad let loose with a roar. "It's got absolutely nothing to do—"

I slammed the door behind us.

Aunt Jeanine turned from handing Aaron a stack of plates. "Something wrong?" Her pleasant tone matched the kind expression in her enormous dark blue eyes and round face with a knobby chin.

Leaning on the counter, Uncle Hank grinned. "Probably running from a pack of rabid ants in the flower bed."

Rusty and I glanced at each other as I hung up my keys on the line of hooks by the back door.

In the silence, Carrie's higher shouts punctuated Dad's deep bellows.

Losing his grin, Hank said, "Jeanine, you'd better ..."

"I'm going, I'm going." Wiping her hands on a dishcloth, Jeanine rushed out the door, strands of red-gold hair flying behind her.

My backpack slid from my shoulder. "This isn't typical, is it? Don't Dad and Aunt Carrie usually get along?"

Hank opened a cupboard door and took out a glass. "They fuss at each other like they're still kids, but, well ..."

"I've never seen them fight like this," Rusty said in a quiet voice.

Suddenly, the kitchen seemed too small. Or I'd become the elephant in it.

No voices penetrated from outside.

"Carrie should cut the Big Guy some slack." Hank opened the freezer door. "If he's holding back some facts about how you got here, we should respect that."

"Oh, hey." Gram climbed up from the basement, carrying a jar of apple butter. "I didn't realize you and Mal were home, Rae." She hugged me. "Happy birthday." Releasing me, she turned toward the stove. "Now you'll have to tell me how close I've come to your mom's recipe."

Since I'd told Gram that stuffed green peppers were my favorite dinner, she'd been trying to duplicate Mom's recipe, which wasn't easy since she hadn't written it down. Gram had to work off my memories and taste tests.

The back door opened, and Jeanine, Dad, and Carrie filed in.

"We're just about ..." Gram's relaxed smile faded.

Aunt Jeanine passed a weary hand down the side of her face. Aunt Carrie clutched her gardening gloves as if she hoped to squeeze the life out of them, and Dad—he looked like his rage was mixed with a heaping helping of something else, but I couldn't read exactly what it was on his flushed face.

"We're just about to eat." Gram's voice was usually quiet, sort of dreamy. Now it was just sad. "Mal, sweetie, you have time to change."

I went to my room and changed into jean shorts and a sleeveless blouse.

All eleven of us sat at the long plank table, said grace, and passed around the stuffed peppers—without rice—roasted cauliflower, cathead biscuits, honey from our hives, and homemade apple butter.

Saying the meal was tense was like saying a hurricane was breezy. Carrie and Dad sat at opposite ends of the table, Carrie chatting with Aaron and Micah so easily no one would ever guess she'd come from a shouting match with her big brother in the front yard.

"How was work, Rae?" Jeanine plopped a spoonful of apple butter on her biscuit. "Has the summer reading club started?"

Jeanine didn't really fit with her superhero siblings. Shorter than Carrie and slender, she looked too fragile to tackle the bad guys. Maybe that was why she only did it through her mystery novels and short stories.

I said yes and forked the spicy meat from the green pepper on my plate.

Dad, who sat at right angles to me at the head of the table, shot me reassuring glances.

Everyone at my end kept asking me questions, and I kept answering, but I actually wanted to slide onto the floor and sneak into my bedroom until tomorrow. Even though Carrie was kind to me, I was still the source of her anger.

Gram and Jeanine wouldn't let me help clean up the dishes, so I waited at the table until they cleared it.

"Present time!" Micah bounced beside the chair Dad had just left.

Aaron brought over a box about the size of a loaf of bread wrapped in lime green paper. He set it in front of me as the family gathered around. "It's from all of us."

Micah sidled up to me. "Dad said you'd like this." But his sentence held doubt.

"I'm sure I will." I ripped off the paper. My breath disappeared. "It's a macro lens," I whispered.

Micah frowned, glancing over the family. "I told you she wouldn't like it."

"Oh, I do, I really do." I rubbed him on the back. "I'm just...surprised."

The lens was worth at least $700. I'd drooled over pictures of it often enough to remember the price. From what I'd observed of the finances of Dad, Gram, and the Norrises, Carrie must have paid for most of it.

"Thank you. Thank you all so much." I tried to look into everybody's face and stopped at Carrie. "You didn't have to."

"Of course, we didn't." Uncle Hank put on his cowboy hat. "That's why it's called a present and not a payment."

Pressing up against me, Micah peered at the lens. "Aaron said you can take good pictures of bugs with it. How come you wanna take pictures of bugs?"

"Not just bugs. Anything small." Scooting back my chair, I stood. "I'll show you. Let's—oh, wait." I looked to Gram. "Are we doing cake now? Or pie?"

"I'm glad you said pie because that's what I made—apple and cherry."

"I'm definitely a pie person."

"I thought so. We need to wait so everyone has room for it."

"I definitely need to wait." I lifted the lens from its box. "Before I show you how it works, Micah, us kids need to meet upstairs."

"How come?" said Micah.

"Father's Day secrets," I whispered and motioned for them to follow me.

Dad said, "I'll keep Hank busy on your room, so he can't spy on you all."

"Like I'd ruin my girls' surprise for me," Hank said, faking offense. "But I've got to get back to planting."

I knew farming depended on the weather, but I'd never realized how hard farmers had to work when the weather was right. Uncle Hank and his father had been planting in a frenzy since last Wednesday. He'd had to debate taking time off for the parade and picnic.

Up in the playroom, Amber, Coral, Rusty, Aaron, Micah, and I cleared enough toys off the floor for us to sit. Since Dad and Gram had thrown up a temporary wall for her temporary bedroom, there was even less room for the avalanche of toys my brothers had acquired.

Sitting cross-legged, I said, "Thursday after work I'm planning on driving to the mall in Lancaster to get our photos printed and buy frames for our Father's Day gifts. Does anybody want to come with me?"

"I will," Amber said without a second's hesitation, like I knew she would.

"Do you need help picking out a frame?" Rusty sounded puzzled.

"Not help exactly. I just thought since the four of us are giving one gift, y'all might like to pick out the frame for the photos I took of y'all."

Micah spun wheels on a toy car. "I don't want to go shopping at the mall."

"Then I'll choose the frame for the four of us," I said.

"It doesn't really matter what we give Dad," said Rusty. "He'll puddle up if it's a dirt clod."

He wasn't far from the truth. When I'd given Dad a photo for his birthday, he got all misty-eyed because it was the first gift from me. Now I'd be giving him his first Father's Day gift with the sons of his late wife. Better have a mop handy.

Coral propped her elbows on the railing of the stairs. "If Amber's going, I'm going."

Amber sat up. "You hate malls and shopping."

"If I don't go, you'll pick out a pink frame with unicorns dancing around the edge." Coral rolled her eyes. "I know what Dad likes."

"I know Dad as well as you do." Amber's voice grew shrill. "And at least I have taste."

Drawing in my lips, I tamped down a groan. Refereeing my cousins was not how I wanted to spend my shopping trip.

Chapter Twelve

"Coral, you have no sense of style at all." Amber's eye roll seemed calculated to annoy her sister even more than usual. She snatched the multi-photo frame from Coral's hands.

When I'd picked up my cousins after supper, I'd vowed I'd let Amber and Coral fight out any disagreements between themselves. No way was I getting sucked into playing ref.

But now I was a hostage. I'd spent five minutes selecting a frame that could hold the four photos of me and my brothers. Amber and Coral were going on twenty minutes of arguing about a frame for their photos.

"So ugly is a kind of style." Coral put a hand on her waist. "What's wrong with a wood frame?"

"Just because we live on a farm doesn't mean every single decoration has to be rustic." Amber held up a sleek, black metal frame. "Rae, won't our photos pop in this frame if we use white mats?"

Actually, I hated black frames with white mats because too many people displayed photos that way. "This is for your dad, not mine. Y'all need to agree on something."

"It's not my fault we're still standing here." Coral flounced against a shelf.

"You're too loud." Amber glanced around as if she was afraid the entire junior class of Marlin County High School would troop down the aisle of the craft store and watch their fight.

I really couldn't abandon them. Their parents would notice if I came home alone. "I'll be waiting by the registers when y'all decide on something."

At the front of the store, shoppers milled in and out and down the broad hall of the mall. Some kind of grand opening was going on at a store two doors down. Senator Schuster greeted people as they filed in. More damage control?

Bruce Schuster handed out a piece of paper like a bookmark, chatting with anyone who stopped longer than to take the item. His appearance had improved since Monday. His black polo shirt was the right size for him and untucked, hiding his bulging gut, and his black, wavy hair had been combed.

The senator glanced up and spotted me, his smile widening as he waved in my direction.

I smiled back to be polite, then looked over my shoulder to the frame aisle.

From the head thrusts and thrown out arms, it took me most of a second to deduce my cousins had decided on nothing.

Returning my attention to the outside of the store, I found Bruce Schuster in front of me.

"Sorry about the picnic," he mumbled, rubbing a hairy hand along his jaw. "I mean, what I said at the picnic."

He didn't sound sorry. He sounded more like someone had forced him to make an apology. Probably his brother. Maybe he needed to be on good terms with other elected officials like the sheriff?

"It's all—" I shouldn't say it was all right just to get rid of the guy. "Thank you. I—uh—thank you for taking the time to come over here and tell me that."

"I got all the time in the world until the mall closes." Spreading his legs a little apart, he crossed his arms over his gut and gestured toward his brother. "Since Brad's divorced, our family helps out when he does events. He says he should give off a family man vibe. Voters around here like that." He chuckled. "Keeping Brad in office has sort of turned into a family business."

"Oh—uh—I didn't know that." I edged backwards.

"Yeah. And I really am sorry about Monday. When I get too many cans in me, I never know what's gonna come out." If helping his brother was the family business, he seemed in no hurry to get back on the job. "Everybody in the county was shocked when Mal said he had a baby with Bella. I mean, he was pretty wild in high school, but I didn't think he was in Bella's league. I oughta know." A self-conscious laugh came out like a cough. "She turned me down often enough, and I was just a dumb high school football player like Mal."

Why was he telling me all this? Did he really think I wanted to know all these private details?

I inched further back.

"You know—" his hazel eyes studied me "—you don't look much like your mom. Not much like Mal either."

"Dad said I take a bit after my grandmother. Excuse me. My cousins need my help." I spun around and said over my shoulder, "Thanks again."

As soon as I entered the aisle, Coral grabbed my arm. "Rae, wouldn't a wood frame look better?"

"There's nothing evil about metal, Coral," Amber said in a groan.

So nice to hear them arguing. Nice and normal and not at all weird like my previous conversation.

I picked up a frame that would hold two 5 x 7 photos. "Both your photos will look good in this—it's wood painted black."

"And white mats," said Amber.

"No," said Coral.

I removed a mat from the rack. "How about cream as a compromise?"

They argued another five minutes about the color, and then, finally, agreed on cream. By the time we went to a register to pay, Bruce Schuster wasn't nowhere in view.

We wandered into the mall, past the grand opening of what looked like a store featuring local arts and crafts and OSU merchandise, and I treated Amber and Coral to frozen yogurt.

Licking our treats, we left the mall by a side entrance closest to where I parked my truck.

"Can I drive?" Amber wiped cherry yogurt from the tip of her freckled nose with a napkin.

"The Rust Bucket's very sensitive." I swallowed a lump of my chocolate yogurt. "Too sensitive. I should—"

Amber yelped as two men—one blond, the other fat—popped out of an alley and knocked into her as they pounded into the parking lot.

"Hey!" Coral flung out her arms and some cotton candy yogurt too. "Watch where you're going."

I glanced down the alley, which seemed to be a delivery area behind this wing of the mall, and blinked, looked, and blinked some more.

Gripping a wall, Troy hauled himself off the ground, blood smearing his face.

I ran over to him. "Are you all right? Should I call an ambulance?"

For the first time, I was close enough to him to see that his pale green eyes had the same burst of yellow in the centers that Walter's had.

Holding his head, he said, "Rae Riley? What are you doing here?"

"Shopping." I handed him an unused napkin. "I'll call an ambulance."

"Please don't." He held the napkin against his bleeding lip. "Thank you."

"Did those guys beat you up?" Coral whispered.

He tried to grin and winced. "You three don't need to get involved in this. Your parents would not want you talking to me."

"Shouldn't we call the police, Rae? Those guys just committed assault." Amber glanced over her shoulder.

The two men had run out of sight.

Troy held up a hand. "This is my problem, girls. I don't want you kids to get in trouble because of me." He weaved his way out of the alley to where it joined the parking lot.

"Don't you want to press charges?" I wiped the dripping yogurt from my fingers.

"Against who? It's a case of mistaken identity. They thought I was Matt Malinowski—he's the oldest son of my half-brother Cal. Your dad put Matt in prison over a year ago."

I took a quick peek at my memory. "He's one of Dad's cousins who jumped him."

Troy nodded, then closed his eyes and clasped his forehead. "I told them they'd grabbed the wrong guy. They didn't believe me, but before they could do more damage or I could show them my ID, you girls appeared."

"So you won't go to the police?"

"That's a nice idea, but it doesn't work for Malinowskis." He huffed a pathetic laugh. "You wouldn't understand since you're a member of the respectable side of the family, but most of the time, cops are as dangerous to us Malinowskis as our enemies."

"You could tell Dad."

He chuckled deep in his throat. "You have a lot of faith in Mal. That's the way it should be."

He stopped beside a powder blue hatchback and dug into the front pocket of his jeans. Then his eyes rolled up, and his knees buckled.

I grabbed him by his elbow. "You can't drive. Let me call an ambulance."

He shook his head, winced, then opened the door, and fell into the driver's seat, his feet resting on the pavement as he took some deep inhales.

He was in no condition to get behind the wheel of any vehicle.

I tugged on my earlobe. "I'll drive you home."

Three gasps escaped together.

"Uncle Mal told us." Coral bent toward me as if she needed to get closer for me to hear her. "He told all of us that Troy's dangerous, and we should stay away from him."

"I know." I forced my imagination to hold off on the manufacture of the many potential responses Dad would have to this decision. But if I had a concussion, I'd like someone to help me. And since Troy was injured, he wasn't much of a threat.

Troy dabbed the bloody napkin at a cut through his eyebrow. "Actually, I'm not dangerous at all."

Coral aimed a solid glare at him. "Uncle Mal also said you're a con man."

"Amber, you drive the Rust Bucket." I handed her my keys. "Stay right behind me. If it looks like I'm in trouble, call the cops." Although what kind of trouble Troy could make when I had control of the car, and he could barely stand, I couldn't imagine.

"Absolutely." Amber's single word rang with a thrill.

I fought a groan. Amber could overdramatize anything, and I didn't need her to imagine driving Troy to Walter's house was an epic adventure.

"Thank you." Troy held out his keys.

I took them and asked him to stand and move away from the car. I handed Coral my cone and then looked and felt under the driver's seat. Then I went around to the passenger side and reached under that seat.

"What are you looking for?" Coral said through a mouthful of yogurt and cone.

"A gun." I opened the glove compartment. "Or any kind of weapon."

Troy gasped. "I know your dad doesn't like me, but I'd never hurt family."

A burn started up my neck, but when I told Dad about this, I wanted to reassure him I'd taken every precaution. Dad had said during his instructions on self-defense to follow my instincts if I was suspicious. If I was wrong, I could always apologize.

Satisfied the car was unarmed, I returned to Troy, who watched me with wide eyes. He wore a white polo shirt, belted into faded jeans. Not many places to hide a weapon.

"Lift your pant legs." My manners kicked in. "Please."

Still staring. Troy did as I asked without a word, revealing bare feet in his deck shoes.

When Amber pulled up in the Rust Bucket, Coral got in, and then Troy and I slid into the hatchback.

As I scooted the seat back, Troy sucked in a breath. "The—the way you turned your head—you looked exactly like Bella."

"No, I don't." I slammed the hatchback into gear.

The evening light filtered through lumps of iron clouds on the western horizon while feathers of white clouds drifted east against a deepening blue sky.

Patting his wounds with the napkin, Troy said nothing until I drove onto the state highway.

"If Mal gets ugly about this, tell me. This is all my fault."

"My dad doesn't get ugly with me." If I looked straight ahead, maybe Troy would shut up.

"I'm glad to hear that." His relief sounded genuine. "I've seen Mal angry and—well, I'm glad you haven't."

"I've seen him angry. It's nothing."

That wasn't quite the truth. I didn't like dealing with his anger, but it usually was his outside expression of his inside worries. Knowing that made it easier to take. Usually.

"I don't want to hurt your relationship with Mal."

"You can't," I said to the grimy windshield.

"I bet you're right. I hear all over the county how pleased Mal is to call you his daughter, despite how it might hurt his career. I've heard—"

"What do you mean by 'call' me his daughter? I am his daughter. You said yourself that I'm a Malinowski."

"Totally true. Anyone can see you're related to Walter. I just meant ..." Frowning, he tugged at his ear.

My heart seized up. No one in the family or Mom made that gesture when they were thinking. Of all the mannerisms I shared with Dad, that wasn't one of them.

Dad ...

Troy and Mom ...

A cold stole over me, shriveling my senses, forcing my mind to consider only one thought.

No, Father. That can't be, that can't be ...

"I just meant that I don't belong to the camp that thinks Mal and you should have done a DNA test." Troy's voice seemed to reach me from the bottom of a well. "If you're happy with calling Mal your dad, then—"

A car veered into my lane, horn blaring.

I swerved onto the shoulder.

The car followed, crowding me.

I whipped the hatchback into the long weeds and tall, fuzzy pink flowers lining the shoulder and stomped on the brakes.

The car, a dark four-door, blasted its horn as it shot by.

Chapter Thirteen

Staring after it, I said, "I think those were the guys who ran out of the alley." My words were squeaks, and I released a breath I didn't know I was holding. "The passenger could've been the fat guy who ran into Amber. Did you see who it was?"

The Rust Bucket flew by. Hadn't Amber seen me get run off the road?

"Wasn't that your truck?" Troy peered through the windshield.

I stretched my right arm into the backseat and hauled up my backpack. As I took my phone out of a side pocket, it rang, and I swiped it on. "Amber, why didn't you stop?"

"It's Coral. Amber told me to tell you we're following the car that tried to hit you to get their license plate."

"You're what?" My shout made Troy jerk under his seat belt.

"Amber thinks it's the guys who beat up Troy. She wants to make sure."

"Tell her to stop chasing them right now and pull over as soon as you can."

"We're getting off the highway."

I sagged over the wheel. "Good. Where?"

"I don't know."

"That road that's near the big antique mall," Amber said in the distance. "I think I can get close enough to see who's driving."

I sat up like the springs in the seat had delivered an electric shock. "Stop now. Are you crazy? I'm coming. Keep talking, Coral." I shoved the phone at Troy. "Put it on speaker and hold it." I stared over my shoulder at the traffic flying by on the state highway, then turned back to the phone. "These guys are dangerous. This isn't smart, Amber."

Amber's faraway voice came to me. "We aren't going to confront the guys. Just get their license plate and see if they could be the guys who beat up Troy."

"They have to be." I roared into the right lane of the highway. "I've never been run off the road before."

Accelerating as fast as I dared, I raced down the highway. In a few minutes, the antique mall, empty at 8:30 in the evening, appeared on my left, beside the northbound lanes. I switched on my right blinker when I saw the sign for the only road that met the southbound lanes.

Turning, I said, "Amber, did you get off at Tarkiln Road?"

"I think so."

"Stop driving. Are you still on Tarkiln?"

"No. I took the first road on the right. I can't—" Her words evaporated.

"Coral? Amber?" I scanned the right edge for a break in the woods that hemmed the road.

No answer.

"They probably drove into a spot with no reception." Troy thumbed a button. "I'll try to call them back."

I screeched onto the first road on the right and hadn't driven far before the hills closed in on the crumbling asphalt and human habitation disappeared.

"It's a black hole." Troy set the phone in the slot in his door. "You've lost service now. I'm sure they're fine."

The road climbed into the darkening hills. No sign of my truck.

Father, let them be all right. And, please, don't let Troy be my father.

I crested a hill. Near the bottom, the Rust Bucket was pulled over on the right. Dropping one hand from the steering wheel, scraps of the fake leather coming off with it, I followed the road down the steep slope of the narrow valley and parked behind my cousins. I slammed out of Troy's car and ran up to the driver's side.

A perplexed expression wrinkling her lightly freckled face, Amber looked up and down the road.

"Amber, what did you think you were doing?" My question ended in a screech. I swallowed.

"I told you we were just getting close enough to get their license plate number and see if it was the same two guys from the mall."

"We only saw those guys for half a second. We can't identify them."

"Well, no, not in a lineup. But if I'd gotten close enough to see the driver and the passenger, and they turned out to be two women or two kids or something, then we'd know you getting run off the road wasn't connected to Troy's attack."

I pulled a hand down the side of my face. "Thanks for finally stopping."

"She only did that—" Coral poked an accusing finger at her sister "—because she wasn't sure if the car had kept going on this road or turned off on that one." Now the finger pointed to a gravel road that sliced between the spires of pine trees.

"It doesn't matter now." I pushed off the truck. "We're going home."

Sighing, Amber grabbed the gearshift. "I'm sorry I couldn't get closer."

"I didn't want you to get closer." The screech fought for release.

Amber shoved the gearshift. No movement. Then she pushed it, pulled it, and shoved it again. "Rae, I think it's stuck." Her pale face reddened, like the western sky behind the trees. "Sorry."

I groaned loud and long. "Turn it off and stand on the brakes. Coral, hand me the flashlight in the glove compartment."

As Coral fished it out, Troy appeared by the truck. "What's the flashlight for?"

"The gears won't mesh." I crouched in front of the hood.

"We shouldn't linger." Troy's gaze darted over the woods that dwarfed us. "That car could come back this way."

The gaps between the trunks were already black, and the darkness was rising, as if pushing the scarlet off the trees' limbs and out of the sky.

"I'll be as quick as I can." Although out of all the times the gears had slipped, I'd only fixed it twice myself.

I laid on my back and scooted under my truck. Holding the flashlight, I grabbed the gears with my right hand and pressed so hard that my fingers grew sore. I crawled out and sat in the thin stems of purple dame's rocket hanging over the fragmented edge of the asphalt, shaking my fingers.

"You can all fit in my car, and you can still drive, Rae." Amusement touched Troy's battered, tiny mouth. "Since you frisked me, you know I'm completely—"

The sound of rattling leaves reached us.

Troy went rigid, all his attention on the sharp slope of the hill that descended right beside my truck. "Someone's coming." He spoke in a croak.

Amber threw me a panicked look and I manufactured a reassuring smile.

Troy was awfully anxious for not knowing the identities of the two men. Getting a split lip was unpleasant, but Troy acted like he knew they could do a whole lot worse.

Coral frowned at him. "That's a squirrel."

Only Troy's pale eyes moved as he scrutinized the pines and shrubs growing at precarious tilts above us. "How can you tell?"

"The sound of somebody stepping on leaves is a ton different from that sound. Which was leaves or pine needles shaking."

"It sounded way too big to be a squirrel."

"Squirrels make a surprising amount of noise for their size." I stretched my fingers.

Troy finally moved, half turning to me. "Are you a Girl Scout too?"

"No, I've just been in the woods a lot." I shoved myself under the hood.

Pointing the beam of the flashlight up, I went to work on the gears.

"Did you hear that?" His question whipped the air. "I'm sure it's—"

"Another squirrel." The frown in Coral's voice was unmistakable.

"It sounded like a bigger animal to me." For the first time, Troy's understanding, apologetic tone revealed strains of impatience. "It could be something as big as a deer."

"A deer won't come and beat you up."

I had to tell Dad, Uncle Hank and Aunt Jeanine that they didn't need to worry about Troy conning Coral.

My fingers slipped, and I rub them on my shorts.

What would the three of them say about this mess? Amber was at fault for not listening to me, but she wouldn't have been driving without me if I hadn't tried to help Troy. An image of Dad turning deep red and releasing his opinion at top volume cut the air in my lungs.

I gripped the gears again, and they meshed together.

Thank You, Father. I needed something to go right about now.

I slid out from under the hood. "Start it up, Amber. You follow me and actually do it this time."

"I will." Amber held up her right hand. "I swear."

Anyone who didn't know her might think she was mocking me. But Amber didn't mock, especially not me.

"I'm counting on you."

Troy strolled back to the passenger side of his car, not even a tremor of unsteadiness.

My body went limp. Had he played me? I hadn't considered that possibility because I couldn't see how conning me gave him any advantage. Unless he thought driving him would get all of us in trouble with our parents.

"You look like you've recovered." Anger simmered in my words, stiffening every muscle, and I made zilch attempt to hide it.

"I am feeling better." He touched his split lip.

"You can drive yourself home."

"I'll try." He lowered his voice. "I won't tell anyone how you girls helped me."

"Fine. We will." I jerked open the back door of Troy's car and snatched out my backpack.

If Troy had faked his dizziness, I'd fallen for it like a duck with two broken wings.

As I marched to the Rust Bucket, Amber revved and revved the engine. But it wouldn't catch.

Oh, please, Father. Not this.

Amber leaned out the open window. "Am I doing something wrong?"

"Probably not, but let me try."

Amber and I exchanged places. I turned the key, punched the gas, but no go. I smacked the steering wheel.

"What do we do now?" Coral's frown deepened.

"We all get in Troy's car. I drive to where I can get reception, call the cops, and see if they want to track down that car. Then I'll call Dad." My stomach took a dive.

I locked the truck, fighting an urge to scream at Amber, at Troy, but really, at myself. I'd tried to do the right thing, and it had bit me. Big time.

I called to Troy, who hadn't gotten into his car. "We'll ride with you. I'm driving."

"I am desperately sorry, Rae." Amber's voice was breathless as she adjusted her grip on the shopping bag with the frames. "I thought it was a good idea to get their number."

"Amber." I made every effort to sound kind. "If those guys ran me off the road, they could've recognized you from the mall and run you off the road too."

"I hadn't thought of that." Her voice shrank. "I guess I just got caught up in all the excitement."

And, I bet, she wanted to impress me, doing something she thought I would have done. My anger fizzled. If circumstances had been a little different, I might have.

Amber and Coral slid into the back, and Troy and I resumed our seats.

"This is all my fault." Troy turned sideways. "I wasn't thinking clearly when I agreed to let you drive me. I'll tell Mal that." He looked into the backseat. "And Jeanine."

Flooring it up the hill, I said, "Great. You can also tell the cops about your attack when I tell them about getting run off the road."

"You're calling the cops?" A trace of genuine surprise might have echoed under the question.

I clenched the wheel. "About time somebody did."

"But you have nothing to tell them. I mean, you didn't see who was in the car or get the license plate number."

"It was a Ford," said Coral. "Dark blue."

I glanced back at her. "Did you notice anything else?"

"I think the first letter of the license plate was a 'D'."

"You couldn't have seen all that." The right side of Amber's mouth twisted as she rolled her eyes.

"Why not?"

"I didn't. How could you?"

"Coral wasn't driving." I tried to head off a fight. "Was that all?"

Coral was silent for a moment. "I think they were poor. The car had a lot of paint missing from different parts and I saw rust spots."

Amber groaned. "Coral, our cars have paint missing and rust spots, and we're not poor."

"Yeah, we are."

"No, we're not."

"Yeah, we are."

I started to tell them to quit arguing when Troy's face tensed, and he rubbed his right temple.

With a hard grin, I let them argue all the way to the antique mall.

Chapter Fourteen

At the mall, its cluster of long, low pole buildings dark and locked, I pulled into the empty parking lot and called the police. I only mentioned getting run off the road. I could explain to the officer in person about the guys who beat up Troy. The dispatcher said a patrol officer would meet us in fifteen minutes. I told Amber to call her parents on her phone.

With my mood wallowing at ground level, I swiped Dad's number.

"Hey, Rae. Coming home?"

"Not yet, Dad." I adopted a smile, hoping that would relax my voice. "We've got a bit of a problem, but we're okay." I recounted what had happened, starting with when we left the mall with our frozen yogurt.

"Troy was in no shape to drive, so I decided I'd drive him to Walter's in his—"

"You got in a car with Troy?"

Dad's shout forced me to hold my phone away from my ear. And he kept shouting, louder and louder, until I got to the part about us waiting for a cop at the antique mall.

He took a long breath. "So you're all right?"

"Yeah." I saw the depressed look on Amber's face as she returned her phone into her purse. "Amber just got off the phone with Uncle Hank and Aunt Jeanine."

A phone rang behind Dad. "That's probably them now," he said in a growl.

Troy held out a hand. "Let me talk to Mal."

I turned my back on him and said, "We'll wait for y'all to come. Dad."

"You promise you won't go anywhere with Troy if the officer leaves before we get there?"

"Yes."

"You mean it?"

My mood sunk into the dirt. "Yeah, Dad."

As I tucked my phone into my backpack, Coral said, "I knew he'd be mad. We should have left Troy where we found him."

"You're absolutely right," Troy said with a sigh.

Coral folded her arms and glared. "You could've said that back at the mall."

"I was too confused by the blows."

She shifted her weight to her back leg. "Uh huh."

The patrol officer pulled in and was wrapping up his questioning when Dad drove up in his huge, black truck with Hank and Jeanine right behind in the Norrises' maroon SUV.

The officer closed his pad. "Not much I can do at this point without a license number." He eyed Troy. "Are you sure you didn't know either of the men who attacked you or could recognize them from photos?"

"I'm sure, officer." He shook his head. "Even if I could, none of us can say they were the ones who forced Rae off the road."

"'Course not." Dad joined us under a high streetlight. "Rae gets run off the road all the time. Could've been anyone."

Troy opened his mouth, but Amber planted herself in front of Dad, arms spread out. "I am entirely to blame, Uncle Mal. Rae told me not to follow that car, and I didn't listen. If you want to be angry at someone—" she raised her fine chin "—be angry at me."

Dad's eyes looked heavenward but didn't complete a roll. "Amber, I appreciate you sacrificing yourself to my wrath for Rae's sake and all, but your parents will take care of any punishment."

"You bet." Tilting his cowboy hat further down his forehead, Uncle Hank frowned at his oldest daughter.

Lowering her arms, Amber seemed to wither.

"It's actually my fault, Mal." Troy stepped in front of me like a shield. "I shouldn't have let them help me."

"Your concern for the girls' safety is touching, Troy. And way too late." He showed his badge to the officer, and they walked away, talking.

Uncle Hank said, "Here's what we're doing. Jeanine'll drive Troy's car to Walter's. Mal will drive Troy in the Beast. You girls are riding with me to wherever Rae's truck is, and I'll see if I can get it going."

Amber and I gathered the shopping bags from Troy's car. Amber and Coral sat in the back of the SUV while I sat beside Hank up front.

"I'm so, so sorry you had to come out here." I clicked the seatbelt.

"Not your fault your truck broke down in the middle of nowhere." Uncle Hank looked back at Amber.

"You're right." She sat up perfectly straight, pressing her hands against her chest like she was taking some kind of pledge. "Dad, I take full responsibility." Then the noble ring faded from her voice. "What are you and Mom going to do?"

"We've been discussing not letting you drive by yourself for a month."

A protest seemed to rise to her lips, but then Amber pinched them together and sank back in her seat.

On the lonely country road, Hank got the Rust Bucket running in ten minutes.

As he closed the hood, I said, "You'll have to show me how to do that."

"Be glad to." He wiped his hands on his jeans.

"I really did try to keep Amber and Coral safe." I held the flashlight up so we could see each other's faces.

"I know. If Amber had listened to you, most likely they'd've been fine. But Mal told you to steer clear of Troy. Why didn't you listen?"

Too bad I'd aimed the flashlight so Hank could read every detail of my embarrassment. "I thought he needed help. God expects us to help people. Even our enemies."

"But He also expects you to be smart. If Troy wasn't in no shape to drive, you should've called the cops."

"But he wasn't drunk or high."

"You thought he was a danger behind the wheel," said Hank. "You can call the cops for something like that."

"Oh. I—I didn't know that." I let the flashlight drop.

How much dumber could I've been tonight?

Hank broke into his extra wide grin, a relief to see. "Jeanine figured you didn't. Your dad couldn't believe you didn't know that, but Jeanine told him that as smart as you are, if you thought you could call the cops, you would've."

That's was a flattering opinion, but it might not be true.

I drove the Rust Bucket behind the Norrises' SUV to the highway. As we snaked our way through the rolling hills, I replayed everything that had happened.

Why had Troy faked being too injured to drive? To get us in trouble? Or to get me alone and insinuate that he was my dad?

My air clogged my throat.

That couldn't be true, but I had evidence other than Troy's word. When I researched the stalker, Walter said Troy and one of Dad's first cousins bragged they had slept with Mom. And Troy had brought Mom to Walter's house a few times. Jason Carlisle had said he'd seen Troy sneaking out of the abandoned children's home Mom had used as a sort of headquarters for all her covert activities. And Troy had tugged on his ear when he thought, just like I did.

Sections from Mom's letter to Dad, apologizing for trying to blackmail him with her pregnancy, rose in my mind.

"I don't remember why I targeted you that night. I was pretty drunk, but I do remember I was in a meaner mood than usual, and I knew you were from a nice family. Back then, I hated nice families."

I took the exit from the highway.

"If Bella was as drunk as all of us were that night you two hooked up, how could she be sure you're the chick's father?" Bruce Schuster's question rammed around my brain.

Could Mom have gotten drunk another night and not remembered she slept with Troy or another Malinowski? Dad admitted he was drunk the night I was conceived. Were he and Mom so trashed that they couldn't remember not sleeping together and Mom only guessed they had when she became pregnant?

I drove past the barn and up to the house.

This was such a mess. If I only could be sure of Mom's judgment. After she wrote the three letters, I'd asked her point-blank if one of the three men was my father.

She had said, "Yes."

So she was convinced that it was either Dad, Jason, or Professor O'Neil.

Leaning against the headrest, I closed my eyes.

Troy had no more proof of his paternity than I did, so why would he care? Dad said he hadn't seen Egypt and China in almost two years, so he wasn't exactly burning with a desire to play dad.

My air jammed again. What was Dad going to say to me when he got home?

"Are you all right?"

I started, bumping my knees against the dash.

Gram placed fingers on the edge of the open window. She gave me that calm-waters look of hers.

"Yeah." I got out, dragging my backpack and the shopping bag over the seat. "We're all fine. Troy didn't try to hurt us or anything."

"Troy's weapons are his words." Gram patted my back. "He'd never use physical force unless he was sure he could get away with it."

Now she told me. He'd packed a fully loaded weapon tonight.

Passing through the living room, I said hey to Rusty, who was in his usual nighttime spot, stretched out on the couch, reading a fantasy novel.

In my bedroom, I shut the door, laid my stuff on the bed, and switched on the green-shaded lamp on the narrow desk under the window. Using the small key on my key chain, I unlocked the center drawer and reached to the very back of it. I pulled out an envelope, opened it, and removed the copies of the letters Mom had written to the three men she'd blackmailed. As long as the letters were, I had them memorized, but I still wanted to re-read Dad's in case I had forgotten something.

Five minutes later, I returned the envelope to the back of the drawer.

Mom was very clear. She had been drunk, although she knew that was no excuse.

But had she gotten drunk often, so often she wouldn't remember who might have been my father? There was no way of knowing now.

Through my closed door, I heard Rusty say good night to Gram.

I couldn't even try to go to sleep with so many questions and concerns stealing my peace.

I opened the door connecting the old bedroom with the new one. The electricity wasn't hooked up yet, so I took the desk lamp and an extension cord from the lamp beside the bed, plugged it in near the doorway, and set the lamp on the floor, tilting back the shade to aim its beam on an unfinished section of drywall. I picked up the paddle from the spackle container and worked the material into a seam like Dad showed me.

I spread and smoothed, spread and smoothed.

Father, should I investigate Troy's insinuations? Or just ignore them?

Voices eventually reached me, and I recognized Dad's deep one. Then his huge frame filled the doorway between the two bedrooms.

Lowering the paddle, I faced him, although my feet seemed reluctant to turn in his direction.

He peered at my work. "You do a good job when you've just learned how to spackle."

I couldn't stand small talk. "I'm sorry. I had no clue helping Troy would make such a mess."

Dad leaned against the door frame. "Most of the mess was Amber's fault. You know why she was determined to go after that car, don't you?"

I twirled the paddle between my fingers. "She thought it was something I'd do, and I think she wanted to impress me. I told her not to."

"I know you did. You can't control Amber. I just want you to understand how Amber ... hero worships you. The choices you make have a bigger impact than you may think."

"Like since I helped Troy, Amber may try to help another sketchy relative?"

"Possibly." Dad released a sigh from somewhere deep. "I told you to stay away from him. Why didn't you?"

"I really thought he was hurt, so he couldn't be much of a threat. The Bible says to treat others as you would like to be treated. It also says to be kind to your enemies."

"I know. But Jesus also said that we have to be as wise as snakes when we go out among the wolves. You've got to be wise about how you help people. Rae, you worry me. You were ready to get yourself involved in a possible domestic situation in the middle of the woods. You drove Troy when I specifically told you he was dangerous. Even if he'd been genuinely injured, and Amber had listened to you, you still would've been run off the road."

"That's true." I reached up to tug on my earlobe but dropped my hand. "But is there anything in the Bible about circumstances where you shouldn't help your enemies?"

"Well ... not that I can think of." The left side of Dad's face contracted.

We shared that mannerism, and Gram said it signaled that we knew we had to do something we didn't want to do. "But God doesn't expect you to let people take advantage of you."

"I get that." I clenched my jaw, considering how Troy had played me. "But doesn't He expect you to risk yourself sometimes? The good Samaritan did. A pastor said in a sermon that the Samaritan risked getting attacked when he stopped to help that guy. You risk your life every time you go on patrol to cover gaps in the shifts."

"I'm trained to assess risks and respond appropriately."

"But you aren't trained for every type of situation that might come up."

"Well ... no." The left side of his face bunched up again. "But if something unusual happens, I rely on my experience. You don't have any experience dealing with grifters." He stepped into the room. "What did Troy say to you?"

Not "Did he talk to you as you drove him?" Dad seemed to know Troy well enough that if he got me alone some place, he'd put his mouth to work.

"He talked about how much I remind him of Mom. He keeps flattering me." My hand twitched for my earlobe, but I ignored it. "Maybe so I like him or trust him?"

"There's a reason 'con' is short for 'confidence'. Anything else?"

Something in my gut tightened. I did not like him grilling me like a suspect. "He kept saying how he'd fix things with you if you were angry with me, like I needed protection. More flattery, I guess. He also said the two guys who beat him up thought he was Matt Malinowski."

"Yeah, he told me that too." Dad huffed a laugh. "Matt's at least four inches taller and fifteen years younger than Troy, so both those guys are either stupid or nearsighted. So Troy's lying." His voice grew quiet. "Were you flattered?"

The something in my gut snapped, and I stabbed my gaze at Dad. "I may have been dumb tonight, but I'm not that dumb."

"Sorry." He was still quiet. "Troy's spent years perfecting his lies. Don't think you're dumb if you buy some of them. And don't ever think you're not susceptible to them. It's when you think you can't be conned that the con man gets to work. But if you're never around him, he can't do a thing."

"Unless he cons people into doing it for him. You said Troy prefers to operate that way."

"True."

"I can't suspect everybody is working for Troy."

"I guess not." Admitting that sent a spasm across his face. "Can I give you a hug?"

Any resentment in me melted. "Always."

He wrapped his powerful arms around me and gave me a good steady squeeze. He said in my ear. "Rae, you have a gift for mercy. We should study that so you can use it wisely. I've got a study Bible, and Ma does too. We can both look up verses and pray about them. If I learn something, I'll tell you, and you'll do the same. What do you think?"

I wasn't sure I had a choice. "Sure."

He kissed me by my ear. "It's not your job to help everybody, and there are some people you can't help."

I rolled that around my mind as I brushed my teeth in the little, sky-blue bathroom Gram and I shared.

True. There'd be situations where I couldn't help someone because I wouldn't have the expertise or the person would refuse, but shouldn't I help as much as I could when I could?

I turned off the bedside lamp, but instead of lying down, I stared at the closed door to the half-finished bedroom, replaying my conversation with Troy.

All his talk amounted to a boat load of nothing. Some weird comments and a shared mannerism didn't justify jumping to the conclusion he was my dad. Or even that Troy thought he was. If I brought that to Dad, he'd think I was even dumber than I'd already shown. And what could he say? If he actually thought I might be Troy's daughter, he wouldn't throw me out. He was too kind for that. But would he keep me because he loved me or because he felt it was his duty? Like Jason.

I held my hand against my stomach.

I couldn't stand it if I knew Dad was just tolerating me because he thought he had to.

Was there any way to disprove my theory? If I knew Troy's blood type, that could shoot down his insinuations in an instant since mine was rare. And if I could ask someone about Mom's drinking habits when she lived in Marlin County, that would at least let me know if it was likely she could have made a mistake.

Father, if I shouldn't pursue this, please let me know.

I tried to release my ideas to Him, but they kept changing, twisting, turning, morphing until sleep overwhelmed them and me.

Chapter Fifteen

Walter stalked into the library the next morning, almost barreling into Devon as she unlocked the doors to the lobby.

As he headed for the desk, Devon raised her voice. "Sorry, I was in your way."

"You wasn't." He threw it over his shoulder.

I shuffled sheets of paper together and set them aside. "Walter, have you met my friend, Devon Majors? Devon, I don't know if you've met my great-grandfather, Walter Malinowski Jr."

"I've seen Mr. Malinowski in town a few times." Devon pushed back a sleeve of her blouse, her moss green eyes sparking.

He glanced at her. "Call me Walter. Everybody does."

That was no lie. Every single family member I'd met used his first name instead of "Dad" or "Grandpa."

Planting his broad, calloused hands on the checkout desk, he said in his cellar voice, "I thought you was smart, Rae. You solved that case with that stalker. Giving Troy a ride was just plain dumb." He glared at me from the bottoms of his deep-set eyes.

Fighting an instinct to back away, I said, "I thought he was really hurt, and I didn't know I could call the cops if he was too hurt to drive safely."

Sorting newspapers behind Walter, Devon lifted her eyebrows at me.

I groaned inside.

I'd have to explain what happened last night, letting yet another person in on how Troy had conned me.

Walter leaned toward me. "You 'n' Amber 'n' Coral are just lucky y'uns only got run off the road. Troy could've done a whole heap worse. Like when he set up Mal."

Deciding it wasn't worth correcting him over who got run off the road, I said, "I'll know better next time."

"If you don't go near him, there don't have to be no next time."

I was getting Dad in an older, more terrifying version.

My phone vibrated under the desk. Carrie. She'd said she'd call before she came with the Carlisle kids.

"Excuse me, Walter." Picking it up, I swiped to answer.

"Hey, Rae. The kids and I are parked in the lot behind the library. Jason's Land Rover stands out like the Amish at the Pentagon, so I thought if I parked back here, Ashley and her prince might not notice, if they're trying to snitch a sample from Sylvie. Any sign of them?"

"Nope. Only Walter is here."

"All right." She sucked in a breath. "We're coming in." She hung up.

Carrie sounded like she had just accepted an order to carry out a secret mission as a member of the SEALs.

"Who wanted to know I was here?" Walter said.

"Carrie. She just wanted to know who was in the library right now."

"I heard she's pretendin' to be babysittin' those Carlisle brats." His statement ended in a snarl.

My eyes widened. Walter wasn't friendly to anyone, but that sounded like a serious dislike for all the Carlisles. Why? Maybe Aunt Jeanine would know. I'd ask her if I remembered.

Alli and Richard entered the little vestibule between the two sets of double doors with Carrie balancing Sylvie on one hip and a canvas bag packed with books in her other hand. As Alli stepped into the library, Richard darted past Carrie, back out onto the sidewalk. Dropping the bag of books, Carrie spun around, lost her footing, and fell on one knee. Sylvie sprang free and ran into the library.

I hurried from behind the desk as Carrie dove for the leash—uh— strap dangling from the fluffy yellow backpack Sylvie wore and missed.

Alli wrapped up her little sister.

"Lemme go." Sylvie twisted in Alli's arms.

"Daddy said you can't run away."

Richard reentered the library, clutching something in his hand.

On her knees, Carrie said, "Richard, why did you run out there?"

"This. It's for my collection." Richard held out his hand, a tiny red thing—it looked plastic—resting in his palm.

Alli said, in a voice that made her sound like a grumpy-middle aged teacher correcting a student, "I've got Sylvie, Carrie."

Hooking her white-blonde hair behind her ears, Carrie reached for a book on the floor. "Thank you, Alli. I know I can count on you." She seemed to aim for a cheerful tone, but it sounded strained.

"You want help?" Walter loomed over Carrie in the vestibule.

"Thanks, Walter. If you could pick up the books."

I told Walter to take what he picked up to the desk and carried ten or so to the counter as Carrie corralled the Carlisle kids.

With big brown eyes and full cheeks, the Carlisle kids could have been cast as adorable orphans in movies where the orphans sang and danced about their poverty. Although these were exceptionally well-scrubbed and well-dressed orphans—hardly any scuff marks marred their sandals.

Scooping up Sylvie, Carrie said, "Richard, you told me you have collections of feathers, cool sticks, seashells, and shiny stuff. How does a red lion fit into those?"

"Wanna pway." Sylvie bent backwards in Carrie's arms.

She put her free hand behind the two-year-old's back. "In a minute."

Richard stared at the toy, then smiled. "I'll start a new collection. Red things."

"You can't." Alli tapped her foot. "You've got too many already."

"Daddy didn't say so."

"Richard." Carrie kneeled beside him. "Remember what your dad said about always staying with me when we're not at home?"

"I shouldn't have gone out to the sidewalk?"

"No, you should've stayed right beside me."

Richard looked at the plastic toy, his eyes growing troubled. He switched his gaze to Carrie. "You're not mad at me, are you? You still like me, don't you?"

Carrie's harassed expression faded under her smile, which sent a glow over her whole face. "I'll always like you, Richard. Even if you forget to listen to me, I still like you."

"Go pway." Sylvie crossed her arms, pooching out her lips.

"That's what we're going to do, but together." Straightening her navy blue t-shirt, Carrie held a hand toward Walter. "Kids, this is my grandfather, Walter Malinowski."

Alli's jaw dropped. "You have a grandfather?"

Carrie stared. "How old do you think I am?"

Sylvie wriggled. "Gotta potty."

Carrie's face froze. She waited while Richard dropped the lion in his camo green backpack with a T-Rex on it, then speed-walked toward the children's room with Alli and Richard, but turned right at the hall that led to the bathrooms.

Walter muttered something and then, with his knuckles pressed against the counter, said, "Stay away from Troy, Rae. There's no telling what he might do to you."

He shoved off the desk and stomped out of the library.

"Your great-grandfather more than lives up to his reputation." Devon joined me behind the desk.

"But I think he's actually concerned about me." Although he acted more aggravated than concerned. But Dad acted angry when he was worried, so maybe Walter truly ... cared? That didn't seem to be the right word, but why else had he come to the library to holler at me?

Mr. Olson hurried in, and I took his stack of westerns. A few more patrons drifted in and out. Rocketing through the double doors after delivering his usual gripe about the poor quality of our library service, Mr. Olson collided with Rick Carlisle.

Rick kept on coming as if he hadn't noticed the 300-pound man who'd knocked into him. "Is Carrie here with the kids?" His question came out breathless.

"Yes," said Devon. "They've been here—oh, what would you say, Rae? Ten minutes?"

"Then why won't she answer my texts?" Rick held up his phone.

"What's the problem?" I set aside a pile of program fliers I'd been sorting.

"I was in my office and I saw Steve and Ashley walking down Main—"

"I thought that was you, Carlisle," said Steve Conrad as he and Ashley Carlisle strolled, hand in hand, into the lobby.

Chapter Sixteen

Rick folded his arms, straddling his stance like he'd have to throw up some kind of defense at any second. "What do you want?"

Conrad held up his hands. "Let's not get off on the wrong foot, Carlisle. We saw you come in here and thought maybe we could talk to you about your brother's custody problem, without our lawyers and all the formality. Just a quiet conversation, and you can tell your brother what we'd like."

"We know what you'd like." Rick tilted back his head as if to get it into a better position to look down his thin nose at them. "You want Jason to test Sylvie, so you don't have bother with the expense and embarrassment of dragging a little girl, who may not be your biological daughter, into an ugly court case."

I crouched behind the desk and texted Carrie.

Prince charming and ashley in lobby with rick

Conrad spread his hands. "One test would simplify everything."

Carrie didn't text back.

"No, it wouldn't," said Rick. "Not for our family and definitely not for Sylvie. Do you have any idea what it would do to a two-and-a-half-year-old to be ripped from the only family she knows?"

"It would take her a while to get used to us." Conrad used a patient tone, like an adult humoring a bratty kid. "But a child should be with her parents."

"Sylvie already is."

Still no response from Carrie. Had her battery run down? That seemed unlikely.

"I told you this wouldn't work." Ashley's squeaky voice was sullen. She entwined her arms around one of Conrad's bulging biceps and put on a pout, identical to the one Sylvie had used this morning. "Jason just wants me to suffer."

Rick rolled his eyes. "Yes, of course, Ashley. Everything in life revolves around you."

I glanced down the hall that ran to the children's room. No one was visible, and I couldn't hear voices of any kind.

"Careful, Carlisle," said Conrad. "You're talking to my fiancée."

"In case you didn't know," Devon said in a bright tone that held the glitter and strength of steel, "fighting in the library is strictly prohibited."

Conrad gave her a broad grin, the picture of a car salesman about to launch into his pitch. "No one's fighting, miss. Just discussing a difference of opinions." His tone was confidential, like he and Devon were the only two people present.

I grabbed a loaded book cart. Carrie and the kids couldn't still be in the bathroom, could they? The bathroom was in the center of the building. It could have blocked signals. I couldn't send or receive texts in the employees' kitchen below it.

"I think you're right, Ashley." Conrad covered her hand on his arm. "I think Jason did a private test, knows Sylvie's ours, and is holding onto her just to hurt us."

Rick seemed to grow taller, drawing away from them. "It's never occurred to either of you—has it?—that Jason would love Sylvie regardless of her DNA?"

Conrad's salesman grin faded. "Why would anybody want to raise someone else's kid?"

Pushing the cart out from behind the desk, I said, "I'll be back in a minute, Devon."

"I'm fine. Just waiting for a reason to call the cops."

"We won't give you a reason." Conrad spoke with a warm assurance.

When I reached the hall that branched off to the right, Carrie stumbled out of the women's restroom with the three kids.

I said in cheerful voice, "Will you come back with me to the videos?"

Wrapping the band around one of her braided pigtails again, Alli said, "We don't get videos much. We can stream at our house."

"Maybe we have videos you can't stream." I looked directly at Carrie.

She gave me a brief nod. "We might as well check it out, kids."

Alli and Richard ran ahead, and I fell in step beside Carrie. "Prince Charming and his consort are in the lobby. They're talking to Rick."

"Why didn't you text me?"

"Rick and I both did. I think the bathroom blocks reception."

"Wan' go with Awwi and Rich'd." Sylvie pushed against Carrie's shoulder.

Carrie pulled the strap of Sylvie's backpack over her wrist and allowed the little girl to slide to the ground.

She whispered, "I drove around ten minutes looking for a tail before we came here." She broke into a jog to keep up with Sylvie.

I picked up my pace. "Mr. Conrad and Mrs. Carlisle act like they don't know the kids are here." I explained how Rick ended up in the library. "I really think Conrad saw Rick walking in here and just decided to talk to him."

"We'll look at videos until you give me an all clear." Carrie lurched over Sylvie, who'd come to an abrupt stop beside Alli.

I left the cart loaded with adult nonfiction by the teen books and pushed an empty cart back to the lobby.

Rick, Conrad, and Ashley had remained where I'd left them, but they were looking up at the balcony.

"—care how civil you've been." Barb's voice was strictly no-nonsense. "You are disrupting the operations of this library. Leave now as I've asked."

"We don't want to cause any trouble," Conrad said. "I can see now that it's useless to talk to either of the Carlisle brothers." Taking Ashley's hand, he turned toward the doors.

Over her shoulder, Ashley threw Rick a glance of pure poison, her lips pressed in a nasty smile.

Rick fired an expression of his own, but it wasn't just poisonous. His expression should have killed her on the spot.

My cart bumped into the checkout desk.

With Rick, it wasn't just that he looked ready to kill his ex-sister-in-law. He actually was capable of murder. At least he was twenty years ago.

Once the couple had left, Barb said, "Goodbye, Rick." Her icy words dropped like pellets from the balcony.

Gazing up at her, he said, "I'm not disrupting the library."

The silence Barb exuded was as frozen as her words. "Fine. See that it stays that way." She spun on her heels and disappeared into the shelves.

Rick's face remained lifted to the balcony.

"You can tell Carrie they're gone, Rick." I rolled the cart behind the desk. "She and the kids are in videos. She didn't get your texts because they were in the bathroom."

A moment passed, then Rick gave a vague nod and left the lobby.

"Always nice to have a front row seat to the drama in the county." Devon typed on a keyboard. "I hate getting my news second and third-hand." She cocked her head. "Why didn't Rick want Ashley and her boyfriend near the kids? Is he and Jason afraid of kidnapping?"

"No." I wasn't sure how much Jason wanted me to reveal. "One reason is that he doesn't want his kids to see their mom and get their hopes up that she's coming back to live with them."

"I don't think he needs to worry about that. Their mother's been gone so long, she's pretty much a stranger."

My mind flashed back to those days in school when someone's dad would stop by. I'd ached for one of my own, and I hadn't even met mine yet.

My heart warmed. Nice to be able to add "yet."

"They'd get their hopes up," I said. "I know. I was like—"

Laughter caught my attention.

Rick, holding Sylvie, and Carrie stood in the hall.

"I'm sorry that my effort to help only made matters worse." He kissed Sylvie on the cheek, making her giggle.

"I appreciate your concern, but I had Rae covering the front." Carrie grinned up at him. "We're good."

"I guess I'm apprehensive."

"Totally understandable."

They looked good together—his brooding, dark good looks and Carrie's sunny prettiness and blonde—what was I thinking?

I turned to the hold shelf. If Carrie ever got interested in Rick, I'd have to tell her about his past.

Rick allowed Sylvie to leap out of his arms, and Carrie sprinted after her as they headed for the children's room.

Passing our desk, Rick said, "I'm sorry you both had to witness that."

"The library's a public place," said Devon. "We've seen the public act way worse."

Rick broke into a grateful smile and pushed through the doors to the sidewalk.

Chapter Seventeen

Twenty minutes later, Carrie brought the kids and a bag sagging with books to us. Placing Sylvie on the counter, she looked down at Alli and Richard. "I left your summer reading records on the table. Would you get them?"

Richard dashed off. Alli pursed her lips, as if she disapproved of Carrie's forgetfulness, and followed her brother.

Carrie said, "Ashley and Prince Charming have spotted the Land Rover in the parking lot out back. I saw them from the windows at the back of the children's room. They're hanging around a little convertible parked on Woodward. I was afraid they might find us, since they were already at the library. Rae, I need your help to get the kids to the Rover without the happy couple approaching them. Can you leave the desk for fifteen minutes? Devon, can you watch the kids while I talk to her?"

"Anything to help Jason." Devon removed a scanner from Sylvie's plump hand.

Alli and Richard ran back to us, reading records flapping in their hands.

"Come around here, kids." Devon waved them behind the desk. "I'll show you how we check out books while Carrie talks to Rae."

In the women's restroom, Carrie told me what she wanted me to do. It sounded simple enough, and like Devon, I wanted to help Jason and his kids.

Back at the desk, I picked up Sylvie, Carrie grabbed the bag of books, and we descended with Alli and Richard to the basement by the back staircase. As we stepped outside, a white glare of heat smacked us. With the door recessed, no one could see us from the street.

"Wait for your cue." Carrie lugged the book bag to the Land Rover.

"Why do we have to wait?" Alli crossed her arms.

I repositioned Sylvie more comfortably on my hip. "It won't be long."

After Carrie deposited the bag in the cargo area, she slipped her wallet into a pocket of her cargo shorts and strode toward the street.

Sylvie twiddled her fingers in my hair. "Your hair pwetty."

"So's yours." I tried to free my hair from her fingers.

Alli's left sandal tapped the cement slab. "What are we waiting for?"

"Carrie said to wait, so we have to wait." Richard didn't look up from the dinosaur book he was flipping through.

"It's hot." Alli's arms crossed more tightly. "The car's right there. Why can't we go to it?"

"We won't have to wait much longer," I said as Sylvie lurched toward Richard's book and I grabbed her with my other hand to keep her from pitching out of my arm.

Now that I'd seen the kids' mother, I found no resemblance between her and them. Alli, Richard, and Sylvie all seemed to be variations on Rick's and Jason's features—dark brown hair, velvet brown eyes, and Richard and Sylvie had Jason's round face. Sylvie looked more like Jason than either Ashley or Steve.

"Good morning, Mr. Conrad." I could just hear Carrie's cheerful voice, loud but not unnaturally so.

"Come on, kids." I jogged to the Land Rover, glancing at the street.

A tiny mint green convertible was parked across from the opening to the lot, but Ashley and Steve were nowhere in sight. Carrie had maneuvered them out of view of the Land Rover like she planned.

"I'm Carrie Malinowski, and I'm the babysitter."

Alli climbed into the backseat.

"You're a bodyguard?" Conrad's question exploded the quiet morning.

"What's a bodyguard?" Richard turned to me with his foot planted on the edge of the car's floor.

"Ask Carrie when you get home." I hoisted Sylvie over her brother and placed her in her car seat.

"Jason is crazy." Conrad again, sounding even more outraged.

"No. Simply cautious," said Carrie. "I thought you should know."

How many straps did a car seat need to keep a kid safe? The answer seemed to be about 100, each with a clip or buckle, wound in and around the plastic seat.

"I'll do it." Alli snatched the snarled straps from me.

"This is insane." Conrad seemed intent on announcing his opinion to the entire world. "Anyone that paranoid should not raise children."

Carrie's reply just reached me. "Jason isn't the one stalking three little kids."

"That's it." Alli fastened a buckle with a resounding snap.

Richard peered around me to the lot. "Is somebody looking for Daddy? He's in Columbus."

"Carrie's just chatting with some people." I shut the passenger door, hopped into the driver's seat and pressing the brake, pushed the ignition button.

Wow. That was smooth. It worked just like Carrie described it to me.

I cranked up the air conditioning and looked out the window.

Carrie rushed toward us, leaving Conrad and Ashley on the

sidewalk. Ashley watched Carrie with a mouth opened so wide a robin could have built a nest in it, her small white purse with gold accents dangling in her hand. Conrad yelled something, but the closed doors muffled it. I put the SUV in reverse, and the screen in the dash lit up with the view from the backup camera.

The rich really did live differently.

I backed out the Land Rover and drew up to Carrie.

She jumped into the passenger seat. "Floor it before Prince Charming tries to block us."

But as I touched the pedal, Conrad marched to the middle of the opening to the street and stood with his legs spread, his overly muscular arms folded across his t-shirt.

Carrie opened her door and raised herself above it. "I can call the cops." She held up her phone.

"What charge?" he barked, his flat face as harsh as his voice.

"Oh well, let's see. Menacing, disturbing the peace—"

"Menacing? How do I menace a bodyguard?"

She waggled the phone. "Do I call?"

Ashley wasn't gaping anymore. She stood rigid on the sidewalk, her only movement the breeze wafting her long, highlighted bangs.

The corners of Conrad's mouth pulled down, tightening his furious expression. "Jason can't keep us from our daughter." Then he pivoted on one foot, standing to the side.

Carrie shut her door, and I pressed the gas. Conrad barely gave me enough room to squeeze onto Woodrow Avenue. One glance at his burning eyes made me keep my attention on the street. I turned downhill and then turned right at the bottom.

"Was that guy talking about Daddy?" said Alli.

Carrie threw a give-me-guidance glance at the ceiling, then transformed her expression with a grin. "That man was confused."

Turning right again, I drove up Sugar Street until I found an empty parking space and pulled over.

As Carrie and I unbuckled, Alli said, "I thought I saw our mom."

Richard pulled against his belt, craning to look out the windows. "Where?"

"Outside the library."

"Are you sure? Did she want to see us?"

"I don't know. Why do you want to see her?"

A nine-year-old shouldn't sound so bitter.

Sinking back into his seat, Richard seemed to shrivel.

A seven-year-old shouldn't look so depressed.

Carrie turned to the kids. "We've got a ton of stuff to do at the house today before I leave." Her grin widened, illuminating her round face.

"We'd better get home."

She spoke with so much enthusiasm that Sylvie clapped her hands and Richard managed a smile. But Alli stared out the window, her brown eyes aging her, making her expression more appropriate for someone hardened into middle age.

Maybe an irresponsible mom did age a kid. Losing my mom to cancer was horrible, but losing a mom to her own selfishness was way, way worse.

Carrie took over at the wheel. I waved from the sidewalk, and she beeped as she pulled away.

As I reached the intersection at Main Street, Conrad and Ashley roared by in the mint green convertible, flying in the opposite direction to Carrie and the kids.

Pushing the door to the library, I prayed the Carlisle kids wouldn't be hurt any more by their mom.

Chapter Eighteen

Just before noon, Dad called. "Can you come over to my office for lunch now? I'll be free in a few minutes."

He sounded so serious. Not like he wanted to have lunch with me because we could talk without the boys interrupting. I groaned. I knew exactly why Dad wanted to see me in the middle of the workday.

I said, "I need to ask Devon if she minds taking her lunch at one."

"I don't." Devon looked up from the book drop box.

"I'll see you in a few minutes, Dad."

I swiped off and clutched the edge of the counter.

"What's wrong?" Devon slid a jumble of books onto it.

"Dad's being overprotective."

"He does that a lot, doesn't he?"

"Yeah." I straightened, brushing back my hair. "But I'd rather him be overprotective than not care."

As the clock in the courthouse played the state song of Ohio, I crossed Main Street in front of the library, carrying my backpack and lunch bag. The sun poured white heat onto the black asphalt and cracked sidewalks, while a line of smoky gray clouds slid along the western horizon, like scouts, checking out the territory.

At the corner of Main and Sugar, I entered the white two-story building and greeted Liz as she typed at her desk. The tilted steps to the second floor always seemed ready to slide me off like in a funhouse. The door to Dad's office was open, and he flipped through papers at his desk, biting into a sandwich.

I shut the door behind me. "Which bothered you more—me being in the lobby when Rick argued with Mr. Conrad and Mrs. Carlisle or me helping Carrie with the Carlisle kids?"

Blinking, Dad stopped chewing, a clump of food caught in his cheek. Then he swallowed and gave me his lit-from-within grin. "Your intelligence keeps surprising me."

"That didn't take intelligence." I dropped into a chair. "That—that—I guess you'd call it a confrontation—had to be all over the county two seconds after it ended."

"Got that right."

"And—" a smile rose, despite my annoyance "—I've gotten to know you."

His face brightening, he said, "I hadn't heard that Rick argued with Conrad and Ashley in the library. The stories Liz got said they had it out by the courthouse, or in the bank, or outside Rick's office. What happened?"

Unpacking my lunch bag, I told Dad what had occurred from the time Rick ran into the library until I got out of the Land Rover.

He made some notes. "Did Conrad sound serious when he said he thought Jason had privately tested Sylvie and knew she was biologically his—Conrad's—daughter?"

I replayed the scene in my mind. "Yes, and he said the same thing to Carrie as I drove away."

"This is getting uglier and uglier."

"Do you think they would try to kidnap Sylvie if they believe she's their daughter?"

"Not unless they want to run and hide the rest of their lives, which I don't believe for a minute." Dad sat back in his swivel chair. "Steve Conrad is a very successful businessman. He owns eight dealerships in Columbus, and in the last six months, bought two more in Cincinnati."

"You've been researching him?"

"I asked Jeanine to, when she had the time. Just for my own private information. I sense something's going to break, and I want background information. Conrad's not only successful. He likes to flaunt his wealth. Jeanine found lots of photos on his social media pages that show him and his wife at the time attending charity events and playing with their newest car or boat. He even owns a plane. Jeanine also said, and I noticed it too, that even though these are Conrad's personal pages, they're all professionally managed. He's smart enough not to post anything that undermines his image as an entrepreneur and community benefactor." Dad picked up his turkey sandwich but set it down without taking a bite. He leaned toward me. "You didn't have to help Carrie. She should've known better than to ask you."

My gut tightened. "Please don't get into a fight about it with her. She asked me. She didn't pressure me. I wasn't in any more danger than when Rick and Mr. Conrad were in the lobby."

Rick's expression bloomed from my memory, and I put a container of chips back on the desk, losing my appetite.

"What is it, Rae?"

Was my expression that obvious?

Dad already had trouble forgiving Rick for nearly killing Mom when she was pregnant with me. I didn't want to prejudice him more.

But Rick's face ... "Maybe I'm imagining things because of what I know about Rick, but he looked—he looked—"

"Ready to kill Conrad and Ashley?"

Forcing myself, I nodded. "But looks can't kill, and on Christmas Eve, Rick was coming to confess to you before I'd told him Mom had forgiven him and the statute of limitations had run out on his crimes."

"True. But when all is said and done, Rick got away with attempted murder. And this time, he and Jason have even more to lose if they love Sylvie, regardless of her biology."

Could Dad love me regardless of biology?

Clutching my apple, I dug a huge chunk out of it. Why did I have to think of that? Troy had no proof, and neither did I.

"Rae, I don't want to fight with my sister." He sighed, his broad shoulders seeming to dwindle beneath the crease of his black shirt. "Lately I can do nothing, and Carrie will still find a reason to be mad at me. I can't even kid her anymore. I get she's disappointed in me, and I don't blame her. But I can't change the past."

"I'm sorry."

He shot me a questioning look. "Are you sorry out of sympathy, or do you actually think you've done something wrong?"

"Out of sympathy." But, although it made no sense, I did feel like I'd done something wrong.

Dad smiled. "Glad to hear it."

"So you won't talk to Carrie about me helping her?"

He looked down at his desk, scratching an eyebrow.

"I wanted to help." I lowered my half-eaten apple. "I feel awful sorry for the Carlisle kids."

He met my gaze. "Rae, that's a credit to you, but you can't help everyone."

"But Carrie was with me. You can't say I can't trust my own aunt."

An hour seemed to pass, and then Dad got out, "No." Then he asked if I noticed anything else about the confrontations.

Scrolling through the morning's events, I said, "Just one thing. Mr. Conrad yelled at Carrie that he thought Jason hiring a bodyguard for the kids proved he was an unfit parent."

Dad huffed a laughed. "Very few judges would think that when so many kids get abducted by non-custodial parents each year."

Throwing my apple core and napkin into the trash can by the desk, I said, "You don't have to wait up for me tonight."

He stared, then said, "That's right. You're going to your movie tonight. I don't mind waiting up. I can sleep in since tomorrow's Saturday."

I started to open my mouth to protest but decided against it. The only way he'd go to bed before I got home was if Gram waited up for me.

Walking back to the library, I kept thinking of Rick.

Had I misread him all these months? If he wasn't actually sorry for

attacking Mom, as I believed, would he commit the same crime again?

Chapter Nineteen

After work, at her one-bedroom apartment, Devon fixed the best tacos I'd ever eaten—sorry, Mom—and Amber, Liberty, Serenity and I devoured them. Amber and I helped the girls put on a fashion show for Devon with the Barbie dolls Amber had brought from her house. Then a half hour before showtime, Devon and I left for the theater.

More dark clouds had invaded from the west but were thin enough to allow some shafts of golden evening light to touch the clock tower on the courthouse. Humidity had risen, dogging us like a whiny kid, all the way to the corner of Main and Sugar. Catty corner from Dad's office sat the stately Opera House in crimson brick. Three steps and gilt-encrusted doors took us to the lobby. Although small, the Opera House had all the gold-coated fixtures and intricate details expected in a theater preserved to look the way it had when it opened over a hundred years ago.

An enormous chandelier glittered above us as dual red-carpeted staircases swept up to the balcony. I unrolled the sleeves of my denim shirt. The lobby was so arctic that the chandelier might have been gleaming from a sheen of ice.

Devon bought me a soda and popcorn, and we settled in the front row of the balcony, my favorite place to watch a movie.

I drained the soda in the first fifteen minutes. Halfway through the movie, I was ready to burst and creeped out. I hurried to the women's restroom tucked under the left staircase. Stepping out of a stall, I found Ashley Carlisle leaning toward a mirror, applying mauve lipstick.

Dropping the cylinder into a small, white Coach purse with gold bling, she gave me a dazzling smile. "Hey, I've seen you around, but I haven't introduced myself. I'm Ashley Warren, Jason's ex-wife." She held out a hand with two jewel-dappled rings.

I took her hand just to be polite. "I know who you are."

"I know you're a friend of Jason's. I saw you talking to him at the beach and the lodge."

"Yes." I edged around her to the sink.

"Well, I was wondering if you could give him a message for me."

I glanced over my shoulder. Her careless tone sounded like she was asking me for a few bucks to buy popcorn, but her smile didn't match it. It seemed slapped on.

Reaching for a paper towel, I said, "If you need to talk to him, shouldn't you tell your lawyer?"

As I threw the paper towel away and turned to the door, she grabbed me by both arms, her smile erased. "I have to talk to Jason. Things are such a mess." Tears rose in her eyes, and she swallowed.

She would have alarmed me if I hadn't been certain I could flatten her with one blow.

"My kids don't even recognize me. And I wouldn't hurt them. Jason didn't need a professional bodyguard." She took a big sniff. "Jason's blocked my number. Could you tell him to unblock it so I can call him?"

"But—but—" Her 180 spin in behavior made me dizzy. "You don't want to use your lawyers?"

"I don't want to talk about Sylvie and Steve. It's—" She bit her lip. "I have to talk to him."

Dad would yell until the roof blew off if I got involved.

"Please." She released my arms. "Please tell me you'll do it. I have to get back before Steve gets suspicious."

I studied her, searching for a false note in her request. How could I believe her when she'd changed her tune so quickly? "Are you afraid of him?"

Her eyes widened, but she was silent, as if she had to either process my question or manufacture an answer. "Please tell me you'll give Jason my message."

"If you need protection, I can tell my dad. He's the sheriff."

Blank stare. "Your dad and your brother are both cops?"

"My brother? My oldest brother is thirteen."

"Who was with you at the lodge?"

"My dad."

Her mouth fell open.

To get back on track, I said with a dismissive wave, "He had me in high school. If you're scared, you should go to him."

She grabbed my arms again. "Just tell me you'll talk to Jason. Please. You have a kind face."

Was she flattering me? Her whole body was wound tight, and she balanced on her toes, waiting for my answer.

Father, there's no problem, is there, in delivering a message? No danger.

Running the consequences in my head, I couldn't see any. My Father didn't bring anything alarming to my mind. "I'll tell him."

"When?"

"After the movie. Tonight."

She let me go, the tension holding her taut vanishing, like her bones had been stolen.

I started for the door, but she clutched my left arm.

"Promise me you won't tell anybody but Jason that I talked to you."

Her perfectly manicured nails bit through my shirt.

"I won't tell anyone but Jason and my dad."

"You can't tell your dad!"

Under the glare of the bathroom lights, her age showed. The make-up couldn't hide the tiny wrinkles radiating from her lips, and the few strands of silver the stylist had missed glinted in the unforgiving light.

I said, "He can help you if you let him."

She pushed my arm away.

"If anyone asks me what we talked about, I'll say make-up." Her voice held a brittle edge that aged her even more. Her gray eyes had turned to granite, and I found myself staring at Alli. "If you say I said anything else, I'll say you're lying." The desperation leaped into her face. "But please talk to Jason."

"I said I would."

She flung open the thin door with a frosted glass pane and hurried out.

I followed her. "But, Mrs. Carlisle, if you need—" I bumped into her because she'd halted just outside the restroom.

A phone to his ear, Steve Conrad looked straight at us. "Is she bothering you?"

Ashley glanced at me, as if surprised to find me behind her. "No." She broke into a girlish giggle. "Why would you think that?"

"Oh, I don't know. Because everybody in this town is a flunky of your ex. I have to take this."

"Who would call you on a Friday night?" she said.

"Someone who won't be working for me long. Tom," he shouted into the phone. After a pause, he looked at the screen. "No signal? But I got the call in the balcony."

I said, "Coming down to this floor must have made you lose it."

He stared at me like I'd announced with deep conviction that the world was flat.

"If you walk around outside," I added, "I'm sure you'll pick it up."

"This place is crazy." He stamped though the gilded front doors.

Ashley raced up the stairs ahead of me, like she was scared I might continue our conversation. She dove into a seat at the very back of the balcony.

I resumed my seat next to Devon.

"I thought you'd fallen in," she whispered. "You aren't sick or anything, are you?"

"No." I popped a few pieces of popcorn into my mouth.

The superheroes saved the day. I didn't notice how, focusing on Ashley Carlisle. Warren. Whatever.

Why did she need to talk to Jason so urgently? Was she playing me like Troy had? Her merry-go-round of emotions left me spinning.

"I think I'm getting too old for superhero movies." Devon stretched her arms as the house lights came on. "I just can't get into them."

"You're only thirty-three." I gathered the empty containers. "Weren't they making superhero movies when you were a kid?"

"Not like they do now." She blinked against the stunning illumination of the chandeliers as we reached the top of the staircase. "Did you like it?"

"Yeah. Not one of the best, but pretty good. Thanks for the gift."

Outside, a cool breeze and soothing darkness had wiped away the heat and humidity of the day.

"Let's take a shortcut." Devon crossed the street, and I followed her to the alley that ran behind the shops on Main Street all the way to the library.

We both stopped at the mouth of it.

Conrad squatted beside a mint green convertible that was parked in it. Ashley looked over his shoulder, huddled in her teal jacket, clutching the strap of her purse.

"I thought it would be safe parked off the main road." Her voice was so timid I barely heard her. "Will it cost much to fix?"

"Oh, of course not." Conrad snapped to his feet. "A custom paint job like that won't cost anything at all."

"I'm sorry."

"It's not your fault. The paint might have been scratched anywhere in this insane county. Vegetation and trees aren't cut back from the roads. You never know when you're going to lose reception. You should have sued Jason for mental cruelty when he made you live here." He spotted Devon and me. "What're you looking at?"

"If you two are so miserable here—" Devon put a hand on her hip, giving them her thoughtful frown "—why don't you go home and harass Jason in comfort?"

A vein bulging on his wide forehead, his hands balled into fists, Conrad marched over to us.

My muscles coiled, and my focus zeroed in on him to anticipate his next move.

He loomed over Devon.

A noisy group of kids passed the alley, chatting.

Stepping back, he threw back his head and laughed. "You should see your faces. What did you think I was going to do with all those people coming out of the theater?" He laughed, loud and sharp, as if the noise could skewer us.

Devon's moss green eyes took on heat. "Glad us simple peasants amuse you."

Conrad calmed enough to say, "You can tell your boyfriend that my lawyer thinks Ashley has an excellent case for filing to get sole custody of all three kids. It's irrational to hire a bodyguard for them."

"My boyfriend?"

"We saw you with Jason at the parade."

"His daughter and my daughter are friends. That's all."

"And his money has nothing to do with them being friends."

Devon's lips pulled in to fire back, but Conrad went on, "We would have settled for Sylvie, if he'd let her get tested to see if I'm her father. But now that Jason's shown how crazy he is, he may lose them all."

"The Carlisle kids aren't prizes," Devon shouted, "that you can take or keep depending on your mood." She looked around Conrad to where Ashley sat holding herself on the convertible. "He's talking about your kids, you know. It will ruin them if you take them from Jason."

Ashley made not one movement to indicate that she'd heard a word Devon said. She held her purse against her side, staring at her high-heeled white sandals.

Conrad held out his arms. "How can living with your own mother ruin you?"

Devon snorted. "I won't state the obvious. Kids don't care about biology. They only know that the adults who take care of them and love them are their parents. A legal document won't change that."

"Yes, it will." His blazing glare met Devon's defiant one. "My daughter should live with me. I've built everything I have—ten dealerships, a house in New Albany, one in Mexico, and a condo in Vegas. I've spent twenty-five years building my empire, and I'm going to pass it on to my kids, who will pass it on to their kids. I didn't work this hard just to have it all die when I do."

"You don't have any children?" I covered my mouth, surprised I'd broadcast my thoughts.

"Yes, one. And we're going to get her back. And if we have to rescue her brother and sister from a nut case, we'll do that too. No matter how long or how much money it takes." He wheeled away and slammed into the convertible.

Ashley scrambled in, and they roared down the alley.

"Come on," Devon muttered, and she quick-stepped around a dumpster.

My legs were so much longer than hers that I didn't have to hurry to keep up. "Dad doesn't think Mrs. Carlisle has a case." I explained how a parent might take precautions because of fears that the non-custodial parent might kidnap the child. "Although Dad thinks Mr. Conrad has so much money and power and prestige, he wouldn't risk it all to kidnap a kid he isn't sure is his."

"If he's that wealthy, and if he can find the right lawyer, he could legally kidnap her," Devon said in a grim tone.

We turned right into another alley and headed downhill.

Rubbing a silver stud in her ear, Devon said, "Have people been talking about me and Jason as a couple? It never crossed my mind that they would, which was stupid. I know how people talk."

"Some people have made comments. I tell them what you told me—Shayne was the only guy for you."

"Wonder why no one has said anything to me."

"Most people aren't that brave."

Devon watched me a moment, then chuckled.

A few minutes later, we reached the parking lot for Devon's apartment. Now would be a better time to call Jason than waiting until I got home.

I pulled my phone from my backpack. "I need to make a private call in my truck. Would you tell Amber to wait in your apartment until I'm done?"

"Of course." She turned onto the short walk to her apartment.

Once she was inside, I slid behind the wheel of the Rust Bucket and swiped Jason's number.

After several rings, he answered. "Rae? Is something wrong?"

"Not with me." I explained how I met his ex-wife and what she asked me to tell him.

When I finished, a silence opened up on the other end.

To fill it, I said, "She might've been playing me, but she seemed—"

"She was playing you." Jason's voice shook with an anger I'd never heard before. "That's all Ashley knows how to do. She's never been honest in speech or action since I met her. Both times she left me, she sneaked away while I was at work."

She'd left him twice? News to me, and I couldn't ask him about it now. "You could be right." But the woman hunched in her jacket and who broke into false giggles when she saw Conrad came back to me. "Jason, she seemed genuinely scared. Or at least miserable."

"She made her bed. She can lie in it. She can die in it for all I care." He sucked in a deep breath. "I appreciate you delivering her message." That sentence held a little more of his usual friendliness.

He hung up.

I laid my phone against the steering wheel, staring out through the dusty windshield.

I'd done what I'd promised. Now I just had to figure out how to tell Dad that Ashley acted afraid of Conrad without him exploding over me getting involved in a nasty domestic dispute.

Chapter Twenty

Driving toward the Norrises' farm, I tested possible approaches in my mind as Amber told me about how she and the girls spent the evening. She spoke with her head against the headrest and without her usual animation, like I was getting only a photo version of their time together instead of a fully edited movie.

"Tired?" I said.

She brought up a yawn from her flip-flops. "Fourteen hours of babysitting Serenity is way, way too long. Liberty is a piece of cake. Give her craft supplies, coloring books, and a big stack of kid novels, and she's the easiest kid I ever watched. But I have to keep my eye on Serenity every single second. I went to the bathroom after supper, and when I came out, Serenity had put half the food in the apartment on the counter because she was going to 'whip something up'." She stared at the passing trees, barely discernible outside the beams of the headlights. "They don't have very much food."

"Devon doesn't make a lot." I took a left turn too tight, making the tires squeal. "It's nice you're letting them borrow your Barbie dolls."

"They're just collecting dust in the basement. Coral never liked to play with them much. When we were little, and she liked me, we played with them because she wanted to hang out with me, not because she really liked dolls."

"'Liked me'? You don't think she does now?"

Amber released a little laugh. "She thinks I'm a wimp because I care about how I look and prefer the arts to breaking my back on the farm."

"But you help out, especially with the horses."

"Coral still thinks I'm a wimp."

So both my cousins had misconceptions about each other. At least I hoped they were misconceptions.

I dropped Amber off at her farm and then drove home, rehearsing how I was going to tell Dad about the incident with Ashley.

Not that I really wanted to, since I wasn't sure of his reaction. But if she wouldn't go to the cops, I should tell one cop, just out of kindness and a sort of duty as a responsible citizen.

Mouthing the words of my speech, I stomped on the emergency brake and got out of the Rust Bucket in front of the garage.

To my surprise, Dad was reading on the front porch, using the little lamp Gram had set on a stump she had leveled and varnished as an end table.

He gave me his lit-from-within-grin. "How's my girl?"

"Pretty good." I rested against the porch railing and nodded at the door to the new bedroom. "You put an outside door to my bedroom so I could come and go as I want. Are you still going to wait up for me after I move in there?"

Sighing, Dad dropped the fishing magazine into his lap. "I'll have to stop someday, won't I? I'm just not there yet."

Gripping the railing with both hands, I looked down at my sandals.

"Something wrong, kiddo?"

"Not exactly. But since you want background information on Mr. Conrad and Mrs. Carlisle, I thought you should know about this." Taking a deep breath, I plunged into my story. "So I promised her I'd only tell you and Jason. Then she—"

"You promised to help her?" Dad's question was sharp. And loud.

Even in the poor light of the lamp, I could see red flooding into his face.

Steeling myself, I met his glare. "Yes. I did. Then she wanted me to—"

"Rae, what's the matter with you?"

Although I expected the roar, it still made me jump.

"This is a domestic problem, one of the most dangerous calls a cop—"

"There's wasn't any danger, Dad. I thought—"

"I already warned you when you were going to interfere in that fight in the woods. Now you—"

"I thought it all over before I—"

"Are you trying to get yourself killed?"

Tears surging in me, I ran into the house, through the living-dining room, and slammed the door to my bedroom. I pressed back against the door, a tightness latching onto my chest, a tightness that grew hotter and hotter.

He had no reason to discipline me. I wasn't a stupid teenager who broke curfew. I'd held a job for years, paid my own way until I moved to the farm.

Anger evaporated the tears.

"Rae?" Dad was very quiet on the other side of the door.

Too bad he hadn't thought of starting that way.

I flung the door open. "I am not an idiot. I thought about the consequences of helping Mrs. Carlisle and prayed about it and realized there was no danger. And you'd realize it too if you let me finish." I gripped the edge of the door until it bit my palm. "I've been on my own since I was fifteen because most of that time, Mom was too sick to take care of me, and I've been completely on my own since right before my eighteenth birthday, and I've survived fine without you being around to yell at me."

My chest heaving, I glared up at Dad.

He didn't move. He met my glare with eyes overloaded with surprise and something else—maybe a whole bunch of something elses. I couldn't place his expression at all.

"What's going on?" Rusty stumbled to the foot of the stairs.

"Nothing." Dad still stared at me. "Rae and I will keep our voices down."

"Is anything wrong?" Gram came down the stairs, tying her peach bathrobe. "Was somebody yelling?"

"I was, Gram." A new burn, one red hot with embarrassment, shot up my neck. "Sorry."

"Why are you yelling in the middle of the night?" Rusty said through a yawn.

"It doesn't matter, Rusty." Gram watched us through squinting eyes, freeing long strands of smoke gray hair from under her bathrobe. "Go back to bed."

He shrugged but trudged into the bathroom first.

"Is there anything I can do?" Gram hovered on the steps.

"No, Ma." Dad suddenly sounded exhausted. "Rae and I just need to talk."

"Okay." But Gram didn't sound confident in that word. She went back upstairs.

Dad said, subdued, "I'm sorry I yelled at you. You're right. I should've let you finish. Let's sit down."

"I'm sorry too." I followed him to the couch. "I shouldn't have yelled either."

"I understand why you did." He glanced at me and then at the coffee table. "Tell me what happened from the beginning."

I waited until Rusty went back to his bedroom, and then I told Dad the entire story.

He sat with his profile to me, nodding now and again, so I knew he was listening, but I got the feeling half his mind was somewhere else.

"I thought I should tell you because if Mrs. Carlisle is that scared, she needs help."

Another nod. "We can only help her if she lets us. You told her to contact me if she wants to. Since she didn't mention any kind of crime, the ball's in her court." He heaved himself upright, like it took enormous effort. "I'll let you get to bed." He dragged heavy steps into the kitchen.

Something was wrong. Very wrong.

I got up and followed him.

Dad was usually so affectionate. Why hadn't he given me a hug or a kiss or just squeeze my hand to go with his apology? Was he still mad at me for fighting fire with fire?

He opened a cupboard and got out a glass.

No, he didn't act like he was bottling his anger. More like he was depleted, like something had gone out of him and left him very weary.

"I really am sorry." I curled my fingers against the top of the bar that separated the kitchen from the dinner table.

The left side of his mouth lifted. "I know you are. One apology is enough." He filled the glass with water. "Good night, Rae." He went downstairs.

In my bedroom, I replayed the entire scene as I kicked off my sandals. Maybe I'd startled him with my outburst. It was the first time I'd ever fought with him.

I sank onto my bed.

If it was my last, it'd be perfect.

Chapter Twenty-One

Dad was still asleep by the time I left at 9:30 the next morning, so I couldn't tell if he still seemed drained.

Despite the humidity mounting all day, we were pretty light on patrons at the branch library in the village of Barton. At 4 p.m., Leandra Hamilton locked the front doors of the narrow storefront of the branch. As she pulled away from the curb on the side street where staff always parked, I rummaged in my backpack for my keys.

Heat blurred the blue sky. No clouds floated by to shield the street from the intense afternoon sun. Sweat beaded under my hair.

"It's Miss Riley, isn't it?"

I glanced up, fingers freezing among tissues, wrappers, and camera accessories.

Steve Conrad strolled down the uneven sidewalk, his salesman grin providing a sizable dent in his flat face. Chuckling, he said, "I just want to ask you a question, Miss Riley. Not eat you."

Thawing instantly, I bent my face over my backpack to hide the blush I felt forming.

"What question, sir?" I collected my wits, assembled my expression, then met his gaze with my professional manner.

"Nothing scary." He leaned against my truck, folding his arms, striated muscles bulging from under the sleeves of a collarless white shirt with two buttons unbuttoned. "I wanted to know what you and Ashley discussed in the bathroom last night."

My air disappeared. This was what Dad warned me about, getting involved in a situation I had no idea how to handle.

Hoping my friendly neighborhood librarian demeanor was still holding, I said, "Didn't Mrs. Carlisle tell you, sir?"

"She's Ms. Warren, and yes, she did, but I happened to drive by just now and saw you and thought I'd ask you too." He used the confidential manner he tried with Devon in the library, like we were good friends sharing something private and valuable.

Yeah, right, you just happened to drive by. How had he found me? A few questions asked of whoever was working at the main library today would do it.

"Mr. Conrad, if you don't believe your fiancée, I can't help you." I used the pleasant but firm tone I reserved for difficult patrons and big-mouthed tweens and teens.

A truck rumbled by, and the voices of kids carried to us from a yard somewhere across the street. I wasn't alone.

"Why so secretive, Miss Riley?" He chuckled again, like I'd treated him to a good joke.

"I don't want to be involved with you and Mrs. — your fiancée."

Shoot fires, I seriously did not want to be involved.

"Fair enough," he said with a nod.

He was giving up?

Before he changed his mind, I unlocked my truck, swung open the door, and found several bills thrust at me, fanned like a deck of cards.

"I don't suppose you make a lot of money at the library. $100 can buy you new jeans or some make-up, if you're careful with it."

I goggled at the bills. This was completely nuts. And I could buy two or three complete outfits for $100. Where did he think I shopped?

"What did you and Ashley talk about last night?" His voice was still friendly and sort of exclusive, as if he was giving me the chance to do him a special favor.

Ripping my gaze from the money, I said, "I'm not getting involved, sir."

"$200? $300?" He pulled folded bills from his wallet.

"I have to go." I slid under the wheel.

"The offer stands." He held out a card. "Call me any time you change your mind."

I slammed the door shut, jammed the key in the ignition, and prayed it would start.

As I cranked the key, Conrad placed his card under my windshield wiper and then saluted me with two fingers.

I shot away from the disintegrating curb. What was more disturbing — his question or his bribe? The whole encounter was like I'd walked out of the library and into a story I hadn't read before. I had no clue how much had happened before I'd stumbled into it, so I couldn't judge what my role was. Too weird.

Driving to the intersection, I looked in my rearview mirror.

Conrad remained on the sidewalk, still wearing his grin.

I clenched my teeth. I wanted that grin gone and wanted him to know I wasn't interested in his money.

Making sure no one was behind me, I clicked on my hazards and stopped at the intersection. I got out, and watching Conrad, removed the card from under my wiper. Then, with big gestures, I tore the card and let the halves drift to the ground.

A jerk stiffened him, and the grin vanished. His lips moved, but I didn't hear what he said. Then he darted across the road and toward a

Hummer painted in brown and green camo.

A vehicle that expensive had to be Conrad's. Was he going to follow me? Leaping into the Rust Bucket, I slammed it into gear and glanced in the rearview mirror.

He stood with the door open to his Hummer as an old car rattled by. Then he looked in my direction, and throwing back his head, laughed.

Anger and relief twisted in my gut, and I whipped the Rust Bucket to the right and tore out of town.

~~~~~

I drove as fast as I dared, taking turns at random in case Prince Charming decided to follow me. That had to be why he'd run to his Hummer. Or had he just wanted to scare me? When I thought I'd driven far enough and only had a vague idea where I was, I pulled over at the first spot I could find—a weed-choked gravel patch in front of a boarded-up house.

What should I do now?

I clutched the steering wheel as the air conditioning did its pathetic best to lower the roasting temperature in the cab.

I did *not* want to get into another fight with Dad. I couldn't take him yelling at me again or be sure I wouldn't yell back. We didn't need any more strain on our relationship right now, and I knew how he would react if I told him about this.

Was Ashley in danger? Conrad hadn't threatened her or me. Should I try to tell her Conrad didn't trust her? That would seriously tick Dad off, and he was in a perfect position to help her. Besides, if Conrad knew I approached her again, that'd only make him more suspicious.

Even more important, I really didn't want to get involved. Things were getting out of focus, getting beyond what I could help with any confidence.

I wiped sweaty strands from my face.

I wanted Dad's advice badly. Back in the winter, Dad had said that if I needed to discuss female problems with someone, I should pick a woman I trusted. This wasn't the same thing, but I needed advice on law enforcement from someone reliable.

A name popped into my head.

I dug out my phone. No reception.

I shoved the Rust Bucket into gear and drove until the phone got some bars as I cleared the woods and climbed a ridge. At the crest sat a little white church, and I parked in its lot.

I texted a request for a call. In less than a minute, my phone rang, and I answered.
~~~~~

Chapter Twenty-Two

The next evening, after supper, I had just punched the buttons to start the dishwasher when the landline rang and Gram picked up.

"Lydia Malinowski speaking. Oh, hello, Jason. Yes. He's here." Gram called for Dad, and he took the phone.

I lingered by the dishwasher.

After a few comments, Dad's expression turned perplexed. "You're welcome to come over. With the kids. Ma and Carrie can watch them ... Yes, Carrie's back from Columbus. She came in this evening and had supper with us ... A half hour is fine."

Dad set the landline on its base, still looking puzzled.

I put the box of dishwasher soap under the sink. "Jason's coming over with his kids?"

"Uh, yeah." He studied the countertop, fingering a scar that ran along his left eye.

Although it was none of my business, I said, "Is there a problem?"

"I'm not sure." He brought his gaze to mine. "Jason wants my advice because I'm a married man."

"Did he say why?" Gram snapped a lid on a plastic container.

"No. But he said it wasn't something he could ask Rick about. Or Father Keir." Dad shook his head, then said to Rusty, who had come out of the basement, "Aaron and Micah went up to the playroom with Carrie. If they want to play football, they need to come down now because the Carlisles are coming over."

"How come?" Rusty jogged to the stairs.

"Don't really know." Dad said to me, "Hopefully, we can get that walk in after they leave."

Dad had made special efforts to spend extra time with me the past two days. Maybe he felt he had to, to show he was really sorry about Friday night. It wasn't necessary. The apology covered it.

Putting my arm along the small of his back, I said, "Walk or football — doesn't matter. It's still quality time."

"Even if we crush you?" Aunt Carrie thundered down the stairs with my brothers.

The evening was bathed in a sleepy gold, thick cloud cover flattening the sunset light.

Playing football on a slope added an interesting element of surprise to a game that was always startling because Aaron liked to experiment with the rules and Micah played like there weren't any.

Dad, Micah, and I played against Carrie, Gram, Rusty, and Aaron. Carrying the ball, Micah ran down to the fence for the alpaca pastures.

"You're out of bounds," I yelled.

"Who says?" he yelled back.

The gray Land Rover turned onto the drive. As it pulled up to the garage, Alli and Richard leaped out, Richard holding a plastic box about the size of a shoebox.

He ran straight to Carrie, who was pulling clover from the ends of her long hair.

Richard held out the box to her. "I got something for you. Seashells."

"Richard, you already gave me the little lion you found at the library."

Jason got out of the Land Rover and looked ... a complete wreck. I'd never seen him with a t-shirt or dress shirt untucked, but now his cornflower blue polo hung loose, and his hair, which usually had so much product in it that it resembled the molded hair of a Ken doll, had a slight rooster tail rising in the back and the bangs fell across his forehead.

Shoving these aside, Jason carried Sylvie to the porch. "Carrie, can you come with us to church from now on?"

This wasn't like Jason at all. No greeting or pleasant chitchat before getting to the point of the conversation.

"Sure. Did something happen?" Carrie closed the lid on the box of shells. "I didn't see any reason you and Rick couldn't keep track of the kids there."

"Apparently, I can't." He lowered Sylvie to the ground while still holding her hand. "After mass, I had to take Sylvie to the bathroom and Richard went with us. While I was helping Richard at the sink, Sylvie got away from me. We couldn't find her for five minutes. She'd shut herself in a classroom. I can't afford to make a mistake like that again."

"I'd be glad to. No charge."

"I can pay." He crouched to remove a worm from Sylvie's grasp.

"I know. But I can give you two hours gratis."

"Thanks."

Carrie went on, "I had an idea about getting the kids out of the house this summer. I talked it over with Ma, and she said it'd be fine for me to bring the kids over here. There's a ton to do, and the farm is very —" her eyes shifted to Alli and Richard as they talked to Aaron and Micah "— secluded."

Dad brushed dirt from his jeans. "Can you keep track of the Carlisle kids with three extra kids? Four if Coral comes over."

Carrie rolled her eyes. "Yes, Mal. I thought of that. Rae, you're off tomorrow, aren't you? Could you help us as we try this out?"

I hadn't made any plans other than working with my new lens, so I couldn't wriggle out of it. "I can help."

"Great." Raising her eyebrows, Carrie looked at Jason.

"Well ..." He pushed his hand through his hair, and it moved enough to look even more disheveled. "The kids would enjoy it. Don't eat that." He removed a peony blossom from Sylvie's hand. "Can you watch them while I talk to Mal?"

"Absolutely." Carrie handed Richard his box. "Who wants to come down to the creek with me and the Carlisle kids?"

Richard said, "Don't you want a shell?"

Carrie bent down to him, her hair falling over her shoulders. "Richard, you don't have to keep giving me things for me to like you. I like you just as Richard."

A sweet smile spread across his round face.

Carrie picked up Sylvie. "Have you kids ever caught crawdads? Aaron and Micah can show you how. Richard, did you bring your backpack? I'm sure there's tons of stuff at the creek for your collections."

"Daddy." Richard looked down at his buttoned, short sleeve shirt and khaki shorts. "We didn't bring our old clothes."

Jason swung his bangs out of his eyes. "It's okay for you to wear what you have on."

Richard's big brown eyes bolted open as Alli said, "It is? But we'll get muddy."

"Mud washes out." Gram tossed the football onto the porch. "If your clothes are really muddy, you can borrow some of the boys' clothes to wear home."

Alli wrinkled her nose. "I don't wear boys' clothes."

Gram and Carrie led the Carlisle kids and my brothers toward the woods. If I had to help out tomorrow morning with the kids, I didn't want to spend this evening with them too.

"Let's take a hike, Carlisle." Dad moved down the drive.

"Or I can," I said. "I can go out and take pictures, and y'all can have the house to yourselves." Hopefully, when they were done, I'd have a chance to ask Jason a question about Mom.

"Thank you, Rae," said Jason, "but a walk sounds good."

They headed down the drive, Dad ambling along while Jason trudged.

Having the house entirely to myself was as delicious as a scoop of dark chocolate ice cream with dark chocolate chunks. I fired up the desktop computer, stuck in my camera card, and reviewed the photos from the parade in peace. Absolute peace.

I'd settled on four photos to send to the newspaper when a herd of kids burst into the kitchen.

"Do you want pie, Rae?" Aaron pulled out a chair at the dinner table.

"Do you have to ask?"

Gram sat Sylvie in a chair. "Are Jason and Mal back?"

"No." I stepped over to a double-hung window that looked out onto the front porch.

The setting sun had dipped below the lid of cloud and stretched the shadows of the surrounding trees to such gigantic proportions that they coated the front yard in cool twilight.

No sign of Dad or Jason. But Aunt Carrie was on the porch, wiping at her eyes.

Should I ask if she was all right?

A frustrated scream welled up in me.

Why did most of my life lately seem to hinge on whether or not to help?

I slipped out the front door. "Is everything okay?"

"Oh." Carrie started, her fair face red-eyed and streaked with tears. "I'm fine." She wiped tears from her cheeks with the heels of her hands. "The kids just got to me for a moment. I mean, their situation did."

I sat on the porch swing. "You feel sorry for them?"

Carrie nodded with a big sniff. "Ma and I were bringing the kids back to the house for a snack, and Richard asked if I'd marry his dad." She growled, brushing her wrist across her nose. "Jason even warned me, and it got to me."

"Warned you? Why?"

"Richard is so desperate for a mom that he asks any woman he likes if she'll marry Jason. Jason said about two weeks after he started kindergarten and first grade, Richard asked his teachers that question. I've got them beat. Richard asked me after only five days."

She dropped onto the swing. "They're really great kids, but Ashley's made Alli bitter and suspicious of women—she questions and judges everything I do. Richard's dying for a woman to pay attention to him, and Sylvie—she may be too young to be affected by her mom's absence, but it'll hit her someday. I'm sure Angie Gibson is a wonderful babysitter, but they need more than that. Their mother—" fury flashed like heat lightning over Carrie's face, "—their mother ought to be knocked upside the head every hour, on the hour, for treating her own kids like—like last year's fashions."

"Is Ashley's mom in their life? I know Jason and Rick's mom doesn't live close."

"Ashley's parents divorced when she was in high school. Her mother eventually remarried and moved to Arizona. She and Jason's mother do the grandma thing—you know, cards and gifts and calls. But they only visit a few times a year."

I watched Carrie's profile and decided it couldn't hurt to ask. "I've been wondering why Mrs. Carlisle and Conrad want to test Sylvie now. Why not when Mrs. Carlisle left Jason for Conrad right after Sylvie was born?"

"Because she didn't."

I stared. "When did she leave Jason?"

"It's not the when. It's the who. Jason's convinced Ashley left him for someone other than Steve. After what I've learned about Conrad, so am I.

"Right after Ashley and Steve contacted Jason," Carrie went on, "Rick dusted off his investigative journalist skills and got digging. He even interviewed Steve's ex-wife. Rick believes Ashley started an on-again-off-again affair with Steve when she left Jason the first time, right after Richard was born, and moved in with her father. Steve was married at the time. Daddy died about a year later, so here came Ashley back to Jason. She got pregnant with Sylvie. At the time of Ashley's pregnancy, according to Steve's ex-wife, Steve and she were attempting to get pregnant after a four-month separation. By the time Ashley had Sylvie and left Jason, ex-wife was pregnant. So even if Ashley came to Steve then, claiming the baby was his, he would have turned her down because his wife was pregnant and he's crazy to have an heir."

"I've learned that." I repeated what he'd said to Devon outside the theater.

Carrie huffed. "That's nothing compared to what his ex-wife told Rick. After four miscarriages, she refused to get pregnant again and wanted to adopt. He said he wouldn't leave his business to a stranger. So he filed for divorce."

My eyelids stretching, I stared at the darkening fields and woods, fireflies providing specks of light.

"Yeah, just when you think he can't sink any lower, Prince Charming does."

My expression must have been easy to read, even in the deepening dusk.

"But back to your question," said Carrie, "Jason believes Ashley left him the second time for an unknown boyfriend. Boyfriend X must have paid for everything and really well because Ashley never bothered to take part in the divorce proceedings to get alimony. From what Rick and Jason have told me, I think Boyfriend X dumped Ashley recently or maybe she's had a string of boyfriends and the most recent one ditched her. Since Ashley has never supported herself, she had to find a new boyfriend who would. She looked up Steve, found he was almost done divorcing his wife, and told him Sylvie may be his. As soon as his divorce was final, Ashley moved in with Steve, and they contacted Jason."

I tiptoed through my next words. "Remember what Mr. Conrad said about Jason keeping Sylvie from him out of revenge? I don't think Jason would do that. But do you think he would fight to keep Sylvie, even if a DNA test proved she wasn't his, because—because he's raised her? He's the only parent Sylvie knows."

Carrie passed her hand over the top of her white-blonde hair, blowing out her cheeks. "I certainly hope so. I honestly don't see why not. Her DNA doesn't change who she is. She's still the little cutie who likes to take off and wants to play like a big kid. Knowing the science doesn't make her any different." Carrie looked to me. "Can you imagine turning any kid, not even one you've raised as your own, over to Prince Charming? I'd feel like I was handing a baby over to a—a—a Sith lord."

But even if Jason felt a responsibility not to let Sylvie go to an unfit family, could he still treat her like Alli and Richard? Could Dad treat me the same as the boys if I wasn't his biological daughter? Or would he just put up with me because he knew what a nightmare Troy was as a parent?

"Where are the kids?" said Dad.

He and Jason came around from the far side of the garage.

"They're inside." Carrie stood. "Ma's giving them pie for a snack."

Dad said, "Jason, I'll get my Bible," and went inside.

Carrie followed, and Jason was about to when I said, "Could I ask you a question? About my mom? I know it's not a pleasant topic, and if you don't want to, that's fine."

He studied me a moment, threads of tension rippling through him, winding him tighter. "I guess I have to hear it before I can object."

I said in a rush, "Did she get drunk very often?"

Jason pulled back, his small brown eyes widening. Clearly, he wasn't expecting this question. "Uh—well, no. Very rarely. I didn't realize it at the time, but if she stayed sober at a party when everyone else was drinking, she had a lot of power."

"But you did see her drunk?"

"Only two or three times. And it was—it was scary. She'd drink so much that she'd pass out. One time I thought she'd stopped breathing. She passed out on the floor of the children's home, and I sat with her until dawn because her breathing was so shallow."

"That was very kind of you."

"Does this ... help you?"

"Yes." I opened the screen door. "We'd better get inside if we want any pie. Dad says he can stop at one piece, but he doesn't usually have the willpower."

As soon as we entered, Sylvie wriggled out of her chair at the dinner table and ran over to Jason, grabbing his hand. "Get pie, Daddy."

Jason didn't move. He stared at Sylvie as she tugged on his arm, his face blank.

She groaned, pulling. "Get pie."

He watched her, like he couldn't comprehend who she was or what she was doing.

"There's lemon meringue," Alli said from the table, a dollop of custard in the corner of her mouth. "And strawberry-rhubarb."

Jason started and broke into a dilapidated version of his million-watt smile. "Sounds delicious."

I scooped a slice of strawberry-rhubarb pie onto a plate for him and then loaded another plate for myself.

What had Jason been thinking as he stared at Sylvie? Maybe about how much he didn't want to lose her. Or maybe how much he didn't want to raise Steve and Ashley's kid.

After we had demolished both pies, Jason scooted back his chair, Sylvie sitting on his lap and licking her fingers, and told Alli and Richard to find their muddy shoes.

Picking up the heavy Bible beside him, Dad got up from the table. "I put the bookmark in Hosea." He held it out to Jason.

With Sylvie yawning on his shoulder, Jason looked at the Bible like it was a mysterious package that may have been ticking.

"Compare it to your Bible at home," said Dad. "Nothing wrong with doing some Bible research of your own."

Frowning, Jason tucked the Bible under his arm. "Thank you."

Later, while brushing my teeth before going to bed, I turned over what Jason had said about Mom.

It was possible that Mom could've slept with a guy and not remembered, but not likely.

Coming out of the little bathroom, I went to the desk and switched on the light.

Back in the winter, Dad said I couldn't mess up our relationship. I'd been his daughter since my conception, and nothing could change that. But that's when he thought I was his daughter.

Did Jason feel the same way about Sylvie?

I prayed that if he didn't, he would.

I opened Gram's study Bible, which I really liked, because a lot of times, I didn't understand the verses on mercy I'd been looking up and needed the explanation at the bottom of the page.

But instead of flipping to the index for more verses, I turned to the table of contents and found Hosea. The book was short and had two parts. One was the story of Hosea and his unfaithful wife Gomer, and the other were warnings from God about how Israel needed to turn from their sins and return to Him.

Had Dad chosen this book to help Jason handle Ashley's unfaithfulness? But that happened over two years ago.

I reread the first three chapters and grew still.
Hosea took Gomer back.
Was Jason thinking of doing the same with Ashley?

Chapter Twenty-Three

Really?

The ringing landline made me roll over and check my clock. 6:30. On my day off.

I glared up at the ceiling, although I knew it was perfectly innocent of this disgusting crime.

Thank you so much, person who has to call the sheriff directly instead of going through Dispatch.

"What?" Dad's question penetrated my bedroom door better than the ring had.

I swung myself upright.

When Dad got ready in the morning, he was very conscious of keeping quiet. The caller must have said something truly shocking. Although what could truly shock a cop?

Pulling on my aquamarine bathrobe, I shuffled to the door and opened it.

Dad was bent over the kitchen counter. "Tell Zagoric I'll meet him at the lodge." He hung up.

"What's wrong?" A yawn stretched the last word.

Staring at the counter, Dad said, "Steve Conrad called Dispatch a few minutes ago. Said Ashley Carlisle is missing."

Another yawn froze in my mouth.

His blue eyes shifted to me. "Conrad took a sedative and went to bed early because he hadn't been sleeping well. At 10 p.m. He doesn't know when Ashley went to bed. He woke up at 5:30. Thought it was weird that Ashley was up already—she's not an early riser, and the restaurant doesn't start serving breakfast until 7:30. Her purse, jacket, and car are gone. He says she left everything else. He heard nothing during the night."

"Then she hasn't ditched him."

"It doesn't look like it, but I'll know better once I get there." His eyes were aimed at me but unfocused, as if lost in thought. Then he finished tucking in his shirt. "I was afraid something bad might happen. The situation was getting too tense."

"Like what happened to my mom." I spoke in a whisper of a whisper, as if the event was labeled taboo by law. "And me."

Dad closed the cooler he carried his lunch in. "Her boyfriend says she's missing, and Ashley has a verified habit of running out on her men.

119

That's all I have to go on for the moment."

"There's something I should tell you." My muscles knotted all over, but if a crime had actually occurred, maybe this was something Dad needed to know. "It happened after work on Saturday." I told him about Conrad approaching me with his question and his money.

Dad's eyes swelled, and a couple times, he attempted to swallow, like he was trying to get down a whole cantaloupe.

My words picked up speed. "When I drove away, I wasn't sure what to do. Conrad hadn't committed a crime. I'd only gotten scared when I saw him run for his Hummer, but then he just laughed at me. He creeped me out, checking up on his girlfriend like that." I clenched my hands. "I really didn't want to get into another fight with you, but I wanted a cop's advice, so I texted Chris, and he called me."

Dad's massive shoulders dropped, and his face, so taut, went slack. "You did? He hadn't left for vacation yet?"

"He had, but he'd stopped at a rest stop when I texted, so he could talk. He said that I was right, no crime had been committed, although Mr. Conrad sounds like a hero." I grinned. "That's how he put it. But he said I'd already told Mrs. Carlisle to come to the police if she needed to. No one can make her leave her boyfriend, no matter how scared she is." I frowned. "If she wasn't just acting for me."

Dad's eyes went back to their sightless expression.

This wasn't much of an improvement over the yelling.

"Uh, thanks, Rae. I never know what intel might prove important." He fumbled for the handle of the cooler.

Something was wrong again, like on Friday night. But what? I'd done what he'd advised—talked to an expert in an area I wasn't an expert in.

I dodged toys and reached the kitchen.

Dad carried his water bottle and cooler to the back door.

"Did I do something wrong?" I huddled in my bathrobe.

He aimed a split-second smile at me. "No. You turned to a good source of help when you needed it. Kincaid is an incredibly dedicated and intelligent officer for his age. I'll see you at supper."

Dad latched the door behind him so it made no noise.

I sank onto one of the high stools by the bar, too many thoughts swirling in my mind.

What had I said that had thrown Dad for a loop? And what did Ashley's disappearance mean?

A shiver shook me.

It was eerily similar to what happened to my mom. Was that why Dad worried about me feeling sorry for people and trying to help them? Because helping the wrong person in the wrong way could lead to even more trouble?

~~~~~

When Gram got up at seven, and Micah did a few minutes later, I was well into making chocolate chip muffins.

Agreeing to help with the Carlisle kids now seemed like a stroke of genius. Staying busy was the best way to keep from wondering about Dad's reaction and Rick's possible guilt.

His strawberry blond hair sticking up like a cardinal's crest, Micah hopped onto a stool across the counter from me. "Chocolate chip?"

I nodded and slid some over to him.

He opened his grin and popped them in.

Gram strode into the kitchen, braiding her hair. "Did I hear the phone ring this morning?"

"Yes." I told her about Ashley's disappearance.

She paused in tying a leather cord around the end of her braid. "That's ... worrying. If she was breaking up with her boyfriend, she wouldn't leave her clothes. And why would she leave the lodge in the middle of the night?"

Had Conrad threatened her, and she'd been so scared that she'd taken off?

As I placed the muffin tin on the oven rack, guilt sent prickles out of my heart.

I'd been so caught up in analyzing the puzzle, and possibly my role in it, that I'd forgotten about the woman who was missing.

I shut the oven door and closed my eyes.

Father, I'm sorry. Forgive me for being self-centered. Please help ... please help ...

"Are you praying, Rae?" Micah said.

I opened my eyes. "Yes."

"I pray before I go to bed."

"You can pray anytime." Gram plugged in the griddle and set it on the stove.

But what should I pray? If Ashley had dumped Prince Charming, that might get him to leave Jason and the kids alone. The best thing for the kids was for Jason and Ashley to reconcile. But only if Ashley wanted to be a mother and wife this time. It would be beyond horrible if she came back and then left her family for a third time.

I twisted the timer. "Gram, I'm going to shower. Can you take the muffins out when they're done?"

"Of course."

I returned to my bedroom. The sun had risen high enough for the morning light to turn white, picking out every detail of the hunter green quilt on my bed and the desk with books, papers, pencils, cords, and camera cards. I needed to organize all that stuff at some point.
~~~~~

Father, keep Ashley safe and work out this mess for the best for everyone involved. Only You know what's best, and only You can do it.

At 9:30, Carrie pulled up in the Land Rover, and Richard burst out like a paroled prisoner, his backpack bouncing against him. Alli exited as if she was too old to get excited about anything, while Sylvie twisted every which way to escape Carrie's arms.

Dividing to conquer seemed the best way to help Carrie to keep track of all the kids. So Rusty and I led Alli and Aaron to the barn to perform the chores for the alpacas, while Carrie and Gram took care of Richard, Micah, and Sylvie.

When we were done in the barn, we hiked over to the Norris farm and hunted around for Coral, finding her with her grandfather in his tractor shed, both of them elbows deep in an imposing tractor.

"Hey, Coral, Mr. Norris." I gave him my best professional expression and bent down to pet Chestnut, a small brown and cream husky kind of dog, one of the many dogs that circulated between the two Norris farms.

Mr. Norris nodded, but that was all. Shorter than Uncle Hank and skinnier, Luke Norris had Uncle Hank's huge brown eyes set in a gaunt face. But Hank's eyes always reflected his easy-going, good humor. Mr. Norris's brimmed with disapproval. If they ever brimmed with anything else, I hadn't seen it because whenever he saw me or Dad or my brothers, his expression made it clear what he thought of the Malinowskis. Carrie said it had taken him ten years before he'd finally decided Aunt Jeanine wouldn't leave Uncle Hank and their daughters for the first guy who flirted with her.

"Are you going to be done soon, Coral?" I said, as Gimli, a basset hound mix, rubbed against my calf. "Alli would like to see the baby foxes, and I'm not sure I can find the way."

Coral backed away from the tractor, studying it. "We're almost done. I'll take you as long as that rich chick isn't there." She wiped her greasy hands on a greasy cloth. "Some people act like they own the whole outdoors."

She could have been talking about herself. "I'm sure she won't be there," I said.

"You can clean up in the house." Mr. Norris had a quiet voice, the words slipping to you, instead of landing on you.

The hike to the clearing took almost a half hour, but the baby foxes, as if I'd invited them to perform ahead of time, pounced and rolled over each other in sunbeams.

"They're so cute," Alli squealed, earning a hush from Coral, as the five of us crouched behind a fallen tree. "They won't come over here and bite us, will they, Rae?"

"As long as we don't get too close, they won't." Coral extended her hand toward the biggest fox lying at the edge of the sunlight. "The parents are the ones you gotta worry about, and we're not very close."

"Foxes are the most distant relative of the domestic dog." Aaron began telling us fox facts until Coral looked ready to slug him, so I told him to be quiet.

When Aaron said he was bored, we played "Spy" in the woods and then made our way back to the Norris farm. All the horses, including Alli's horse, Tornado, which she boarded at the farm, were in the pasture. Coral got some apples, and we petted and fed the horses until lunchtime.

By the time I'd scarfed down pepperoni rolls, a yogurt, and a pickle, I needed a break from babysitting. As soon as I'd helped Gram get the kitchen back in shape from lunch, I asked Rusty if he'd like to come with me while I worked with the macro lens.

Glancing into the living-dining room, where Aaron and Alli were trying to outshout each other in an argument over what to play next, Rusty muttered, "I'll get my binder."

Rusty and I hiked to the creek that bordered our farm and our cousins'. Dusty beams of light breached the canopy of sycamores and ignited Rusty's gorgeous shade of dark red hair. He found a comfortable log, opened his three-ring binder, uncapped a pen, and wrote on the next installment of what had to be the world's longest fantasy novel. I squatted beside a short dogwood where a bee landed and lifted from its white blossoms.

Rusty was just about perfect company on a shoot. He didn't talk much, usually caught up in whatever he was writing.

When inspiration dried up for Rusty, we wandered further into the woods. I snapped photos here and there. We explored a shallow cave made by an overhanging slab of rock jutting from a cliff face.

Rusty sat on a rock outside of the cave. "I should write down my first impressions of the cave before I forget, so I can use it in a setting for my book."

"Just call when you're done."

I strolled on. The light seemed to fade, intensifying the shade under the mature maples and tulip trees, and a breeze wound among their thick trunks.

I stopped beside a half-rotted log, recognizing the clearing where the foxes lived.

Something rattled in the thicket sheltering the den.

Crouching, I lifted my camera. Could be something good, although with the macro lens on, I wasn't sure how any shot at a distance would come out.

The thicket stilled, and a man's voice said, "Rae?" The snaking branches parted, and Troy emerged.

My mouth worked a moment before words came out. Despite his surfer dude appearance, Troy did not seem like a nature lover to me. The den was a good fifteen-minute hike from Walter's house. Had he followed me and I hadn't seen him before now?

"Rae, I'm so glad to see you." He approached, a smile spreading all over his face.

I backed away.

"Rae, you don't have to be afraid of me." Sighing, he stopped with a crunch on last year's leaves. "I bet Mal let you have it for helping me."

"My dad doesn't let me have it." Even if I thought that, I would never admit it to Troy.

"If Mal makes trouble for you, you can call Walter anytime and leave a message for me. I'll tell Mal again that it was completely my fault."

A furious fire broke out in my chest. "I don't need any protection from my own dad."

Relief swept over Troy's face. "I'm really glad to hear that. Just remember, you've got a friend in me."

Dad said to avoid Troy, but I was sick of his insinuations. Maybe if I dragged them out into the light, they'd burn up like vampires. Shoot fires, I wished he'd burn up like a vampire.

Locking onto his eyes, I marched up to Troy. "Why do I have a friend in you? You hate my dad, my aunts, my brothers, everybody in my family."

"That's Mal talking. I'm in your family too. You're Bella's daughter. She'd want me to look out for you."

"No, she wouldn't. She knew what you're like. Once she became a Christian, she wouldn't want you anywhere near me."

Troy's gaze softened. "You can't know for certain what your mom would say about me. Don't believe everything Mal tells you."

"Why? I keep asking you questions, and you don't really answer any of them." Stepping closer, I crowded him. "I know what you think."

"Really?" He raised his eyebrows.

"You think there's a chance I'm your daughter." I flung it at him.

He started, then broke into a slow grin. "You've got your mom's brains, that's for sure. All right. I didn't want to say so, but yes, I was with your mom a lot more than Mal, so just statistically speaking, you are far more likely to be mine than his."

"Mom left clues that don't point to you at all. My mom wouldn't lie to me."

"Of course she wouldn't. But I've heard she didn't tell you about her past until right before she died. If she was that sick, she might have confused her facts."

"She didn't."

"Your faith in Bella is inspiring, but you can't know that." He sidled closer, shoulder to shoulder. "If you ever want to know for certain, call me, and we'll send in a DNA sample for a test. Nobody ever has to know. It'd be for your peace of mind."

"My mind is at peace." But the way I shouted it wouldn't have convinced anyone.

"I didn't mean today or anything. Think it over. We can do it anytime you—"

"Leave me alone." I whirled around, tripped on something, staggered around, and then ran.

Chapter Twenty-Four

It's not true, it's not true, it's not true.

Father, Troy can't be my father. You wouldn't have led me here just to rip the rug out from under me, would You?

I caught my foot on a root and grabbed at a bush before I pitched headfirst down a short, steep slope.

I checked my camera and lens. No damage.

I ran on.

But then why had He let Mom die, leaving me with no one for eighteen months that felt like decades? Was He punishing me for something?

Dad called me a blessing, Father. He and the whole family are that to me. My finding them couldn't be wrong.

Gray clouds marbled the sky. The breeze had grown stronger, pushing between the spindly spice bushes, white-blossomed dogwood, and long, tapered leaves of the pawpaws.

Troy had no proof, just insinuations and lies. But if I could find out his blood type, that might end my worries quick.

I stumbled down a hillside. At the bottom, I cupped my hands around my mouth and yodeled. At least, I attempted my best version of it. Gram had taught me how to do the call, but mine still didn't sound like hers. But it carried better than shouting names, which was why, Gram said, her great-grandmother used it to call her children in the mountains of West Virginia, and the Branson family had passed it to the next generation ever since.

A faint return call reached me, and I homed in on it.

Nice to carry on the family tradition.

My stomach sickened.

If Gram was a part of my family.

As I hiked into view of the cave, Rusty glanced over his shoulder. His forehead wrinkled, just visible beneath his heavy bangs. "You okay?"

A faint growl of thunder rippled above the stirring leaves of the enormous maple tree that overshadowed the cave.

Rusty closed his binder. "I think we'd better get home."

Aunt Jeanine knew a lot of family history. Maybe she'd know Troy's blood type.

"We don't have to go back home." I put my camera in the backpack. "Let's go over to the Norris farm."

A few fat drops had splattered us when the small, light blue farmhouse came into view. Chestnut and Gimli trotted from behind the stable and escorted us inside.

One glance at the piles of clothes on the couch, muddy boots by the TV stand, and assorted dishes on the coffee and end tables told us that Aunt Jeanine was nearing some kind of writing deadline and Amber and Coral hadn't covered for her.

"It's me and Rusty," I called.

If Aunt Jeanine was deep into her writing, it might take her a few minutes to surface. If she heard us at all.

Rusty and I skirted the boots and entered the hall to the bedrooms.

A peek in Hank and Jeanine's room showed Jeanine slumped in a high-back swivel chair, frowning at a computer screen.

"Writer's block?" I said.

"Oh, hey, kids." With a vague wave, she continued to stare at the screen.

"Amber and Coral aren't here?" Rusty brushed raindrops from his hair.

"Amber's babysitting, and Coral's over at her grandfather's." Jeanine tapped a pencil against her teeth.

I explained how the threatening storm drove us here, and then, aiming for a casual tone, said, "Do you have the same blood type as mine and Dad's?"

"No." Jeanine hit a few keys. "Mine's the same as Ma's, A positive."

Rusty sat on the unmade bed. "I don't know what mine is."

A burn leeched into my cheeks. I was a crawling sneak. I didn't care about Jeanine's blood type. But I didn't want anyone to know what Troy had been insinuating. At least, not until I felt I needed to tell Dad.

But I should still be honest. "I know Walter is AB negative, and I think your dad was. Is Troy?"

"All of Walter's kids have his blood type, except Lily. He wasn't sure if she was his daught—" Her wide blue eyes shifted to me, startled. "I'm sorry. I'm just bringing up old gossip."

Rusty sat straighter. "Walter doesn't think Aunt Lily is his daughter? Why?"

"He does now. Her oldest son, Lee. J., looks like his stand-in, and her next son, Larry, is a close second." Jeanine removed her mottled brown reading glasses. "It's not a big secret or anything. When Walter's second wife, Aunt Lily's mother, left him for Jeff Buchanan, a lot of people said Aunt Lily looked like a Buchanan. At some point, Walter had Lily's blood typed and found out it didn't rule him out as her father, but it wasn't the same as his."

"Walter didn't mind not knowing for sure?" I said.

"I don't know. Walter would never discuss something that personal." Her small face brightened, and she scooted to the edge of the chair. "There's about a six-inch height difference between you and Rusty, right?"

Rusty and I glanced at each other, and Rusty shrugged. "I guess so."

The question had to be related to her story.

"Great." Jeanine pushed her chair back. "I was stuck on a fight scene between my deputy marshal and a fugitive. You two have the right amount of difference in height. You can help me act it out."

She started for the doorway but turned to us just short of it. "I'm sorry. Will you help me act out the fight scene?"

"As long as you give us credit in your acknowledgements at the end," I said.

"Unfortunately, this is a short story. So all you have is my undying thanks."

Rusty brushed past her. "Do snacks come with your undying thanks?"

As we entered the living room, Jeanine halted beside a rocking chair buried in clothes.

"Oh, boy." Her gaze swept over the room. "I knew it was bad, but I didn't realize it was a disaster."

"We can help you clean up," I said.

Rusty threw me an annoyed look.

Jeanine pushed the rocker against a wall, and Rusty and I took the dishes to the kitchen, then moved the coffee table. She told us how and where to grab each other, trying to construct a realistic fight scene.

So my two questions about Mom left me with just the possibility that she was too drunk to remember that Troy might be my dad.

Fighting a sigh, I fell to the floor as Rusty faked a kick at my stomach.

I'd been counting on the blood type eliminating Troy from contention. I was no better off than before I'd asked Jason and Aunt Jeanine.

We left Jeanine to get home near supper time, the rain amounting to just an annoyance that was now replaced with watery sunshine.

Rusty and I emerged from the woods edging the pasture farthest from the barn. Onyx, the solid black alpaca, and Patches, a brown and white one, trotted up to us, and we petted them on their poofy heads as Dad's patrol SUV came to a stop in front of the garage. I was waving to him when our guard llama shot out of the barn.

Swinging his bangs out of his eyes, Rusty said, "What's wrong with Hor — someone's riding him."

Horace galloped up the drive toward the house with Micah clutching him around his thick neck, bouncing against his back and yelling with every bounce.

Chapter Twenty-Five

Rusty and I raced after them. Dad pounded down the drive, straight at Horace, from the opposite direction. As Horace bore down on Dad, he swiped Micah off the llama, pulling the blanket Micah sat on with him. Horace slammed into Dad and kept going.

"Dad!" Rusty yelled.

He lay on the drive with Micah on top of him.

Micah rolled off Dad and peered at his face. "Are you okay? Is your face messed up?"

Rusty and I dropped to our knees beside Dad as he raised onto an elbow and his dark blue eyes popped open.

"Are you all right?" I said.

Dad gave me a thumbs up, but he didn't attempt to right himself.

Running up to us, Aaron yelled, "I told you not to ride Horace."

Micah glanced over his shoulder. "You're too bossy, Aaron."

"His face is fine, Micah." Rusty put a hand on Dad's shoulder. "It's not like when he got beat up at Walter's."

Dad dragged himself to his knees, hauling in a gallon of air. "I told you." What would have been a normal, shattering shout only came out at half volume. "Last fall, I told all three of you boys. No riding on the alpacas and Horace."

"No, you didn't." Aaron picked up the blanket, which had straps dangling from it. "You said we couldn't ride on the alpacas. Horace is a llama."

Dad growled. "Same thing." He took another deep breath and got to his feet.

"No, it's not. Gram said it was okay to make a saddle for Horace."

Dad squinted at Aaron, like he always did when his conversation with him turned into nonsense.

"Why is Horace loose?" Gram trotted off the front porch.

Dad glared at her. "Aren't you watching my kids?" His shout, now back to full strength, made all of us but Gram jump. "Did you tell Micah he could ride Horace?"

Gram froze. Not just on the surface, but as if every atom in her had ceased to move. Except for her eyebrows, which rose as she delivered the mother of all mom looks.

Dad snatched a breath and focused on his shoes. "Sorry. That was out of line."

Gram relaxed in a blink. "Thank you, sweetie. Let's get Horace, and then you can tell me what happened."

"Hold on, Gram." I touched Dad's arm. "Are you sure you're all right?"

Gram's face tightened. "What happened?"

"Horace ran over Dad."

"Oh, sweetie." Gram reached for Dad's hand.

"I'm fine, Ma. My spine cushioned my fall. Let's get Horace."

The llama had quit running and now wandered along the fence corralling the female alpacas. When Gram was close enough to grab his halter, Horace wheeled away, looking down his long nose, as if every human in sight disgusted him. After several failed attempts, Dad finally snagged the halter, led Horace through the barn, and released him into the pasture with the females.

Back in the barn, he turned to Aaron. "What exactly happened?"

"It's all his fault. Now we can't make any money." Aaron shoved Micah, who swung back, so I got between them.

Crouching to be at Aaron's eye level, Dad said, "Let's back up. How would Micah riding Horace make money?"

Still glowering at our youngest brother, Aaron said, "I told Alli how Gram has the 4-H club come over, and she trains the kids on how to show alpacas at the fair, and most of the parents stay for the whole lesson. And some of the 4-H kids have little brothers and sisters, who make trouble. So Alli said if we gave the little kids rides on Horace and charged them a dollar, we'd make money, and they'd stay out of trouble."

Gram said, "I told Aaron he could make a saddle, and we would test it. Horace will have to be trained, which won't be easy, since he's funny about things on his back."

"We'll never do it now." Angry tears rose in Aaron's light blue eyes. "'Cause Micah jumping on his back will make Horace too scared to take riders now."

"We were about to see if Horace would tolerate the saddle." Gram put her arm around Aaron. "Then I had to put the casserole in and told the boys not to do anything until I got back."

"So you didn't listen to Ma." Dad stood, looking at Micah, who was swinging on a stall door and staring at the ceiling of the barn as if no one had spoken to him. "Micah, go with Ma and pull two extra chores from the chores jar."

Using his foot as a brake, Micah stopped the door, then slunk by Dad and left the barn with Gram.

Aaron wiped at his eyes and turned the homemade saddle over. "I don't think he damaged it." He looked up at Dad, brightening. "Maybe if we give Horace a break, like a couple weeks, we could try again."

"Check with Ma first."

Dad, Rusty, Aaron, and I climbed the hill to the house. As Rusty and Aaron pulled ahead, I fell in step beside Dad. "I guess you haven't found Mrs. Carlisle."

"Nope. I'm going back out to look as soon as I eat."

"Can you tell me anything?"

He studied me for a moment. "Well, I believe less and less she left with a new boyfriend. Deputies in Franklin County went with Conrad to their home in Columbus. If she took any clothes from there, it wasn't much."

Rusty and Aaron banged into the house.

My breathing picking up speed, I said, "Are Jason and Rick suspects?"

"I haven't ruled them out."

"But Jason has no motive if he was going to take Mrs. Carlisle back."

Dad stopped dead with one foot on the first step to the front porch. He scrutinized me, then said, "You heard me mention the book of the Bible I wanted Jason to read. Then you read it."

I shoved my hands in my front pockets. "I got curious."

"That could be your motto."

"Were Jason and Ashley going to reconcile?"

"I can't say. Jason expects me to keep our conversation private." His eyes bored into mine. "You can't repeat your suspicions to — look who I'm talking to." Dad started up the steps. "The only teen in America who doesn't spill her guts all over social media."

"Amber and Rusty don't."

"They aren't allowed to. You actually have the freedom to make a choice."

"When you said I should be careful who I help, were you thinking of Rick?" I joined him on the porch. "Because I let the statute of limitations run out on his crimes, I've given him the chance to commit crimes again?"

"No." He unbuckled his utility belt. "You've given Rick a second chance. If he fails to take advantage of it, that's on him. What I worry about is that you'll try to help in a situation where you can't or you might actually do harm. Or the person you help doesn't need it or tries to exploit your kindness."

"Like Troy." I sighed. "He so played me. And I can't be sure that Mrs. Carlisle didn't. But don't you have to take risks sometimes when you're merciful?"

"Yes. You showed a lot of wisdom dealing with Ashley and Conrad." He watched me a moment more, as if he was weighing saying something else. Then he said, "I'd better wash up."

He hadn't had to pause and think before he announced that. What had he wanted to say?

As we entered the living room, I said, "Do you think Mrs. Carlisle could've been in an accident in a really remote part of the county?"

"Very possible, although it doesn't explain why she left the lodge in the middle of the night. Conrad had their phones set up so they could track each other. The last known location for her phone is the lodge." Dad headed to the kitchen. "So the phone could now be in a location without reception. Or she could have met someone near the lodge, been attacked, and left in the woods. But that person would have had to dispose of her car. I'm leaning toward her leaving the park, but I can't overlook any scenario at this point."

He hung up his keys on the hooks behind the kitchen door. "All the employees at the park who can spare some time have been combing the area around the lodge. The patrols are covering the county roads, trying to spot evidence of a car leaving the pavement. I posted on some local pages that if anyone wants to volunteer to check along roads or search the hills around the lodge, they can call Liz at our non-emergency number, and she'll assign them an area."

"I could do that after supper," I said.

"Which? Checking out the roads or the state park?"

"Where do you need the most help?"

Dad rubbed his chin. "Probably the roads. I think it's much more likely she's nowhere near the park. But I don't want you driving that heap of yours. See if Jeanine or Carrie'll go with you and take one of their cars."

"For sure."

Chapter Twenty-Six

As soon as supper was over, Dad left, and I called Aunt Jeanine. She said both she and Carrie wanted to help, so Gram dropped me off at the Norrises' farm. My aunts met me by their vehicles, Carrie's mellow yellow Jeep and the Norrises' maroon SUV.

Jeanine said, "Rae, you'd better drive Carrie. She's beat."

Carrie handed me her keys. "You wouldn't think watching three little kids would be more exhausting than tracking fugitives, but keeping myself positive and cheerful— " she plastered on a way too perky smile "—while maintaining order is a serious strain. I mean, when a perp got out of line, I'd just take control until I got compliance. But I can't throw the kids to the floor and cuff them when they aren't listening."

"You might lose your job that way." Jeanine grinned and gave Carrie a scrap of paper. "These are the roads Liz gave us to search." She looked westward, dark clouds blocking any view of the sunset. "We may have two hours of daylight left, but if more clouds move in, we won't."

We mounted up.

Aunt Carrie's Jeep handled so smooth, no groaning or chugging or collapsing. That kind of reliability must have been a serious comfort to her.

I aimed the Jeep northwest, and in a few miles, the farm fields had grown smaller and the woods lining the road thicker.

Swerving around a pothole, I said, "Did Jason tell the kids about their mother's disappearance?"

"Good grief, no. It'll just produce a lot of unnecessary anxiety. But Alli and Richard can see something's up with Jason. He's wound so tight that I expect him to snap at any minute."

"Do you know who was the last person to see Mrs. Carlisle besides Mr. Conrad? I forgot to ask Dad."

"He might not tell you, although I'm sure it's all over the county by now. The last person, who's not a suspect, to see Ashley was Dalton Edwards, the clerk working the front desk at the lodge last night. He said he saw Ashley and her prince come into the lobby about 8 p.m. They got in the elevator. Then Ashley called down for a bottle of Scotch to be delivered to their room. Edwards took it up, and she answered the door. That's the last anyone saw of her."

I tugged on my earlobe. "We only have Mr. Conrad's word that Mrs.

Carlisle left their room before 5:30. Are there any security cameras at the lodge?"

Carrie gave a contemptuous laugh. "Probably in the gift shop and maybe in the lobby. No, I don't think there's any footage of Conrad carrying Ashley's body into the woods." Her voice grew quiet. "Jason worked from home today, so he could be available to talk to Mal when he wanted him. While the kids were eating lunch and watching TV, he talked to me in his office. He told me about Ashley speaking to you at the theater."

I turned onto a road of chip and tar, pale blue hyacinth scraping the tires and sides of the Jeep. "Do you know if Jason unblocked his ex-wife's number and if she called him? Or maybe he called her?"

Carrie dragged two fingers through her hair, then turned up a hand. "Since you already know she wanted to talk to him, I don't see the harm in answering. No one but you, me, and Mal knows this. As soon as I got off work, I called Mal and told him what Jason told me to make sure Jason is telling the cops the same story."

"I won't tell anyone anything."

She exhaled in a huff. "I know that from personal experience." She looked out the window. "Ashley called Jason around 2:30 on Sunday morning. They talked only for a few minutes. At the same time, this morning, Jason called Ashley. She picked up at once. Again, they talked only a few minutes. Ashley told Jason she couldn't talk longer, but she'd call him back in an hour. She never did."

"Did she say where she was when she answered?" I pulled away from a fallen branch poking into the road.

"No, but Jason said he heard road noise and got a sense she had to meet someone. That's why she wanted to call him back."

Although I could guess, I said, "Did Jason say what they talked about?"

"No. He didn't volunteer that information, so I didn't ask. I assume Mal pressed him for the details."

"So she never came back from her meeting. At least, she never came back to Mr. Conrad."

"If you believe Jason."

I looked at Carrie and hit a pothole.

"Watch it." She bounced against the door.

"Don't you believe Jason?"

The trees encroached closer as the road fell steeply away.

"He's the ex-husband, making him a very likely suspect in her disappearance. If she's disappeared."

"But what's his motive?" I applied the brakes. "If he was afraid Mrs. Carlisle and Mr. Conrad would take Sylvie from him, I think he'd take out

Conrad. He's the force behind all this."

Out of the corner of my eye, I saw Carrie give me sidelong scrutiny. "You really like Jason, don't you?"

"Well ... yeah. But like an uncle." No way I wanted her to think I was attracted to a guy the same age as my dad. "He's been nice to me since I was hired at the library, and he's always helped me with any trouble I've had at work."

She watched the side of the road. "I find it hard to believe too, but I know Jason's extremely worried that Conrad might persuade Ashley to sue for custody of all three kids on the grounds that hiring a bodyguard for them was crazy. I told Jason it didn't make him look paranoid. For Pete's sake, his ex-wife and her boyfriend are hanging around his kids when they have no reason to. Any parent might worry about kidnapping. But my opinion didn't seem to reassure him."

Carrie and I finished checking out the roads Liz assigned us, noticing no signs of an accident by the time the thick clouds brought night on early. I drove to our farm, got out, and Carrie left in the Jeep.

No one was up but Rusty, stretched out on the couch, hidden behind a fantasy novel thick enough to stop a bullet.

I fell into the green recliner. "Where's Gram?"

"Taking a shower. She said she was really tired and wanted to go to bed early."

I went to the computer table by the front door and pulled two sheets of blank paper from the printer. Resuming my seat in the recliner, I placed the paper on a picture book I'd found on the floor and used it as a tiny desk.

Gram said good night to us on the way to her makeshift bedroom upstairs. We had to get my new room done, so she could have her old bedroom again. Every time I offered to move upstairs, she turned me down, saying I needed more privacy than she did.

Rusty had been reading, and I'd been writing a while when Dad trudged in the back door.

I hopped out of the recliner. "Any news?"

"Nope. Nothing new. Rusty, you should be heading to bed." He trundled down the basement steps.

I gave Dad five minutes, then went downstairs and knocked on the door of his bedroom.

"Come in."

Entering the basement bedroom, I was glad again Gram had given me her room, instead of Dad. Although the room had sandy walls, blond wood furniture, and a decent-sized window, it still looked like a cave, especially at night. Standing in it for only moments had already depressed me.

137

Dad switched on the lamp by his double bed. He'd changed into running shorts and a gray t-shirt with a hole in the right sleeve. He could go from neat, trim officer to disheveled dad in ten seconds.

Holding the picture book and sheets of paper, I said, "Carrie told me that Jason talked to Ashley early Sunday morning and this morning. But he didn't tell her what the conversation was about. Did he tell you?"

"Yes, but I can't tell you what he said." He yawned.

"I know. But do you believe him?"

His mouth hung open for a moment, then Dad finished his yawn. "I don't know."

Needles of dread made me clutch the picture book to my chest. "Can you tell me why Rick and Jason don't have alibis?"

Dad eyed me. "Why do you want to know?"

I showed him the chart I'd made. "I'm trying to organize the information so I can make sense of it, maybe see some connections.

Suspect	Opportunity	Means	Motive
Jason	Alone Sunday night and Monday morning	Lured her from lodge and ...	Protect kids
Rick	Alone early Monday morning	Lured her from lodge and ...	Protect kids
Steve	Alone with Ashley Sunday night and Monday morning. Said he took sleeping pill.	Didn't need to lure her from lodge.	?—Has every reason to want Ashley alive
Boyfriend X	?????	Lured her from lodge and ...	Jealousy? Ashley knows something she shouldn't? ?????

His spine snapped to attention, and his eyes ballooned. "Rae, you can't conduct a private investigation. This is an official—"

"I wasn't going to investigate." I sat beside him on the bed. "It's just—well, I'm interested. And puzzled. And I thought if I organized the information, I might understand it better. If I think of anything, I'll tell you right away. I won't question people or anything."

Dad tried to give me his special lit-from-within-grin, but for some reason, the power wasn't there. "I'm sure Jason's and Rick's alibis are all over the county by now, so I don't mind telling you. Jason was alone with his kids from the time he left the farm last night until Carrie arrived to watch them this morning. From about 9:15 p.m. to 8:30 a.m. Rick went to a fundraiser in Columbus last night, representing Carlisle Quarry and Concrete. He ran into some journalist friends. They went to one man's home for drinks after the fundraiser. Rick left a little after 12:30. He got home around 2:30. He was alone until he entered the newspaper office at 7 a.m. today, although he spoke to a reporter at about 6:15, when she called him about the report of Ashley's disappearance."

I added the information to the chart. "If either of them, or both of them, had plotted to hurt or kill Mrs. Carlisle, you'd think they'd have alibis."

"You'd think Rick would. This is his second run at it."

My stomach took a sick twist.

Dad pointed at a column. "Who is Boyfriend X?"

"Didn't Carrie tell you?" I explained Jason's theory that when Ashley left him after Sylvie was born, it was for some man other than Steve Conrad.

"Makes sense. Although Conard wouldn't be the first man to lead a double life."

"You mean living with his wife in Columbus and supporting Mrs. Carlisle someplace else?"

He nodded. "Although if Ashley really thought Sylvie might be Conrad's and they've had a relationship for the past two years, you'd think she'd have mentioned it before now. Maybe she did leave Jason for someone else and has since broken up with him."

Remembering Conrad's conversation — if you could call it that — with Devon, I said, "Mr. Conrad acts like that king of England who kept marrying to produce an heir."

"Henry VIII. He did away with a few wives. But that makes zero sense for Conrad. Without Ashley to support his claim that he's Sylvie's father, I don't know if he could bring a case to force Jason to test Sylvie."

I tugged at my earlobe. "Even if he found out Ashley wanted to leave him, I think he'd try to bribe her to stay with him, like he did with me. He's a salesman." Conrad's outraged expression as I tore up his card loomed in my mind, and I scooted closer to Dad. "But Jason and Rick have no motive since Ashley wanted to come back to Jason."

"You're assuming facts that haven't been substantiated."

"I know you can't say, but Carrie told me about the calls. From the times, and Jason coming to talk to you, I'd say Ashley asked Jason to take her back when she called early Sunday morning. Jason came to you to ask for your advice. When he called her at 2:30 this morning, they discussed the idea, but not for long. Ashley had to go but said she'd call back. Something stopped her."

"Not bad," Dad said. "We'll assume that you're correct — that Jason came yesterday evening to ask for advice about taking Ashley back. He could have lied to me. If he was plotting to murder Ashley, he couldn't do better than enlisting the sheriff as a witness to support him."

My stomach twisted tighter. "Do you think he lied?"

"I have no idea. I just have to be suspicious of anything a suspect tells me. If you think of anything else that might help, let me know. I'll check with Carrie and Jason about Boyfriend X."

"She said there could've been more than one. Mrs. Carlisle was gone for over two years."

"Sadly true." He squeezed my hand, appearing ready to say something. Then it dissipated, and he got the deflated look again. "Anything else you think I ought to know about this?"

He had been planning on saying something else and changed his mind.

I said no, kissed him good night, and went upstairs.

Why did he keep doing that? Prepare to say something and decide not to.

Rusty had fallen asleep in a huddle on the couch. I got him up and walked him to his bed.

Then I settled into the recliner and reviewed my chart, a depression dripping over me.

Awful to realize, and maybe Ashley hadn't, but there was no shortage of people who'd like her to disappear.

Chapter Twenty-Seven

Crossing the library parking lot the next morning, I read all the texts that had pinged once I'd left the farm and driven into an area with reception. Chris had sent me several photos of white caps breaking before a lighthouse on Lake Michigan. Beautiful, well-composed shots for a phone camera.

As I was punching in the code to the employees' entrance, Devon walked up, her face pink. "I'll take the dry heat of the southwest over humidity any day."

Humidity? A few feathered clouds decorated a hazy blue sky, and some sweat had beaded on the back of my neck since the air conditioning in the Rust Bucket had taken a vacation. I wouldn't have said the humidity was even noticeable yet.

We met Barb coming down the back stairs.

"Good morning." Barb resettled on her nose the pale blue glasses that matched her light-weight blazer. "Rae, would you come up to my office?"

"For sure."

She had just closed the door to her office when she asked in a harsh whisper, "Have they found Ashley yet?"

"Not that I know of. And Dad would call me if they had. He knows I'm interested."

Barb took two paces, then paced back to me, then away. Forgetting to invite me to sit showed she was monumentally preoccupied.

"You've noticed how similar Ashley's disappearance is to your mother's?"

"Yes, ma'am." A nauseating chill made me gulp.

"Do you know where Rick was during the time she disappeared?"

"Dad's not sure she has disappeared, as in someone's kidnapped or killed her." I explained the theory of the car crash.

"But I heard she left the lodge in the middle of the night. She must have had a reason other than driving off the road. Unless it was suicide, but nothing I've heard about Ashley from Jason or Rick indicates she would do that."

"We only have Mr. Conrad's word that she left in the middle of the night. The desk clerk Sunday night saw her come back with Mr. Conrad to the lodge at eight and then he took a bottle of Scotch up to her room, which she took from him. Those are the only facts Dad has about when she was last seen."

Barb wrung her thin hands. "Rick told me he went to a charity event in Columbus and stayed late at a friend's house. He didn't get home until 2:30."

I didn't see any harm in saying, "That's what he told Dad." I tugged on my earlobe. "Do you mind if I ask when Rick told you that?"

"I called him." She flung out an arm. "The woman who was threatening to take away his beloved niece, and possibly all of his brother's beloved children, disappears, and you don't think my first thought is Rick Carlisle has struck again?"

I tried to assemble some kind of response, but Barb kept going, pacing again. "Do you know if his alibi checks out?"

"No, ma'am. Dad wouldn't tell me one way or the other."

Barb spun to me. "Do you think he killed Ashley?"

Agony echoed behind that question, an agony that had to have grown since Barb first heard Ashley was missing yesterday. And Dad and I were the only two people she could discuss it with to relieve her pain. But she seemed to hate Rick since she broke up with him. Why all the anguish? Unless she had second thoughts too.

Father, help me help her. But let me be honest.

"I don't know."

She squeezed her eyes shut, like the sentence stabbed her.

"But I doubt it. He seems changed to me, and Jason told me how grateful Rick is for a second chance. I don't think he'd want to jeopardize it."

"Perhaps that's what you want to believe since you gave him the second chance." Barb's words dripped ice water

Keep my mind clear, Father.

"I really believe it. I could be wrong, but I'm not trying to lie to myself or you."

Tears brimmed in her eyes, and she yanked off her glasses. "I'm sorry, Rae."

"No problem. I'm sorry you're so upset."

She turned her face to the ceiling, sniffing. "Please don't repeat this conversation to anyone."

"I won't except for my dad."

Barb drew a breath, like she was about to object, and then said, "I understand."

I shut the door to her office behind me and headed for the lobby.

Chapter Twenty-Eight

The next morning, Gram stumbled into the kitchen, surprising me with her bleary eyes.

"Didn't you sleep well?" I drained my mug of chai.

"No. I seemed to wake up a lot," she mumbled.

"Maybe you'd sleep better in your own bed."

"It won't be long now." Gram removed a mug from the cupboard. "I can wait until your room's done."

"Would you like me to take care of the alpacas this morning?"

Gram broke into her dreamy smile. "That would be so nice."

I threw on a t-shirt, jean shorts and hiking boots but took my time reaching the barn, strolling down the drive as the morning light seemed to freshen everything—leaves seemed greener, flowers seemed brighter. Even the tired red paint on the barn appeared more vibrant.

Inside, I went to the stall for the two males and opened the door that led to their pasture, and Steel and Slade trotted out. I started to unlatch the gate to the females' bigger stall when someone walked into the barn from the drive side.

Turning, I said, "Gram, you don't have—" and the rest of the sentence died on my tongue.

Two men had entered—one middle-aged with a gut straining the buttons of his open-collar dress shirt and one probably in his twenties with a blond buzz cut.

"Good morning, Miss Riley," said the middle-aged guy. "We'd like to speak to you."

His brown, wavy hair shined from too much product and had only a few silver strands, but his face looked like every sin he'd ever committed had stamped it with a seam, pouch, or broken vein.

He advanced into the barn while Blonde Guy lolled against the half open sliding door, a leer on his chiseled face making all my brain cells scream a warning.

"Who are you?" I fought to sound unconcerned. "How do you know my name?"

"Don't tease us, Miss Riley," said Greasy Guy. "We know you know who we are. We've talked to your cousin. You've been wise not to identify us to the cops." His lips lifted to display dark-stained teeth. "We want you to continue being wise."

My cousin? They had to mean Troy. Only God knew what he'd told these guys about our family connection. But Troy knew I couldn't identify them. Neither could Amber or Coral. Why was he setting me up?

Blonde Guy broke into a caveman snicker, pulling back a side of his gray sweat jacket to reveal a pistol tucked in the waistband of his jeans. "I can make you wise if I have to."

My heart contracted as adrenaline tightened every muscle fiber. "My grandmother's expecting me to come back up to the house in a few minutes."

No way could I get past Blond Guy. I started for the males' stall to go out by the pasture door, but Greasy Guy planted himself in front of me in the aisle.

"Does she have you working on a time clock? I don't think so."

"Excuse me." I tried to push past him, but he placed a hand on my arm, and I recoiled from it, my stomach jumping. "You can't keep me here." Shoot, my voice shook.

Blonde Guy pulled the gun from his waistband. "I can."

My blood drained from my head, leaving me dizzy.

Father, help me. Help me think.

In his separate stall, Horace snorted, making Greasy Guy back away.

"What kind of farm is this, anyways?" Blonde Guy swept out the hand holding the gun, and both men watched Horace with the kind of suspicion you'd use for a large, loose dog who was barking at you.

I'd been around him so long that I'd forgotten how intimidating Horace could be. He was as tall as both men and twice as heavy.

Horace gave another snort and pawed at his straw bedding.

The two men tensed.

I reached over the stall to pat Horace and brushed my hand against Aaron's llama saddle draped over the side of the stall.

The Lord hit me with an idea so hard, I flinched.

"This is an alpaca farm," I said. "If you won't let me leave, I still have to release the females and our llama into the pasture. The males are already out, and they're getting impatient."

The bloodshot gaze of Greasy Guy raked Horace. "Go ahead, miss. But if you do anything—let's call it 'unexpected,' my friend will make you regret it."

Yeah, and I had a friend that could make them both regret a whole ton more.

Removing Horace's halter from the nail outside his stall, I noted where the shovel for cleaning soiled bedding leaned against the males' stall, behind Greasy Guy.

"We want you to understand that keeping our identities to yourself is your best policy." Greasy Guy reached toward my face, and I twisted backwards.

He chuckled, smoothing the side of his glistening hair.

Swallowing a lump of panic, I said, "I understand," and swung open the gate to the stall.

Horace tossed his head, making Greasy Guy jump back a step.

Squashing a grin, I pulled the halter over Horace's head.

"I hope you do, miss. I don't want to hurt you. An unpleasant part of my business, but any job has its drawbacks."

Gripping the halter, I guided Horace into the aisle between the stalls.

"You're not taking that thing out past my friend." Greasy Guy scooted away from us.

"No. He can go out with the females, through that door in the barn wall." I positioned Horace on the dirt floor, aiming him like a missile.

Father, keep Horace safe. Let me get to the shovel in time.

"Oh, I forgot." I lifted the saddle from the door.

Greasy Guy stuck his hand into his sports coat. "Keep that thing away from —"

A huge hand shot into the barn, grabbed Blonde Guy by the shoulder, and jerked him out of sight.

As his partner yelled out, the Greasy Guy spun to him, and I dropped the saddle on Horace's back.

Releasing a whinnying squeal, Horace reared and plowed into Greasy Guy as he turned back toward me. The fat man fell into a post, smacking his head, and hit the rough ground like a hay bale dropped from the loft.

Snatching the shovel, I shouted, "Who's out there?"

"Me 'n' Gyp." Walter's cellar voice brought a rush of relief that left me as light-headed as my fear.

"Can you come in here, Walter? I need you to cover this other guy."

"Gotcha."

Blonde Guy stumbled into the barn, blood dripping from his nose.

With Egypt beside him, Walter stalked in, holding the man's gun. "You sit."

As Blonde Guy obeyed, a shiver crawled from my scalp to my knees, weakening them, but I tried to sound strong. "Walter, please watch them both. I'll see if this guy has a gun."

Greasy Guy hadn't moved. I rolled him onto his back and pulled a pistol from a holster under his left arm.

Shaking off another shiver, I said, "Thanks, Walter. You too, Egypt. I thought I could take out this guy —" I pointed a toe at the inert man "— with Horace, and that would give me enough time to take out the other guy with that shovel. But I was afraid I wouldn't make it, and Horace would get shot. You saved me and him."

"I wasn't tryin' to save no dumb animal." Shoving his free hand into his jeans, Walter kept the gun trained on the men. "You hurt? They didn't do nothin' to you, did they?"

"Just scared me."

Egypt sniggered, but a fierce glance from Walter killed it.

Holding a hand against my stomach, I said, "What are y'all doing here?"

Walter backed against the sliding door. "Gyp saw Troy get into a car with these two yahoos, and it looked like maybe they forced him. So we followed them. When they parked out on the road and headed into the trees, I knew they was up to no good, or Troy was, because there was no reason for them to come to your farm. Gyp and me tracked them and saw them come in here. When I could, I took out this idiot."

Blonde Guy sat on the floor, his back against a stall, the jut of his lower jaw making him resemble a preschooler in time out.

I said, "Where's Troy?"

"As soon as the guys came in here," Egypt said in her usual acid tones, "he hightailed it into the woods."

My shoulders sagged. "He really did set me up."

How many other opportunities to help would come back to bite me? A burn flooded my face and raged inside me, hollowing my gut. If I could get more stupid, it'd take real effort.

"Bet you wished you hadn't been so dumb and helped him, don't you?" A sneer marred Egypt's pinched face, which wasn't all that pleasant to begin with.

"I'd better call Dad," I said in a flat voice. "Can you watch them?"

"Glad to." Walter's lips parted, revealing his long, strong teeth.

As I trudged out of the barn, Gram raced down the drive, carrying a rifle, and Troy ran with her.

"I'm fine," I called. "We took out the two guys."

"We?" Gram called back, and Troy echoed the word.

When she reached me, Gram hugged me, and then we stepped back into the barn with Troy.

Greasy Guy still lay on his back, but the labored breathing through his open mouth proved he was alive. Blonde Guy glared like a ticked-off, spoiled brat.

Troy started at the sight of Egypt and Walter, who loomed over the two men with the pistol in his calloused hand.

"When did you two get here?" Troy said.

A change had come over Troy. His voice wasn't as measured. His face didn't register the usual patience or noble suffering or wistfulness. He sounded like he was honestly shocked and had reacted before he could filter it through his con man's techniques.

"You'd like to know that, wouldn't ya?" Walter's sneer made Egypt's seem amateurish.

Peering at the two men on the ground, Gram said, "We can sort out the details when Mal gets here."

Troy turned to me, reaching for my arm. "I'm so glad you're—"

I jerked away. "Save it." I snatched a lead rope from a hook. "Gram, I'll get Horace." Too bad I couldn't glare Troy to death. "Save it for my dad, Troy."

Chapter Twenty-Nine

Forty-five minutes later, Dad was taking Troy's statement outside the barn after hearing from me, Walter, and Egypt.

Houston placed Blonde Guy into his SUV, and the paramedics loaded Greasy Guy, who was just conscious enough to mumble, into the ambulance.

Gram had gone back up to the house to keep my brothers from joining the excitement and had called Carrie to tell her not to come with the Carlisle kids.

Houston turned to me as he shut the back door. "You always seem to find the action around here."

"I don't try to." Clutching my arms, I toed the ground.

He leaned closer, his sea green eyes softening. "Real glad you're okay."

My heart shook for a moment. "Thanks." It came out in a whisper.

Straightening, he gave me his good ol' boy grin. "Next time I'm in a tight spot, I'll look for a llama."

A laugh escaped my lips but died as a spike of guilt killed it. What would Chris think? He couldn't know Houston could affect me this way because ... because ... I just didn't want him to.

Houston's SUV ground down the drive to the road.

The sun had climbed high enough for us to remain shaded in the barn's shadow.

"So let me say this in my own words, Troy." Dad's powerful baritone probably carried to the alpacas and Horace in the farthest corner of the pasture. "When you left Walter's house this morning, you were cornered by —" Dad flipped a few pages back in his notes, " — Frank Joseph, a PI from Arizona, and Austin Falk, who seems to work as his henchman. They still think you're Matt even though you are not twenty-eight or six-foot-two. They demanded money from you — over $20,000. Since they wouldn't believe you weren't Matt, you played along, claiming you'd get the money by next Tuesday or Wednesday, but they didn't buy it. Fearing for the safety of your daughters and Walter —"

Walter spat. "I bet."

" — you tried to scare them off by telling them one of the girls they ran into at the mall could identify them as the men who beat you up and ran you off the road. Instead of scaring them, the men insisted on seeing this girl and intimidating her to keep silent. They forced you into their car. Since you couldn't persuade them to leave the county, you decided to bring them to my house so I could arrest them. Unfortunately, as you three approached the house, they recognized Rae and followed her into the barn. You sneaked into the woods, heading for the house, while they were threatening my daughter." Dad's voice rose at the end of the sentence, his glare sharpening. "You got turned around in the woods a few times, which delayed you getting to the house. When you finally made it there, you told Ma what was going on. Have I got that right?"

Troy nodded. "Absolutely correct."

Dad's glare should have sliced Troy in half. "In all my sixteen years as a cop, I've never heard so many lies, so fast." He broke out into a roar. "Micah could've invented a more believable story, and he's seven."

Troy reared back. "Why would I lie?"

A contemptuous chuckle echoed deep in Walter's throat as Dad said, "Oh, I don't know. Try my deductions on for size.

"Joseph and Falk traced you to Walter's place. They threatened you because you owe them money or owe money to somebody who hired them. You couldn't get them to give you more time, and for some reason, you didn't want to file assault charges against them. Maybe you thought, as the single witness, the charges wouldn't stick, and you really needed them to stick. So you finessed the situation to let me and my family take care of your problem." His jaw clenched for a moment.

"You told the men that Rae could identify them, but you'd persuaded her not to go to the police. But you weren't sure she'd keep her lips zipped. I bet you even let them sort of beat it out of you where Rae lives. You let them force you into their car and brought them here. I'm not sure how you wanted the situation to play out from there. I am sure you wanted the two goons to threaten someone in my family or maybe my whole family, then you'd have more than one witness to bring charges, and I'd take them out of circulation, removing the threat to you."

Troy had listened to Dad's explanation with widening eyes. Then he said in a stunned voice, "I'm glad I never became a cop. You can believe anything bad of anybody, including family." He met Dad's furious glower. "Do you have any proof of your theory?" His laid-back tone had the tiniest undercurrent of a sneer.

"For a court, no. But I've known you all my life, Troy. I know how you operate."

"I can say the same thing." Again, under the casual words, a hint of smugness.

Dad moved in on Troy, who tried to hold his ground, but Dad forced him against the fence. "You are very lucky Rae wasn't hurt, and Walter and Egypt followed you."

"I know." A great wash of relief filled his voice. "I wish now I'd handled this better. I'd never want to endanger family."

"You need to come up with better excuses." Dad put away his notepad. "You made a mistake two years ago, and I got jumped. You made a mistake today and put my daughter in danger. You can't keep saying you make mistakes, Troy. You're forty-three. Not fourteen."

Troy sighed, his tiny mouth drooping. "I'm just not as smart as you are. Or have your dark turn of mind to suspect everyone of being up to no good."

"Mal's right in your case." Egypt slouched against the barn, arms crossed.

Troy gave her a warm smile. "I know we haven't been getting along, honey, so I appreciate you coming to help me."

"I came to help Walter." Egypt pushed off the wall. "He's the one who wanted to follow you. I would've said nothing 'cept I knew Walter'd want to know."

"Well, I very much appreciate it, Walter." Troy maintained the same smile, but the words rang false. "But I'm confused. Why did you follow me?"

"Why do ya think?" Walter growled. "It looked like you was in trouble, and you're my kid, even if the trouble's all your own doing. Malinowskis should stick together."

"Yes, we should." Troy nodded like he'd just received wisdom from Solomon himself. "And I know you'd do anything to prevent losing another son."

My ears caught the false note again, and I jerked to attention.

A very slight taunt had crept in under the patient observation. A subtle version of the tone I'd heard way, way too many times from China.

Or was I imagining it because I was furious at Troy?

I glanced to Dad. He'd turned to a block of ice as Egypt spluttered, "You—you're—it wasn't Walter's fault Reuel died."

Fists raised, she threw herself at him, but Dad grabbed her.

Morphing into a tornado, Egypt twisted, hurled obscenities, and struggled against Dad's iron arms.

Walter spun on his heels and stalked down the drive, his back to us.

Dad shouted, "Egypt, Troy's not worth a prison sentence."

The tornado subsided as Troy said, "I would never press charges against my own daughter."

"I'll give you five minutes and see what your story is then." Dad kept Egypt wrapped up. "I know you hate Walter, Troy, but he did come to help you. It just so happened he helped Rae."

A mystified expression smoothed Troy's Californian good looks. "All I made was a simple statement. Reuel's death has haunted Walter because he knows Reuel only went to that bar because Walter badgered him to. I was simply acknowledging the fact."

No, he wasn't. And how rotten of a monster did you have to be to figuratively spit on people who helped you?

Dad released Egypt, who jerked out of his arm, snarling. But she didn't go for Troy.

I side-stepped closer to Dad. "Maybe I should follow Walter."

"That's the last thing he'd want."

Walter was already out of sight, probably heading for wherever he'd parked his truck.

Dad said, "I need all of you to sign your statements, but I'll get Walter to sign first before he leaves. Egypt, go on up to the house and wait for me there. Troy, you wait here."

"Why do I have to go to the house?" Egypt tossed her head, her long sepia hair swinging by her embedded frown.

"Because I won't be here if you try to take out Troy again. Go up to the house and cool off while I have a private word with Walter."

"I don't have to listen to you."

"No, you don't. But I do have to arrest you if you commit assault." Shifting his weight to his back leg, Dad hooked his thumb on his belt.

I turned and dragged my feet up the drive.

How could helping someone have turned out so badly, Father? Wasn't I right to help Troy? We're supposed to love our enemies.

"Can I get coffee?" Egypt caught up to me.

"Yeah, or tea. Gram also has muffins and scones. She might be making oatmeal today."

"Sweet old lady." Egypt smirked. "Does she tuck you in at night?"

I was in no mood to endure anymore insults, taunts, or threats. Those were the only things Troy and his daughters had in common. They all used their mouths as weapons.

"Only when she isn't toting a shotgun. You should remember that."

"Don't try to scare me. You don't have any llamas around for protection."

"Believe me, if I think you need one, I'll get one." I flung open the front door and stomped inside.

Chapter Thirty

"How's my girl?" Dad gave me one of his shoulder-crushing, one-armed hugs as I finished signing my statement on the kitchen counter. When he usually asked that question, it was a greeting. Now he said it more seriously.

Walter, Egypt, and Troy had already left, and Gram had herded my brothers outside to stop the flow of endless questions.

"I feel completely stupid. And I'm really, really sorry." I hooked hair behind my ear. "I never would've helped Troy if I knew it would put Gram or the boys in danger."

"I know, kiddo." Another squeeze. "But I'm not sure you're helping Troy made much of a difference in this situation." Concern deepened his voice.

"But if I hadn't driven his car—"

"If Troy really wants to use us to protect himself, he'll figure out a way to do it. If he hadn't thought of you, he'd've tried something with Amber or Coral." His boyish face was a mass of tight lines.

"I'm really confused, Dad. Jesus said to love our enemies. And when I've been looking up those verses on mercy, I haven't found any exceptions. Like don't help people who could hurt you. So why did loving my enemy go so badly? Although ... " I rubbed my shell locket between my fingers, "when I prayed for a clear mind, I got it. I thought of Horace, and God kept him and me safe. And the rest of the family."

"God didn't say loving our enemies would be easy. But He does want us to be wise, to avoid danger whenever we can."

I locked gazes with him. "Are you mad at me?"

"No." He hugged me. "I'm not going to yell. I'm really trying to watch that." His gaze intensified, as if he thought he didn't have my full attention. "But even when I'm mad, that doesn't mean I don't love you."

"I know. You said I was yours since Mom told you about me and I can't do anything to change it."

"That's right. Nothing can."

Did he mean that? Absolutely nothing? Like endangering the family or not being his biological daughter?

Father, should I tell him my fear?

The left side of Dad's face contracted. He was thinking about something he should do, but didn't want to. What could it be?

The landline rang.

Dad picked up and listened. His entire body went rigid. "Yes, she's fine, Simcox. Everyone in my family is."

My eyebrows rose.

The Chief of Police hadn't called out of any concern for Dad's relatives. Not when he was still fuming over losing the election to Dad.

Dad listened again, his face growing redder and redder. "Excuse me for a moment." His voice was hoarse.

He handed me the phone and placed my hand over the mouthpiece. Then he went out the back door.

My thoughts whirling, I lowered myself onto a stool by the counter.

A sharp roar made me jump, and in another minute, Dad returned to the kitchen. The deep scarlet in his face had faded to puce, and he gestured for the phone.

"I'm back, Simcox. Sorry for the delay. No, I don't think I need to call BCI in on this case. Houston can handle it." Dad went quiet, said good-bye, and hung up.

Bending his head, he gripped the counter.

"What did the Chief say?"

Dad shoved himself upright. "The case with Joseph and Falk is too tough for my department, so I should call in agents from the attorney general's office for help. That's just an excuse for him to remind me that he thinks I'm unfit for office." He shook his head. "I shouldn't let him get to me. Usually, he doesn't because I've come to expect his insinuations. Today, I took it wrong." He glanced at the clock on the microwave. "You'd better getting moving."

I got off the stool. "If you find out anything from those two guys—"

"I'll tell you. But I'm sure what Troy told us will mostly jibe with anything Joseph or Falk will say. If it doesn't, he'll just claim they're lying."

A half hour later, I pulled into the library parking lot, and my phone pinged.

A text from Chris.

I opened it

A picture of the Badlands—dry, dusty, gorgeously bleak.

I texted that to Chris as the courthouse chimes struck noon. Cutting my response short, I bolted for the basement door.

Although Devon and I had to get a meeting room ready for a musician performing for a children's program in the evening, I spent most of the day deflecting questions in the variety of "Have the cops found Ashley Carlisle?" and "What happened at your farm this morning?"

Just before five, Bruce Schuster strode up to the desk with several thick paperbacks held in the crook of his arm.

I cringed inside, but since Devon was also working the desk, hopefully, the conversation wouldn't veer into the weird.

Bruce dropped the books, all romance novels, onto the counter. "Heard about what happened out at your farm, Rae."

Pulling the novels toward her computer, Devon said, "Don't waste your breath. Mal's told her not to talk about the case, and she won't."

Bruce gave me a suspicious squint. "Why doesn't Mal want you to talk about it?"

I opened my mouth to answer, but Devon beat me. "Because it's an active case and Rae's a witness. If she flaps her gums, she can mess up the prosecution's case." She glanced at the novels. "Conducting research, Bruce?"

"You're too funny, lady. Naw, they're for my mom. She's recovering from hip replacement surgery." He glanced over at an overweight man with fly-away mouse brown hair, who slid a magazine back to its place on the shelf. "Dalton, has Mal told you not to tell anyone you're the last person to see Ashley Carlisle?"

I thought that man looked familiar. Dalton Something was the manager at the lodge, the guy who told Egypt to get back to work when Dad and I had breakfast there on my birthday.

"No." Carrying three DVDs, Dalton walked toward—no, he actually waddled toward the desk. "Why would he? There are no secrets in this county."

"Well, I just found out—"

"I still can't believe Ashley Carlisle is missing." Ms. Hancock, who might have been the Algebra teacher Amber had complained about, scurried over to the growing group at the desk.

But between Bruce, Dalton, and their guts, there wasn't much room for the thin, middle-aged woman.

"Dalton, did you see a lot of Ashley and that new boyfriend of hers at the lodge?" Ms. Hancock pushed her head forward like a curious heron.

Bruce said, "Think he did something to her, Dalton?"

Two more patrons crowded in, and Dalton Edwards—that was his last name—was surrounded like a celebrity. Becoming the Last Person to See the Victim Alive had obviously elevated his status.

Reddening but smiling, Mr. Edwards said, "I didn't see them that much. Steve Conrad has a temper, but he only threatened with words."

Ms. Hancock's beaky nose quivered. "What kind of threats?"

"The standard. If staff doesn't do this or that, he'll have our jobs. Nothing unusual."

The group pelted him with questions until Mr. Edwards said he would be late for supper.

Devon left for home at the same time Mr. Edwards did, but Bruce, Ms. Hancock, and other patrons gossiped several minutes longer before going their own ways.

At 7 p.m., the lobby was peaceful with most of the patrons in the basement meeting room for the children's program. A lid of pewter hid the evening sun, bathing the courthouse and the street in soft grays.

Houston sauntered in. "How're you doing?"

He probably meant if I was a nervous wreck from this morning's mess. "Not bad. I don't feel jittery or anything. It all happened so fast, I didn't have time to feel scared for long. Have you learned anything from those two guys?"

He rested an elbow on the desk. "The doctors say Joseph has a concussion, but I still think he's milking his injury, so he doesn't have to talk to us. He says everything's so foggy that he can't even remember what case brought him to Ohio. Falk's talking but doesn't know much. I don't think he's acting. The only thing he told us of any significance was that he and Joseph were looking for Troy Malinowksi, not Matt."

"Troy will try to talk around that somehow."

He slid me a grin. "Be fun to watch him try. The search of Joseph and Falk's hotel room in Zanesville didn't produce anything. We don't know if someone hired Joseph to look for Troy or he's the one who wants your uncle's hide."

I frowned. "Too bad you didn't get any more information. Thanks for the update."

He spun a pencil on the counter. "You probably don't feel like it tonight, but later in the week, you could come over to the house, and we could work on some projects and surprise Chris."

A thrill spiraled from my heart. This was the first time Houston had asked me to do something other than lunch in months. Then memories from the beach party surfaced—him flirting with Liz, with Hayley, with every woman present. And what would I tell Chris? We were just two friends helping him out? Would he believe that?

The thrill died as panic gripped me. I wouldn't want Chris to think ... but what would Houston think?

"Rae? You drift off somewhere?"

I gave myself a shake. "Sorry. But I can't work on Chris's house until my new room is finished. I've got to give Gram her room back."

"Nice of you to be concerned for her." He still lounged against the desk, but his sea green eyes narrowed.

Should I invite him to help work on my room? But if Dad thought it would look bad for Chris to come over, the same would apply to Houston. Would Chris think there was something between us? Did I want something between me and Houston? Not when flirting seemed to be as instinctive as breathing to him.

A girl who was in the marching band with Amber dropped her

novels on the end of the desk.

I hit keys to bring up the check-out screen. "Maybe when Chris gets back, we can get together to jam."

A spasm crossed Houston's face. "I don't have the drum set any more. My friend wanted it back."

"Oh." Or maybe he was just saying that because I'd ticked him off. Or I'd just stomped all over a sore spot.

"See you around." He ambled out.

His words were harmless, but his tone indicated that he couldn't have cared less if he ever did.

As I tore off the due date slip for the girl, my phone pinged. I opened it to a photo of Mount Rushmore. Another thrill zinged me, and my fingers stumbled over themselves to respond.

Chapter Thirty-One

When I got home at 8:30, my brothers ran out the front door, Gram bringing up the rear.

"I thought we were tackling the floor tonight, Gram." I removed my denim shirt from over my sleeveless red tank top.

"We did. The boys and I got quite a bit accomplished. So we're taking a break for firefly hunting."

"C'mon, Gram," Micah yelled before he plunged between the pawpaws looming above our four hives.

A tide of weariness smacked into me, and I pulled my hand down the side of my face. "I wanted to ask you something. I asked Dad, and I wanted your opinion too."

Gram's smile turned expectant, and I rolled the hem of my shirt. "Do you think I was stupid to help Troy? It's been on my mind all day. I keep going over the verses I've found on mercy, and none of them say anything about evaluating the risks of helping someone. But I put the whole family in danger."

"Troy put the family in danger. Not you. If you could do it over again, would you help him?" Her question was soft, gliding to me in the darkening dusk.

"Well, I'd call the cops instead of driving him."

"What if you could see he was really hurt? Like his head was split open. And you couldn't call anyone for help. Would you help him, knowing what you know now?"

My brother's voices wafted to us like the fireflies that hovered about the peonies.

I bit my lip, then said, "I think I'd have to. I—I can't see myself leaving somebody in trouble." I kicked at a pebble on the sidewalk by the flowerbeds. "No matter what kind of jerk he is."

"Why? Why do you feel you have to?"

I touched my locket. "Because God expects it."

"Why does He expect it?"

Shoot, Gram's questions were harder than anything I'd had to figure out in calculus. There had to be an answer in one of those verses I looked up.

You do not stay angry forever but delight to show mercy.
But in your great mercy you did not put an end to them or abandon them.

Let us then approach God's throne of grace with confidence, so that we may receive mercy and find grace to help us in our time of need.

"Because ... that's what He does?"

"More than that. It's who He is. As you get to know Him better and want to obey Him, it will be who you are too."

"I don't think Dad will like that answer."

"My sweet boy," Gram said with a sigh, "needs to trust his worries to God. He tries, but he has a trust issue with God because he lost Reuel and Em."

"I can understand that. I still don't know why God didn't heal Mom, since she was all I had. But He did let me find you all."

Gram reached up and held my face in her hands. "You're like a counterbalance to our losses. No one in the family, least of all Mal, ever expected such a gift." Her smile took an amused twist. "I don't know why. God's always surprising me with—I'd guess you'd call them plot twists. Jeanine calls Him the Original Author, and He's got His plot twists worked out perfectly."

Aaron called, his orange hair vivid against the dim pawpaws. "Are you guys coming?"

I helped Aaron and Rusty helped Micah track the fireflies in the deep shadows thrown by the broad leaves of the giant bushes.

I was wiping a third firefly into Aaron's jar when Dad tromped down the hillside to where Gram sat in the cool grass. The hills ringing the farm to the north and west still clung to peach light while behind the house the sky was turning from cerulean to slate.

As Dad lowered himself with a grunt to the ground, Gram said, "You're back earlier than I thought."

"Well, when you feel like slapping yourself to keep awake on the road, it's time to go home."

"Nothing new about Ashley?" I screwed the lid on the jar. "Houston stopped by the library and told me he hasn't learned anything new about those two guys."

"Yeah." Dad pulled his uniform shirt free from his pants. "We're not exactly cracking either case. Now that we've arrested Joseph and Falk, hopefully, Troy will move on."

Gram said, "I've been praying he'll leave. You said he'd only come here for one of two reasons: he was hiding out or running a con."

Aaron raced up the hill to Dad. "I've been thinking."

"Oh, goody." Dad pressed the heel of his hand against his right eye.

"Since Horace was so good at taking out the guy in the barn, do you think you could use llamas in law enforcement?" Aaron's eyes glowed as they always did when a new idea excited him.

Dad slid a hand over his mouth to hide a smile. "You mean use them instead of dogs?"

"They're too big." Micah dropped into Dad's lap with his jar. "They'd never fit in the back of the patrol SUVs. Maybe you could use alpacas."

"Alpacas are scared of everything," said Aaron. "I thought llamas could be used like horses for crowd control." He crouched beside Dad, rocking on his heels. "If you had a line of llamas—like twenty of them—and a mob wouldn't disperse, you could have the llamas charge them."

"And make headlines around the world. The real drawback with your idea, Aaron, is that you can ride a horse and use them for other things besides crowd control, like search and rescue. A llama just isn't as useful."

Rusty hiked up to us. "I wish I could've seen Horace take out that guy in the barn."

Dad peered into Micah's jar. "He probably looked about the same as I did when Horace flattened me."

After the boys filled the jars with grass and leaves for the fireflies to eat overnight, we climbed the hill to the house for a snack. Dad trudged last, so I hung back with him.

"There's something I don't understand about Walter and Troy," I said. "Walter knows what Troy is like, doesn't want China and Egypt alone with him, but he lets him stay at his house. Why?"

"A couple of reasons I can think of." Dad unfastened his belt and hung it over his shoulder. "But they're only guesses, since Walter will never admit to more than Malinowskis should back each other against the world." We stopped outside the front door, warm light tossing rectangles of illumination on the plank floor of the porch. "First, I think Walter feels guilty. His third wife took off with Troy and Venice when they were four and two, and he had no idea where they were for four years. Second, since his mother threw him out when he was twelve, he—"

"What?" I gasped, putting a squeak on the end.

"You haven't heard this before? Jeanine and Hank are falling down on their job of telling family stories. Yeah, Walter's mother hated all her children, but she singled him out because he was the only boy."

My eyes seemed to swell to apple size. "But—but what about his father?"

"Walter Sr. drifted in and out of the family. He finally never came back."

"What did Walter do when his mother threw him out?"

"Moved in with his uncles, his father's brothers."

"Was living with his uncles any better for him?" Although I was pretty sure I knew the answer.

"If going from abuse to neglect is better, then yes." Dad sighed. "I've told Walter there's a difference between kicking out a kid and kicking out an adult, but that just makes him mad. I know he understands that, but he just can't bring himself to do it."

On your own at twelve. Coral's age. It'd been hard enough at eighteen.

I bit my lip.

"Yeah, it's awful," said Dad.

"It explains a lot about Walter."

We went into the house.

From under the piano, Micah launched himself at Dad's right leg and grabbed it.

Dad let out a yelp of surprise that Micah still hadn't figured out was fake.

"Gotcha again." He tightened his hold on Dad's leg.

"You sure did." Dad rubbed him on the head.

I opened the fridge and moved plastic containers and bags aside. "Gram, don't we have some cantaloupe? I want to give Horace a treat. I still feel bad about using him to take out the fat guy, but I didn't know what else to do."

"We do have responsibility to take care of the animals God's made." Dad clumped into the kitchen with Micah still attached. "But you're more important than any animal."

Dunking a snickerdoodle in a glass of milk at the kitchen counter, Aaron said, "Horace probably doesn't think so."

Chapter Thirty-Two

"Oh-oh, I can't believe it." Leandra stared at her phone just after opening the library the next morning.

"What?" I placed the last item on the hold shelf behind our desk from the inter-library loan delivery.

"My mother-in-law says Chief Simcox is searching Jason Carlisle's house." Her normal bubbly voice grew more effervescent.

"How does she know? Does she live in Jason's neighborhood?"

Leandra thumbed her keyboard. "No. I'll ask."

While she texted her mother-in-law, a symphony of pings chirped from Leandra's phone. I must not have had friends who gossiped because my phone didn't make a peep.

"Dottie says her sister called her after her sister-in-law texted her after her friend Debbie Schuster, who lives next door to Jason, texted her." Leandra's plump face shone with her ever-present smile.

"Debbie Schuster?" My fingers hung suspended over a keyboard. "Is she related to Senator Schuster?"

"Yes. She's his mother. The Schusters have lived next door to the Carlisles for years." Her smile tilted. "I wonder why the Chief is searching Jason's house."

"Something must have happened." I finished my email to the assistant director and then texted Carrie.

Everything all right?
You're not serious. Are you working?
Yes
Coming with kids.

Had Simcox told Dad about his search? His lack of cooperation with the sheriff's department was no secret. Carrie must have told Dad, but to be safe ... I texted Dad the information.

Fifteen minutes later, he hadn't responded, but Carrie tumbled into the lobby, her oversized peach blouse hanging crooked off her powerful shoulders as Sylvie clung to her, a bulging canvas bag of books banging into her shin. Richard ran past her, the straps of his backpack hanging from his elbows as Alli entered last, walking with measured steps, as if she had a book balanced on her head.

"There are cops at our house." Lips pursed, Alli studied Carrie, as if she was determining whether the babysitter was at fault.

Richard placed his fingers on the edge of the desk and rose on tiptoes. "A policeman said they're looking for our mom."

My gaze darted to Carrie, who nodded, her jawline tightening as she disentangled Sylvie's chubby fingers from her hair.

Richard went on, "Alli told them she doesn't live with us, and Carrie told them ..." He turned around. "What did you tell the policeman, Carrie?"

"'Shut your stupid mouth.'"

For some reason, that made Sylvie giggle.

I stared at Carrie. "You said that to Simcox?"

"No, to the officer with the big mouth who was with him. Simcox looked offended, but I don't know why. That has to be the nicest insult he's ever heard. Honestly, he should teach his officers some discretion. Come on, kids." Her bright tone contrasted with her frazzled expression. "Let's see if any new crafts are in the children's room."

Richard dashed under the balcony, while Alli put some distance between herself and Carrie as she followed him.

Every person who came in the door for the next half hour had to say something about Simcox searching Jason's house.

"I heard Jason gave the Chief permission, so he must not be worried about him finding anything."

"No, the Chief has a warrant."

"Carrie Malinowski wouldn't let them inside."

"Carrie Malinowski offered to help them search."

"Rick's at the house with Jason."

"No, he isn't."

The swirling opinions swirled my brain. Was Dad helping Simcox search the house? He could, since he had jurisdiction over the whole county, while Simcox could only operate within Wellesville. The only good thing about the gossip was that everyone seemed to have forgotten about the incident in the barn yesterday, giving me a break.

Mrs. Kenzora was sharing her theories about the search with an elderly woman by the racks of paperbacks under the balcony when Brad Schuster walked in from Main Street.

Practically pouncing on him, Mrs. Kenzora said, "What's the latest about Chief Simcox searching Jason's house?"

"I—uh—uh ..." The pressed dress shirt and khaki pants were the only signs of the smooth politician I'd seen at the picnic and the mall.

"Aren't you staying with your parents?" The elderly woman pressed close. "I thought your dad said you were helping him with Debbie."

"Yeah—uh—yes." His spine lengthening along with a smile, Brad drew himself up into a straight but relaxed posture. "When I left the house, the two police cars were still parked in front of Jason's house." The polished words rolled out with ease. He stepped up to the desk. "My mom just got a text that a book she ordered has come in."

While Leandra turned to the hold shelf, Carrie texted me, asking if I could come back to the children's room. Leandra said she could wait on anyone else who needed help.

I hurried to the children's room. Alli and Richard were gluing squares of tissue paper into a collage while Carrie peeled sticky paper from Sylvie's fingers.

Sylvie looked at the bits of red residue on her thumb and stuck it in her mouth.

Carrie pulled it out. "It's not food."

Sylvie's face scrunched up as Carrie used a wipe to clean her fingers. Then she tied a strap of Sylvie's backpack to her chair and led me to the wall of windows at the back of the room. "The kids are getting bored, and Simcox isn't done. I just talked to Jason. I guess I should take them to the farm, but I didn't want to because they've seen so much of the boys that they're fighting a lot. Are there many people in the lobby?"

"A lot more than normal for a Thursday morning," I said. "And they're all talking about the search."

"No surprise there." Carrie massaged her chin. "I don't want the kids to run a gauntlet to get to the front door. Could you help us sneak out the basement door to the parking lot? I parked there again."

"For sure."

Untying Sylvie, Carrie told Alli and Richard to bring their collages but leave the books they wanted, and I would check them out and bring them to their house later.

"Why?" Alli remained in her chair, applying a blue piece of tissue paper to her artwork. "We've never done that before."

"Special circumstances." Carrie hoisted Sylvie onto her hip.

Alli slid her a suspicious look. "What special circumstances?"

"Circumstances so special that you'll have to ask your dad." Carrie pulled her hair away from Sylvie before the toddler could get a solid hold. "We're going down the secret stairs like we did before to get to the Rover."

Richard grinned and pushed open the door to the stairwell.

"They're not secret," Alli said. "Everybody in the library knows they're there."

"We can pretend," said Carrie.

"Why?"

"Because," Carrie said through a frozen smile, "it's fun."

After I let Carrie and the kids out the basement door, I returned to the lobby with the canvas bag filled with books.

At noon, I texted Jason to see if I could bring the books over. By the time I finished eating my lunch in the employees' kitchen, Jason still hadn't responded. I checked the time. If I walked fast, I could get to Jason's house and back before my lunch break was over. And I wanted to get out and exercise, giving me time to think. The Carlisles' porch was deep. If I set the bag against the wall, the books would be protected from any sudden shower.

I retrieved the bag from behind the checkout desk and went outside to Main Street. Despite the dazzling sunshine, the day didn't feel cheerful. Not a breath of a breeze disturbed the humidity that slunk through the streets as I turned east.

The houses became nicer and bigger as I walked toward Jason's neighborhood. Most were Victorian and craftsman style houses renovated by people who had the extra money to spend on that kind of thing.

One police car pulled away from the curb in front of Jason's tan and cream, three-story house as I turned onto the street. An elderly couple sat in wicker chairs on the front porch of the house to the right of Jason's. A walker waited beside the woman, so they must have been Brad and Bruce's parents. Every other second, one or both of them glanced at Jason's house.

Chief Simcox and Jason walked onto the wide porch. The Chief was built out of sharp, square angles—chestnut flat top, strong jaw, severely cut shoulders.

He trotted down the steps.

My steps stuttered. But I couldn't exactly dive into the Schusters' flowerbed to avoid the Chief.

Simcox rounded his cruiser, swung open his door, and then stared at me. "Glad to see you're all right, Miss Riley."

"Thank you, sir." Based on our past brief history, I reckoned his relief was a mere formality. Like my thanks.

"I just saw your text, Rae," Jason said from the porch. "You can bring the books inside." He spoke a shade too loud. Maybe for the neighbors' benefit?

Hiking the bag higher on my shoulder, I rushed up the sidewalk lined with orange and yellow daylilies to the porch.

Jason appeared to have aged since Sunday. His button-down shirt was wrinkled, his brown eyes were bloodshot, and the grooves across his forehead and along the corners of his mouth looked permanent.

He held open the thick, carved wooden door.

Passing into the foyer, my eyes blinked to adjust from the bright noon street to the glossy, coffee-dark wood interior.

"Eric found nothing incriminating." Jason closed the door behind me. "You can tell that to whoever you want to at the library. That's why I let them search without a warrant. Nathan said I should insist—Nathan Hall's my lawyer—he said I should insist on a warrant, but I had nothing to hide. I want people to know that." He dropped onto a step of the impressive staircase. "Has Mal discussed Ashley's disappearance with you?" His voice became urgent. "I know what you two must be thinking. Bella harassed me, and Rick tried to eliminate her. Now Ashley's missing."

"We've talked about it." I set the bag beside a dignified grandfather clock. "But, well—it's hard for me to believe he'd try to commit murder again after he was willing to confess to Dad about what he did to my mom."

Propping his elbow on his knee, Jason held his forehead. "I keep telling myself that, but until Christmas Eve, I never thought my brother was capable of murder." His voice rasped, as if he was 100 instead of thirty-eight.

At the children's home early Christmas morning, Jason had said that by allowing the statute of limitation to run out on the attempted murder and arson Rick had committed, I'd given his brother back to him. But not the same brother. I hadn't realized that before. Nothing could be the same between Rick and Jason.

"You're perceptive, Rae. Does Mal consider Rick his number one suspect?"

I selected my response. "He's not sure any crime has been committed. He thought the most likely explanation was that your ex-wife left the lodge for some reason and had an accident."

But something new must have happened this morning for Simcox to search the house.

Jason said, "She was meeting someone Monday morning. I know she was. We talked around 2:30 a.m., and she said she couldn't keep talking to me. She had to go, but she'd call back in an hour. But who could she have been meeting? And if that person harmed her, why?"

"That's what Dad's trying to find out."

The ornate hands of the grandfather clock neared the top of the hour.

"I've got to get back to work," I said.

Jason focused on the plush, circular rug in the center of the foyer. Then he shook himself. "Oh, of course." He heaved himself off the steps. "Thank you for your honesty." A laugh scratched his throat. "I keep ending up in your family's debt. I don't know what Rick and I would have done this past week if Carrie hadn't agreed to take the job. She's wonderful with the kids." He offset his jaw. "She's a very honest pers—no, not honest. I mean, I'm sure she's honest, but she's a very natural person. That's the word. She doesn't put on an act to impress or manipulate people. I'd already left for work when Eric called to ask if he could search the house. When I came home, Eric told me that while he and one of his officers were waiting for me to begin the search, his officer told my kids that Ashley was missing. Carrie told him off. Eric was seriously ticked, but she didn't care." A faint smile surfaced.

Did that quality make Carrie attractive to him? Or maybe he just noticed a tremendous difference between Carrie and his ex-wife.

Jason let me out the front door.

The Schusters were still stationed on their front porch. I gave them a brief, friendly glance, which Mr. Schuster returned while his wife stared at the Carlisle house.

Once out of the neighborhood, I hurried into a jog. Why had the Chief conducted the search? And did finding nothing make The Mystery of the Missing Ex-wife clearer or murkier?

Chapter Thirty-Three

After supper, I got the front yard mowed down to the pastures before the kids from the 4-H club, their parents, and a horde of younger siblings descended on us. Rusty and Aaron joined them as Gram trained the kids on how to show their alpacas at the county fair in September.

I monitored the younger siblings whose parents didn't seem all that concerned with what they got into.

The last family had left when Dad's SUV turned onto the drive from the dead end road, the late light of the evening highlighting its coat of dust.

As soon as Dad stepped out of the patrol vehicle, Aaron and Micah attacked, Aaron swinging punches, which Dad deflected, and Micah fastening onto his leg. Rusty opted for just slapping Dad on the arm and asking if there was anything new concerning Mrs. Carlisle.

Dad said nothing he could share and ran into the house with Aaron and Micah under each arm.

Carrie was sitting in the recliner with a magazine. I hadn't seen her arrive.

"What'd you want to see me about, Mal?" She set the magazine on the coffee table.

"Do you want some pie, Aunt Carrie?" Micah said as Dad released him.

"Maybe later,"she said.

"Let's go downstairs." Dad unbuttoned his uniform shirt. "Rae, please come with us."

What did he want me for?

Dad pushed the piano bench aside and stepped over a dump truck on his way to the basement door. "Ma, could you keep the boys up here?"

"Absolutely." Gram lifted a slice of apple pie onto a plate. "When do you want supper?"

"I'll fix something for myself after I'm done talking to Carrie and Rae."

"No, you won't. You'll make yourself a peanut butter sandwich or eat an apple, and that's it."

"I'm not a growing boy anymore, Ma."

"It depends on how you define growing." Carrie grinned at him.

Dad's gaze darted to her.

It sounded like the kind of crack Uncle Hank liked to aim at Dad. But

Dad had said he couldn't joke with Carrie anymore.

The left side of his mouth lifted in a hesitant smile, and then all three of us trooped downstairs.

At the bottom of the steps, Dad took off his uniform shirt and shoes. We gathered around the chunky wooden table used for sorting and folding clean clothes. The bare bulb above us gave off the severe glare of stadium lights.

"This has been weighing on my mind since Conrad reported Ashley missing." Dad leaned back against the washer, hooking his thumbs in his beltloops. "Then Simcox wanted to search Jason's house, and Carrie told me today how funny Rick and Jason are acting. "

"They're both strung up tighter than tennis racquets." Carrie stood with her feet planted, arms folded. "But that could mean a lot of things. They could be guilty of Ashley's disappearance. Or they're innocent, and they're afraid of being accused. I can't tell, but I thought you should know, Mal."

Interesting to learn, but why did Dad want me to hear it?

"I appreciate your observations. Because of that it's made me—well, I've had to reconsider ..." He frowned at the cracked concrete floor.

Carrie said, "I take it you're still reconsidering."

"Not exactly." He gave Carrie a searching scrutiny. "Are you still committed to the Carlisle job?"

She met his gaze with one equally strong. "One hundred percent. If Jason or Rick or both of them have done something to Ashley to protect the kids—I know that'd be their only motive—the kids need someone to look out for them."

Dad nodded as if he expected that answer. "Rae, tell Carrie everything that happened to your mom twenty years ago except for the name of the third man."

Carrie's arms seemed to turn to mush, dropping to her sides.

Swinging to Dad, I gaped.

"Go ahead, Rae. I want Carrie to understand the risks she's running working for Jason."

"What third man?" Carrie's voice went high. "What second man?"

"Okay." In a low voice, so it wouldn't carry through the heating vents, I unloaded on Carrie how I found out about Mom's blackmail, Rick's murderous attack and arson, how Mom never knew who attacked her and raised me on the run—everything except Terry O'Neil's name.

Carrie's jaw just didn't drop. It hung like it was broken with no hope of fixing it. After a few minutes, she felt for support and collapsed against the weathered hutch Gram stored her canning supplies in.

I rolled and unrolled the edge of a shirt left on the table. "Only Dad, Barb Hanson, and I know this. And maybe the priest at the Carlisles' church."

"Barb knows," Carrie whispered.

"Rick told her what he'd done before he went to the children's home for our meeting. He thought he was never going to see her again, so he explained why."

The scene at the home with the Carlisle brothers replayed itself. "Dad, I don't think Rick would pull the same crime again. He was going to turn himself in to you because he couldn't live with his guilt anymore. He was prepared to die for his crimes."

"'Die for his crimes'." Carrie's voice was hollow, but she didn't whisper. "He thought he could get the death penalty?"

"He thought it was a possibility. He planned the murder. He didn't know he hadn't succeeded."

Dad said, "I think Rick might try it, if he thought the cause was good enough, like sacrificing himself for the security of his brother's children." He leaned toward Carrie. "Now, do you understand why we reserved some information?"

Carrie's dark blue eyes sparked. "You don't have to use that exasperated tone." Dad's lips parted as she went on, "Have you told Ma all this?"

Dad took a moment to answer, watching his younger sister. "Everything except the names, which she's probably figured out. I only told her because I wanted her to understand why I believed Rae's story, why I was confident I could invite Rae into our family."

"Fine, fine. I get it. That's dead and buried." Carrie held out her hands. "But why didn't you tell me all this Monday when Ashley was reported missing? I feel like I've been operating blind on this case."

Dad's mouth fell open, his eyes popped, as if his whole face were falling apart. "I shared with you the one thing you've been harping you wanted, and now you're going to complain that—" His voice reached roof-raising decibels, and then he snapped his mouth closed and stormed out of the basement into the backyard, the screen cracking against the sill behind him.

Carrie took two steps, then stopped, her shoulder slumping. She glanced at me. "You probably won't believe this, but I don't like fighting with Mal. He's just beyond frustrating." She rubbed her chin. "I guess he feels the same way about me."

A change of subject was needed, and to keep curiosity from killing me, I said, "Do you know why Simcox asked to search Jason's house?"

She straightened her shoulders. "I've got an almost certain explanation but no proof. When did you arrive in Marlin County?"

Her question surprised me. "L—last June."

She whistled. "You've been sitting on dynamite and never breathed a word of it. I can tell you in complete confidence that no one around here has a clue about the connection between Rick and Jason and your mother. Hank picks up a lot of gossip, and he and Jeanine talk it over. The closest anybody's come to the whole truth is Jeanine. She suspected there were other men involved with your—your paternity case, and Mal saw no reason to air their names. Wow." She stared off, as if the shock was overwhelming her again.

"What about the search?" I hoped I didn't sound as frustrated as I felt.

Carrie shifted her head to me and then blinked, as if to recalibrate her focus. "This is pure guess work, but I think Simcox got an anonymous tip. That's why he asked Jason's permission to search the house. He couldn't get a search warrant on a tip alone. As soon as Jason got home, Simcox and his officer both went straight to the garage. It's the old-fashioned setup where the garage sits at the back of the yard and you access it from an alley. Then they moved to the house. I think someone told them they saw Jason hide something in or by the garage."

"Or the person planted something on Jason and called Simcox. But if they planted it, why didn't he find it?"

"You're both just speculating." Dad returned to the basement, a lot quieter, his face sagging.

Fire lit Carrie's fresh face. "Well, we have to because—" The flames fizzled, and she sucked in her cheeks. "Look. I really don't want to fight with you."

"That's a shock." Dad shoved his hands into the front pocket of his uniform pants. "I don't want to fight either."

"Good."

But neither sounded or looked good, just worn out, like they quit fighting out of exhaustion rather than a serious need for peace.

"For the sake of argument, we'll pretend Simcox got an anonymous tip," said Dad. "Somebody could have seen Jason hide or get rid of something. That person didn't want to catch flak for snitching on a Carlisle. So the person left a tip. For an unknown reason, Jason moved the item before Simcox asked to search the property. So he gave his permission because he knew he was safe. Or maybe the tipster saw Rick up to something, and he later removed the item."

"If someone is trying to frame Jason with an item belonging to Ashley," said Carrie, "or if he's getting rid of her belongings—either way, it means she's no longer alive."

Dad gave her a steady gaze. "That seems more likely with each passing day."

Micah's and Gram's muffled voices drifted through the floor as I clutched myself and the harsh light picked out the concern on their faces.

Chapter Thirty-Four

The next morning, crumpling the quilt under my chin, I lay in bed. Dawn turned from murky gray to murky gold.

Nightmares about the stalker had faded, but now the showdown in the barn enhanced them into full 4-D.

Pursing my lips to slow my breathing, I swung my legs out of bed.

Useless to try to go back to sleep with a panic attack raging through my body.

I pulled on khaki cargo shorts, an olive-green t-shirt, and my denim shirt—my BBC nature photographer outfit. Ever since I'd watched BBC nature documentaries with Mom, I'd wanted to take photos in the wildest places on earth, although the chances of that happening were right around zero.

After a breakfast of pickles and a scone, I pulled on my backpack and hiked to the Norris farm.

In the stable, Coral held a piece of straw for a gray-striped barn cat to bat.

"Feel like acting as a guide?" I said.

She shrugged. "Sure. Where do you want to go?"

"Any place you think has something interesting to shoot."

Coral scratched the cat's head. "Okay."

We walked west, the pillowy clouds behind us already blinding white against a blue sky faded from the humidity that had seeped in with the dawn.

As the terrain grew steeper, I said, "Are you taking me to the foxes? I have plenty of pictures of them."

"No, I wasn't going there. I'm tired of that rich chick thinking the woods are her private office for meeting people. I was taking you to this hill that's close to Walter's place."

Rich chick ... Coral had said Frank Joseph and Austin Falk were poor because of the car they drove. And she also said the rich chick looked older than a girl.

I stopped in a tiny clearing with sunny-headed butterweed brushing my bare legs. "Coral, why did you call the woman you saw by the old bridge a rich chick?"

Coral's eyebrows puckered. "I didn't see her by an old bridge."

Now my eyebrows mimicked hers. "On Memorial Day, when we had to get a ride from Walter, where did you see the rich chick?"

"On this old road. It's all broken up with weeds growing in it. I followed it one day when nobody was there. It goes back to an old oil pump. I didn't say I saw a bridge."

I sorted through our conversation that day. "You're right. I assumed we were near the bridge where the high school kids party because I couldn't think of any other reason a couple would be arguing in the middle of nowhere." My eyes narrowed. "Why did you call her a rich chick?"

"Because of her car." Coral lifted her baseball cap and swiped more hair underneath it.

My breath caught. "What did it look like?"

"A teeny tiny convertible. A really weird light green. It was so low to the ground, I don't know how she got it so far down the road."

I broke into a run. "What's the fastest way to get there?"

Coral said from behind me, "Why?"

"I'm pretty sure I know where Alli, Richard, and Sylvie's mom disappeared to."

I let Coral get ahead of me and followed her sure steps as fast as I could.

We passed the clearing with the fox den and climbed a short slope that ended in an oddly level area that was completely choked with understory plants like honeysuckle and pawpaw.

Coral took her time searching for the easiest route. My adrenaline pumping, I wanted to just charge through all the tangles of skinny branches. But Coral's approach would lead to less scratches and stabs.

We finally forced our way out to a hillside that fell abruptly from our feet. It was actually the top of a small ravine, the sides less snarled in bushes. Below us, an old gravel road, decorated with weeds striving for the few rays the old maples, oaks and tulip trees allowed, followed the bottom of the ravine. And parked on it was Mrs. Carlisle's mint green, two-seater convertible. Empty, except for something bright sitting on the passenger seat.

Turning sideways to the slope, Coral began to hike down. I assumed the same position, using the bushes as handholds, but still lost my footing twice on the steep slope.

Reaching the road, I landed beside Coral and dusted dirt from my shorts.

Coral stepped toward the car.

My hands froze above my back pockets. "You should wait at the top."

"Why? And why would the chick leave her car here?" She moved toward it again.

I grabbed her arm. "This is a crime scene."

Jerking free of me, Coral said, "It's a crime to park your car on an unused road?"

"This is Mrs. Carlisle's car, and she's missing."

Coral's brown eyes rounded, then darted left and right, as if making sure nothing was sneaking up on her. "Do you think somebody kidnapped her?"

That was slightly better than what I was thinking. "Wait at the top of the hill."

Without another word, Coral scrambled up through the dense bushes.

Stepping with the same care I'd use if I was barefoot and crossing a room carpeted in broken glass, I pushed myself toward the car. She might be there, up under that dash.

My skin came under an attack of stinging pinpricks.

Father, please don't let me find a body.

A pang of guilt stopped me. I was more worried about finding a corpse than Ashley actually being dead.

I'm sorry, Father. If she's alive, let me find her.

Leaves and berries decorated the two seats of the little car, and Ashley's lightweight teal jacket lay on the passenger seat. No one, except a child, could fit under the dash.

The pinpricks returned, stabbing harder, as the still air seemed to thicken around me.

Conrad had said all she'd taken with her was her jacket and her purse. She might have met someone here and gone off with him or her, leaving her jacket and taking her purse. Or ...

An animal rattled the high leaves of the sheltering trees.

... she was still here.

Shots of adrenaline fed my muscles, my brain screaming, "Run!"

Clenching my hands and toes, I fought to hold my ground. "Mrs. Carlisle?" It came out as a strangled whisper.

"Do you think she's hiding in the woods?" Coral's incredulous question made me jump like it had grabbed me.

I held up my hand, recruited more air, and called again. After five days, chances of her being alive were miniscule, but Mom had been attacked and left for dead.

Cardinals chirped, and a drab little bird landed on the back of one of the bucket seats.

Should I look for her in case she was injured and still alive? But even if she was, I'd still have to get help. I couldn't do anything for her.

I scurried up the slope, scraping my knees against roots and spice bushes.

"C'mon, Coral." I plowed into the dense understory on the flat ground. "We gotta get Dad."

Coral took the lead, and I ran with all my strength until a side stitch slowed me as we entered yet another line of woods.

Coral stopped as I walked to her with my hands on my head. I said, "Did you recognize the man Mrs. Carlisle was talking to on Memorial Day?"

"I know I've seen him before. I can't remember where."

"Try to remember." Gulping air, I burst into another run.

We raced up and down the wooded hills until, at the edge of the Norris property, I had to walk again. "Have you remembered?"

Coral stared at me. "You wanted me to think about it *now*?"

"Dad'll want to know."

We hiked along the border of the recently planted fields, climbing upward until we entered the woods that lined the pastures and stable for the Norrises' horses.

On the drive, Uncle Hank was bent under the raised hood of his dark green truck. Senator Schuster kept his neat jeans and striped button-down shirt several feet from the grimy vehicle. Hank looked like a hobo next to the politician, wearing tattered jeans and a stained t-shirt.

"I'd be glad to board a horse for your daughter." Hank twisted a tool. "Or I can give you the name of a good stable near Zanesville, if that'd be easier for you." He backed out from under the hood. "Hey, girls. Brad, I don't know if you know my daughter Coral and my niece Rae."

The senator gave us his sleek smile. "I've met Rae, but not Coral." He held out his smooth hand to her.

Coral shook it for a half-second. "Dad, we just found the car that belongs to Alli and Richard and—"

"We gotta call Dad first." I grabbed Coral's hand and started to pull her after me, but she yanked free and raced to the front door.

"What's wrong?" Although Aunt Jeanine was in the kitchen, she could see us burst through the front door. She put down her mug as we pounded into the tiny kitchen.

I grabbed the landline from the stand on the counter that separated the kitchen from the dinner table.

"We found—" Coral looked to me. "Can I tell Mom?"

"Yes." I punched in Dad's number.

Whipping off her cap, she said, "Rae and me found the car that belongs to Alli, Richard, and their baby sister's mom."

Dad's phone went to voicemail, so I dialed again.

"Ashley wasn't there?" Jeanine's enormous blue eyes stared like they'd be incapable of blinking for a while.

"Rae couldn't find her, but she didn't look very hard."

Voicemail again.

"Just her car with her jacket in it." I dialed again.

Uncle Hank moseyed into the kitchen. "What's going on?"

"Holy smoke, Jeanine, what's wrong?" Dad's deep voice was equal parts irritation and panic.

My words froze in my throat. Was Dad going to yell down the phone because I'd gotten mixed up in the case? Again?

"Jeanine? What do you want?" he said.

Swallowing, I braced myself. "Coral and I found Mrs. Carlisle's convertible."

"Rae? Where?"

"It's hard to explain. I can guide you to the place on foot, but I don't know what road it's near so you can drive to it. It's parked on an abandoned road." A chill mingled with sweat on my back. "Her jacket is still in the car ... so I think she's around there too. We came straight here to call you."

"No signs of a struggle?"

"I—I didn't look for that. I didn't notice anything like that. I called her name in case she was lying somewhere injured, but after five days, it isn't likely, is it?"

"Slim to none. I'll be right there."

"Hold on. Coral saw the guy Ashley met there on Memorial Day. Ashley and this guy are the couple I heard in the woods. Coral says he looked familiar, but she can't place him."

Long, heavy pause. "Does she know if he saw her?"

My lungs quit for a moment. "I hadn't thought of that." I lowered the phone. "Coral, do you know if the man saw you?"

She frowned. "I know how to sneak up on somebody."

I lifted the phone. "Coral says he didn't."

"Tell Hank and Jeannie to keep Coral at the house until I get there. Tell Coral to think about who she saw but not to force it. I'll be there in twenty minutes." He clicked off.

I blew out my cheeks. Dad had held it together. Big relief.

Coral was pulling at her lip, her sweaty copper bangs plastered to her forehead. "I think the guy the chick was talking to has come to the farm."

"A farmer?" said Jeanine.

"No." She stared at the kitchen counter, then lifted her head. "I think he came to watch you give somebody a riding lesson, Dad."

My heart solidified and sank.

In four strides, Uncle Hank had disappeared down the basement steps. "I got my list of riding clients on my desk."

"Let me try something." I removed my camera from my backpack, turned it on, and scrolled back to photos of the parade. I held out the camera to Coral, my lungs frozen again.

She peered at the small screen. "That's him. I knew I'd seen him here before."

She laid her finger on Rick Carlisle sitting beside Jason with Sylvie in his lap.

Chapter Thirty-Five

Somehow, I found a chair by the dinner table and dropped into it.

Rick had played me. Like Troy and probably Ashley. All those tears and guilt-ridden explanations on Christmas morning hadn't meant a thing.

Jeanine called for Hank to come back from the basement and then said, "Coral, what did Rick say to Ashley?"

"I didn't watch them very long." She pulled on her lip again. "I got to the top of the hill, and they were down on the road. He said something about he wasn't stupid, and something about giving something to her in installments. She acted like he was driving her crazy and said to leave her alone, and then Rae called me, so I left."

"Mrs. Carlisle said a couple times to leave her alone." My voice was dull. "I only heard her cry out twice. I never heard what Rick said. I could just tell one voice was higher, and one was lower."

Jeanine's small face contracted. "Coral, are you sure Rick was speaking to Ashley Carlisle?"

"It's her car. Who else could it be?"

"We shouldn't assume. Come on, Coral." Jeanine led her into the hall to the bedrooms.

Hank stared after them, bending the brim of his cowboy hat. Then he said, "You off today?"

Work. It had completely fled from my mind.

I called Barb, telling her I'd be coming in late because I discovered evidence in the Ashley Carlisle case.

Barb whispered, "Have you found her?"

"No. I can't tell you anything more than that. Dad wouldn't want me to, but I'll tell you what I can, when I can."

Even though she'd broken up with Rick, his secret meeting with Ashley would hurt like a gut wound.

"I'd very much appreciate it, Rae."

I clicked off and then called Gram to explain why I hadn't come back to the house to change for work. Then I sank back into the chair and held my head in my hands.

"Rick met Ashley," Jeanine said as Coral bounded by her and opened the refrigerator. "Coral identified her from a Facebook photo." She pulled out a chair and sat beside me. "It's a shock. I'm not sure I believe it myself."

"I know I don't." Hank turned on the water at the sink. "I've known Rick, off and on, since we was kids. I can't see him attacking a woman."

I squelched a laugh. I so wanted to let it go, long and bitter. Dad had said the same thing at the children's home on Christmas morning.

Rummaging in the fridge, Coral said, "Mom, are you thinking Alli's mom went back there to meet her uncle and he killed her? But why?"

Dad came in through the back door then with Chief Deputy Harris behind him.

Jeanine bolted to her feet. "Coral identified both the man and the woman—Ashley and Rick Carlisle."

Dad's hand froze, reaching for a notepad. Deputy Harris raised her eyebrows, but as a former Marine, it would probably take a rain of nuclear bombs to shock her.

Maintaining his professional calm, Dad picked up the landline and punched in a number. "Simcox? I've just had a break in the Carlisle case. One of your officers needs to bring in Rick Carlisle for questioning. I have a crime scene to investigate. So hold Carlisle until I can send a deputy to question him. Thanks." Setting the phone in its holder, he said, "Let's talk in your bedroom, Coral." He rubbed my shoulder as he passed me.

"Rae, are you all right?" Jeanine slipped into the chair again. "You seem ... beyond stunned."

What could I say? I stared at my bony hands, holding each other on the table.

"Ya know, it don't have to be Rick." Hank poured himself a cup of coffee. "I mean, he met her on Memorial Day and didn't do nothing to her."

Jeanine frowned. "She met someone else there? I can't believe someone else killed her and just happened to hide her car in the same place she'd had another meeting. There has to be a connection between Rick's meeting and her car left on the road."

Another meeting. Something bubbled in my numb mind, then subsided.

"Harris is going to stay here," Dad said as he returned to the kitchen with Deputy Harris and Coral. "When I figure out where in the world this road is, I'll send back Rae and Coral with the directions. Girls, get some water, and we'll get moving."

Hank pushed off the counter. "I'm coming."

"I don't need you." Dad put away his pad.

"I feel better sticking close to Coral."

Dad tapped his pencil on the counter. "Okay, but once we're there, stay out of my way."

Aunt Jeanine and I filled water bottles, and then the four of us left by the front door and turned right, walking past the stables and pastures and into the woods.

The trees seemed to hold the air, keeping it still, as the sun sent blinding threads of light between any leaves where it found a breach. Four dogs accompanied us, but as we hiked deeper into the woods, they melted away.

Hank said, "Maybe Ashley ain't dead. Maybe she went off with someone. You know, another boyfriend."

"She'd pack clothes if she did that." Dad stretched his leg over a hole in the slope.

Leaving Conrad for another boyfriend.

I lurched to a halt in the dead leaves on the forest floor. "Coral?"

"What?" Several yards ahead, she turned back to me.

"You—you said you d-didn't want to go—" I pressed my lips together, my nerves twitching from an idea that had hit me. "You didn't want to go over by the fox den this morning because the rich chick used the woods for meeting people. Did you mean she's met more than one person there?"

"Yeah." She began walking, but Dad held up a hand.

"Wait a minute. Was there another man with Rick Carlisle?"

"No."

The three of us waited for Coral to explain.

Coral stared back.

"Punkin." Hank bent toward her. "We need more details."

"I told you everything I know."

"Not about Rick Carlisle." Dad glanced about and sat on a fallen log. "We need to know about the second man. Had you seen him before?"

"No. I didn't get a good look at him. He had his back to me most of the time."

"If I showed you some photos, do you think you'd recognize him?"

Coral frowned up at the canopy. "I think so."

"What did he look like? What was he wearing?"

She said he was fat. She could tell that when he turned sideways and saw his profile. He looked old, like a dad. He might've had brown hair, but he was wearing a baseball hat.

Jotting notes, Dad said, "What day was this?"

"It was after lunch one day. Rusty and me were just messing around. He got an idea for his book and sat down to write it in his binder. I decided to see if the foxes were out and I heard—it was the day after Amber got into all that trouble for not listening to Rae." She grinned.

"Okay," said Dad. "That was a week ago. Tell me what you heard."

"Well ... I thought it was weird people being out here again. I mean, if you're going to meet somebody, you do it at an office or coffee shop or something. So I snuck down the slope to the ravine and hid in the honeysuckle to see what was going on. It's so thick they never saw me."

"And they said ... " Dad's pencil hovered over the pad.

"The rich chick was upset again. The fat guy wanted her to do something, and she said she couldn't."

"Do you remember their exact words?"

"Not really. I mean, I might if I think about it."

"Don't think about it. We'll go to the road, and you can hide in the honeysuckle like you did before. Rae and I will stand like Mrs. Carlisle and the other man. Maybe recreating the situation will help your memory."

"That's a good idea, Uncle Mal." Coral's tone implied that good ideas from Dad were as rare as straight roads in Marlin County.

Hank slapped Dad on the shoulder. "That's why he's sheriff. Overloaded with brains."

Dad rolled his eyes, and we were on the move again.

Striding over a fallen log, Hank said, "Punkin, how come you didn't tell us about the second guy back at the house?"

"Nobody asked me. Everybody kept asking me about the guy the rich chick met on Memorial Day."

Dad looked down at Coral as the terrain sloped upward. "Did you only see Mrs. Carlisle in the woods those two times?"

She nodded.

Coral and I led Dad and Uncle Hank across the flat ground choked with pawpaws, honeysuckle, and spice bushes to the top of the ravine.

I pointed. "Can you see it? The mint green?"

Both Dad and Hank bent over to peer through the tangle.

"I see it," said Dad. "Everyone stay here until I call you."

As Dad crashed down the nearly vertical cliff, Hank said, "Coral, show us where you hid to watch Ashley and this other guy."

Coral stepped around saplings, walking along the edge of the ravine. She stopped several times, then plunged down the slope and halted about twenty feet below us.

"I was right across from that rock." She indicated a sandstone boulder protruding out of the opposite face of the ravine. An old tree had spread its roots around the rock, clutching it like a huge hand with spindly fingers.

Dad yelled Mrs. Carlisle's name, and the understory thicket crunched as he pushed through it.

I paced the edge of the ravine above Coral.

Maybe Rick was innocent, maybe he hadn't mentioned his meeting with Ashley because he knew how that would look to Dad since Dad knew his secret crimes.

Dad called for me, and I worked my way down the slope.

Wearing latex gloves, Dad picked up the teal jacket from the seat of the convertible.

"Coral's in position, where she was hiding when Mrs. Carlisle met the other man." I glanced about. "I guess you didn't find her."

"No, but I didn't look very far from the car." He scanned the hillside. "Coral, Rae will be Mrs. Carlisle, and I'll be the man. Tell us where to stand." He said to me, "I can't find her."

"You gotta move up the road more." Coral's order drifted down to us.

Dad and I walked up the road, broken up with butter weed and fledgling shrubs and trees, closer to whatever road it intersected.

"That's about right," said Coral, and we stopped.

Her copper hair peeked through the rich green leaves of the bushes.

Dad said, "Did Mrs. Carlisle drive her convertible to the second meeting?"

"Yes."

"What did the man drive?"

"I don't know. I couldn't see it."

"Then maybe he walked."

"That's what I thought at first," said Coral. "When they heard Rusty calling for me, and they decided to leave, the guy left first. He parked way up the road where I couldn't see his car. I heard an engine start and a car drive away. Then the rich chick drove away."

Dad had gone stone still, but his voice sounded normal. "We'll go over that in a minute. It's a week ago and you can see the man and the woman. What were they saying? Try to remember the exact words."

"Okay, Uncle Mal. You should turn your back to me. That's why I couldn't see the guy's face until he turned to listen to Rusty."

Dad obeyed, and I stood on his left.

"The chick said she couldn't do something."

"Exact words help, Coral," said Dad.

"I'm trying." Her voice soured. "All I know is the guy wanted the chick to—to—to meet somebody." Her tone brightened. "That was it. He wanted her to meet someone here later, and she kept saying how she couldn't, and the guy kept saying she had to. He said something like 'slip him something or get him drunk'." Pause. "How can you get somebody drunk? I mean, if the guy won't drink the booze, you can't—"

"Don't worry about it, Coral. Did either of them use any names?"

"I don't think so."

"What happened when Rusty called you?"

"Well, first, Rusty yodeled for me, and they both froze like the teacher caught them vaping in the bathroom. I couldn't yodel back because they'd know I was watching them. The guy said something like 'How can there be people out here?' Then Rusty started calling me, and the guy turned his head, and I saw the side of his face. And the chick said, 'I have to go', and the guy said ..."

My whole body winding tight, I waited, but Dad showed no signs of tension.

"... he said, '3 a.m. Monday morning.'" Coral announced it like she would the winner of a race. "The chick said she'd try to come to the meeting, and he said 'Great', or 'Good', or something, and he walked up the road and drove away and then she did."

Dad said, "You're sure about the time and day of the next meeting?"

"Yeah."

"Did Rusty come close enough to see them?"

"Naw. I left after the chick left and found Rusty by the creek, a little ways north of here."

Dad looked to the ground, his boyish face lined. "Come on, Rae." He headed for the wall of the ravine. "Coral, you can move. We're coming up."

Once we were at the top, Dad gave Coral a one-armed hug. "Thanks for all the intel. Are you sure neither the man or the woman spotted you?"

"Yeah, they never looked my way. They only looked at each other until Rusty started yelling for me."

Dad said, "Are you sure he called your name?"

Hank and I stiffened.

"Yeah, after I didn't answer his yodel."

"But that don't mean they heard her name." Hank pulled Coral next to him. "Just hearing voices would've spooked them."

"True, but we can't take any chances." Dad got down on his haunches. "Coral, you have to stay with your dad or mom or some other adult until I can figure out who this second man is. No wandering in the woods. You stay at your house or your grandpa's and always with an adult."

Coral's neck strained forward as she listened to Dad's orders. "Why?"

"Because if this man hurt Mrs. Carlisle and heard your name, he might think you can ID him. He might try to hurt you too, but if you're always with an adult, he won't try." Standing, Dad looked to Hank. "Since Carrie's already planning to go to church with the Carlisles, she might as well stay at your place for the weekend. I'll come over when I can, and I'll assign a deputy to patrol near the farm in case of trouble."

Hank tightened his arm around Coral's shoulders. "If you really think it's necessary. It's been a whole week since Coral watched them. If the guy was worried, don't you think he'd've tried something by now? It wouldn't take him long to find the only Coral in the county."

Coral wrapped her arms around Hank's waist. "Would he try to kill me?"

"No." Dad put the full force of his cop voice behind it. "That will not happen. Hank, you're probably right. Ashley and the guy just heard voices without hearing the name because no one has threatened Coral yet. But we'll be cautious until Coral can identify the man." He gave Coral a reassuring smile. "With all the adults in the family keeping you company, and Carrie and me on the job, you'll be perfectly safe."

Coral clutched her dad tighter. "How can I identify this guy? I don't know his name."

"He's somebody Mrs. Carlisle knows, or he was sent by someone she knows. Jeanine can start trawling through Mrs. Carlisle's social media pages and see who she can find. You all wait here. I'll see where this road comes out. Then you three can head back and tell Harris where to meet me." Dad plunged down the slope again.

The three of us didn't look at each other. The air hung over us, stagnant and moist. A red wing blackbird trilled, and a mourning dove cooed, but from the way Uncle Hank's huge brown eyes swept over the woods, I knew he felt any of those sounds could hide a danger to his daughter.

Coral said in a subdued voice, "Do I have to stay inside? All the time?" She watched her dad, panic freezing her freckled face.

That might be worse for Coral than getting attacked. Like the need I had to take photos, Coral had one for going outside. During the winter, unless it was well below zero, she always went out, even if it was just to walk to her grandfather's farm.

"Mal didn't say that." Hank rubbed his daughter on her cap. "You just have to stay with an adult." He glanced about. "I'm surprised Ashley knew about this place. You could tell she hated living here."

"Maybe Rick picked it," I said. "Then when the second guy wanted a meeting, she told him to come here."

We fell silent again.

The long leaves of a pawpaw bush rattled.

I jumped, and Uncle Hank shoved Coral behind him.

A chattering squirrel dashed out of the bush, across the leaf litter, and up an oak tree.

Coral whipped off her hat. "This isn't fair. Why'd they have to meet here? I wasn't doing anything wrong."

"You shouldn't've snuck up on them," said Hank. "I know you were just curious, but you didn't need to eavesdrop."

Coral opened her mouth, then snapped it shut, kicking at the dead leaves on the ground.

Dad's footsteps approached, and he climbed up to us. "The abandoned road comes out on Molly's Bend. Tell Harris. You all can head home."

Hank and Coral pushed past the curving branches of a honeysuckle, but I said, "Can I stay? I've got to know if you find her."

"What about work?"

"I already said I'd be late. Nothing special is going on that we need extra desk coverage. Please. I can't stand waiting to hear from you."

Dad gripped my shoulder. "You can drive my SUV over. I'll need two vehicles to block both ends of the road. Once the news gets around, there'll be people coming to gawk."

"Thanks." I ran to catch up to Hank and Coral.

Chapter Thirty-Six

Aunt Jeanine's creamy complexion went dead fish white as Uncle Hank told her about The Mystery of the Second Meeting.

Coral slouched in a recliner in the living room.

One hand on her belt, Deputy Harris said, "If Carrie's here with you all weekend, and Mal has the patrols stay around here when they aren't on a call, she won't be in any danger."

Jeanine kissed Coral on her forehead. "I'll start checking out Facebook pages right now."

"If you find anyone who might fit the suspect's description," said the deputy, "don't show it to your daughter. Tell Mal or me first. We have to do this properly. Also, since she didn't get a good look at him, she might pick the wrong man if you throw a lot of photos at her."

"I won't show Coral anything. I'll just do research."

"Good deal." Deputy Harris pointed a clear-coated nail at me. "You drive Mal's SUV where I tell you, and you stay by it."

She sounded beyond annoyed, her sculpted face almost betraying that emotion, which was the first time I'd ever seen her look anything but completely cool and professional. Maybe that mask had developed from her Marine background, or her twenty-five years of service as a cop, or being an African-American officer in a county that was at least 90 percent white.

I nodded. My hand itched to salute her.

The trip to Molly's Bend, wherever that was, took more than a half hour as the Chief Deputy and I wound our way onto smaller and smaller roads that cleaved deeper and deeper into the hills. We'd traveled about a mile on a gravel road that seemed to consist of mostly corkscrews when I spotted Dad.

He waved Deputy Harris further down the road. I pulled up beside him and rolled down the passenger window.

He leaned into it. "I found her."

My stomach dropped like I'd crested the top of the highest roller coaster.

Dad reached into the window to squeeze my shoulder. "I didn't have time to get down to the body. I knew I had to stand out here so you could find me. She's at the bottom of a cliff, maybe a quarter-mile from her car."

I sucked in a breath. "Somebody pushed her? Or killed her and then threw her off the cliff?"

"Could be either of those scenarios." He withdrew his hand and scratched his eyebrow. "What puzzles me is why she's not buried. That's what I've been looking for, freshly turned earth. I figured I'd have to call in a cadaver dog. If you lure somebody to a remote spot like this, you'd think the murderer would take advantage of the woods and hide the body."

"He ran out of time?"

"He's had five days. That's a guess. I'll have to wait on the autopsy, but I think she died early Monday morning when she had her meeting." He stepped back. "Park up the road to where you think other drivers have enough time to see that the road is blocked. Not that anyone uses this road. Only one car has passed since I've been waiting for you. But as soon as word gets out, we'll have sightseers. It's probably out now. The driver of that car was Kelly from the lodge, and she tried to grill me about what I was doing out here."

"It was probably all over the county before that." I explained that Senator Schuster was asking Hank about boarding a horse when Coral and I came back to the farm. "Coral said we found Mrs. Carlisle's car before I cut her off."

"I'd hope Brad would have more discretion. Bring the keys to where the convertible is and you can walk home from there."

Dad strode back to the narrow break in the woods the abandoned road carved out. I would have driven right by him if he hadn't stood out on Molly's Bend.

At the top of a hairpin turn, I parked Dad's SUV, removed the keys, and got out.

Another SUV drove toward me. Jason's Land Rover. It stopped beside my open door, and a midnight blue, four-door Volkswagen parked behind it.

Senator Schuster or Kelly or both hadn't wasted any time spreading their intel.

Jason climbed out of the Rover as a woman, a little older than me, leaped out of the car, her black satchel banging her hip.

Shoving his bangs off his forehead, Jason said, "What are you doing here, Rae? Did you find Ashley's car? Have you found Ashley? Do you know why a town cop took Rick to Eric's office?"

"I—I don't know how much Dad wants me to say. You should talk to him."

"I'll find out, Jason." Pulling a tablet from her satchel, the young woman passed the patrol vehicle and headed down the road.

I called, "I don't think Dad wants—"

"She's a reporter," said Jason. "The newspaper office got a tip."

The reporter had disappeared around the bend in the road when another vehicle appeared. Even from a football field way, I could tell it was a Hummer.

Clutching his hair with both hands, Jason said, "Did Mal call Steve?"

"Not that I know of." My muscles snapped to high alert.

Wearing a Hawaiian shirt with palm fronds that outlined his pecs and biceps, Steve Conrad slammed out of the Hummer. "So it's true. The cops have found something."

Jason's brown eyes narrowed to slits. "How did you know?"

Conrad flung out his arm. "You've lived here your whole life and think anything's a secret? That obese clerk who's spreading lies about Ashley and me told me. The whole lodge should know by now." He stabbed a finger at Jason. "Did that brain dead sheriff call you instead of me?"

"A friend called me, and then a reporter from the paper did."

"Did they find Ashley?"

"I don't know." Jason groaned the sentence.

"Then I'll find out." Conrad marched around the Rover and Dad's SUV.

"Sir." I trailed after him. "That's not a good idea."

He spun to me. "So you're a cop now?"

"I just know my dad wouldn't want anybody but his officers down there."

Conrad said, "I know why he wouldn't want Jason down there since he's the prime suspect, but I'm Ashley's fiancé."

"Making you a suspect too." Jason planted both hands on the hood of the Rover, his head bent toward the ground, as if he might lose his breakfast at any minute.

A vein stood out on Conrad's forehead as he charged up to Jason. "I love Ashley. Why would I hurt her?"

Jason shoved off the hood and stared down the road.

Conrad glared at him, the vein still prominent.

I wasn't equipped to handle this situation. We needed a cop, but I couldn't leave. My presence was probably the only thing preventing the two men from losing it.

"Whatever they found — " Conrad strode past the vehicles again " — if they think it's Ashley's, I'll have to identify it."

Another patrol SUV swung into view.

"Mr. Conrad," I said, "why don't you talk to this officer first?"

He looked up the road and frowned, but remained where he was.

The relief of seeing Houston slide out from behind the wheel of the SUV was nearly enough to wipe away all the sweat the humidity and tension had raised.

Ambling toward us on his long, skinny legs, Houston said, "Did anybody from our agency call y'all? Because if they didn't, you have to stay here. Hey, Rae." He flashed me his good ol' boy grin.

"Hey, Houston. No, nobody asked for Jason or Mr. Conrad to come."

His handsome face white, Jason said, "Houston, could you call Mal and ask him what he's found?"

"I can call." Houston reached into his SUV. "Doesn't mean he'll tell you anything."

Should I leave? Somehow, it felt wrong when I knew what bomb Dad was about to drop on Jason. The situation felt so awkward, like going to an event at a stranger's house and not knowing their rules.

Jason was bent over the hood again. His agony seemed so out of place when he'd told me only a week ago that Ashley could die in whatever bed she'd made.

"Mal's coming." Houston hooked the receiver back on the radio. "And, Rae, he said he'd get his keys from you." Houston strolled between Jason and Conrad, probably readying himself to act as a barrier.

Conrad paced the width of the road, but Jason seemed paralyzed in a stoop as he focused straight ahead.

After what seemed like days, Dad's massive frame appeared around the turn with Deputy Harris half-trotting to keep up.

Jason and Conrad both surged past all the vehicles

"Better wait here," Houston called after them but followed like he didn't expect them to listen.

The men and Ms. Harris met in a patch of sunlight the overhanging trees allowed to touch the road.

"I am very, very sorry," Dad said. "We found a body. It will need to be identified by fingerprints or dental records. The body has deteriorated out here in the woods. But I'm sure it's Ashley."

Conrad stilled, blinking, as Jason spun away, releasing a moan.

Conrad snapped out, "What do you care?"

Holding his head, Jason turned side to side. "I have to tell my kids their mother is dead."

Conrad marched toward Jason. "So? You kept Ashley away from them for so long, her death won't mean anything to them. Unless you killed her. Then they'll lose both parents. Except for Sylvie."

Snarling, Jason launched himself at Conrad.

Houston threw his arms around Jason.

Dad and Deputy Harris planted themselves like walls between Jason and Conrad.

Conrad glared around Houston. "See? He can't control his murderous—"

"Shut up!"

Dad's roar dried up Conrad and froze Jason. Being louder than the average human had advantages for a cop.

"Mr. Conrad." Dad brought down the volume, but it was still loud enough to control everyone. "If you want to stay, you will accompany Deputy Harris to where you can wait closer to the crime scene. Jason, you stay here with Houston. Any more outbursts, and I will arrest whoever disturbs the peace. Understand?"

Glancing between the two men, Ms. Harris said, "I'm very sorry for your loss."

Conrad gave her the briefest nod and then opened his arms. "Whatever you say, sheriff. I didn't try to attack somebody."

Houston released Jason, who wheeled away.

Dad said, "Houston, BCI agents are on their way. They may come in on your end, or where Harris parked."

As Conrad and Deputy Harris walked down the road, I edged over to Jason. "I'm very, very sorry."

Jason stared into the woods. "Mal, why did an officer pick up Rick?"

"Because I need to talk to him." Dad stepped close enough for Jason to glance at him. "I'm so sorry, Jason. This won't be easy on your kids, even if you don't see the effect immediately."

Jason lowered his head, his whole body shaking.

Dad said, "Rae, come with me."

I stretched my legs to stay beside him as he led me down the road and out of sight of Houston and Jason.

He took his keys from me. "When you get to the library, you can tell people that you and Coral found Ashley's car, and I found a body that's waiting identification. That's all you need to say. Don't mention how you figured out where it was. No one can know that Coral witnessed those two meetings. If anyone gets persistent, tell them to come talk to me."

Very few people would take up that offer.

When we turned onto the abandoned road, Conrad said to Ms. Harris, "Why does she get to go in there?"

Dad said over his shoulder, "Mr. Conrad, don't ask for trouble."

At the convertible, I hugged Dad, climbed up the slope, and headed for the den and home.

The humidity was piling up like waves on a shore, pummeling me. I stuck to the shade as much as I could even when I reached a field.

Why had Jason acted so crushed? Had he really been hoping to reconcile with his wife? Had Conrad known? If he had, that still wouldn't give him a motive to kill Ashley when he could bribe her to stay with him. Ashley had a record of being extremely bribable. If he killed her, he probably killed any chance of getting Sylvie tested.

Besides, he wouldn't send some guy to set up a meeting in the middle of the woods in the middle of the night. It had to be one of her old boyfriends.

By the time I reached home, sweat had soaked all my clothes, and my brain felt about as fresh. My brothers were running into the woods, guns with foam darts in their hands.

"Hey, Rae." Micah waved to me, and I waved back.

In the kitchen, Gram was emptying the dishwasher. Her usual mellow expression was gone.

Lifting my hair off my neck, I said, "Jeanine told you about how Coral and I found Mrs. Carlisle's car?"

"Yes." She put a saucepan in a drawer. "This is awful."

I told Gram that Dad had found a body.

"We need to pray for Jason and the kids." She placed flatware in the sorter. "But if Ashley died from a fall from the cliff, it might be an accident."

"I don't see how. Someone set up a meeting with her at 3 a.m. Why would he do that if he wasn't planning on doing something—drastic?"

"He, or she, might have another reason for keeping the meeting secret. If she met a man, he might be married, and he can't let his wife know about Ashley." She turned the beaded bracelet on her wrist. "She must not have been afraid to meet whoever it was. Jeanine told me what Coral overheard. Ashley's main objection about the meeting was that she couldn't get away from her fiancé, not that she didn't want to go to the meeting."

"I hadn't thought of that."

As I showered and dressed, guesses at the identity of the man Ashley met and of the person who had sent him twisted around each other like a nest of snakes.

The man didn't have to be local. Ashely might have chosen the abandoned road either because she already knew about it, or after meeting Rick there, she knew its seclusion would be good for any other secret meetings.

Father, please protect Coral. Maybe the man didn't hear her name.

Gathering my backpack, I went to the kitchen and grabbed two pepperoni rolls and an apple. I could eat them as I drove to town.

As soon as I stowed my backpack in the employees' kitchen, I mounted the back staircase and went straight to Barb's office. Her door was open, but she wasn't at her desk. Stepping to the other side of the door, I saw her staring out the windows that overlooked the parking lot for the employees.

"Barb." I murmured, but she jumped.

Holding her hand against her heart, she said, "Shut the door."

I did, and she met me in the middle of the bland beige room. "What's going on? Why was Rick arrested?"

"He wasn't arrested. Dad just wants to talk to him." Then I told her what Dad had permitted me to say about discovering the body.

She listened with a blank face. Then she turned at a right angle to me. "It must be Ashley, or you wouldn't have bothered to come and see me personally."

"I just want you to know the truth. The body still has to be identified."

Barb took in a breath and released it, which made her appear smaller. "Thank you, Rae." She returned to the windows.

I hurried out of the office.

Chapter Thirty-Seven

The four hours I worked Friday afternoon might as well have been forty.

I dodged, ducked, and deflected questions as if every patron who entered the library had been hired on as a deputy and thought they had a right to interrogate me.

The four hours would have seemed like four days if Devon hadn't been backing me. Eventually, she cut everybody off after they asked their first question with, "Mal doesn't want her to talk about it. Go ask him."

When we closed at 4 p.m., I ran for the Rust Bucket like it was a sanctuary. Heading home, I passed a road that eventually led to Walter's place.

I bit my lip.

With everything that had happened, I hadn't done more than thank Walter for saving me. I should bake something or ask if I could help him with a project at his house.

Dad didn't come home for supper, and he wasn't home by the time Rusty and I finished mowing the parts of the yard that I hadn't gotten to yesterday. When we came in, Aunt Carrie was still at our computer. She'd come over as soon as she finished eating with the Norrises. She told the boys she was doing research and wouldn't say anything more, despite Aaron's questions.

But I figured she was doing what I'd wanted to do at the library between patrons—dig into Ashley's social media sites for photos of fat men or any clue to who might have sent him.

Beat from all the walking and stress of the day, I went to my bedroom, picked up my chart, and flopped onto the bed. I stared at it until my writing blurred.

What had Dad learned from Rick? Would he tell me anything? The question of Rick's guilt might crush me if I had to live with it another day.

At 11 p.m., with Dad still out, I sacked out on the couch, hoping to catch him when he walked in.

~~~~~

I jerked upright, awake.

"Oh, I'm sorry, kiddo." Dad stood halfway between the couch and the kitchen, the light above the sink backlighting him. "I didn't see you there."

"What did Rick say?" Most of my sleepiness vanished as I
~~~~~

remembered why I had bedded down on the couch.

"I can't tell you. But his story is plausible. Doesn't mean I believe it." He lowered himself onto the arm of the couch. "I wish Amber didn't know about the danger to Coral. She could let something slip, especially since she's babysitting Devon's daughters tomorrow. Actually, today."

"She'll be too busy watching Serenity to gossip on her phone. But even if she talks to her friends, Amber won't get so caught up in the drama that she'd ..."

Dad gave me a long look.

"Okay, maybe she will get caught up in the drama, but she won't leak anything." I brushed back a mass of my hair. "Did Jason know about Rick's meeting with Ashley?"

"He says he didn't."

"Do you know how Mrs. Carlisle died?"

With a whispered groan, Dad moved to the recliner. "Well, first, it's her body. Her fingerprints were on file with the school. I won't get the results of the autopsy until Sunday or Monday. It looks like right now that the fall might've killed her."

"Could it have been an accident?"

"I'd consider that if I didn't know about her meeting two men there. And if she hadn't disappeared in the middle of the night."

"Can you tell me who chose the abandoned road for the meeting?"

"Rick did. He tied a flag on a bush at the head of the road so she could find it."

"So she probably suggested it to the second man."

"Probably." He pressed his fingers against his eyes. "Rick says he kept quiet about the meeting because he knew what it would make me think. Didn't dawn on him that deceiving me would have the same result. But he should give me credit for knowing how to conduct an investigation." He fingered the scar by his eye. "Once you break someone's trust, it's almost impossible to get it back." He sighed. "I've been too hard on Carrie. I'm the one who kept a huge secret. No wonder she doesn't trust me."

"Gram and Jeanine and Hank do."

A tired smile attempted to lift his slack cheeks. "That shows the kind of people they are, not who I am. Hank thinks the best of everyone unless you give him good proof otherwise. Jeanine is very forgiving, and Ma and I've lived together for seven years. We really understand each other." He gave me another long look. Then he heaved himself out of the recliner. "Good night."

Saying "good night" wasn't what he'd been thinking over.

I watched his back as he went to the basement door.

Should I ask what was on his mind? But I couldn't make him tell me if he didn't want to.

Gathering my pillow and quilt, I tiptoed to bed.

I hated having something unspoken between us, but waiting on Dad seemed my only option.

Chapter Thirty-Eight

After we turned out the alpacas in their pastures Saturday morning, Gram and the boys assembled their suitcases to spend the weekend with her sister in Columbus. She had been looking for a time to visit, and this weekend seemed ideal for trips to the water park and the zoo. My brothers would enjoy everything Aunt Marti had planned, and since they weren't home, they wouldn't wonder why Coral didn't come over to our house or why they couldn't go over to her farm.

Gram began to zip her suitcase, then stopped. "I know it's sensible to take the boys to see Marti and Robert, but I feel like I'm abandoning family when they really need me."

"Both Dad and Aunt Jeanine approved." I lifted a black duffel bag from the floor. "I can take this out."

"Thank you. Now you won't stay here all day by yourself? I know there's no reason to think it's unsafe, but ..." She touched my arm. "Too many scary things have happened lately."

"I'm spending the day with Coral. Maybe I can keep her from focusing on how she can't roam like she usually does."

Once Gram and the boys left, I took apart the twin bed Gram had been sleeping on in the playroom. I carried the frame to my new room and then wrestled the mattress and springs, which kept getting caught in the stair railing, down the steps. I assembled the bed on the part of the floor that was finished. When Gram came home, she couldn't argue with me since I'd already moved in.

Then I drove over to the Norris farm. With Amber watching Liberty and Serenity since Devon was working at the main branch, I was Coral's chief entertainment. We cleaned the stable. I saddled Pokey and led him into the corral. Balancing herself on the top board, Coral gave me a lesson.

"Heel down," she said as I trotted past her.

I obeyed. When Pokey and I rode by again, Coral didn't look at us but stared beyond the corral to the woods, like a prisoner gazing at the landscape between iron bars. Aunt Carrie circled the corral the entire time, the husky and a Doberman mix keeping her company.

Dad and Deputy Harris stopped by for lunch and showed Coral several photos. She shook her head at all of them.

By the middle of the afternoon, as my chocolate chip muffins were cooling, I told Aunt Jeanine I would pick up Amber.

"You don't have to leave yet."

"I'm going to drop off these muffins at Walter's." When alarm made her catch her breath, I added, "I'll make sure Troy isn't there first. If he is, I'll leave."

Her mouth twisted in a grimace. "I guess that's okay."

As I neared Walter's property, I studied the road for a convenient place to pull over, planning to walk through the woods to see who was at his house. But with a scary drop on one side of the road and a steep hillside on the other, the best I could do was park at the foot of his drive, which was so long that no one could see the Rust Bucket from the house.

I hiked through the woods until I could view Walter's house through a screen of white honeysuckle blossoms. Not only was Troy's hatchback parked by the garage, he was drinking coffee on the front porch.

I sneaked down the hill to my truck and drove away.

Dad had thought Troy would leave now that Joseph and Falk had been arrested. He'd obviously come to Walter's to hide from Joseph. So why did Troy stay?

He either owed money to Joseph or to a client who had hired the PI. Maybe Troy was still hiding from the client. But wouldn't it have been smarter for Troy to leave since he couldn't know if Joseph had told his client where he'd found Troy?

So Joseph might have been the person Troy was hiding from after all. But if that were true, he wouldn't be hanging around Marlin County out of warm feelings for his daughters and Walter.

The puzzle was still bothering me when I parked in the lot for Devon's apartment.

A few minutes after 4 p.m., Devon turned into the lot, her cheeks pink from the heat.

"Any news on the case?" She stopped by my open window.

"Which one?"

"Any of the 300 cases you're involved in."

"Nope."

"Is that true or is that a kind way of saying 'None of your business'?"

"It covers all 300 cases."

Amber came out a few minutes later, wisps of red gold hair escaping from her long, twin braids, hauling a canvas bag stretched to its limit.

"I'm glad that's over," she said with a groan. "Six days straight with Serenity can kill you."

I shifted into first. "I know Devon appreciates having a reliable babysitter."

"The pay isn't great, but I'd rather babysit than work retail or at the state park." She scooted the bag, crammed with craft supplies, to one side in the footwell. "And Uncle Mal doesn't need to worry. I didn't talk about

Coral at all." She rolled her eyes, her usual breathless voice harsh. "Not to the girls, or on the phone, or in texts."

"I told him he could trust you."

She turned to me, pulling against her seat belt. "You did? You think you can trust me after that mess with Troy?" Her brown eyes shone.

"Well, I trust you to keep your mouth shut about something so important."

She relaxed into her headrest. "Thanks."

We rolled out of town.

Flocks of dove gray and snow white clouds chased each other across the sun, making the road ahead flash from shade to sun and back again.

Amber leaned toward her open window. "So much has happened since yesterday that I can't remember if I told you how smart you are — to figure out from 'rich chick' that Coral had seen somebody other than a high school kid." Her admiring smile brought a glow to her storybook beauty.

I tucked ruffling hair behind my ears as we rattled around a pothole. "It was just a guess."

"A really smart one."

I turned off the state route behind a hatchback that looked horribly familiar.

Amber peered through my bug-spattered windshield. "Isn't that Troy's car?"

"Yes," I said through my teeth.

"Wonder where he's going."

I stared at her. "You don't really want to know, do you?"

She turned a puzzled face to me, then started. "No. No, of course not." Sitting back, she waved my question away with a sweep of her elegant hand. "Delete that. Erase it."

~~~~~

After supper, Dad and Deputy Harris stopped by with more photos to show Coral.

As they took her to a bedroom, Hank, Jeanine, Carrie, Amber, and I remained in the kitchen. We'd been cleaning up the supper dishes, but now we hung in the room, still, suspended.

In a few minutes, the three of them came into the living room. From the way Coral flung herself onto the couch, I knew she hadn't identified the mysterious second man.

Dad crouched beside her. "Don't get discouraged, Coral. It's only been one day. We'll find this guy."

With her chin sunk low, she said, "I'll be dead by the time you find him."

Dad patted her shoulder and then joined us in the kitchen. "We're not
~~~~~

licked yet. We'll keep digging into Ashley's past and see if we can find likely candidates. Rae, are you staying here until I get home?"

I told him yes, then he left with Deputy Harris by the back door.

Wiping her hands on a dishcloth, Amber watched Coral as her sister sat collapsed on the couch. "Coral, would you like to watch a movie? Your choice."

This was a sacrifice. Coral only liked adventure movies or ones with horses in them. Amber preferred epics and romances.

Coral stared at the woven rug under the coffee table. "You hate all the movies I like."

"We both like *The Two Towers* and *The Return of the King*, but I'll watch whatever you pick."

Coral lifted her head. "You will?"

"Yes."

"Okay." She bounced to her feet. "*The Two Towers*. As long as we fast forward through the talking trees part."

Hank said he'd join us when he could, so Jeanine, Amber, Coral, and I clambered down to the basement, past Hank's desk, littered with papers and a computer for all his farm information, to where Amber had created a homemade theater with black sheets to wall off a small section from the rest of the basement.

Jeanine and Coral settled into beanbags arranged in a semi-circle in front of a desk that supported a small TV and DVD player. Amber placed the disc into the player, and I turned off the lights.

As the movie opened with a battle scene, Troy and his motivations would not leave my mind. Dad had said Troy only had two motives for returning to the county—lying low or pulling a con. But could he have had a third one?

My conversation with him at the fox den sparked a theory. During one of the battles with cavalry, I slipped upstairs.

Carrie sat at Jeanine's desk in her bedroom, staring at the desktop monitor.

"Any luck?" I leaned against the desk.

Sighing, Carrie pushed the swivel chair away from the desk. "No new, overweight men with a connection to Ashley."

"I had an idea about the identity of Boyfriend X."

"We're not sure there is a Boyfriend X."

"But there could be. What if it was Troy?"

Carrie's entire body jerked, rolling the chair back a few inches.

"I met Troy by the fox den the day you brought the Carlisle kids to the farm for the first time. I thought it was strange, him being out there, although it's walking distance from Walter's house. But the den is very close to the abandoned road. What if Troy persuaded Ashley to leave

Jason, and she helped him with his cons? She finally got fed up working for him and left him for Conrad. Because she'd actually helped him commit crimes, Troy was afraid she'd reveal something that would put him in prison. So he sent Joseph to set up a meeting with her. Then Ashley met Troy on the road, and he killed her.

"When I met him at the den, he could have been coming back or going to the crime scene. Maybe he took something of hers then to plant it on Jason."

Carrie held her forehead. "I am losing my touch. You're the third person who's told me that theory, and it never occurred to me."

Now I jerked. "Who else did?"

"Jeanine came up with it and told me before supper. She was going to tell Mal, but he'd already thought of it and brought a photo of Joseph for Coral to look at this evening. And now you. All three of you thought of it independently. I'm not surprised Mal did, but I'm the private investigator. It's sort of humiliating that my sister, the writer, and my niece, the photographer, put the pieces together before I did."

"But Coral didn't identify Joseph."

"Nope."

My shoulders slumped.

"But keeping thinking, Rae." Carrie moved to the edge of the chair. "We've got to find this guy. I don't know how long Coral will survive under house arrest."

I trudged into the kitchen and popped popcorn. As I was emptying the bag into a bowl, Dad called, telling me he was home. I said I'd be over after the movie.

The heroes saved the day again. Coral figuratively rode along with the cavalry, and Amber got to admire a warrior princess and drool over epic hunks, although any guy with hair longer than mine is not all that attractive.

Dad was already asleep by the time I came in the kitchen door. I was glad. If he didn't get a break in the case soon, it would break him.

Chapter Thirty-Nine

The next morning, Carrie accompanied the Carlisles to mass as Sylvie's bodyguard and Dad acted as one for Coral at our church. Who knew Marlin County would have such a demand for personal security services?

Dad went back to the office after lunch and still hadn't reappeared when I finished cleaning out the stable with Uncle Hank after supper.

Picking up the handles of the wheelbarrow, Hank said, "Thanks, Rae, for spending so much time over here this weekend. It helped all of us from thinking too much."

I poured grain into a feed bucket for Pokey. "That's what families are for."

Nice that I could say that. After Mom died, I'd figured I never could again.

"Hey, Rae." Amber jogged into the stable. "Gram just called. She and the boys are home."

She helped Hank and me finish giving the horses fresh hay and grain.

As Hank slid the wide doors of the stable shut, Amber ran ahead of me into the house.

Three whole days under guard. How much more could Coral take? She slunk around like her depression added ten pounds to every step. Carrie had gone with her over to Mr. Norris's house so Coral could help him work on an old tractor they were restoring. Maybe doing something normal like that would—

Gunfire exploded behind me.

I threw myself to the ground in the flower bed beside the front porch.

Who'd shot at me? Had someone shot at me? Was someone hunting in the woods? But it sounded so close.

From my snail's eye view, I glanced around as best I could.

Hank lay on his back in front of the stable.

The air froze in my throat.

Father, no.

I commando-crawled across the grass.

Blood was smeared across his forehead as he rolled into a sitting position.

He couldn't have been hurt bad if he could sit up. But how was that possible if he'd been shot in the head?

"Uncle Hank, are you hit?" My question sounded strangled as I reached him.

"Hank?" Aunt Jeanine's voice came from the house. "Did you hear—"

"Stay inside." Whipping around to his knees, he shoved on the stable door. "Get in here, Rae."

We scrambled into the stable, and the wood door ground in its track as Hank shoved it closed.

Panting on the dirt floor, Hank said, "Are you all right?"

"I'm not the one bleeding." I pointed at his forehead.

Hank wiped at it. "I hit something when I hit the dirt."

"So someone did shoot at you?"

Dragging in air, he nodded. "I heard the bullets hit above my head." He pointed up. "Either he wasn't aiming for me, or he's the world's worst shot."

I followed his finger. Several small holes, punched near the roofline, allowed the setting sun to shoot gold rods through them.

"You saw it was a man?"

Hank shook his head. "Could've been a woman. Someone was hiding in the woods." He took a length of rope that lay on a hay bale and knotted it through the handles of the two sliding doors. Then he motioned to me, and we crawled to the opposite end of the stable, where the doors led to the corral.

Pokey snorted, and Knight tossed his head, but the gunfire didn't seem to have affected the horses.

Hank half collapsed against a hay bale outside the stall used as a tack room.

"You're still bleeding." I kneeled beside him. "Are you sure you're okay?"

"Despite what the Big Guy would say, I would act differently if I was shot in the head." He pulled off his ragged white t-shirt. "Why would the fat guy shoot at me? He couldn't have mistaken me for Coral. She's been at Dad's since we finished supper." He pressed the shirt against his forehead.

"It could've been an accident."

"I'd believe that if it was hunting season. But me and Jeanine have lived here seventeen years and nobody's ever taken a potshot at us. It's got to be connected to the guy Coral saw." Hank lowered the t-shirt from his wound. "Is it bad?"

A jagged cut bisected a swelling bruise.

"It's not pretty, but I don't think you need stitches."

He started to reapply the t-shirt but let his hand drop. "We gotta warn Dad and Carrie." He leaped to his feet and hauled open the door to the corral.

"Uncle Hank, I think Aunt Jeanine would've called them right after she called Dad."

Shifting his jaw, he looked down at me. "You're right." He pushed the door closed. "Coral's safe with Carrie and Dad."

We sat in silence except for the munching of the horses enjoying their suppers.

"Do you think we could sneak to the house through the corral?" I said. "He hasn't fired again."

"We' re gonna sit tight." Uncle Hank used the firm tone he reserved for correcting his daughters and horses. "We'll wait until the Big Guy gives us the all clear. Besides, I don't want two brushes with death in one day."

I lowered my eyebrows in question.

"First the shots, and then the Big Guy trying to remove my head because I didn't keep you safe here in the stable." He tried to break into his ornery grin, but it fell apart. "Now that I think about it, he'll try to kill me anyway because you came over to help me instead of running into the house for cover."

"But you were lying on the ground. I couldn't leave you."

This time, he gave me a grin that stretched to its limit. "You're a good kid, Rae."

As I rested against the post for a stall, flames touched my cheeks.

We discussed who might have been the man Coral saw, and the cut on Hank's forehead finally clotted.

"What I don't get," said Hank, "is why hurt Coral now? He's had more'n a week."

I tugged on my earlobe. "Something must have happened to make him think she's a threat."

"We gotta get him." Hank's extra big brown eyes became incinerating and he set his extra-wide mouth in a snarl, an expression I'd never seen on his face before. "My little girl can't live in a closet for weeks and weeks."

I pictured my chart, shoving together and pulling apart the information. Did the discovery of the body prompt the man to take action? If so, why attack Hank?

A vehicle approached, and then the engine turned off. Someone got out and pulled on the outside handles to the doors by the drive.

"Hank? Rae? You all right?" Dad called.

Hank got to his feet. "Don't tear the doors off the hinges. I ain't made of money." He untied the rope.

As soon as Dad entered, he grabbed me in one of his bone-obliterating hugs.

"I'm fine, Dad," I said against his bullet-proof vest.

"I am too," said Hank. "Just in case you were worried. Did you catch him?"

Releasing me, Dad said, "You saw who it was?"

"No. I just thought it made more sense saying 'him' than 'them'."

"Phelps is still going through the woods, trying to figure out where the shooter stood when he fired." He squinted at the cut on Hank's forehead. "Did you get grazed?"

"By a rock when I dove out of the way. Not that I needed to." Hank pointed at the holes in the wooden walls. "I don't think he was trying to hit me."

Dad gazed up. "Kincaid is driving Carrie, Coral, and your dad over. I'll have him and Phelps look for the bullets." He slapped Hank on the arm. "Glad you injured a nonessential."

Hank looked at me. "What'd I tell you?" Then his easy-going smile faded. "Now I don't want you to get on Rae's case. You've got a kid with real guts. She could've run into the house, but she said she couldn't just ditch me and you should—"

Blood flooded Dad's face. "Rae, you could've made it to—" The decibels rose, then he clamped his mouth shut, his face deepening to scarlet.

I'd braced myself for an outburst, but Dad's attempt to master his mouth didn't seem much better.

"You can go ahead and yell," I said.

"No." It came out husky. "Not appropriate."

"It's better than watching blood squirt out of your ears."

Dad shot me a look as Hank burst out laughing. A grin spread over Dad's face, displacing the flush.

Hank fell back on a hay bale as he placed a hand against his chest. His laughter subsiding, he released a long breath, resting his hands on his knees. "Man, I needed that. Rae and me were talking—nothing else to do while you were playing CSI—and we can't figure out why he'd attack now, after a week's passed."

"I know why." Dad reached into the back pocket of his jeans. "When I turned onto your drive, I noticed that the door to your mailbox was open, and there was something inside. Since it was Sunday, and I remembered how Rae got threats from the stalker, I stopped to get it." He held out a plastic bag with a white sheet of paper inside.

In black crayon, it said, "Not a penny."

Chapter Forty

"'Not a penny'?" Mr. Norris looked up from the plastic bag up to Dad. "Not a penny for what?"

"Blackmail," Dad and Carrie said together.

The small living room in the Norris farmhouse had about reached capacity now that Chris had escorted Coral, Carrie, and Mr. Norris from the old man's farm.

Mr. Norris drew back. "My son ain't never done anything he could be blackmailed for."

"Hank isn't the victim." Carrie took a seat beside Amber on the faded blue loveseat. "The shooter is the victim and thinks Hank or Jeanine is the blackmailer."

The corners of his eyes wrinkling, Mr. Norris pulled at the right end of his mustache. "That's ridiculous."

"'Course it is." Hank sat between Coral and Jeanine on the frayed, beige couch, two bandage strips across his forehead. "I only blackmail after the harvest and before we start working the fields in the spring. I'd never blackmail anyone in June."

"Henry, that's not funny." Mr. Norris tried to sound severe, but a relieved smile his white and black mustache couldn't hide prevented him. "What will Walter think?"

Walter? Why was Mr. Norris concerned with what my great-grandfather—oh, that's right. He meant Dad. Mr. Norris was the only person on the planet who called Dad by his legal first name.

"Not much, Mr. Norris," said Dad. "I've known Hank since birth." He gestured with the bag at Chris, who was waiting by the front door. "Kincaid, see if you can recover the bullets fired into the stable."

"Right." He aimed his quicksilver smile at me. "Glad you're okay, Rae."

"Thanks." Was I smiling too much? My cheeks sent out stabs of pain.

As Chris walked out the door, I turned back to the seven people in the living room. All but Mr. Norris were giving me odd looks, ranging from Dad's cocked eyebrow to Amber's clasped hands and sparkling eyes.

Dipping my head to let my hair fall by my face, I pressed against an ivory wall. Maybe it would swallow me.

Dad set the bag on an end table. "That man Coral saw must have received a demand for money."

"Or the man Ashley met at 3 a.m. did," said Carrie. "Since the fat guy remembered hearing Coral's name—"

"—he figures either Jeanine or Hank or both are the blackmailer," Dad finished, "because a twelve-year-old isn't likely to be one."

I said, "The demand must've been recent since he hasn't done anything before now."

Mr. Norris bore a searching glare at me. "Or the shooter was after Rae. She had a stalker after her just a few months ago."

"That case was solved." Dad put some punch behind his statement.

"Hank and Jeanine ain't never had this kind of trouble before." Mr. Norris kept his gaze on me. "It seems a whole lot more likely that the shooter thought Rae was still with Hank and fired at him by mistake."

By mistake. By mistake ...

"Dad." Hank pressed a finger against the bandage. "He couldn't have made a mistake like that. Rae was nowhere near me. He had a clear view of her."

"Mal, what are we going to do?" Jeanine had enveloped Coral in a hug, smoothing her hair. "Is it safe to stay here?"

I was a complete idiot.

I ran out of the living room and into Jeanine's bedroom, grabbed a piece of paper from the printer on her desk, found a pen under the monitor, and drew.

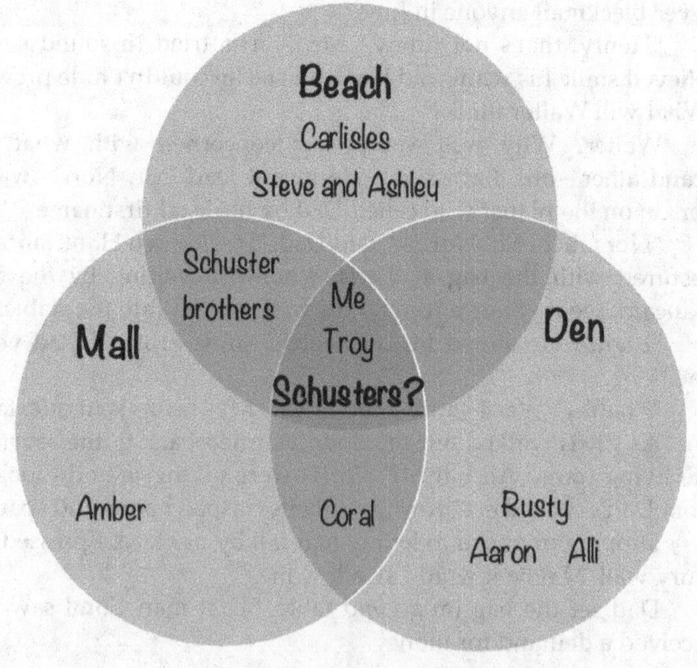

"Rae?" Dad appeared in the bedroom doorway.

"Just give me a minute." I scribbled in words.

"You thought of something?"

I finished my diagram and thrust it at him. "See?"

"Uh, yes, but what does it mean?"

"Would a con man turn to blackmail?"

Dad's eyes narrowed. "Ye-es. It's the cowardly kind of thing Troy would love. Almost no risk. But what proof do you have?"

Jeanine peeked over Dad's shoulder. "What's going on?"

I pointed to my diagram. "I've been looking at Troy the wrong way. When I was at the lake on Memorial Day, Troy was there. When I was at the mall, Troy was there. I forgot the Schusters were at both those locations too. When I met Troy by the fox den, I wondered if he was following me."

Dad straightened to attention. "When did you meet him there?"

"Last Monday. I didn't think about it until yesterday, and my theory about him was the one that you'd already come up with, so I didn't mention it to you." I waved it away. "You said Troy came to the county either to hide or run a con. What about both?"

"Possible."

"Hey, if Rae's got something," Carrie spoke from behind Dad, "we should all hear it."

We returned to the living room, and I positioned myself in the center of the woven rug like I was doing a presentation at school.

"I think Troy came to Walter's house to hide from Joseph," I said. "But at the parade or picnic, he heard about the investigation into Senator Schuster's campaign finances, so he started following him to see if he could catch him doing anything he could blackmail him for. Troy went to the lake when the Schusters had a party. He went to the mall when the senator opened a store. So if Troy was at the fox den, which is so close to the crime scene, maybe it was because the senator was there."

"Wait a minute." Hank came forward in his seat on the couch. "A guy could be out in the woods for a ton of different reasons."

"But we have a note referring to blackmail." Carrie pointed at the bag. "And a known con man in the vicinity of the crime."

"But Brad is skinnier than I am. Ashley couldn't have met him."

"Not the senator," I said. "It had to be—"

"Hold it, Rae." Dad touched my arm. "Don't say anything else. We have to do this right. We'll go to my office. I'll have Harris meet us and get photos ready for Coral to choose from. The Norrises will ride into town with me. Carrie, Rae, and Mr. Norris—you can all come in another vehicle, and I'll get Kincaid to bring up the rear."

"Do you know who I saw, Uncle Mal?" Coral scooted to the edge of the couch.

"I'm praying we do."

Chapter Forty-One

Coral didn't have to say a word when she ran into the lobby of the sheriff's department after looking at the photos Dad had showed her in his office. Her mile-wide grin said it all.

Lifting her eyes to the drop ceiling, Jeanine murmured something, and she and Aunt Carrie hugged each other as they sat in the lobby's mismatched chairs. Uncle Hank let out a victory whoop, putting one arm around Amber and the other around Coral. Mr. Norris's gaunt face held the traces of a smile. I sagged against one of the desks.

Thank You, Father.

Dad strode into the lobby with Chris and Deputy Harris. "Coral positively identified Bruce Schuster as the second man who met Ashley in the woods."

Mr. Norris twisted the end of his mustache. "Bruce Schuster killed Ashley Carlisle?"

"I don't know, Mr. Norris. He may have just set up the meeting, and Brad killed her. All I can do at this point is ask him why he never mentioned he had a meeting with Ashley in the place where we found her body. We'll see what he says. Kincaid, Harris, Phelps, and I will go to his home to talk to him. I want everybody to wait here until he's in custody or cooperating or both. Carrie, you can update Ma. But nobody else." Dad's steeled gaze swept over us. "I don't want Bruce or Brad to get wind of what we suspect. Or Troy. If he's the blackmailer, and he catches on we're on to him, he'll bolt. So not a word to anyone. Got it?"

We all nodded or said, "Yes."

Hank snapped his fingers. "So Brad asking if his daughter could board her horse with me was just a story to see if Coral was my daughter."

"You got it," said Carrie.

Hank broke into a fierce grin. "Mal, all I need is about five minutes with Brad before you take him in."

"As I've said before—" Dad started for the hall "—I have no desire to arrest family, and that includes in-laws."

I grabbed Dad in a hug. "Be careful."

That launched a whole round of hugging, which Deputy Harris watched with crossed arms.

I looked to her and Chris. "Y'all should be careful too." My eyes met Chris's black ones.

His professional expression didn't alter by an inch, but he inclined his head to me and then disappeared into the hall with Harris.

Releasing Dad from her hug, Coral said, "Uncle Mal, I'll never spy on anybody ever again. I already told Mom and Dad that. I swear it."

He struck down the bill of her cap. "Thanks, kiddo."

After he left, Coral fell into a chair with a dull silver metal frame. "How long do we have to wait?"

"It's hard to say." Carrie rummaged in her small purse. "It depends on how fast they find Bruce and if he cooperates."

Sitting back in a wooden chair with nubby brick red fabric, Mr. Norris said, "Why would either of the Schuster brothers kill Ashley Carlisle?

"It's just a guess, Mr. Norris." Carrie pulled her phone from her purse. "But when Ashley abandoned Jason two years ago, she probably left him for Brad Schuster. Brad could have set her up as his mistress in another city and led a double life—one with his wife and kids in Zanesville and one with Ashley."

Once again, Mr. Norris's usual disapproval of all things Malinowski produced a severe stare. "We shouldn't discuss this in front of children."

Carrie rolled her eyes, but Jeanine said in a quiet but firm voice, "I don't like my girls hearing about this either, Luke. But we're involved in this mess up to our necks, so they have to know."

Mr. Norris's lifted nose showed his silent disagreement.

"How could Brad afford to do that?" Hank angled his head to one side. "Do state senators get paid that much?"

"I doubt it." Carrie thumbed on her phone. "But he could if he was using his campaign finances for something other than his campaign."

Hank whistled. "That'd be a motive for murder. Especially since I heard talk of there being an investigation into his political donations." He shoved back his hat. "If Bruce was helping Brad set up Ashley, then Brad must trust Bruce to keep his mouth shut."

I perched on the edge of Liz's desk. "At the mall, when Troy got beat up, Bruce was handing out stuff at the store opening. He said that the whole Schuster family helps his brother with public appearances since he's divorced. Bruce said—" I closed my eyes to piece together his exact words "—'Keeping Brad in office has sort of turned into a family business.'" I opened my eyes. "I thought he meant the whole family helped with his campaigning like any of y'all would for Dad."

"This is all just speculation." Carrie held her phone to her ear. "I'm going to update Ma."

Hank glanced at Jeanine. "You gotta use this in a story."

While Carrie spoke to Gram, Hank, Jeanine, and Amber discussed story ideas. I pitched in a couple.

Coral went into the hall that led to the back door and restrooms, and

Mr. Norris followed her.

"Now you meant what you said." Mr. Norris's quiet voice barely reached me. "You won't sneak up on people to eavesdrop on them no more, will you?"

"No, Gramps. I swear I won't."

"Good. Because I don't know where I'd get another mechanic and farmhand so good."

Amber leaned against the desk beside me. "Chris Kincaid is very handsome. He's gorgeous in his uniform."

Her insinuating smile made me squirm down in my chair. If I faked my death, would she get the message that I didn't want to talk about this?

Returning to the lobby with her grandfather, Coral said, "Rae, can I play games on your phone?"

I dove for where I'd left my backpack by an end table. "I'll play with you."

We passed around phones, playing different games, until Carrie's phone rang. We froze as she answered.

Carrie's end of the conversation consisted of mostly monosyllables. "Got it. Hope everything goes smoothly." She swiped off and aimed a big grin at us. "Bruce Schuster is under arrest. Mal and Harris pulled into the drive—no sirens, but Bruce panicked, fired a couple shots over their heads, and ran. So Mal arrested him and took his gun. He told Bruce he was going to compare bullets from his gun with the ones found at the stable. Bruce has opened up and can't talk fast enough."

Uncle Hank tried to hug Jeanine and his daughters all at once. A crisscross pattern of hugging took place among all of us, except for Mr. Norris, who restricted himself to blood relations and his daughter-in-law.

"But—" Carrie raised her voice "—none of us can mention anything about Brad, Ashley, and Troy. If anyone asks you about the shooting tonight, you say it's under investigation, and that's it."

I had a feeling that sentence would be worn to a thread at work the next day.

Chapter Forty-Two

"Brad and Bruce Schuster," Gram murmured after she'd taken a sip of tea at the dinner table. "I can't say I'm surprised if Brad misappropriated funds to support a mistress. The Schusters have always been concerned with appearances. I've always wondered how Gary and Debbie could afford their house on a trucker and dental hygienist's pay. But I don't see either of those boys becoming violent."

I sprinkled sugar into my tea. If I'd learned anything since I'd come to Marlin County, it was you never knew what people were capable of.

My brothers had gone to bed, so Gram and I could talk freely. Dad still wasn't home.

"But why else would he meet her in the dead of night?" I stirred my tea. "He's divorced now, so he's not hiding an affair from his wife."

Gram stared into the dark living room. "If he spent political money on her and was about to be investigated, he wouldn't want anyone to know about her. But if he married her, she couldn't testify against him. He might have set up the meeting to propose. Once they were married, it wouldn't matter who knew about their affair."

Sipping, I rolled that around. "She met him Monday morning, he proposed because he doesn't want anyone to know he spent campaign money on her, she turned him down, and he killed her."

"I don't know." Gram's veiny hands cradled her mug. "Ashley Carlisle never struck me as intelligent, but she's a survivor. She wouldn't do anything to anger him in such an isolated place. If she was afraid of him, she wouldn't have gone at all."

"True." I tugged my earlobe. This case wasn't as slammed shut as I thought. "I'm sure the blackmailer is Troy. So he was there. Maybe he killed her, so he could have something more serious to blackmail Mr. Schuster with."

"Troy would only commit violence to protect himself." Gram squirted a dollop of honey into her tea. "If Ashley was alive, he might've been able to blackmail her too, threatening to reveal to her fiancé that she was cheating on him."

"Bruce set up the meeting. He might've come to it without Brad knowing. Ashley didn't answer the way Bruce wanted, so after Brad left, he killed her. But he'd only do that if he'd gotten a share of the political donations."

"I'm sure BCI agents are combing through Brad's campaign finances at this very moment," Gram said. "And Mal is checking on where Bruce was early Monday morning."

"Maybe the autopsy will point to the killer. Dad said he thought he'd get the results by Monday."

She reached across the table for my hand. "Let's pray there's conclusive evidence. Whoever is innocent doesn't deserve to have this mystery hanging over them."

We prayed, and then I went to my almost finished bedroom. My move into it had surprised Gram, but she hadn't protested.

Since the electricity wasn't hooked up to my room yet, I took the books I was reading—the sci fi short stories, a book on shooting portraits, and a collection of photos of West Virginia—and carried them all to the couch.

I opened the West Virginia book.

I'd catch Dad when he came in to find out what he could tell me about the latest developments in the case.

~~~~~

"Hey, Rae."

My heavy-lidded eyes found Micah an inch from my face.

"Will it bother you if I watch a show?"

I slapped the end table for my phone. Only eleven minutes until my alarm went off.

"Go ahead." Swinging my legs onto the floor, I ran my tongue around my dry mouth. "But be quiet. Dad must've come home late. I never heard him."

I hoped he was still sleeping and hadn't left before dawn.

By the time I showered and dressed, Gram was up and cooking bacon.

Snagging a warm slice, I saw a note on the dry erase board that hung on the fridge.

"Don't wake me until nine."

I started to set a mug of water in the microwave when the landline rang. I picked it up.

"Mal? Ed. I got the autopsy report on Ashley Carlisle. She definitely died from the fall. Occurred within twenty-four hours of when she was last seen. That's as narrow as I can—"

"Excuse me, sir." I hated to interrupt, but Dad would want me to. "This is Rae Riley. My dad's asleep. Can I take a message?"

"Oh, sure. Have Mal call me when he can."

"And you're the coroner?"

"Yes." He chuckled. "When you live long enough in one place, you think everybody knows you. I'm Ed Hawthorne."
~~~~~

I jotted down the information, thanked him, and hung up.

Gram looked around me to the note. "I don't see any reason to wake Mal early. Ed didn't say it was urgent."

At the library, as Devon and I logged onto the computers at the check out desk, she said, "So what happened at Jeanine's house yesterday? People have texted me a hundred different versions. Was there really a shooting?"

"Yes." That was public information.

"And Mal arrested Bruce Schuster for it?"

"He was arrested for shooting at Dad and Deputy Harris." I bent over the drop box and lifted out a pile of books.

"But not for the shooting at the Norris farm?"

"That's under investigation."

"Does that mean I should stop asking questions?"

"I guess." I scooted the pile onto the counter.

"All right." She gestured toward the two-story window and the dingy gray morning. "How about this weather we're having?"

Scanning a large print book, I had to laugh.

The bombardment of questions from patrons was even worse than it was on Friday because now they had four points of attack — the thugs in the barn, the discovery of Ashley's car, the shooting at the Norris stable, and Bruce Schuster's arrest. I couldn't blame them. If all that had happened to someone I knew, I might try to pump the person, but hopefully, my manners wouldn't let me.

All morning I waited for someone to hurtle through the front doors with the announcement that Brad or Bruce Schuster had been charged with Ashley's death.

But by noon, I alone was the trending news topic. Three families, two elderly men, Ms. Zollars, and Mr. Edwards had come in, and everyone but Mr. Edwards had asked me about the shooting.

Fielding their questions, I glimpsed Mr. Edwards flipping through magazines and scowling at me. No one bothered to ask him about Ashley and Steve. Apparently the public had decided that The Discoverer of the Body, which I wasn't but nobody could remember that, ranked higher than Last Person to See Victim Alive.

The patrons had thinned to just one old man leafing through the Columbus newspaper when Mr. Edwards pushed a few cookbooks and several thrillers at me.

"I'm surprised Mal's deputies didn't find Ashley Carlisle's body before you did."

Mr. Edwards's comment was at least different from everybody else's.

"The wife and I probably would've found it," he went on, "even if everyone hadn't been crowded around that spot on the road. I mean, the opening is wide enough to drive a semi through."

My hand hovered above the cookbook I'd reached for. "There was a crowd?"

Dad had said there would be, but it was still creepy. No, more ghoulish than creepy.

"Sunday night there was. Your dad should review search procedures with his deputies."

His criticism of Dad probably stemmed from his irritation with me for stealing his spotlight. I could criticize him and the wife for being a pair of ghouls.

Just to be nice, I said, "Did you see a lot of Mrs. Carlisle and Mr. Conrad before she disappeared?"

His paunchy face brightened. "Yeah. A whole lot. Everyone at the lodge learned to expect the unexpected. They ran hot and cold."

His answer came out so fast that he must have perfected it after being asked about the couple a hundred times.

"Sometimes they were as sweet as honey. Other times—" he shook his head "—they were the kind of guests you couldn't wait to check out. Like the last night I saw her. She and Steve came in around 8 p.m., and she told him that if he'd been sleeping so badly, he should take one of her sleeping pills. She said the walls are so thin that she'd had to take one every night since they checked in. Then she aimed at me this nasty smile."

I put the due slip in the top book, but Mr. Edwards kept right on talking. "Then a half hour later, she called and asked if I'd deliver a bottle of Scotch to their room. And she couldn't have been nicer. She even gave me a $20 tip."

Ashley had taken Bruce's suggestions seriously, encouraging Conrad to take a sleeping pill and then getting booze. Small wonder he never heard her leave.

"Now Steve would get angry if he thought we weren't giving them five-star service." Mr. Edwards showed no signs of leaving. "For crying out loud, this is a lodge at a state park. I spent a lot of time making peace with him since I'm the assistant manager. None of the staff wanted to deal with him when he was in a nasty mood. Except for Egypt Malinowski. She's your cousin, isn't she?"

"My half first—yes, she is." No point going into our exact biological relation.

"Egypt had no problem waiting on them when they got demanding, but I should've stopped her." He shook his head again. "Egypt has a really short fuse."

Unfortunately, my first-hand experience could verify that. "No joke."

"I sent her to take Steve extra towels on Tuesday afternoon. No, it was Monday, the day Ashley went missing. He was really worried. I got a call that there was a fight going on in the hall where Steve and Ashley have their room. I raced up there, and Egypt and Steve were standing in the hall, giving each other looks to kill. Then Steve laughed, and I thought Egypt was going to claw his throat open. I told her to leave, and when she had gone, he said he appreciated me stepping in, just as nice as can be, like he hadn't chewed off my ear five minutes earlier on the phone over the towels."

I hadn't thought of Egypt as a source of intel on Steve and Ashley. Had Dad? Almost certain since he knew she worked there. But he'd have a tough time trusting any information she gave him.

I said, "Did Mr. Conrad or Egypt say what they were angry about?"

A big grin pushed back Mr. Edwards's bulky cheeks. My question must have made his day, meaning I was gossiping and shouldn't have asked it.

"Steve said she didn't knock, just barged into his room. Egypt said she did knock, and the door wasn't latched, so it moved when she hit it. She called to him, still standing in the hall. Steve came out of the bathroom and accused her of snooping and—well, she didn't say so, but I'm sure Egypt told him he was wrong in very explicit terms. I've worked with Egypt for two years. But Steve didn't complain about her mouthing off to him, just said that I should reprimand her for snooping."

Aiden, a junior high kid, who seemed to live at the library, asked if I could help him find a video game.

Giving me a snappy nod, Mr. Edwards gathered his books and strode through the double doors.

We must have been friends now since I'd let him dish his dirt.

~~~~~

Dad's patrol SUV was parked by the garage when I pulled in after work.

Glad to see he made it home for supper.

Since he'd been working so much, I didn't butt in on my brothers' time with him. They wrestled, worked on a city of plastic bricks in the playroom, and helped Dad finish the floor in my bedroom.

At nine, as he and the boys were cleaning up tools, Dad said he was going to bed early so he could get a few hours' sleep before he went on surveillance.

"Who are you surveilling?" asked Aaron.

"Is it dangerous?" Rusty looked up from where he'd dropped a hammer in a toolbox.

"Not at all." Dad aimed a punch at Rusty's head, which Rusty tried to block, and smacked him in the ribs instead.

Rusty swung back, his concerned expression gone.

I helped Dad carry the tools to the garage.
~~~~~

As we placed them on the tool bench, I said, "You haven't gotten any proof to charge Bruce or Brad Schuster with killing Ashley?"

"Not yet." He scrutinized me. "This is for your information only. Got it?"

"For sure."

"Brad is cooperating with us and under constant watch until he leaves the money for the blackmailer. If we can catch him, and I'm sure it's Troy, I might leverage the truth out of him. Right now, Bruce and Brad are pointing fingers at each other or the blackmailer." He sighed. "Sad how they turned on each other. The autopsy didn't provide any evidence as to who's responsible. But if I nab Troy, I'll have independent verification. Troy won't know what the Schuster brothers told me, and Brad and Bruce don't know who the blackmailer is."

"Have you talked to Egypt about Steve and Ashley?" I repeated what Mr. Edwards had told me about Steve accusing Egypt of snooping in his room.

"I told her to keep her eyes open. But I can only trust what she says if she doesn't have a grudge against him."

"I hope your strategy works."

Sighing again, Dad shoved the toolbox to the back of the bench. "Right now, it's all I got."

Chapter Forty-Three

Sleep came to me Monday night in spurts. I tossed and turned, something poking me awake all night. Something about the case didn't sit right. But what?

I woke up before my alarm, staring at one of the sheets Gram had hung over the windows in my bedroom until we bought drapes.

Was it something Dad had said or Mr. Edwards? Maybe Egypt had seen something when Steve had gotten so angry? Should I ask her? She might not have told Dad because it didn't seem important.

Maybe it was the conversation with Dr. Hawthorne? A twenty-four-hour window of opportunity meant Ashley might have died hours after her meeting with Senator Schuster.

Digging in my backpack, I found my chart and unfolded it.

Suspect	Opportunity	Means	Motive
Jason	Alone Sunday night and Monday morning 9:15 pm-8:30 am	Lured her from lodge and ... met her at the abandoned road	Protect kids
Rick	Alone early Monday morning 12:30-7 am	Lured her from lodge ... and met her at the abandoned road like before	Protect kids
Steve	Alone with Ashley Sunday night and Monday morning. Said he took sleeping pill	Didn't need to lure her from lodge	?—Has every reason to want Ashley alive
~~Boyfriend~~ ✗ Brad	????? Met Ashley at abandoned road	Lured her from lodge and ... attacked her	~~Jealousy?~~ <u>Ashley knows something she shouldn't?</u> ~~?????~~ Had an affair with her. Supported her with campaign finances?

Suspect	Opportunity	Means	Motive
Bruce	Set up meeting on abandoned road	Attacked her after Brad left?	Benefited from Brad's political office?
Troy	Seen near abandoned road	Attacked her after Brad left?	Blackmail Brad?

But no new revelations dawned on me as I studied it.

The unsettled feeling traveled with me all day, weighing on me, like the humidity that had sunk over the county. The sky was a marbled gray running from slate to pearl hinting at rain, but never delivering.

After work, I came home and found the kitchen quiet. Strangely quiet.

Gram stirred a jumble of colorful veggies and meat in a frying pan, but beside the sizzle of cooking food, the house was silent.

"Where are the boys?" I inhaled the salty aroma of hot soy sauce.

"At Jeanine's. They're having supper with them, so it's just you and me and Mal."

After a week of wall-to-wall kids, I could hardly believe so much peace was possible.

Dad arrived ten minutes later, and we sat down to the stir fry and Gram's homemade naan with a cherry chutney

Gram asked me about my day, and I told her, and she told me about hers, and Dad stayed silent, like the burden of the case had closed his mouth, except for receiving food.

Gram spooned chutney on the bread. "I'm going over to Jeanine's after supper, Rae, if you want to come along. Hank's giving Alli a riding lesson. He finally has time. The boys can play with Richard, and Carrie can watch Sylvie if Jason needs her to."

Dad stopped chewing. "Jason will be at Jeanine's? What about Rick?"

"I don't know about Rick. But Jason will definitely be there."

Swallowing, Dad toyed with his fork. "When's the lesson?"

I tore a round of naan in half. Why so interested?

"I think 7:30," said Gram. "What's wrong, sweetie?"

He scratched an eyebrow. "I'll go over with you."

Gram's puzzled look had to match my own. "What alarms you about Jason bringing his kids over?"

Staring at his plate, he released a pent-up breath. "This goes no further than this table."

"Of course." Gram laid her fork beside her plate.

I sat down my glass of water. "For sure."

Dad rested his elbows on the table. "I won't go into details, but I think Troy is blackmailing two people, someone besides Brad Schuster."

I mulled that over as Gram said, "Is this a deduction, or do you have proof?"

"I have almost conclusive proof, but it doesn't point to a particular person. It just indicates Troy is blackmailing someone else, and it has to be concerned with Ashley's death."

I said, "Troy saw someone else at the meeting Monday morning, someone who came with Senator Schuster?"

"If Brad had had anyone accompany him, he would've given me that name Sunday evening and insisted he or she was the killer. This is someone Brad doesn't know about, but someone who could be accused of the crime because Troy is blackmailing him. Or her."

"You think it could be Jason." Gram's voice dropped. "Or Rick."

"They're the most likely suspects. Jason's phone call to Ashley last Monday morning could've been to set up a meeting. Ashley suggested the old road because she knew where it was and was already meeting Schuster there. After Schuster left, Jason or Rick came and killed her."

"It could've been another boyfriend," I said. "No one knows how many Mrs. Carlisle had."

"True." He sighed again. "I don't like suspecting the Carlisle brothers. If they killed Ashley, they would do it out of a mistaken idea they're protecting the kids. It would crush those kids to lose their father and uncle."

I pushed peppers and broccoli around my plate, my stomach closing for business. The Carlisle kids had lost their mother forever. What would happen to them if Jason and Rick were guilty? Would they end up with a grandmother they barely knew?

Dad said, "I can't make a move until tomorrow. Once I nail Troy for collecting blackmail money from Brad, I'll have a way to pry the truth out of him. Until then ..." He spread his hands on the table. "I'll go watch Alli's lesson."

After I helped Gram and Dad clean up, I shouldered my backpack. "Going to take some pictures."

"Keep an eye on the weather." Dad shut the dishwasher. "We're supposed to get storms. They could be severe."

I couldn't tell as I followed the slope from the back of the house down to the woods lining the creek. The sky was the same twenty-seven shades of gray it had been all day, and the Ohio humidity had finally decided to copy its relative in the south. It didn't cling to my skin. It leeched through it, layering itself over my bones, making them sweat as I climbed the wooded hills to the west.

All the facts, all the clues, all the conversations twisted and collided as I tried to figure out what was bugging me about the case. A part of the puzzle that had snapped easily into its place wouldn't now. Which part was it?

Should I see if Egypt was home, try to get her to tell me if she saw anything in Conrad's room? But what could she have seen?

I still wanted to thank Walter and see if I could help him with any chores. I turned in that direction, the humidity tagging along like a thug waiting for a chance to attack.

When I emerged from the woods lining the drive to the ramshackle house, only Walter's truck and a battered, orange, four-door I didn't recognize were in sight.

I wavered by the woods, then marched toward the house.

I would never find Walter alone. If the owners of the orange car made trouble for me, Walter would stand up to them. The important thing was Troy was gone.

As I neared the house, Walter stomped onto the front porch, but since he didn't throw the screen door open, it was probably just his usual stiff way of walking.

He was on the grass before he noticed me. "What're you doing here?"

"I—I—I—" I cleared my throat. "I wanted to thank you again for rescuing me on—on Wednesday. And I wondered if I—I could help you around the house here as—as a thank you."

Walter had watched me with eyes of stone through my stutters. "How come? You're scared of me."

Despite the humidity, I froze. My manners fought with my fear to deny it, but Walter would know I was lying

More throat clearing needed. "Well, that's true." I forced a smile. "But I'm not scared as I used to be."

He still watched me. "You don't need to do nothin' for me."

"But—but I want to. I'd like to help my great-grandfather." I paused as a more convincing idea surfaced. "Malinowskis should help each other."

The left side of his mouth twitched, but nothing more. "I been working in the woods. You can help me clean up the tools. There's a storm comin'."

He stalked down the hill the little house sat on and stepped into the garage built underneath it, grabbing a baseball hat off a hook.

Egypt appeared out of the door that opened to the basement. "Jack wants whiskey, and he's getting mad that he can't find his car keys."

A rough chuckle scraped Walter's throat. "Tell him to come talk to me."

Lounging in the doorway, she said, "What's she doing here?"

"Ain't none of your business, but she's helping me."

"St. Mal won't like it." A sneer made her perpetual frown even more unattractive.

Before she could line up more insults, I said, "I was talking to Mr. Edwards yesterday, and he said you dealt a lot with Steve Conrad and Ashley Carlisle."

"Yeah. So?"

Hard to believe how much nastiness she could pack into two syllables.

"Well, he said Mr. Conrad accused you of snooping in his room, and I know you didn't." I had to add that because Egypt jerked upright and started to tremble, like she was boiling. "So does Mr. Edwards. But I thought if you happened to see anything that might help Dad's investigation of Mrs. Carlisle's death, you should tell him."

"I didn't see nothing 'cause I wasn't in his room." She spun her back to me and left.

If she was lying, I'd probably ruined any chance Dad had of getting it out of her.

Walter led me to a small clearing where he'd left a stack of wood, a chainsaw, an ax, and wedges. I took the tools to the garage and then carried the wood to the shelters where they would stay dry. A trickle of a breeze brushed against the long honeysuckle leaves.

"You better get home." Walter eyed the sky that had darkened to a uniform charcoal. "You might make it before the storm breaks if you leave now." He tucked the chainsaw under a shelf in the garage. "Mal know you come over?"

"No."

"Then don't tell him." He shoved a plastic bucket of wedges onto another shelf. "He'll have a fit. You're an adult and can do as you please, but you and him are off to a good start." He lowered his stony gaze to meet mine. "Don't mess it up."

"I can't." The sentence launched from me without a thought.

"What do ya mean, ya can't?" He squared himself to me, reminding me of just how formidable his size made him. "'Course you can. Just 'cause you're gettin' along now don't mean you always will."

He'd learned that with his mother. If they'd ever gotten along at all.

"That's true. We can do things the other person won't like." I rubbed my locket. "But that won't change our relationship."

"Sure it can. Nothin's set in cement if people are in it."

All my doubts about Dad and Troy and Mom came roaring back like a hurricane. And in the eye of that storm stood Dad's promise.

"No, it can't."

A faint rumble scurried out of the west.

"Dad said nothing would change it, and I believe him." About time I tried that, if for no other reason, because I hadn't yet. "Just like I know it's safe to come over if you're here. You're my great-grandfather, and nothing will change that."

He gave me an x-ray sweep of his deep-set eyes. Then he hung the ax on two prongs on the wall.

"Do you have my number?" I said. "You can call or text me if you'd like me to come over and help with something."

He grunted. "I don't think I got it."

I found a scrap of paper in my backpack, wrote my number, and handed it to him. "Thanks again."

He took the scrap and went to the basement door. "You're welcome." The phrase creaked, like Walter had unearthed it from a box in the back of the garage where it had sat unused for years.

He went inside.

Chapter Forty-Four

The clouds piling into a mountain range in the west weren't gray anymore. Just plain black. Lightning flickered at the horizon.

I broke into a jog, although getting soaked would feel refreshing, dissolving the tight sheath of humidity that had plastered over me.

I slowed as I neared the fox den, conversations and comments about the case cycling in my mind. Then I hiked up the short bank, pushed my way through the dense thickets on the flat stretch of ground, and at the edge of the ravine, stared down on the abandoned road. The strip of weed-infested gravel between the slopes was surprisingly dark for 8 p.m. on a June evening.

The wind pushed against me as I remembered the mint green convertible, where Coral directed Dad and me to stand on the road, the fight out on Molly's Bend.

Conrad: "So it's true. The cops have found something."

Jason: "How did you know?"

Conrad: "You've lived here your whole life and think anything's a secret? That obese clerk who keeps spreading lies about Ashley and me told me. The whole lodge should know by now. Did that brain dead sheriff call you instead of me?"

Jason: "A friend called me, and then a reporter from the paper did."

My muscles went rigid as a gust of wind grabbed my hair and flung it into my face.

Conrad said Mr. Edwards told him where the police had found the convertible.

But Mr. Edwards said he and his wife probably would have found it even if there hadn't been a pack of ghouls gaping at it, as if they'd gone looking for it. As if they didn't know where Ashley's body had been found.

Both statements could not be true.

Mr. Edwards had no reason to lie.

But Conrad did if he killed his fiancée.

But why?

Lightning winked again. Thunder rumbled closer, and the wind rattled the leaves of the surrounding pawpaws.

What if Conrad followed Ashley? He was already suspicious of her. Maybe the scratches on the bottom of her convertible made him wonder where she had been. Then she pushed sedatives and Scotch on him.

Suppose he only pretended to take the pill and the drink? He could have witnessed her interview with Brad Schuster and hadn't liked what he heard.

Dad said Conrad would go into salesman mode like he had with me outside the Barton branch. He'd let Schuster leave and then come out from hiding and talk to Ashley privately.

Privately.

That was the problem.

I wheeled and crashed through the understory plants to the fox den.

I had to tell Dad.

Sprinting when I could through the hilly terrain, I tore through the woods. A side stitch bit into my right side, but I ran against it. My heart hammering, I burst through the woods hemming in the alpaca pastures.

Outside the barn in the field with the female alpacas, Carrie and Sylvie swung open the door to let them inside.

A crack of thunder would've made me jump if I wasn't on a mission.

I climbed through the fence and pounded across the pasture, startling Carrie and most of the females wandering into the barn.

"Good grief, Rae." Carrie placed a hand to her chest as she held Sylvie on her hip.

The toddler laughed as she patted Amethyst on her pompom head. "Fwuffy. 'Pacas fwuffy."

"They sure are, sweat pea." Carrie bounced her a moment, making Sylvie giggle. "Rae, I thought you—"

"Is Dad here?" I placed my hands on my head to ease the side stitch.

"No, he's still at Jeanine's. Sylvie and I came to put the alpacas in before it storms. I wanted to save Ma the trouble. What's wrong?"

"Steve Conrad killed Mrs.—"

More giggles from Sylvie cut me off. Her big brown eyes crinkled in the corners as she tried to pat another alpaca.

"I have to talk to Dad." I ran to the next fence, squirmed through it, raced past the male alpacas, through another fence, and then headed up the hill to the house.

I'd reached the breezeway when the roar of an engine turned me around.

Headlights puncturing the growing gloom, a truck plowed up the drive and slammed to a stop in front of the barn.

Still holding Sylvie, Carrie stepped out of it.

My heart flew into my throat as lightning cracked the black clouds.

That wasn't a truck. It was a Hummer. And Steve Conrad had no reason to be here.

Carrie ran back into the barn.

Conrad hurtled out of the vehicle.

"*No!*" Dropping my backpack, I rocketed out of the breezeway.

Steve glanced at me, then darted into the barn.

I tore down the drive as a pop like a firecracker reached me.

Conrad ran out of the barn with Sylvie, who was shrieking, threw her into the Hummer, and then flew backward down the drive.

When I reached the barn, he'd disappeared onto the dead-end road.

Carrie staggered into the entrance, blood staining the right sleeve of her loose peach blouse.

Fear tightened my throat. "Are you shot?"

"Yes." She shoved her keys at me. "Get my Jeep. We're not losing him."

"But your arm—"

"Go." She pushed me with her good arm.

My lungs bursting against my ribs, I raced to Carrie's Jeep, slid the key into the ignition with shaking fingers, then shot down to the barn. Carrie had rolled up the blood-soaked right sleeve of her blouse and was clutching to her wound as she climbed in.

I pressed the gas to the floor.

We flew onto the dead end road, taking the turn so wide I scraped the right side of the Jeep on straggly bushes lining it.

"Whatever you do—" Carrie fished into her right pocket with her left hand "—don't lose them." She pulled out her phone.

Lightning splintered ahead, and thunder cracked like it hoped to break the sky. A waterfall dumped on us, blinding me.

"What are you slowing down for?" Carrie shouted.

"I can't see." I fumbled for the wipers.

"You know this road." She cranked a knob. "Floor it."

Windshield wipers working in a fury, I could just detect the red taillights of the Hummer.

"No reception." Carrie placed her left hand, which held her phone, on the dash. "This is insane. Why is he doing this? It only makes sense if ..." her voice dropped "... if he knows Sylvie is his."

I whipped my head to her. "How could he? He hasn't been near Sylvie to—"

"Eyes on the road." The order came in a bark.

I obeyed, gripping the steering wheel tighter. "You haven't let him near Sylvie."

The Hummer turned to the left, and when I reached the intersection, I skidded around the corner.

"He must have gotten a sample at church that Sunday she got away from Jason," said Carrie. "That church is wide open. All the outside doors were unlocked when I went to mass with the Carlisles. Prince Charming must've sneaked in by a side door and then grabbed Sylvie and took a sample." She glanced at her phone. "I've got a signal."

We shot up the hill onto a ridge. The Hummer disappeared over the descending side.

Carrie yelled into her phone. "This is Carrie Malinowski. We are chasing Steve Conrad because he kidnapped Sylvie Carlisle. We are heading south on Sutton Ridge Road." She reported the make, model, and license number of the vehicle. "We will maintain pursuit. Mal and Jason Carlisle are at Jeanine's house."

Roaring down from the ridge, I glimpsed the taillights turning right.

"We're turning off Sutton Ridge," Carrie told the dispatcher.

I veered onto the new road, and she fell into me.

"We took the first right at the bottom of the hill." Still holding the phone to her ear, Carrie righted herself. "No, it doesn't have a sign post."

The road had a sharp bend, and I skidded into the wet weeds, pulling around it. Thunder rolled like a giant truck was racing above us.

Again, a hint of red light through the walls of rain was my only sign of the Hummer, and I followed them onto a gravel road.

"Lost signal." Carrie pressed her left hand against the dash. "Prince Charming won't have an empire for his heir to inherit if he's doing time for kidnapping. This is completely stupid."

"I think—" I plunged down the road "—he's escaping before the cops figure out he killed Mrs. Carlisle and Troy bleeds him dry. He decided to take Sylvie with him."

"What are you talking about? Troy's blackmailing Brad Schuster."

"Dad said at supper he thinks there's a second blackmail victim. It's Mr. Conrad."

"Do you have proof?"

I crested a short hill. Carrie glanced at her phone and then held the dash again.

The rain let up a little, and I pressed the gas pedal farther, explaining that Conrad lied about how he ended up at Molly's Bend on Friday.

The Hummer made a quick right.

"Good grief," Carrie said in a breath. "So Conrad came back to the crime scene, maybe to get something else to plant on Jason, and when he saw everybody, he had to create an excuse for being there."

"I think so. Or maybe he was looking for clues to who the blackmailer was if he'd received a note from Troy by then."

I braked, and we slid around a turn on slick gravel.

"But what's his motive?"

"I think it was an accident. I've seen Mr. Conrad angry, and every time, when he realized he wasn't alone with whoever he was mad at, he'd laugh at them. On that abandoned road, in the middle of nowhere, when Mr. Schuster left Mrs. Carlisle, there was nobody to keep Mr. Conrad from unleashing his anger on her."

"Except for Troy, and he wouldn't help anybody but himself."

The gravel road we followed was barely wider than the car. Arching over the road, the trees formed a green tunnel. The headlights revealed no vehicle in front of us.

"He must be lost or trying to shake us." Carrie swayed beside me. "He has to get out of the county, and he's got to know these rough roads won't lead him out."

I chanced a peek at her. Her complexion had turned a dull gray. Mom looked like that when she was in severe pain.

We flew through the rain in the growing dark over a rise. A stop sign reared up in my headlights. Screeching to a halt, I looked both ways on the gravel road we'd dead-ended into.

No lights to the left or right.

Growling, Carrie shoved open her door and got out. The rain drenching her, she squinted down both sides of the intersection, pressing the sleeve over her wound.

She got back in the Jeep. "Turn around. He must've turned onto one of the two roads we passed, maybe to wait us out. We weren't this far behind him. We should be able to see his lights. The road's fairly straight."

I wheeled the Jeep around and roared back the way we came.

Father, let us find him.

"We are not losing Sylvie." Carrie spoke as if countering a statement I'd raised. "I haven't tracked drug dealers through the hills of Mexico to lose a baby on my home turf. Turn right."

Although the rain had slackened to a shower, I almost missed a dent in the forest, revealing a lane.

I began to turn, and headlights came flying toward me.

Chapter Forty-Five

A vehicle—a truck—smashed into the Jeep's right front fender, slamming me into the door and Carrie into me.

The other vehicle backed away.

"Block the road." Carrie leaped out.

I shoved the pedal to the floor, but the Jeep only whined forward by inches.

The headlights raced in.

Throwing the Jeep into neutral, I threw myself onto the wet gravel and weeds. The truck smashed the front fender again.

Carrie shouted something as I scrambled to my feet.

Thunder and lightning combined into one blinding explosion, and I ran toward Carrie.

An old man in a baseball cap and crooked beard catapulted out of the driver's side.

Carrie rushed him.

The old man was Conrad. He swung his right arm around.

"He's got a gun!" I screamed as lightning forked above us.

Grabbing the hand, Carrie slammed him into the opening of the truck and head-butted him, full in the face, the cap flying off and the beard falling away from one side of his jaw.

"Get Sylvie," she shouted. "And my gun."

Her gun? Where? I ran between the vehicles as Carrie rammed her knee into Conrad's groin.

The lights were on in the truck. Sylvie sat strapped in a car seat, her brown eyes bulging from underneath a baseball cap, glued to the battle going on outside the open driver's door.

I jerked on the handle on the passenger door. Locked.

Spinning around and getting slapped across my face with strands of wet hair, I scanned the ground for something heavy.

But the shattered glass would cut Sylvie.

A howl came from Conrad as he collapsed to the ground.

Carrie lurched toward the Jeep. "I'll get the gun. You get Sylvie."

No one was blocking the driver's side.

I slid across the hood of the truck and leaped into the cab.

Sylvie wore a Star Wars shirt. She hadn't been wearing that or the cap at the barn.

I unsnapped buckles, lifted her from the seat, and pulled her out of the cab.

"Get up the hill." Carrie had propped something — it must have been her gun — on top of the open door of her Jeep, surveying the woods beyond the illumination of the headlights.

Conrad was nowhere to be seen.

"Get across the road, Rae, and up the hill. Wait for me there."

Pressing Sylvie close to me, I ran around the Jeep. The hillside dropped at an almost vertical angle beside the road. Grasping at honeysuckle, I propelled us up the slope, dead leaves making me slip. I struggled to get under the trees where their top branches would give us some relief from the rain.

In the gloom of the woods, I spotted a fallen log and dropped onto it.

During the entire climb, Sylvie hadn't made a sound. Shouldn't she be crying or something?

Branches broke below us.

I got to my feet, straining my eyes against the dark.

Then the Branson yodel, hoarse but clear, came to me.

Releasing a huge breath, I sat down again and called back.

The canopy reduced the rain to a drizzle.

A struggling form grunted and crashed up to us.

Switching Sylvie to my left hip, I skidded a few yards below the log, and Carrie fell through a thicket of honeysuckle.

I caught her under her good arm and helped her to the log.

For a minute, we just gasped. Sylvie rested her head against my chest, silent.

"Is Sweet Pea okay?" Carrie managed between pants.

"She's really quiet. Mr. Conrad seems to have tried to disguise her."

"What?" Carrie flipped on the light of her phone and shone it over the little girl, who watched her without a word.

Carrie removed the cap. Sylvie's rich brown hair hung in jagged hanks. The halo of illumination also revealed that the left side of Carrie's face was swollen and blood stained the corner of her mouth.

"That — that — what are you doing?" Carrie said as I placed Sylvie in her lap.

"I've got to fix your arm." I started to untie my denim shirt from my waist.

"Use my shirt. You'll need yours to carry Sylvie. Be quick. Don't pull the sleeve off my right arm. Just wrap the rest of the shirt around it."

I helped her slide her left arm out of the blouse and bumped her knee. She flinched.

"Is your leg hurt?" I ripped the left sleeve from her blouse.

"Not as bad as Prince Charming's knee."

As I wrapped the rest of her blouse around her wound, she said through teeth so tight I could barely catch the words, "I think I know why Conrad didn't kill me in the barn. He wanted me to report he'd snatched Sylvie in the Hummer. Then he switched vehicles, disguised himself and Sylvie, and planned to drive out of the county."

"I'll tie the sleeve around the rest of your shirt to hold it in place." I bit my lip. "It'll probably hurt."

"Make it tight." Carrie gripped the log with her good hand.

I passed the sleeve over itself and slowly tightened. Shudders rippled through Carrie, her eyes and mouth squeezed into threads.

"Is it too much?"

"No." It was just a grunt.

I knotted the sleeve and turned off the flashlight.

Carrie wobbled, as if the strengthening wind was pushing her one way, then another.

"I'll check and see if one of the cars—"

"They're not drivable." Her voice was dull. "My Jeep and the truck are jammed tight, and they're blocking the road for the Hummer. I'm pretty sure that road dead ends at Devil's Creek, so he can't get out the other end. You gotta go. Tie your denim shirt around Sylvie to give you some support."

As I sat Sylvie on my lap and untied my soaked shirt from my waist, Carrie went on, her words slow and thick. "Prince Charming may try to get out of here while he can or he may try to get Sylvie back. He thinks I have a gun."

"You don't?"

"I haven't needed a gun for this job. Kidnapping wasn't supposed to be a threat. I yelled I had one after I knocked his gun out of his hand, hoping I'd make him take off. Which he did. But he might find his gun."

"But I saw you with a gun."

"Just my phone. Do you have yours?"

"I—uh—no. It's in my backpack." I tied the sleeves of my shirt behind Sylvie's back. "If I carry her in my left arm, I can support you—"

"I'm not going with you."

"What?" Freezing prickles crawled down my face, and it wasn't the rain.

"Shut up." The wind seemed to buffet Carrie. "We can't let Conrad see or hear us. We've had the light on too long. Look. I'll slow you down. Besides, I can leave a false trail."

"But you've lost blood." My gut got a hollow feeling, like fear was scraping it out. "I can't leave you all alone."

Carrie laid her hand on mine and clutched it. "Only one thing matters: getting Sylvie home. You got me?"

"B—b—but ..." I started to shake.

"I'm counting on you. So's Sylvie. And the whole Carlisle family." She released my hand. "I'll walk along the road, the way we came. That's the route Conrad will expect us to take. You stay high on the hillside. Keep the down slope on your right. If you do that, you won't get lost. When you get to the intersection, turn left. There are drives along that stretch of the road. Go to the first house you find. Keep checking the phone for a signal. Repeat what I said."

I did in a whisper. "How will we find you if I take the phone?"

"I'll follow the same path you're taking, just by the road. Unless I need to double back, that's where you'll find me."

Father, what's going to happen? Don't let Carrie die.

She grabbed me by the shoulder. "God goes with you, Rae. Even if you think you can't do it, He can. And He'll be with me, so I'm not alone. Go." She handed me the phone.

My knees trembling, I stood, placing my left arm under Sylvie's bottom. "Are you sure I can't help you if—"

"Go." She put so much force behind it I flinched. Struggling to her feet, she kissed Sylvie, who made no sound.

My heart collapsing on itself, I said, "I'll be back as soon as I can."

"I know you will." She limped straight down the slope. "Get higher up, then follow the direction of the road. Use the flashlight only when you have to."

My mud-caked sandals dragged as I put inches, then feet, then yards between us and Carrie.

I swallowed tears.

I can't help her, Father. You have to.

Chapter Forty-Six

The wind pushed whatever debris that wasn't drenched down the hillside, making it sound like an army of squirrels seeking cover from the storm.

Thunder grumbled, issuing a warning of worse things to come.

Sylvie stiffened against me.

"Thunder won't hurt us, Sylvie."

I climbed higher, then stopped and checked the phone. No signal.

I shoved the phone into my back pocket and rushed on, stepping, slipping, squeezing Sylvie to me as I crossed the slope, perpendicular to it. The rumbles continued like a pack of angry wolves regrouping for another attack.

I can't do this, Father. What if Conrad attacks? What if I get lost? I can't let Sylvie and Carrie down. It's too much. I can't help them. I can't help anybody.

My right leg skidded out from under me completely, and I fell on my backside, Sylvie jarring against my chest.

Something rattled behind us.

I flipped around, yanked out the phone, and turned on the its light.

Father, I need You. I need You right now.

I shone the beam up and down the hillside. Few understory plants here. The trees near us had wider trunks with thicker canopies blocking the sun and, right now, the rain.

Sylvie didn't move, breathing against my soaked sleeveless shirt.

Holding the light near her face, I dredged up a cheerful tone, "This rain is lousy, isn't it? I'm going to get you out of the rain and take you to your daddy."

Her big brown eyes met mine, as if trying to determine if I told the truth.

Father, hold me together for her sake.

I dragged myself to my feet.

I know You'll help us, Father, because — because ...

Rushing across the hillside under the bigger trees, I tried to remember the Bible verses I'd copied on mercy.

A crash came behind us. I picked up speed.

Not a single verse came to me.

"We'll be out of the storm soon, Sylvie."

A roar like a waterfall competed with the drumbeat of the rain on the overhead leaves.

Father, You are merciful. I'm counting on that. Have mercy on us.

I turned on the light again.

A few feet ahead was a gash in the slope, rainwater gushing through it.

No way to cross here.

I faced uphill. Higher up, the water had less land to cross and less time to join into a torrent.

I scrambled up the slope, dead leaves and mud squishing through my sandals.

You are merciful, Father. Have mercy on us.

The cascading water became slower, more shallow as I climbed. When it lessened to a swift stream, I turned the light on the ground and found a thick stick. Supporting us with the stick in my right hand, I stepped into the current.

Cool water streamed through my sandals. Trying to feel the uneven rocks with my feet, I stepped, steadied us with the stick, then stepped again. A year later, we reached the other side. I dropped the stick and ran down the slope, then turned perpendicular to it again.

Thank You, Father.

Pounding through the thickening dark as the trees tossed their heads, we popped out on a clear corner of the hillside.

Corner?

Below us, just visible, were iron gray bands alleviating the charcoal gray woods.

We'd reached the intersection.

"It won't be long now, Sylvie."

You are merciful. Have mercy.

Slipping, sliding, using my free hand to catch us before we wiped out entirely, I shadowed the road below.

Thunder unleashed, and the wooded hillside lit up like we were under the climax of a Fourth of July celebration.

Sylvie trembled in my arms.

"We'll get out of this soon."

Darkness merged the trees into a black wall.

More detonations, more flashes of lightning like a dawn that lasted only seconds.

"There's got to be a house somewhere close, Sylvie. There's got to be."

You are merciful, have mercy on us.

The wind mustered strength, ripping a limb from a tree that spewed debris as it hit the hillside.

I jumped, lost my footing, but fell against a tree trunk.

"We'll make it." I broke into a run. "We'll make it."

I raced into a clearing and collided with a sapling—no, a post.

I whipped out the phone's flashlight, which showed that the post belonged to a clothesline.

Hugging Sylvie, I shone the light in a panorama.

Down a steeply pitched back yard sat a two-story house.

"We made it." I ran to it, flung back the screen door, and pounded. "We need help."

No answer. The house appeared completely dark.

I pounded again, the little roof over the door providing small cover from the increasing rain and wind.

There couldn't be anyone at home.

Standing sideways to the door, I turned Sylvie's face away from it and punched a hole in the small pane of glass near the knob with the phone. I swiped the phone around the opening, knocking out the remaining shards of glass. Then I reached inside and unlocked the door.

We tumbled inside, and I fell back against the door, closing it, clutching Sylvie. "You're safe. Let's get you dry."

Thank You, Father, for getting us here.

I flipped the switch by the door, but the room stayed dark.

I checked the phone. One bar reception. If I went upstairs, I might get more.

Turning on the flashlight, I avoided an oval table loaded with unwashed plates, half-filled cups, and at one end, several pieces of mail. I set down the phone and read the addresses: Howard Oller, 67926 Devil's Creek Road.

This had to be Bean Oller, who cleared snow from the library parking lot.

"It won't be long now, Sylvie. You'll see Daddy soon."

At the front of the house, a set of stairs came down by the front door. I hiked past clothes piled on the steps and found a cluttered bathroom right beside the head of the stairs.

Laying the phone on the sink, the light beaming upward, I discovered towels in a skinny cupboard beside the tub.

I untied my shirt and laid Sylvie on the floor. Her cheeks were cold, her eyes closed, but as I removed the sopping wet clothes and rubbed her dry, she opened them a few times.

Leaving her wrapped in a towel, I went to the bedrooms in search of dry clothes.

The Oller family appeared to have no one younger than ten living in the house. I took a t-shirt with an American flag on it and pulled it over Sylvie like a dress. Then I wrapped her in a comforter, decorated with neon racing cars, I'd pulled off a twin bed.

I had a lot to explain to the Ollers.

Fingers trembling, I dialed 911. I'd have to dry off soon.

When the dispatcher asked for the location of the emergency, I gave her the Ollers' address and said, "This is Rae Riley. I have Sylvie Carlisle."

"Thank You, Lord," Gloria Helmick said. "Mal and every officer in the county have been going crazy trying to find you. Someone will be there shortly."

Lights outside drew me to the small window that viewed the front of the house. The Ollers must have just pulled in.

Through the driving rain, I saw a truck parked on the drive, but the hood pointed toward the road, like it had just come out of the garage. A person ran around the hood.

I dropped the phone, my throat swelling.

The headlights didn't show much, but it was enough.

Steve Conrad had found us.

Chapter Forty-Seven

I backed from the window.

Father, we were so close. So close.

"Rae?" Gloria's voice came from the phone on the floor. "Did something happen?"

I creeped up to the window, compelling myself to look out.

He was gone, but the truck on the drive was running.

I dropped to my knees.

What do I do? What do I do? I thought You were merciful.

"Rae? Rae?"

I looked at Sylvie. Her long dark lashes lay on her cheeks as she sucked two fingers. I touched her cheeks. They had warmed.

The boiling panic subsided and became as still as glass.

You said You're merciful. So You are.

I got to my feet.

Just tell me what to do.

I ran to the head of the stairs, listening.

With no appliances running, the house was silent. I would have heard Conrad, despite the storm, if he'd gotten in yet.

All I had to do was slow him down. A cop was coming. Conrad could only approach us by the stairs. They dropped down to the front door like the ones at home. The ones at home ...

I darted into the kids' bedroom, reached under the fitted sheet, and jerked the mattress from the frame. I wedged it in the stairwell, my wrestling match with the twin mattress at home reminding me how hard it can be to maneuver a mattress. Then I jammed a second one above it.

Now weapons. Teachers told us during intruder drills at school that anything can be a weapon.

In the bathroom, I pulled out drawers from the sink.

"Rae, are you there?" said the voice on the phone.

I hadn't hung up?

I picked up the phone. "Steve Conrad is here. I'll hold him off as long as I can."

"Oh—uh—I'll stay on the line."

A door creaked below.

"Rae?" My name drifted up from the dark depths of the house.

I went to a bedroom and pulled out drawers from a desk.

"She's my daughter, Rae."

Slow, uneven steps dragged across the first floor.

I stacked the drawers at the head of the stairs.

"I've got thousands of dollars with me. I can give you some. Just give me Sylvie."

I grabbed drawers from a dresser.

"I hot-wired an old truck I found on the drive. We'll be gone in seconds."

Panting, I hauled more drawers into the upstairs hall.

Why was he talking? Why not just charge up the stairs and—he might not have a gun. And he couldn't know if I had one.

"I know you're up there."

I leaned one eye past the wall beside the stairs.

He wasn't visible. Just the shadowy outline of the front door.

If I could keep him talking, that would delay him even more. Maybe I could get him talking about Ashley's death. Dad needed some kind of proof.

I retrieved the phone from the bathroom. "Keep listening," I whispered.

Setting the phone on the flat top of the railing, I said, "I won't give Sylvie to a murderer."

"I'm no murderer."

"I know you killed Mrs. Carlisle."

"You can't know—you're the blackmailer!" His roar smacked me, and a dark figure charged up the stairs.

I grabbed the first drawer I'd taken from the sink.

"You know, I didn't mean to." He pushed the first mattress aside. "You know I didn't mean to knock her off that cliff when I hit her."

I flung the contents of the drawer at his face.

He fell against the railing.

I threw the drawer at him. It slammed into his head.

He howled and skittered down the stairs.

As he moaned on the bottom step, I said, "I'm not the blackmailer. But I know you came to Molly's Bend when you couldn't have known where we'd found her car unless you'd killed her."

"That fat clerk told me." He gasped between each word.

"No, he didn't. I talked to him yesterday. He didn't know the location of the scene of the crime until Sunday." I picked up another drawer. "Why did you hit her?"

"You were there. You heard the skinny senator propose marriage, and she said she'd think it over. Think it over!" He hit the railing.

"If it was an accident, why didn't you go to the police?"

"In Carlisle's county?" His laugh was unsteady. "They'd never believe me, and I'd get charged with murder." He grabbed both railings at the bottom of the stairs. "You don't have a gun."

"Neither do you. And I'm not hurt."

"You're the blackmailer." He took a step. "I wish I could have seen your face when you went to get my money today and found nothing."

He bolted upward.

I tossed the contents of a drawer.

He ducked.

I threw the drawer.

He jerked to the side.

But the second drawer I heaved knocked him off balance, and he fell past the mattresses to the bottom.

Resting my hands on my knees, I groped for air.

Give me strength, Father.

Groaning, Conrad pulled himself vertical with the bottom post. "What's in this for you? Do you think Jason will reward you for keeping her from me? I can give her everything. Jason will never do that when he finds out she's mine?"

His panting sounded like a dying dog. Then his dark outline twisted, as if something had poked him. He limped out of sight.

My ears tried to grow out from my head. Conrad must have heard something. What?

Swearing flew up the stairs. "She's mine. I'll get her. I'll rebuild my empire and come back for her." He crashed through the house, shoving furniture across linoleum and banging them into walls.

There it was. Below the rain's drumbeat, the hum of another engine joined the one from the truck on the drive.

The back door shut with a crack.

I rushed into the bathroom, stepping over Sylvie, and looked out the window.

An SUV, headlights shining on the house, rolled to a stop in front of the running truck.

I slid to the floor.

You did it, Father. You did it.

Chapter Forty-Eight

"Conrad," Dad shouted as thunder nearly drowned out his call.

I struggled to stand. My muscles had turned to spaghetti. I opened the small window.

Laying his arms over the hood of the SUV, Dad had his pistol trained at the house.

"Dad, he left by the back door. He's limping, so you might catch him." I trembled, and it had nothing to do with being soaking wet.

"Are you all right?" The rain and the dark blurred the world, but I could still see Dad's relieved smile.

"Yes. He doesn't have a gun."

Somebody slammed out of the passenger side of the SUV.

"I know," Dad yelled back as he ran around the house. "Gloria told me."

Gloria!

I returned to the hall and picked up the phone from the railing. "Gloria, Dad's here."

"I know. Hayley had Mal on the other line. She's been relaying information from me to him and him to me."

Frantic pounding hit the front door.

I worked my way through the wreckage on the stairs. "Did you hear what Conrad said?"

"I heard everything you said. I sometimes lost Conrad's words. But the call is recorded. We can review it."

I opened the door, and Jason burst in. "Where is she?"

"Upstairs. Thank you, Gloria."

"Just doing my job." She clicked off.

"Sylvie's fine." I led Jason to the bathroom. "She got cold in the rain, but she's warmed up. She just seems exhausted."

Jason picked up the bundle from the floor.

Sylvie murmured something, then snuggled deeper into the comfort.

"Oh, sweetheart. You're okay, you're ..." He choked, pressing her head against his cheek.

"Mr. Conrad tried to disguise her as a boy." Holding up the flashlight, I explained how Conrad had cut Sylvie's hair, changed her shirt, and traded vehicles.

Jason ricocheted between cradling his daughter and gaping. "Mal must be right. He said Conrad would only make this move if he'd had Sylvie tested and knew she was his."

"Carrie thinks he sampled her at the church when she got away from you."

"That's the only time I can think of." He kissed Sylvie on the forehead and then whipped his head from side to side. "Where's Carrie?"

My trembling grew fiercer. "She's out there." I told him how Carrie had acted as bait.

"She did that injured?" Jason's voice was barely a whisper. "Chris reported finding blood at the barn. Mal and I hoped it was Conrad's."

"We've got to find her." I backed out of the bathroom. "I need to get dry."

"Go ahead. I'll tell Mal Carrie isn't here."

I went to Mr. and Mrs. Oller's bedroom.

Jason shouted from the room next door. Must have been out the window. "Carrie's not here. We have to find her."

Mrs. Oller was a lot shorter than me. Her sweatpants hung on me like capris. I grabbed a man's t-shirt and hoodie from a dresser.

In the bathroom, I wiped off with some dry towels, changed into the borrowed clothes, and wadded up my wet ones. Racing out of the house, I found Dad beside the Ollers' truck.

Jason was cradling Sylvie in the front passenger seat, kissing her plump cheek as I leaped into the back seat.

Stroking her face, he said, "I think she's unconscious. I carried her out here, and she didn't wake up."

"She opened her eyes a few times while I got her dry."

A light flashed inside the cab of the old truck as the windshield wiper on the SUV whipped uselessly against the pouring rain.

Dad popped the hood, worked under it a minute, and then ran to the SUV with two backpacks and threw them onto the seat beside me. "Are you okay, Rae? Really?"

"Yes. You couldn't catch Conrad?"

Dad slammed into his seat. "Never saw him. After Jason told me he shot Carrie—" the words fought through his teeth—"he doesn't matter anymore. But I've got his money and passports. And I removed the rotor from under the distributor cap. He's not getting out that way."

Jason repeated in a hollow voice, "Passports?"

"How bad is Carrie hurt?" Dad flew down the drive backwards.

"Conrad shot her in the arm," I said. "I think it's broken. He hurt her knee, and the left side of her face is swollen." My guts turned to icy slush, and tremors pulsed through me. "I—I couldn't help her and Sylvie too. She told me to leave her. I—I didn't want to but ..."

"You did the right thing, Rae. Carrie was in charge, and you had to listen to her." Dad squealed onto Devil's Creek Road. "Which way do I go?"

"You're heading in the right direction. Take the first right. Carrie said she'd follow that road to the intersection."

Dad braked. "Watch the sides of the road. See if she's made it this far."

"You take the left, Rae," said Jason. "I'll take the right. What did you mean about passports, Mal?"

But Dad had picked up his radio. "Kincaid, where are you?"

"Can't get to you, Mal. There's a tree down on Devil's Creek Road. I'm trying to remove it. It's the only way you can get out of here. Phelps tried to come in from the other end, and it's flooded."

"Get all the help you can." Dad also updated the alert for Steve Conrad.

The tympani-pound on the roof softened as Dad had slowed the SUV. "Passports. Conrad had those two backpacks in Ollers' truck. One was full of cash. The other had clothes for both him and Sylvie and two passports. They must have cost him a fortune. He was disguised in his photo, and Sylvie had a boy's name. He owns a plane. He must've planned to fly her out of the county."

"He had more than that planned." My gaze glued to the dark woods, I told him about Conrad switching vehicles and what he said about rebuilding his empire.

"I can't believe it." Although it didn't seem possible, Jason held Sylvie closer.

"It might have worked." Dad's voice was low. "If he'd gotten out of the county, away from people who know Sylvie, with the disguises and the change in vehicles, he might have made it to his plane."

"I'm so sorry." Jason's tone was hushed, horrified. "I never, ever thought kidnapping was a danger. If I had, I know Carrie would have taken different precautions."

"Sylvie wasn't in that kind of danger until Conrad received the blackmail note." Dad's head swiveled from his window to Jason's.

I blinked and then refocused my eyes on the passing tree trunks. "You know he's the second blackmail victim? Then you know he killed Mrs. Carlisle." I pointed to the right. "Here."

Dad swung the SUV onto the gravel road. "I don't know anything. It's just what Jason and I discussed while trying to find you all. Conrad would only jeopardize his empire if he was under extreme pressure. The only pressure I could think of was his guilt from killing Ashley. He tried to frame Jason and called an anonymous tip to Simcox, but something happened to the evidence he planted. Then he got the blackmail note. Caught between the cops and a hard place, Conrad decided to clear out." He glanced back at me through the plastic partition. "We'll have to review the recording to learn how much of Conrad's confession we got." His tone shrank. "When Hayley reported what Gloria said Conrad was saying, I knew he had no intention of leaving you alive."

I huddled in the sweatshirt.

Jason's lips moved, but no words came out. Then he said, "Rae, did he tell you why he killed her? It seems too dumb for him to do."

"They were alone," I said. "Every time I saw Mr. Conrad get angry, an outsider appeared to rein him in." I explained what happened outside the theater and in Barton. "And when he and Egypt were ready to go at it, Mr. Edwards appeared. The senator must have left the meeting first. When Ashley was alone, Mr. Conrad couldn't control himself, and with no one around, he didn't have to."

"She must have been running away from him, and he caught up with her," said Dad. "He struck her, and not realizing where they were, she fell over the—" He stomped on the brakes, throwing me against the partition.

"What's ..." The word died in my mouth.

Where the road had been, a lake churned in front of us.

Chapter Forty-Nine

"Oh, no," said Jason in a gulp.

Dad leaned on the steering wheel, peering between the frantic wipers. "Are you sure this is the right road, Rae?"

"Absolutely. She's out there. She'll be on the right side, on the hill, the way I came."

Dad flipped a switch, and the lake blazed brighter. Spotlights on the vehicle's light bar reached farther than the headlights.

"There!" Jason and I yelled, flinging out our hands.

A human figure lay on a nearly sheer slope, either tangled in or clutching a bush. The flood waters swirled around her legs up to her knee. The figure made no movement.

My stomach lurched, and I slapped a hand over my mouth.

Dad backed the SUV.

"What are you doing?" I yelled.

"The water is rising." He said it so quietly that he didn't sound like himself. "Rae, you sit here while I get Carrie. Keep the SUV out of the water."

We both got out, and then I sat behind the wheel.

"I'll help." Jason opened his door and laid Sylvie in her cozy cocoon onto the seat.

"Stay here. No argument." Dad went around to the back of the SUV and opened the hatch.

Jason joined him, shouting over a clap of thunder, "On that slippery slope, you may need help."

I twisted in the driver's seat to look back. "Dad, there's a ravine with rushing water in it. I had to climb up high to cross the stream where it was still small. You may need help to get Carrie over it."

Dad stared at Jason as the rain poured over them. "You do exactly what I say, Carlisle, when I say it. Got it?"

"Perfectly."

Dad pulled a rope, a shotgun, and flashlights from the back and shut the hatch. He came around to my side. "Get out."

As soon as I stepped out, he draped his raincoat on me and handed me the shotgun. "It's live. Fire it like your rifle. I don't think Conrad has followed us, but he's proved he's lost his mind. Stay out here and watch for him and the water."

"Be careful." I hugged him.

He kissed me on my soaked hair, then handed Jason a flashlight.

They ran up the slope, Jason slipping after two steps, but he scrambled to his feet, and they raced out of the wide circle of light.

Holding the shotgun across me, I looked to Carrie on the slope.

The water lapped above her knee. She hadn't moved an inch, a mud-coated form, half-hidden by the bush. She was either too injured or too exhausted to save herself.

Sylvie slept on, wrapped in the racing car comforter.

Father, have mercy. Don't let us come this far and lose Carrie.

The waters chopped against her leg like a thousand piranhas jockeying for the first bite.

I placed the shotgun in the backseat and reversed the SUV a few feet.

When I got out, Dad and Jason were nowhere in sight.

My breathing sped up, and I looked to Carrie.

Her right leg moved. Maybe she was conscious enough—no. The swirling water was tugging on her, pushing her leg. It could rise high enough to sweep her away before Jason and Dad got to her.

A scream fought for release.

Don't let her die, don't let her die, don't let her—

Somebody slid down—Jason!—slid down the steep slope, stopping his descent by straddling the bush. He plunged his arms through the tangled branches and pulled Carrie up against him, lifting her clear of the water.

I sank to my knees, something between a scream and a laugh erupting from me.

In a minute, a rope flopped on top of Jason, and he wrapped it under Carrie's arms.

He yelled something, but rolling thunder drowned him out and lightning lit up the scene better than a hundred of Dad's spotlights. The flash revealed Dad pulling on the rope, which was tied around a tree.

The rope went taut, pulling Carrie, as Jason crawled beside her, one hand on the rope, the other under her right arm.

I backed up the SUV again.

Dad reached a thick arm into the beam from the spotlights and grabbed Carrie. He and Jason carried her out of view.

Gripping the wheel, I laid my head on it and shook until my teeth felt loose.

She'll be okay, won't she, Father? She's safe now.

Making a cooing sound, Sylvie stretched a little, rolled onto her side, and kept sleeping.

Getting out, I checked on the water's progress and reversed the SUV back toward the intersection.

Lights bobbed far up the hillside, and under the never-ending pound of the rain, crashing steps came to me.

Finally, Dad and Jason appeared among the shiny trunks, smeared with mud from their faces to their shoes. Dad held Carrie, and Jason carried the flashlights. Turning sideways, Jason hiked down the hillside first, right in front of Dad. He reached back and steadied Dad each time he started to lose his footing.

I opened the back door, and Dad laid Carrie on the hard, plastic seat. He said, "Try to hold her still. I'll get blankets and bandages. Wrap clean bandages around her wound and tie her arm to her body so it doesn't move."

I crouched on the floor by the backseat, and Jason settled Sylvie in his lap.

Carrie looked dead. She had that awful, unnatural stillness that gripped Mom when her pain grew beyond endurance.

Dad shoved a first aid kit and two space blankets at me and placed a wad of cloth under Carrie's head.

As I spread the blankets, Dad got in and roared back to Devil's Creek Road, shouting into his radio, "Kincaid, that tree had better be out of our way 'cause I'm not stopping for it."

Chapter Fifty

Sirens screaming, the SUV flew past what might have been the Ollers' drive as I unspooled a stretchy bandage.

Hooking the receiver, Jason said, "Gloria said she'd notify everyone we're heading for Mercy Hospital." He rubbed a grimy hand on his pants.

Focused straight ahead, Dad said, "How's Sylvie?"

"Still asleep. Or unconscious." Holding her close to his face, he kissed her.

I wrapped the bandage around Carrie's wrist and tied it to a belt loop on her shorts. Her breath quivered.

"I owe you, Carlisle." Dad's voice shook. "If you hadn't grabbed Carrie while I was tying the rope, the water might have swept her away before I could use the rope to reach her."

"You owe me?" A laugh twittered in his throat and then swelled to a full-fledged roar. "Rae's saved my brother, Carrie and Rae have saved my daughter—I think I'll be in your family's debt until I die." His laughter quieted. "I'm glad I could pay you back."

"Rae, tell me if Carrie wakes up at all," said Dad. "What happened at the farm?"

Bracing Carrie as best I could, I explained everything that had happened since I'd realized Conrad had lied the day we found Ashley's body.

We shot onto a road with streetlights. Lightning stretched from one horizon to another.

My knees ached from my awkward position, and I finally thought to say, "I'm sorry, Jason." That was rather vague when so much had happened. "About Sylvie and Ashley."

"You don't have to be about Ashley." He sighed. "She was going away with Brad. I can't believe she left me—well, yes, I can believe she left me for Brad. What I can't believe is how Brad approached me over the past two years for campaign donations."

"You don't know that was her intention." Dad veered around a car that had pulled over to let him pass. "Brad and Conrad both said she wanted to think it over. You can believe two independent sources. I think she was genuinely torn between him and your offer of parole."

"Parole?" I said.

Dad took a turn tight, and I spread my arms to hold Carrie in place.

She hadn't even murmured.

"That's why Jason wanted to talk to me that evening. Ashley asked if she could come back, and Jason didn't know what to do. So we worked out a parole: Jason would help her get an apartment and a job and then she had to support herself for a year and stay sober. He'd contact her regularly, and if she lasted a year, they could discuss her seeing the kids."

"I really didn't want to get entangled with Ashley again, but—well, after reading that book in the Bible, I felt maybe I owed it to her and the kids." Jason wiped a spot of mud on his cheek and turned to me. "Thank you for being sorry for what Conrad did to Sylvie, but the important thing is you saved her. She'll recover. I'll do whatever it takes."

Watching Carrie seem as good as dead, I said through my teeth, "I wish Conrad could hear you say that. He said you'd never treat Sylvie right once you knew she was his, biologically."

"Oh, she's mine." He touched his forehead to hers. "I don't know why I thought the DNA mattered. As soon as Gloria called Jeanine to tell us Conrad had kidnapped her, all I could think of ..."

The wipers whipped, and the road glittered under the headlights.

"... was getting her back," he whispered.

"You know," said Dad, "we only have Conrad's word about the test. He stole a sample under less than ideal circumstances. We don't know what lab he used. I'd ignore anything the man said."

Jason looked to Dad, a smile crinkling his left cheek. "Thanks, Mal. But it doesn't matter. It never did."

The radio squawked to life.

Dad unlatched the receiver. "What is it, Kincaid?"

"Your uncle Troy just called Dispatch. He says he has evidence in Ashley Carlisle's death, but he'll only tell you."

"What?" The word was just a gasp from Jason.

Muttering, Dad hit the steering wheel. "Call my grandfather's house. That's where he's staying. Tell him to stay there until I come, which could be a good long while. If he leaves, I'll get a material witness warrant issued." He clicked off and growled. "He's up to something."

"But what?" Jason sounded stunned. "Conrad did it, by his own admission. What could Troy—" He sucked in the word. "Could he be the blackmailer?"

"I'll find out," was all Dad said.

Chapter Fifty-One

We pulled into the hospital, sirens and tires wailing, the wet pavement shining under the searing lights of the parking lot.

Hospital staff pushed a stretcher out to the SUV, loaded Carrie on it, and rushed her inside.

Jason followed them with Sylvie.

Dad and I entered the waiting room where Gram, Jeanine, Hank, and Walter met us, and a stench hit me, a stench I hoped never to smell again after Mom died.

"How bad is she?" Walter watched the doctor and nurses wheel Carrie away.

"She's shot in the arm and lost a lot of blood." Dad put an arm around Gram, who leaned into him. "But Carrie's tough. I think she'll be all right."

"You think." Walter spat the sentence. "You a doctor now?"

"Is Sylvie okay?" Jeanine wrapped her arms around me.

Jason had disappeared into an exam room with her.

"Mr. Conrad didn't hurt her." I held my head between my hands, the odor clawing down my throat. "She got cold when I carried her through the storm." My stomach churned like the floodwaters.

"Rae, are you all right?" Jeanine stepped back.

I pulled away, edging toward the entrance, that cold, antiseptic stink suffocating me. "Yeah, fine. I'm—uh—going to wait out in the SUV."

"What's wrong?" said Hank.

"I hate hospitals." I bolted out the sliding doors, my hand over my mouth.

My stomach intent on reversing operations, I glanced every which way and spotted a trash can, the rain still pelting everything in sight.

Pulling back my hair, I heaved into it.

Someone took hold of my hair.

When my stomach had emptied itself, it seemed to take all my strength with it. My knees folded, and lying in the cool, soaked mulch of the hospital's flower bed seemed much more welcoming than the waiting room.

But Dad put his arms around me and pretty much carried me to the awning over the entrance to the emergency room.

He held me close, and I listened to his heartbeat through his drenched shirt.

"You really do hate hospitals," he said quietly.

"They haven't made me throw up before," I murmured. "They smell like death."

"I have to go back to the county and get Troy. But you can sit in whatever car Ma drove."

I nodded against his chest. Despite being sopping wet, he felt warm. And safe.

"I was so scared when Gloria called." He stroked my head. "Then Kincaid went to the farm while Jason and I headed to Sutton Ridge and told us about all the blood ..."

I leaned back and looked at him. "You're not mad I helped Aunt Carrie, are you?"

"Oh, no, kiddo. No. Not at all." His hug tightened to lung-squishing force, and I didn't care. "If anybody's in trouble, I know you'll be leading the rescue party."

I giggled. No idea why. Then I said, "What do you think Troy's up to?"

"Taking care of number one. I think somehow Troy caught on to our surveillance. Or maybe Conrad not paying off worried him. Since he'd rather be charged with failing to report a crime than murder, he'll come to us now and tell us what he saw. Not that it matters with the confession we've recorded from Conrad."

"He'll have to invent an excuse for why he didn't come to you last week."

"He'll probably claim he feared for his life. No. He feared for the lives of his elderly ..."

"... father and daughters." I snorted.

"I agree. I doubt I'll ever have the proof now to charge him with blackmail. But catching Conrad is top priority. If he lives." Dad gazed out into the parking lot.

"You think he'll kill himself?"

Now Dad snorted. "Not Conrad. Anyone who went to this much trouble to escape won't turn himself in because of the storm of the century. But he's a fool not to. He's injured in unfamiliar territory."

I watched his damp face. "Do you really think Aunt Carrie will make it?"

"Yes." He sharpened the word. "We've got no reason to think anything else." He looked away, swallowing, and then squinted through the rain. "Barb?"

Barb Hanson splashed under the awning. "Is Sylvie all right? I told Rick I'd wait for her and Jason to drive them home, so he could stay with Alli and Richard."

"I think Sylvie's just exhausted—sensory overload. A doctor's examining her now."

She removed her rain-dappled glasses. "I'm glad you're okay, Rae. How's Carrie?"

"We're waiting for the doctor to tell us."

Barb nodded and passed through the automatic doors.

Dad's phone rang.

With his arm still around me, I heard Gloria Helmick say, "Oh, Mal. I've made a mess of things, or Bean Oller's dumber than he looks. He called to report vandalism to his home and truck, and I tried to explain what happened, but he's got it into his head that you and Rae are on some kind of crime spree, and he wants to call in the FBI."

"I'll call him before I leave the hospital. What's the number?"

I held his phone as he jotted it in a moist notepad.

As he swiped off, I said, clutching myself in Mr. Oller's OSU hoodie, "How am I going to pay for all the damage I did?"

Dad stared, then the left side of his mouth rose. "Do you really think the Carlisles will let you pay for any of it?"

Chapter Fifty-Two

"Is this too big?" Micah held up a chunk of pineapple that he had cut for our Father's Day breakfast.

"That's perfect." I opened the stove and removed the loaves of apple bread.

Feet thudded up from the basement.

"It's done." Aaron held out the frame covered in wrinkled birthday gift wrap.

I shushed Aaron. "Gram wanted to sleep in. She's beat from spending so much time at the hospital."

"Sorry." Rusty sat on a stool by the bar.

I studied the gift wrapping job. "You had to use birthday paper?"

"It's either that or Christmas paper." Rusty swiped a chunk of pineapple.

"Birthday paper is fine." I wouldn't mention that somehow Rusty and Aaron's wrapping job had converted a straight-edge rectangular frame into a rhombus.

The phone rang, and Rusty answered. He held it out to me. "It's the coroner."

I dropped cooked bacon on a paper towel. "Is it Dr. Hawthorne? Tell him we have to wake Dad, but he'll call him right back."

As Rusty relayed the information, Aaron and Micah raced into the basement.

When Rusty and I reached Dad's bedroom, our younger brothers were bouncing up and down on Dad's horizontal form as he made groggy noises.

Rusty hauled Aaron off. "You're gonna kill him before we can tell him we love him."

I grabbed at Micah. "I guess love hurts."

Dad might have said something with "stop" in it.

I bent over him. "Dad, Dr. Hawthorne wants you to call him right away."

A good five minutes passed before Dad was conscious enough to stumble upstairs. He punched in the number and grew more alert through the brief conversation.

Setting the phone in the holder, Dad expelled a long breath. "It's Conrad. The fingerprints match."

"That's the guy who beat up Aunt Carrie, right?" said Aaron. "What'd he die of?"

"They're still conducting the autopsy, but so far, everything is consistent with dying from the fall into the ravine where Houston found him." Dad thumbed in another number. "I'll tell the Carlisles that both Ashley's and Sylvie's cases are closed."

We'd probably hear the Carlisles rejoicing without the help of the phone. Since Jason brought Sylvie home from the hospital early Wednesday morning, the Carlisles had been in lockdown. No one but Rick had left the house.

I placed a wire rack on the counter and dumped the loaves of apple bread onto it.

"Glad to give you good news," Dad said into the phone. "Enjoy your Father's Day ... thanks. Yes, I'll let you know if Carrie is released today." He hung up. "I don't think I've ever heard anybody sound more relieved."

"Rae." Micah leaped off the bar and onto Dad's back. "Can we do the present now?"

Reaching for Micah, Dad said, "Wake up your grandmother first."

I sliced the apple bread. "Gram told me to let her sleep until nine."

Dad sat at the head of the table, and Aaron handed him the frame that used to look like a rectangle.

Micah hopped onto his right leg. "Rae said you'd like this." He used the same doubtful tone when he'd talked about my birthday gift.

Dad set the gift on the table. "So this was Rae's idea?" His eyes grew moist.

Here it came. His reaction to the first Father's Day gift from me.

Micah peered into his face. "You're puddling."

Squeezing his eyes shut, Dad pressed the lids with his fingers. "I am not."

"It still counts if you hide it," said Aaron.

"Lying on Sunday makes it worse," Rusty said with an ornery grin.

"Wanna know what's worse?" With a roar, Dad swept all three of my brothers onto the floor, and the wrestling match was on.

Stepping around the wriggling, laughing mass, I went to the kitchen and got bowls for the fruit salad.

I'd finished setting the table by the time Dad had immobilized all my brothers in a bear hug.

Gram shuffled into the living-dining room. "Is something wrong? Oh, you're wrestling."

Guilty looks started with Dad and spread to the boys.

Freeing my brothers, he said, "Sorry, Ma. I got carried away."

Tying her bathrobe, she came over to him and kissed him as he swiveled to a seat on the floor. "You're allowed on your special day."

The phone rang again. I recognized Carrie's number and picked up.

"I just got the all clear." A little more energy brightened her voice, but it still sounded like a shadow of Carrie's usual spirit. "But you all can come after church. Was that body identified?"

"Yes. It's Conrad."

Carrie released a long breath. "It's terrible to say, but I'm thankful. The Carlisles would have no peace unless they knew what had happened to him. He was an idiot not to give himself up."

No joke. Three weeks ago, Conrad and Ashley had had a future. With his temper and their combined selfishness, it didn't amount to much, but they'd had time to change. And maybe Ashley would have accepted Jason's "parole". But we'd never know. The time to change had run out.

"Like I said, don't rush." Her tone soured. "Not like I'll leave here without you."

"I'll tell everyone. It'll be good to have you home."

As I put the landline back in the base, I reported what Carrie had told me.

Tears glistened in her eyes as Gram smiled. "Even more reasons to celebrate today."

Dad returned to the chair at the table, took the gift, and ripped off the paper. Our four photos looked back at him—Micah catching crawdads in the creek, Aaron inventing something destructive, Rusty writing, and me glancing up from my camera. As a beginner, Rusty had done a good job taking my portrait.

Inhaling deep, Dad propped the frame on its stand and inched his chair back.

"What do you think?" said Aaron.

"Give him a minute," I said. "He's puddling."

Chapter Fifty-Three

"Are you comfortable, Aunt Carrie?" Amber stepped away from the recliner Hank had moved into her room. "Do you need anything else?"

"I think another pillow under my knee will do it."

Since Amber's bed was drowning in lavender and ash gray throw pillows that matched her quilt and walls, we had a lot to choose from.

As I lifted Carrie's braced knee to place a cylindrical pillow under it, she said, "I appreciate you giving up your room to me, Amber."

"Not a problem." Amber beamed at her and then waved at the posters on the wall. "You fit in perfectly. You both do."

A warrior princess from *The Lord of the Rings*—I couldn't keep the names straight—and Wonder Woman gazed down on us.

Pink tinging her pale cheeks, Carrie arranged her sling on the arm of the recliner. "I just did my job. Rae's the real hero. I recruited her on the spot, and she came through with no training whatsoever."

Amber moved the beam to me, and I fought the urge to glare at my aunt.

I'd been getting this all week. Rick kept fumbling over his words if I bumped into him at the hospital. Patrons would gush at the desk or just stare like they couldn't quite believe my trek with Sylvie through the storm was true.

What do you say? I did what my Father wanted me to do. I could have messed it up in so many ways if I'd tried to help on my own.

Hank poked his head in. "Need anything, Care?"

"Nope. Thanks for putting the recliner in here. I might sleep in it."

"Whatever works. If you don't need Amber, Dad and me are going on a trail ride with the girls."

"Go ahead. It's not like I have a shortage of relatives."

As Amber brushed by Hank into the hall, he said, "Thanks again, Rae, for taking the girls' photos. It's a great Father's Day gift."

He had turned to go when Jeanine leaned in, covering the mouthpiece of her landline. "Jason wants to know if he can bring the kids over to see you."

Carrie sat up, grimaced, and fell back in the recliner. "Like this?"

Along with the sling and knee brace, the left side of her face was less swollen, but parts had turned from disturbing black to sickly yellow.

"Rick knows what you look like, Carrie. I'm sure he told Jason, and

Jason knows what his kids can handle."

Carrie grimaced again, but it didn't appear to be from pain. "First time in my life, I have two stunning guys hanging around me, and I look like I ran head on into a rhino."

Stunning? I'd go as far as handsome, but stunning seemed a bit much.

"You know they don't care." I picked up a yellow mug filled with daisies and an arrangement of sunflower blossoms in a clear bowl from the floor.

The room was also drowning in flowers arrangements, close to half of them from the Carlisle brothers.

"Are you too tired to have company?" said Jeanine.

"No." Carrie smiled despite the huge bruise on her face. "It'll be nice to see the kids."

Jeanine disappeared into the hall.

Sighing, Carrie let her body sink into the recliner. "My brain's been swimming in so much pain killer, I can't remember what I've said or what people have told me. Has Sylvie made any improvements?"

I shook my head, scooting two vases to the back of Amber's desk to make room for the daisies and sunflowers. "She still hangs on to Jason, no matter what. Rick says she starts screaming if Jason goes to the bathroom."

She clenched her good hand. "Conrad never cared about her. Sylvie was just another acquisition for his empire."

Gram came in with a tumbler of ice water and set it on the nightstand. "How are you doing?"

"Ma, I haven't had time to get any worse or better since I got out of the car ten minutes ago."

Tension in Gram's face cleared, and she bent over and kissed Carrie on the forehead. "That's the most normal you've sounded since you woke up."

"If she was ever normal." Dad leaned in the doorway.

"Can you tell me any more about the case?" Carrie reached for the tumbler, and I handed it to her. "Did you find proof Conrad planned to take Sylvie out of the country?"

"I told you this on Friday," said Dad as Gram patted him on the arm, leaving the room.

Carrie sipped the water and sank back. "The pain-med fog is just starting to clear, so you'll have to repeat some stuff."

"We think he was flying her out of the country. He borrowed a friend's plane. Claimed he was flying to Arizona to pick up Ashley's mother and stepfather for the funeral, and his plane needed repairs. He stocked it with more clothes, cash, and gold. He'd drained his dealerships of money. BCI agents and his managers are going over the accounts, but less than half of the missing money was found in the backpack or the plane."

"He probably stashed it in overseas accounts he could access from whatever country he was fleeing to," said Carrie.

"We still don't know which one. He hadn't filed a flight plan, but from what he said to Rae, he thought he could start over in another country."

"Do you have anything on Troy?" Carrie handed me the glass of water.

"Not for blackmail. Everything points to him without it being proof. The location Houston followed him to in Lake Hope State Park on Tuesday morning was very similar to where the blackmailer's note told Brad to leave his money at Conkle's Hollow on Wednesday morning."

Lifting a terracotta pot with a snake plant in it, I glanced around for a place to put it. "Brad left the money there, but nobody showed for it. Troy said he went to Lake Hope for a hike."

"And when Houston saw him practically tearing up the ground looking for something," Dad said, settling his back against the door jamb, "Troy said he thought he'd dropped his phone."

Carrie pushed her uninjured hand over the top of her hair. "Didn't Troy use the hike excuse for the reason he saw Ashley in the woods?"

"Yes. But he added insomnia. He said he couldn't sleep, trying to figure out what to do with the threats from Joseph. He saw Brad propose to Ashley, and she told him she'd have to think it over. Brad said he had to know by Tuesday, and she agreed. Brad left first. This part of Troy's story matches Brad's and Conrad's perfectly."

Repositioning her sling, Carrie winced. "I bet Brad only proposed to Ashley to keep her quiet about his campaign finances."

"That's how I read it. Brad's being very cooperative with BCI. I'm sure they'll find he also spent political money on Bruce and other family members.

"The rest of what Troy says matches the story Gloria recorded — Conrad burst out of the woods and confronted Ashley. He hit her, and she took off. Conrad followed her. Troy heard a scream. By the time he found Ashley, she was dead. Fearing for the—"

"—lives of his daughters and elderly father," I said, "he kept quiet."

Dad pointed a confirming finger at me.

Micah peeked around Dad. "Rusty found a football. Can you come out and play?" He glanced at Carrie. "I hope your face gets better, Aunt Carrie."

"It will," she said.

"I'll bet out in a few minutes," said Dad.

Micah darted out of sight, and Carrie said, "You're charging Troy for failure to report a crime, aren't you?"

"Yeah. I told Post—the county prosecutor—to fine him. That'll hurt worse than any jail sentence."

"What about the PI and his thug? Did they say anything that could implicate Troy?"

"I'm sure Falk knows nothing. Whatever Joseph wanted out of Troy, he's keeping to himself. They're both taking plea deals."

Shifting in the recliner with a grunt, Carrie said, "You have no one to pin the anonymous tip on?"

"Nope, but I think it was Conrad. Brad and Bruce combined don't seem bright enough to check the road to see if something happened to Ashley after Brad left. Conrad gave me a list of what Ashley had in her purse, so I'm sure he planted one of those items on Jason's property. Something happened, and Simcox never found it. On Friday morning, I believe Conrad was coming to the crime scene either to get another item to frame Jason or bury the body. I bet it was the latter. He had to be preparing his escape by then. Framing Jason wasn't important anymore. But if we couldn't find the body, we couldn't add murder to the kidnapping charge."

"If Ashley sincerely wanted to grow up and come back to Jason," said Carrie, "then this whole mess is a real tragedy."

We were silent. My brothers' shouts echoed from the front yard.

Carrie said, "Mal, I did tell you I was sorry, didn't I?"

"Several times."

She sighed. "I've been an idiot."

"So have I. We must be related."

They both broke into grins.

Chapter Fifty-Four

A half hour later, the Land Rover pulled up, forcing two dogs to trot off the drive. The afternoon light seemed to lull everyone into a lazy rhythm. Our game of catch with Dad was really more like toss, and my brothers sauntered to where Dad lobbed the football, rather than racing for it.

Jason emerged from the passenger side, carrying Sylvie. She had both arms wrapped around his neck. Her hacked hair appeared trimmed.

Shutting the driver's door, Rick said, "We have something to show you, Mal."

His forehead furrowing, Dad stepped over to the SUV.

Richard ran up to me with a lumpy package of tissue paper. "I have a present for Carrie."

Sylvie screamed and buried her head in Jason's shoulder.

Everyone stared, and Rick spun to his brother. "What is it?"

Jason stroked Sylvie's back. "I think—I think it's Rae. She looked in her direction. It's all right, sweetheart." He reopened a door to the Rover. "I'll get her calmed down and come in later."

Wow. How long would it take Sylvie to see me as something other than the monster who dragged her out into a horrible storm?

As Rick pulled a white garbage bag from the back of the Rover, I said, "Richard, I'll take you to Carrie."

Alli joined us as we entered the house. "Daddy says we have to be really nice to Sylvie because she got so scared." A tough smile hardened her face. ""I'm glad you and Carrie beat the guy up who tried to kidnap her. I bet that's why he died."

"No." I led them through the living room. "The coroner thinks—he's the doctor who determines what people die of—he thinks the guy died in a fall in the woods."

When we came into Amber's room, Carrie started, like she'd been dozing. A big smile pushed aside the bruises. "Good to see you."

Clasping the package, Richard stared from the doorway while Alli said, "I thought you'd look a lot worse." The barest hint of approval laced her voice.

Richard darted to Carrie's side. "I brought you a present." He put the package in her lap.

Carrie handed it to me as I took a seat on the bed. "You'd better open it since you have two working hands."

"I hope you like it," said Richard. "I was going to give you the purse I found, but Daddy said it was our mom's and he had to give it to the sheriff."

My hands froze above the gift in my lap, and Carrie went rigid, her eyes widening.

But her tone was casual. "Where'd you find the purse, Richard?"

"By the garage. It was behind some ladders and pieces of wood we keep out there."

"What day was that?" said Carrie.

Alli dropped onto the bed beside me. "You're asking the same questions Daddy and Uncle Rick asked."

"That's because my brother Mal—he's the sheriff—he'd want to know."

"Rick's showing it to him." I tore off the heavily taped pink paper, revealing a small box covered in tiny seashells.

Richard took it from me and handed it to Carrie. "Do you like it? I glued on all the shells myself."

"I helped," said Alli.

"It's beautiful." Carrie turned the box in her good hand. "It's a good size to keep earrings in."

"Richard." Dad entered the room, carrying the white garbage bag, with Rick. "I'd like to ask you some questions about the purse."

Richard left the room with them.

Carrie said, "Alli, how do you think Sylvie's doing?" She used a business-like tone, like she was consulting a colleague.

Frowning, Alli glanced back at the door, then to Carrie. "She won't let go of Daddy. He has to sleep in the recliner with her. She used to talk all the time. Now she doesn't talk much at all."

Heat flared in my chest, and the same anger contracted Carrie's face.

Then Carrie massaged her chin. "You know, Sylvie liked petting the alpacas. She might like petting the dogs around here since you don't have any pets. Why don't you and the boys round up some of the dogs and see if she'll pet them? Might get her to talking."

Alli hopped off the bed. "We can try it."

A minute after she left, Dad and Rick returned.

Dad opened his mouth, but Carrie said, "I'll tell you exactly what happened. I'm sure after a week and a half, Richard can't remember.

"Conrad planted the purse beside the garage and contacted Simcox anonymously. Before Simcox arrived, Richard found the purse, thought I'd like it, and put it in his backpack. Then I told the kids we were going to the library. Richard had his backpack with him the entire time Simcox searched the yard and house. He forgot about it being in his backpack with all the craziness until he wanted to find a gift for me."

"Almost right," said Dad. "Richard said he left the purse in his closet at some point. I'm sure after the search. He didn't remember it until today." He shook his head. "When Simcox didn't find anything, I should've known the kids had something to do with it. I live with four of them." He faced Rick. "I thought you or Jason had found the item and hid it, either out of guilt or fear of being accused."

"You don't think that now?" Rick arched an eyebrow.

"I would after your omission of your secret meeting with Ashley. But you would never involve Richard in any lie to protect yourself or Jason."

"Thank you." Rick's gratitude was ice. "I'm glad you recognize I have some principles. Not like you, though. I would never advise a man to reconcile with the wife who had deserted him twice."

Oh, good. Now things were all evened up between Dad and Rick. Rick could hate Dad for supporting Jason's efforts to reconcile with his wife, while Dad still struggled to forgive Rick for nearly killing me.

Dad met Rick's glacial glare head on. "Maybe Ashley really did want to change. She didn't take you up on your bribe."

"She didn't deserve another chance."

"No, she didn't deserve it. She just needed it. Everybody needs a second chance." Dad put punch behind the last sentence.

The sinews in his throat stood out as Rick flinched.

"You know—" Carrie adjusted her sling "—all this tension is interfering with my healing. Just FYI."

Shifting his gaze, Rick leaned against Amber's desk. "A friend of Jason's is expediting your insurance claim for your Jeep, Carrie." He tried to sound casual, but his face was pulled taut under his beard.

"That's a real help." Carrie tipped her head to the side. "I've been thinking. If you and Jason agree, I'd like to be an aunt to Alli, Richard, and Sylvie. It would hurt them if I just disappear. I can be an aunt to nine kids as easily as six."

Rick's face melted, and he dropped into the desk chair. "That would be ... wonderful. For the kids." He propped his leg on his knee.

Dad watched without expression, then said, "Rae, I need to speak to you."

"Oh, okay."

I followed him to the front door.

Jason sat on the porch steps with Sylvie. Rusty sat beside them, holding Chestnut by his collar, while Aaron, Micah, and Alli held on to three other dogs.

I froze on the sill.

Dad glanced at me. "I have to put this bag in the truck. I'll meet you at the stable."

Nodding, I shut the screen door.

Richard plopped onto the step beside Jason and petted Chestnut's back. "He's a really soft doggy, Sylvie."

Sylvie let go of Jason's neck long enough for a quick pat on Chestnut's neck, then rested her head against her dad's shoulder. She giggled.

I released a slow breath. She hadn't seen me.

Jason kissed Sylvie's cheek.

She chanced another pat and said, "Wike fwuffy doggy, Daddy." She giggled again.

Stroking her hair, Jason said, "I do too."

I backed into the house, turned, passed Gram and Aunt Jeanine chopping vegetables in the kitchen, and went out the back door.

Easing through the crack between the two sliding doors of the stable, I said, "What's up?" I leaned against a post.

Scratching an eyebrow, Dad looked to his shoes. "I've been wrestling two weeks with how to bring this up to you because I didn't want to make things worse. With me working so much and being so tired, I kept putting it off."

I straightened off the post. What was this?

He met my surprised gaze. "We're okay now? You and me."

"You mean when we fought the night Troy tricked me?" I tilted my head, blinking. "I said I was sorry and so did you."

"But you said that night ..." Dad closed his eyes. "'I've been on my own since I was fifteen because most of that time, Mom was too sick to take care of me, and I've been completely on my own since right before my eighteenth birthday, and I've survived fine without you being around to yell at me'."

"Now I know where I get my good memory."

A smile flitted by. "Are you still hurt that I wasn't around to raise you?"

My jaw but flopped loose. "I'm not hurt. You thought I was dead. All I meant was I'd taken care of myself decently until I found you." I sighed. "Not counting the stalker, I usually have good sense."

Now Dad gaped. "That's what you meant?" He pushed a hand through his crewcut. "Wish I'd brought this up sooner."

"Why didn't you?"

"Well, it was like you said. I didn't want to put more strain on our relationship, and I was so tired from all the long hours that I was afraid I'd lose my temper again."

"I don't expect you to be perfect."

"Thanks. But I need to control my mouth." He paused. "I'm very close to Ma, and I'd like to have that sort of relationship when my kids are adults." He held up his hand like I'd protested. "I know it's a two-way street. If you don't want that, I can't make you." He pulled his lips thin, then took a breath. "But I want to do all I can to make that possible. You called Kincaid because you couldn't trust my reaction." He flinched at the memory. "You're an adult. If you prefer to consult a friend, that's fine. But I'd hate—" the ache in his voice made it creak "—I'd hate for you to want my help and think you couldn't come to me. You and I are closer than I thought possible on Christmas Day. I don't want to mess that up."

I fell back against the post. I needed the support. "You're afraid of ... me?"

"Of driving you away, yes."

After all my doubts and worries about our relationship, it never occurred to me Dad would have them too.

"But you can't." I held out my arms. "You acknowledged me. You—you built a room for me. You've rescued me way, way too many times."

"That's what dads do."

"A lot don't." Troy's face, with his fake, apologetic smile, rose from the whirlwind in my mind. I leveled my gaze into Dad's worried blue eyes. "You're my dad. You have been since I was conceived, and you will be forever. So get used to it."

Like the dawn, a grin broke and lit up his face.

"And I finally trust that," I said. "I knew it. I just had to believe it. Even if a DNA test proved I was Troy's biological daughter, I know it wouldn't matter ... to you ... either ..."

He was going to blow. Either out his mouth or through every blood vessel in his brain, but all the blood rushing into his face had to get released somehow.

I touched his arms. "You can yell. It's about Troy."

"What has he been saying to you?"

Good thing all the horses were in the pasture, or Dad's bellow would have launched a stampede.

I told him of Troy's nasty campaign from the beginning until I made my decision at Walter's.

Turning this way and that, Dad seemed too shocked to know what to do with himself.

Funny. After debating the question until it nauseated me, I didn't have any second thoughts about telling Dad now.

As soon as I was done, he gripped my shoulder. "I am so sorry you didn't think you could come to me."

I looked up at him. "That was my fault. I didn't believe your promise."

"Yeah, but if I didn't blow up at every little—"

"I don't know about that. I also thought it was too dumb to tell you how it worried me." A burn creeped into my ears. "I had no proof. Troy had no proof. But I couldn't shake the fear that maybe he was right.

Especially when he tugged on his earlobe."

"But I'm a parent, Rae. I do dumb every day."

I lowered my eyebrows.

The left corner of his mouth hitched. "I can put that better." He put an arm around my shoulders. "Kids get crazy ideas, especially about their parents. I guess we always want to be reassured that they love us. I'd lived with Ma for seven years, and I was sick clear through last Christmas at the idea of telling her about how I'd gotten Bella pregnant. I was mostly worried that she'd blame herself because I hadn't come to her back then. Moms do that. But deep down, I was worried that this time, she'd rake me over the coals, lose any respect she had for me. I don't know why I was so dumb. When I'd told her what happened, all she wanted to do was hold me." Dad gave me a squeeze and released me. "You said Troy tugged his earlobe when you were driving him home. Right?"

"Yes."

"That was the third or fourth time you'd met him?"

"Ye-es." My eyes narrowed.

"I bet he saw you make that gesture at an earlier time and imitated it."

"But how—could he—he was watching me that closely?" I felt so exposed, like when the stalker sent me a photo of myself.

"Oh, yeah. That's the tragedy of Troy. He's intelligent with a talent for understanding people, and he uses his gifts to exploit them and serve himself. His goal was to make you question your paternity. He would study you to see how he could accomplish that."

I crossed my arms over my chest and took hold of them. "But why? I've never figured out a motive."

"First, once he learned we hadn't done a DNA test, he decided to test whether he could con you into liking him and helping him with his scams. Second, if he could hurt me and my family, even better. Since the two goons came to the barn, has he tried to talk to you?"

"No. He hasn't talked to me since that day."

Dad nodded. "You served your purpose. He set the goons on you, and you filed charges against them. He knows you're angry with him, and you're smart, so he won't waste his time trying to convince you that he didn't sic those guys on you."

I wanted to take a long, long shower, as if Troy's analysis of me had left me filthy.

"Rae, why don't we make a deal? If I have a problem with you, I'll just tell you. If I have to cool off, I will, but I won't hang on to it. You'll do the same. I mean—" he cleared his throat "—will you do the same?"

I kissed him on the cheek. "For sure. No matter what the problem is, we're stuck with each other."

He kissed me on the forehead. "We'll go tell Troy that right now."

"We will?"

"You had the right idea, confronting him. I'll explain, in crystal clear terms, that if he wants to celebrate Father's Day, he can do it with Egypt and China. Not you."

Chapter Fifty-Five

I rolled down my window on the Beast as it bounced onto a gravel road leading to Walter's house. "I was thinking Troy would have cleared out of Marlin County by now."

The afternoon was hushed, the shade deep and refreshing under the imposing maples, oaks, and tulip trees inviting.

Dad straddled his huge, black truck around a pothole. "He won't as long as I hold a material witness arrest warrant over his head. Which is no good now that I'm closing Ashley's case."

We rocked up the drive to the delapidated house.

As we got out, the distinctive *thunk* of an ax sinking into wood reached us. We followed the sound to the backyard.

In a sweat-soaked white t-shirt, blotched with paint stains, Walter swung an ax over his head.

"Walter," Dad called, "give yourself a break. It's Father Day."

"Happy Father's Day, Walter," I said.

He brought down the ax, gave us a nod, and then wiped sweat from his upper lip. "A lot of trees come down in that storm. I wanna get the wood chopped and dried." He pulled his arm across his forehead. "What're you doin' here? Didn't Jeanine tell ya I'm comin' over after supper?"

"Yeah. We're actually here to see Troy."

"What's he done now?"

"Nothing criminal. I'm here as Rae's father."

Walter watched us, then dropped the ax. "He'd be better off if you come as sheriff."

He'd taken five steps when Troy came out on the peeling back porch. "Happy Father's Day, Mal."

"Thanks. Just stopped by to let you know Rae's told me how you've been insinuating you're her father."

A spasm passed through Troy's benign expression, and his eyelids fluttered so much that he rubbed his right eye, like grit was in it.

"Why'd you do that?" said Walter. "Ain't like you care about the two you got."

"Of course I care." Troy lowered his hand. "I come to visit when I can."

"When you need a place to hide."

"I told Rae it was a possibility, Mal." Troy turned a few degrees away from Walter. "I felt I had to. I'm more likely to be her father because ..." his face fell, his adam's apple bobbing. "Bella and I were very close."

"You mean—" Egypt tromped onto the back porch with a bang "— Rae could be my half-sister? I don't need another one."

"I don't need any," I said.

Egypt's arms stiffened at her sides, and she drew herself up to fire back, but Walter said, "Let it go, Gyp."

As Egypt glared at Walter, Dad said, "Well, now you know I know, Troy, and the DNA test doesn't matter. Our blood types don't matter. I'm Rae's father, and she's my daughter. We've accepted each other. That's the end of it."

"Perfect," said Egypt.

Troy drew a finger along his scruffy jawline. "But if it doesn't matter, why not do the test?"

Despite looking at Dad, Troy seemed to aim the question at me.

He went on, "A lot of voters have doubts in their minds about the whole situation."

"Then they're stuck with them," Dad said.

Troy studied Dad, then nodded wisely. "You're right, Mal. If a test proved Rae wasn't yours, it wouldn't look good for you during the next election."

Pitching back his head, Dad barked a laugh. "I got to hand it to you, Troy. When one line doesn't work, you keep on swinging."

"Besides," I said, "the fact that you think it's a good idea is the best reason not to do it."

Dad laughed again as Walter released a grating snicker.

For just a moment, a sliver of a second, something other than apologetic understanding lurked in Troy's pale green eyes. Might have been anger. Might have been resentment. But I'd finally struck a blow below the con man surface.

Dad looked to Walter. "You're sure you don't want to come for supper?"

"Yeah. Lily and Cal are coming over, and Egypt and China are making supper, soon as China gets home from work."

"Don't let us stop you." Egypt folded her arms, her jaw jutting forward. "We know you'd prefer eating with all of Reuel's precious darlings."

Snarling, Walter stomped toward the porch. "Did I say that? Did I?"

Egypt glanced at Walter and then seemed to find something fascinating in the woods behind him.

"You and China do a good job with that fried chicken." His tone had eased into its usual harsh growl.

Egypt still wouldn't look at him, but her frown didn't appear as deep.

"If Aunt Lily or Uncle Cal or anybody else wants to come over for dessert," Dad said, "just let Jeanine know so she can tell you if she has enough for everyone."

"Does that invitation extend to me?" said Troy.

"No. I want to enjoy this day with my grandfather and my kids. I don't want to work as a cop and watch you."

"Don't lie." Walter turned on his x-ray scan. "You just wanna spend time with your kids. Ain't got nothin' to do with me."

Dad squared himself to Walter. "I wouldn't have said it if I hadn't meant it. Come on, Rae." He moved toward the front of the house.

Troy said, "Don't worry, Mal. I've told no one around here that I was involved with Bella."

"I wasn't worried." Dad stopped and looked back to Walter and Egypt. "People around here are used to Malinowskis raising other people's kids."

Muscles tensed in Troy's handsome face, hinting again at some reaction he was submerging.

Dad lifted a hand as he moved off. "See ya later, Walter."

As Dad backed the Beast down the drive, I said, "Why was Troy still trying to hurt us? You said I'd served my purpose."

"Not sure. Could just be reflex. He's a con man, and when he realized he could use our decision not to test against us, he tried it. He's also ticked you told me, so he was probably trying to get back at us by driving a wedge between us."

The wind blew strands of hair into my face. "As if."

Dad cracked a grin, and I caught it.

The afternoon light had aged, turning the dust the Beast kicked up to gold.

At the same time, we both burst out laughing.

Acknowledgements

And I thought writing a book during a pandemic was tough. My second novel brought me different challenges from the chaos in which I wrote my first one, and it wouldn't have become the book you hold without the help of many kind people.

Thank you to ...

Charles Carlson, who answered all my questions about identifying bodies, how to determine time of death, and everything else I could think of related to autopsies.

Dave Butler, who answered my questions dealing with police procedures.

Dave Laughlin, who helped me understand divorce and child custody laws in Ohio.

Veronica Harris, who explained how trauma would probably affect a toddler.

I greatly appreciate the time all four experts took to educate me in areas about which I know nothing.

More thanks to ...

Becky Nelson, who give me the inspiration for naming Frank Joseph and Austin Falk.

Mary Ellen Tobin, who suggested the name Chestnut for my literary dog because her dog inspired him.

Debra Guyette and Shelly Cox, who gave me feedback on my title, which I needed because I'm terrible at creating titles.

Tamera Lynn Kraft and Michelle L. Levigne. You both have been so patient and supportive as I've fought my way through finishing this novel.

Ellyn Boynton, Anna Boynton, Theresa Van Meter, and Kip Krueger, who accepted being my beta readers and gave me a treasure trove of insights into improving this book. And for the encouragement I receive from Theresa when we talk about our writing and marketing.

My family, who prove that if it takes a village to raise a child, it also takes a family to raise a book. Thank you to my parents, my sisters, my brothers-in-law, my nieces and nephews for your support and willingness to bounce ideas around with me.

A special thank you to my brother-in-law Mark, and Cheri Clem, my massage therapist, who helped me deal with all the back and shoulder pain I developed from writing.

Another special thank you to my husband Bill. An engineer is priceless for brainstorming. And to my boys, Will and Cole, who supported me through the torturous process of seeing this book to completion.

A very special thank you to my niece Anna and my nephew Peter. I spent four months obsessing about the final clue while I wrote toward the end of the book, and Anna and Peter gave me the breakthrough I desperately needed. I couldn't have finished without you!

And once again, thank you to my Heavenly Father, who makes writing so exciting because I get to learn more about Him.

I pray this story helps you as it has helped me.

THANK YOU!

Thank you for reading this book from Mt. Zion Ridge Press.

If you enjoyed the experience, learned something, gained a new perspective, or made new friends through story, could you do us a favor and write a review on Goodreads or wherever you bought the book?

Thanks! We and our authors appreciate it.

We invite you to visit our website, MtZionRidgePress.com, and explore other titles in fiction and non-fiction. We always have something coming up that's new and off the beaten path.

And please check out our podcast, **Books on the Ridge,** where we chat with our authors and give them a chance to share what was in their hearts while they wrote their book, as well as fun anecdotes and glimpses into their lives and experiences and the writing process. And we always discuss a very important topic: *Tea!*

You can listen to the podcast on our website or find it at most of the usual places where podcasts are available online. Please subscribe so you don't miss a single episode!

Thanks for reading. We hope to see you again soon!

ABOUT THE AUTHOR

JPC Allen started her writing career in second grade with an homage to Scooby Doo. She's been tracking down mysteries ever since. Her Christmas mystery "A Rose from the Ashes" was a Selah-finalist at the Blue Ridge Mountains Christian Writers Conference in 2020. Her first Rae Riley novel, <u>A Shadow on the Snow</u>, released in 2021. Online, she offers tips and prompts to ignite the creative spark in every kind of writer. She also leads workshops for tweens, teens, and adults, encouraging them to discover the adventure of writing. Coming from a long line of Mountaineers, she is a life-long Buckeye. Follow her to her next mystery on Facebook, Instagram, Amazon, Goodreads, Bookbub, and her website, JPCAllenWrites.com, where you can sign up for her newsletter and receive her latest writing news and exclusive content.